MW01075470

# Double FULL

## A *NICE GUYS* NOVEL

# Kindle Alexander

Double Full

Copyright © Kindle Alexander, 2013
ALL RIGHTS RESERVED

Edited by Jae Ashley
Photo credit: Photo of Trevor Adams by wagnerLA
http://www.wagnerla.com/
Cover art and interior print layout by Reese Dante
http://www.reesedante.com

First Edition October, 2013
ISBN: 978-0-9891173-7-1
Digital ISBN: 978-0-9891173-8-8

Published by: The Kindle Alexander Collection LLC

All rights reserved under the International and Pan-American Copyright Conventions. No part of this book may be reproduced or transmitted in any form or by any means, electronic or mechanical including photocopying, recording, or by any information storage and retrieval system, without permission in writing from the publisher, Kindle Alexander LLC, kindle@kindlealexander.com. No part of this book may be scanned, uploaded or distributed via the Internet or any other means, electronic or print, without permission from Kindle Alexander, LLC. Warning: The unauthorized reproduction or distribution of this copyrighted work is illegal. Criminal copyright infringement, including infringement without monetary gain, is investigated by the FBI and is punishable by up to 5 years in federal prison and a fine of $250,000. http://www.fbi.gov/ipr/). Please purchase only authorized electronic or print editions and do not participate in or encourage the electronic piracy of copyrighted material. Your support of the author's rights and livelihood is appreciated.

Double Full is a work of fiction. Names, characters, places and incidents are either the product of the author's imagination or are used fictitiously, and any resemblance to any actual persons, living or dead, events, or locales is entirely coincidental.

Licensed material is being used for illustrative purposes only and any person depicted in the licensed material is a model.

WARNING
This book contains material that maybe offensive to some:
graphic language, adult situations.

# Trademark Acknowledgements:

The author acknowledges the trademarked status and trademark owners of the following trademarks mentioned in this work of fiction:

*Armani*: Giorgio Armani, SPA

*Bentley*: Bentley Motors Limited

*Cheshire Cat*: Disney Enterprises, Inc.

*Christian Louboutin*: Louboutin, Christian

*Coke*: The Coca-Cola Company

*Coppertone*: Schering-Plough Healthcare Products, Inc.

*Corona*: Cerveceria Modelo, S.A. de C.V.

*Creed*: Blue Collar Records, Inc.

*Dallas Mavericks*: Dallas Basketball Limited

*DFW International Airport*: Dallas/Fort Worth International Airport Board

*ESPN*: ESPN, Inc.

*Garth Brooks*: Brooks, Troyal Garth

*Google*: Google, Inc.

*Green Bay Packers*: Green Bay Packers, Inc.

*iPhone*: Apple, Inc.

*iPod*: Apple, Inc.

*Jack Daniels*: Jack Daniel's Properties, Inc.

*Levi's:* Levi Strauss & Co. Corporation

*Linkin Park (New Divide)*: Linkin Park, LLC

*Longboard Island Lagers*: Kona Brewery, LLC

*Malibu (coconut rum)*: The Absolut Company

*Medical City Hospital*: Medical Cities, Inc.

*National Cheerleader Association*: Varsity Spirit Corporation

*NBA*: NBA Properties, Inc.

*NFL*: National Football League

*PETA*: People for the Ethical Treatment of Animals, Inc.

*Porsche*: Dr. Ing. h.c. F. Porsche AG Corporation

*Prius*: Toyota Jidosha Kabushiki Kaisha AKA Toyota Motor Corporation

*Rage Against the Machine*: Rage Against the Machine composed of Tom Morello, Brad Wilk, Tim Commerford, and Zack de la Rocha

*Rose Bowl*: Pasadena Tournament of Roses Association, Inc.

*Speedo*: Speedo International

*SportsCenter*: ESPN, Inc.

*Starbucks*: Starbucks Corporation

*State of Decay*: Microsoft Corporation

*Super Bowl*: National Football League Unincorporated Association

*TMZ*: Warner Bros. Entertainment Inc.

*Walkman*: Sony Corporation

*Wal-Mart*: Wal-Mart Stores, Inc.

*World Series*: Office of the Commissioner of Baseball Unincorporated Association

*Wranglers*: Wrangler Apparel Corp.

*Xanax*: Pharmacia & Upjohn Company

*Xbox*: Microsoft Corporation

*YouTube*: Google, Inc.

*Zombie Apocalypse*: Konami Digital Entertainment, Inc.

# Dedication

This book is dedicated to Perry, I miss you every day.

David, forever isn't long enough...
Autumn and Amanda, you make me so proud.

Kim, I really, really love our boys! Thank you for pushing
when I'm being stubborn. I will always cherish our friendship.
Aidan and Keagan, you keep me sane.

Julie, Angie, Kim, Teri, Beth, Madi, Melanie, Kylie, Renee,
Em, Tee, Magda, VR, to say it's been an adventure is an
understatement...but I wouldn't have missed it for the world.
<3

And as always, to our amazing facebook family and all our
wonderful friends, thank you from the bottom of our hearts.
Without your support and encouragement we wouldn't be
here.

Kindle, you are forever in our hearts.

# Prologue

*March 2003*

Jace gripped the side of the locker, his knuckles turning white as he dropped his head inside the open metal frame. The Texas Longhorn University men's locker room was empty, all except for him and Colton Michaels, who at the moment had his cock buried deep inside Jace's ass.

"*Fuck...* yes!" A loud moan escaped Jace's parted lips. Colt slipped his warm palm over Jace's mouth in an attempt to quiet him. The hard pounding from behind never stopped.

"Shhh... Jace, baby, someone might hear us," Colt whispered. "I've waited too long for this."

"I never knew," Jace panted.

"Shhh... I want this to last."

"I can't... it... dear fucking God, you feel so good." Jace ground the words out, biting his knuckle as Colt's hand slid down to grip Jace's rock hard length, stroking hard and fast in the same urgent rhythm he created from behind.

"Come for me, baby... I'm not stopping until I've had my fill. I've had too many fantasies about this moment." Colt's breath warmed his ear, making his balls ache with every word he spoke.

Jace grabbed for the damp towel he'd just used in the shower, but not for his leaking cock. No, he needed it for other things. Jace crammed the big wad of white terrycloth in his mouth, stifling a long muffled groan as his climax racked through his body. *Damn!* Somewhere in the back of his mind, he swore he could hear Colt's soft chuckle at his over the top response.

Colt held Jace tight, not letting him collapse forward into the top locker when the orgasm caused his knees to buckle. Instead, Colt wrapped his big strong quarterback arms around Jace's chest and pulled him back against his athletic body, keeping him upright. All he could do was drop his head back on Colt's broad shoulder and pant. He wasn't complaining. He'd dreamed about the hot football player for as long as he could remember.

It didn't take too much longer. Colt's grip tightened, and Jace just about went to his knees at the intensity of Colt's release. Completely blissed out of his mind, he smiled to himself as Colt's weight settled on him and his breathing slowly returned to normal.

"I want to hear you cheer my name now, cheer boy," Colt growled in his ear, before turning Jace's head to the side, capturing his lips in a heated kiss.

# Chapter 1

The warm spray of the men's locker room shower soaked Jace Montgomery for the second time in less than an hour. Just like the first time, he was completely alone, and the best he could tell, no one witnessed his complete lack of morals and discretion. But, my god, if they had, who could blame him? That was Colton freaking Michaels who just fucked him senseless at his locker.

Okay, wait, the sentence made no sense. Jace reached down and pinched himself on the arm.

"Fuck! Like your ass doesn't hurt bad enough." Jace halfheartedly scolded himself at how hard he actually pinched himself. It would definitely leave a mark, but instead of thinking about the bruise he just acquired, he chose to dwell on the delicious feel of his aching ass. Colt worked him over like no one ever had before him.

*Where in the world did that come from? Colt Michaels... What?*

Jace reached for the bodywash, soaping his hands. Only their lack of a condom had him in the shower right now. Otherwise, he wouldn't have dared wash for the next week in hopes of keeping Colt's scent on his body a little longer. And yes, he sounded like a girl. And no, he didn't care at all.

Probably not the best move to go without a condom, but he couldn't find it in him to care right now. He was solidly in that after-sex high and decided he'd worry about the lack of protection later. Right now, he just wanted to remember. When they finished, and yes, Jace came not once, but twice, Colt pushed him toward the shower after one hell of a mind-blowing kiss. The kind of lip-lock you read about in super-hot romance novels.

*Hold your horses, hoss.* The thought caused him to cringe, and his reasonable, sound mindset slowly crept back in. Damn, he hated that side of himself, always responsible, doing the right thing all the time. Technically, nothing about tonight classified as making a right decision, so Jace shoved reason aside. He wanted no part of sensible and gently reached back to wash his ass, wanting every thought to stay focused right there on that particular region of his body.

For now, he didn't want to consider how random their little sexual quest turned out to be. Nor did he need to be told they would never do this again. But for the length of this shower, he wanted to bask in the fairytale high of the moment. The one where the handsome prince rode in on his great white horse and swept Jace off his feet, pounding him against his locker. His smile grew bigger.

One very important thing he learned tonight... Colt Michaels had indeed noticed him, just like he'd noticed Colt. As it turned out, they had watched each other for years, but neither had said a word. In what world was that even possible? Apparently in his world! Jace had been given his chance with the gorgeous star quarterback. Clearly, dreams did come true.

It was all down, set, hut, hut, and fuck Jace in the butt, butt! He groaned and then chuckled at the little cheer.

Jace looked down at his water-pruned fingers, still laughing at his rhyme, and decided he needed to celebrate the night. Everything in him wanted to call Haley and maybe Gregory to have a total girls' night. He wanted to share this juicy bit of information so badly. He grabbed his towel and dried off while scolding himself again. This fell conspicuously under the strategic heading of never telling another living soul on the planet. Colt was a testosterone-filled jock with a beautiful girlfriend. He wasn't slumber party gossip material, no matter how bad he wanted to tell someone he'd had hot locker room sex with Colt Michaels.

He never got to be the one with the interesting story! Now that he had one, no way he could ever speak the words out loud. *Dang it!*

Jace wrapped the towel around his waist and grabbed his shower caddy. He stopped by the sink and looked in the mirror. Something he didn't normally do, but with one glance, he saw the ever present grin still plastered across his face. He definitely wore an after-sex glow. Man, he loved having sex with Colt.

Standing in front of the mirror several minutes, Jace just stared at himself. Could this one sexual encounter have altered him somehow? He seemed changed and took inventory of his body. His hair was still short and blond, no change there. His eyes were still a dark green, but they did have a noticeable sparkle, and Jace's smile broadened. His lips were still full, his skin tanned. He lifted up on his tiptoes, rising up to get a better look in the mirror. He was still the same height, about six feet tall. So what was different? Nothing he could see, yet somehow he was fundamentally transformed. *Interesting.*

He gave himself the minute to imagine Colt standing right there beside him, trying to decide how they might look together. The small mirror in his locker didn't do them justice, besides he'd been too far gone to fully absorb what he'd seen. Jace lost himself in the thought. Colt was a little taller, maybe by a couple of inches. They had about the same build. They both worked out more than their fair share. They were lean, defined, and strong. Colt's skin was naturally dark, maybe an olive complexion. His hair was dark, almost black, and his eyes a nice light blue.

To see all of Colt's devilish good looks walking through the locker room had startled him senseless as he'd dressed. Jace had never gotten that up close and personal with the star of the team. And then to have those blue eyes land on him with purpose... Jace had been robbed of his ability to think straight. He still wasn't sure he was thinking straight.

Jace dug for his comb, did a quick brush through of his hair, and wondered if he would ever hear from Colt again. Probably not, but if he did, this whole infatuated schoolboy thing he had going on right now would never do. Reality came crashing forward again in full force. Jace needed to lose the silly grin right now, so he forced the smile away. If Colt made contact with him, he needed to keep it cool, light, and casual. Act as if he did these kinds of things every day, all day. He certainly didn't want to come off as a stage-five clinger. That would scream needy and scare Colt away.

Jace grabbed his shower kit and slowly walked toward his bank of lockers. One glance down the long row and his gaze stopped at the still open locker at the end. All his thoughts of playing the cool guy flew from his brain. He could feel the smile return to his face with the heat of the blush creeping back throughout his body. Colt had banged the shit of him just a few feet away. And man did Jace want a repeat performance!

The small Porsche rocketed through the luxury townhome complex where Colt lived. The car was new, just like the townhome, and much like the big wad of cash burning a hole in his pocket. All were secret gifts no one knew anything about. This was a tricky game, skirting around all the clearly broken rules, but Colt never allowed himself to worry. It was the only benefit of having such an involved, over-the-top father. He took care of all these little details.

Colt zipped into his parking space, bringing the car to an abrupt halt. The townhomes were within walking distance of the university, but he loved driving this thing. He admittedly drove a little recklessly, but what was the point of having a badass sports car if you didn't live on the edge? And Colt had certainly been much closer to falling off the edge tonight.

Maybe diving off the edge was a better way to say it. He'd finally gotten inside Jace Montgomery's sweet tight ass. How long had he fantasized about that one? Since he first saw Jace, that's how long. And the sex was pretty much perfection, just as he dreamed it would be.

Would fucking Jace tonight fall into the top sex of his life? *Hell fucking yeah!* Jace was number one perfect sex right there. Colt always wanted his first man-on-man sexual encounter to be with Jace Montgomery. The current problem? Now that he'd had Jace once, he wanted more. Wasn't that an interesting turn of events? Nah, not really. Deep down Jace had always been one of the most important people in Colt's life.

Funny how he'd never said more than a few passing words to the guy.

Colt pushed open the car door to hear the music of the townhome complex blaring. Spring break had the entire place in full party mode, even as the night had barely begun. None of his neighbors planned to be sober for one minute of their vacation time. It was a quest, and they would most certainly excel in their mission.

The loud music that greeted Colt as he exited the car pulled him from the silence of his thoughts. This was a new experience, he always kept the radio loud as he drove because silence meant thinking, and thinking always had a way of bringing Jace into his thoughts. Jace Montgomery was the secret he held closest to his heart for four long years. The depth of those emotions scared him a little bit. Yet somehow, after tonight, he wasn't afraid of those thoughts any longer. Damn, that felt rockin' good.

"Hey, Colt! Come join us," Gabby, his neighbor, called down from her second floor balcony right next door to his place. Her townhome looked full, packed from the inside out. Colt and his buddies planned to hit Sixth Street tonight, but if his friends saw Gabby already dancing in her bra and panties, they might not ever make it out. That didn't seem too bad either. He'd rather spend all evening thinking about the sexy Jace Montgomery anyway.

"I'll catch you later. I gotta make a phone call," Colt yelled, waving her off.

He headed straight for his place, mildly disappointed when he saw his living room full of people too. Colt navigated through the masses of his friends, winding his way around the living room, and headed straight back to his bedroom. As expected, it was occupied, too.

"Dude, seriously, it's what the spare's for," Colt said, standing at the foot of his bed staring down at Tim, his best friend. Tim gave him a glassy red-eyed stare and the female under him looked about in the same condition. Lucky for Colt, Tim had only gotten as far as getting her top off.

"Come join us. I have a friend," Double-D said, lifting up on her elbows, exposing herself completely to him. From this position, he could guess her breast were real. Funny how that was his only thought.

"Not tonight. Tim, I need my room, buddy." Tim ignored Colt, and turned back to Double-D, continuing his exploration. Colt reached over to pull him off the bed. His buddy squawked, but had no choice except to stand. That was when Colt realized he'd gotten the whole scene a little wrong. Tim's shorts fell straight to the floor.

"*Dude!* Seriously, we've talked about this! The spare bedroom!" Colt winced at seeing Tim hard and ready, sticking straight out from under his T-shirt.

"It's occupied," Tim said, tossing his hands in the air in a shrug. The move had Tim going off balance, and he struggled to stay on his feet with his shorts gathered around his ankles. Colt ran his hands through his hair in frustration. Based on the clock beside his bed, he was at least fifteen minutes from leaving the gym and he wanted to call Jace before he made it home.

"Get the fuck out," Colt said as he began shoving Tim from the room. Double-D was next. She proved to be a little tricky to handle because she was all over him. It took a second to dislodge her and get the door shut and locked behind her.

"Playing hard to get turns me on," she yelled through the door as Colt headed toward his restroom to make his call in as much privacy as he could get.

Colt hoped the closed bathroom door would drown out the party going on in the other room. Colt didn't want Jace to think of him as a party guy. He rolled his eyes at the ludicrous thought. Jace already had to know he was totally a party guy. On a sigh, he dialed, praying Jace would answer.

# Chapter 2

"Damn, you have one fine ass!" Jace did little more than bring his phone to his ear before a voice boomed out the flattering words. He looked down at caller ID, confused when the name *Hottie* appeared. He didn't recognize the name or number on the screen when he answered.

"Colt?" Jace asked, a smile forming instantly on his lips as he said the name. Could this night seriously get any better? He just had his locker room porn fantasy fulfilled by his all-time perfect dream guy, and now the object of his desire called him. No, it couldn't get any better than this.

"I guess I should know who else might be calling. Are you seeing anyone that I should know about?" Colt growled the last part, his deep, sexy voice lowering. Jace couldn't help feeling incredibly pleased Colt would even pretend to care. There was a moment of silence before Jace bit his lip and tried for a cheeky response.

"I'm just seeing every Tom McCorkle, Dick Needham, and Harry Lewis I can." They were ironically all a part of the defensive line Colt played with for the last four years.

"You better not be!" Colt said, laughing. *Score!* He got the response he was shooting for with that little teaser. And did he seriously hear a hint of jealousy in Colt's voice?

"I'm not seeing anyone. What about you? I thought you were going out with Magda McCarthy?" Jace asked. The janitorial staff came banging through the locker room, pushing their large carts, jolting Jace, and he remembered where he stood. He grabbed his gear, shoved his shower kit into the locker, and tossed his duffel bag over his shoulder before heading out so no one could hear him having this conversation.

"Nah, not for a long time now. We just hang out together sometimes," Colt said. Jace actually stopped walking and stood a few feet from the gym's doors as that little bombshell settled. *Colt and Magda weren't a couple*? That bit of information would shock most of the school. Colt and Magda were seen everywhere together. Magda was the reigning Miss Texas to Colt's all-American football hero status. Jace had no idea how to respond. So he didn't and opted for a change of subject.

"My ass hurts," Jace blurted out, looking for anything to say to hide the confusion about Magda and Colt still clouding his mind.

"I hope in a good way." Colt growled. Those few short words had Jace's stomach aflutter. Was he seriously having butterflies over just the tone of Colt's voice?

Better yet, did Colt just really say that to him?

"How did you get my number? Not that I don't want you to have it, because I do. It's just I was wondering, that's all," Jace managed, all of the sudden completely tongue-tied. The need to get out from under all this frantic emotion churning inside him apparently had him rambling.

"When you went back in the showers, I programmed my number in your phone. I got your number. I also looked through your locker. Don't be mad. I wasn't going to. I was just gonna make sure we cleaned it up well enough, but you're a tidy guy. I know we messed it up, so I put it back in order for you." Did Colt just ramble? Wait! An even bigger question, in what world did Colton Michaels notice that Jace Montgomery was an obsessive compulsive freak about his personal organization?

Jace propelled himself forward and shoved open the heavy gymnasium doors. It was dark outside, late in the evening, and the campus was in the beginning stages of spring break. Most of the students had already high-tailed it out of there as soon as their last class ended. Jace walked alone on a well-lit path to his on-campus apartment. He'd taken this path at least a thousand times before. Never had he noticed the branches of the large oak trees swaying gently in the night breeze or the welcoming scent of spring blossoms and fresh cut grass filling the air. He breathed in deeply, not thinking about why he noticed them now, instead letting these things, along with Colt's voice, calm his frantic thoughts.

"Did I just say too much?" Colt asked in Jace's silence. His voice dropped an octave lower again, becoming huskier.

"No… not really." His cock began to stir again, damn he had it bad. He placed the phone on his shoulder and reached down to adjust himself because evidently his dick had taken notice of the change in Colt's voice, too. Which was interesting in itself because he'd just had two earth shattering orgasms less than an hour ago.

"But you're surprised I've been lusting after you this whole time?" Colt asked.

"Yeah, that was pretty shocking. It's kind of unbelievable actually," Jace admitted. He began slowly taking the steps up to his fourth floor apartment. He shared the small quad with four other male cheerleaders. They were all still on campus, senior cheerleaders were required to stay through the weekend for open gym to help any of the new hopefuls in the upcoming cheerleading tryouts.

The silence between them lingered for so long Jace looked down to see if the phone was still connected. After another long moment, he said the first thing that came to mind, "That's why your call came up *Hottie,* instead of a name. I was so confused." Colt still didn't speak. As Jace got to the top floor, he finally asked, "You still there?"

"Yeah, I am." Colt had that same sexy low voice thing going on. "I was just thinking. I'm relieved I finally got up enough balls and made a move. I wasn't lying; I've been watching you since we were freshmen. I couldn't ever get up the nerve to talk to you. I knew if I didn't do it tonight, we'd graduate, and I'd lose my chance."

"I don't even know how to respond to that," Jace said. He stopped again at the top of his stairwell, staring out into the night. His heart thumped wildly in his chest. Those words meant something. They had to! Jace desperately wanted them to mean something because they were about the sweetest words ever spoken.

"Hold up, I'm not finished. Let me get it all out. I wasn't sure you were even gay in the beginning. Then a few years ago, I was on the lawn with some of the guys, and I saw you kissing that redhead from the LGBT group. I would see you at the games, and he would be there too, waving and blowing those fucking kisses. That shit drove me crazy. I couldn't concentrate. I was making so many mistakes, calling the wrong plays, because I couldn't get my head straight about you. God, my dad was so pissed off at me for fucking things up. I finally had to let you go, force you out of my head. But I still watched you with him. I couldn't help it. I admit I was jealous. I hated seeing him in the stands every fucking game. Then I think it was Homecoming when he stopped coming. But I still never said anything. Today when I saw you head into the locker room, I had to take my chance," Colt confessed. His voice sounded different somehow. Not the booming confident one he'd grown to associate with Colt and definitely not the husky, deeply sexy voice from their locker room escapade earlier.

"That's a lie. No way, you seriously watched me that closely? I… Wow. Okay, yeah. That redhead's name is Bradley, and I caught him with Roger, my co-captain and roommate. I broke up with him. I still can't believe you watched me! Wow!" Jace stopped in mid-motion of reaching to unlock the front door to his apartment. The noise inside his apartment made him take a step back; he didn't want to drown out their conversation.

"It's not a lie. It's the God's honest truth. I told you I'd been watching you while were we making love tonight. I don't lie, Jace," Colt stated matter-of-factly. Jace could hear the honesty in his voice and focused on words like 'making love'. Had they made love?

"I didn't believe you, and you took off so fast afterward," Jace said, leaning back against the brick wall.

"I took off fast because I'd already risked so much. For both of us, nobody knows about me…" Colt only slightly paused before he changed the subject. "Now let's go back to talking about your fine ass hurting, shall we?"

"I definitely wasn't complaining. You pounded me good. You know I'm gonna feel you for a while," Jace answered back, teasing Colt, trying to keep his voice down. He was alone outside, but for some reason this felt so forbidden he didn't want anyone to hear him and ruin this moment.

"Let's talk about you. So what, are you like bi-sexual?" *Well that was a little abrupt!* Jace dropped his head back against brick wall. *I'm such a moron.* "I'm sorry, Colt, that came out wrong. You don't have to answer that. It's not any of my business."

"Nah, it's a fair question. And I know I confessed a lot just a second ago, but I'm not really ready to say it yet. I mean, I totally would talk about it with you, if I talked about it at all. I just don't think I can. Not yet," Colt answered back.

"Okay, no rush, I won't push you. I get that's a big step." So, it wasn't a bi-sexual thing. Clearly, Colt was hiding and needed to take those steps to come out on his own.

"Thanks, Jace. Listen, I was thinking. It's spring break. My agent has the hook-up on a place in Hawaii. I'm getting it for like five days starting Wednesday. It's why I'm still here on campus. You should come down there with me," Colt said, and like many times during this conversation, Jace stood there frozen in place. Had he just heard that right? He stared out at the night completely confused. *Vacation with Colt? In Hawaii? Seriously?*

"Are you there?" Colt asked.

"Yeah," Jace responded, unsure how to answer. His heart beat violently in his chest. He wanted nothing more than to go, but he didn't have that kind of money for a plane ticket. What did a plane ticket to Hawaii cost anyway? Certainly more than a couple hundred bucks, right? That was all he had to his name, and his heart sank.

"Does that yeah answer both of my questions, or just one? Did you already have plans?" Colt asked with uncertainty in his voice.

"I was just going home. No big plans. You know, or maybe you don't, I'm here on scholarship. I don't really have the money..." Jace started, but Colt cut him off.

"I got two airline tickets, and the place is covered. We'll just need food and lube." Colt laughed, but Jace remained quiet, wondering why Colt asked him and not one of his friends. Hell, maybe someone else bailed on him and Jace was an easy second because he was clearly a very willing body or bottom, depending on the need. But did Jace even really care about being a second thought? Nah, he didn't. He would be stupid if he passed up his chance to spend a few days in Hawaii, lounging on the beach, sipping Mai Tais and soaking up the tropical sun with the 'hottie' on the phone.

"I was just joking. I'll cover the cost of food, and we don't have to..." Colt started but Jace interrupted him.

"No, I get it. It was funny," Jace answered. Was he seriously going to say yes? Really?

"But not funny enough to laugh?" Colt asked, the humor was back in his voice and Jace realized he was taking too long to answer Colt's question.

"No, it's not that, I just... This just... You shocked me today and now you're doing it again." There, he said it. No more skirting around the biggest point of this entire conversation.

"Is that a bad thing?" Colt asked.

"No, not for me. Would we go all alone? I mean just the two of us?" Jace asked, hopeful.

"Yes, no one else. Just the two of us. So you'll go with me?" Colt's voice lifted, he sounded honestly excited. "Come on, Jace, let's get away. I loved tonight; I want more time with you, alone. I wasn't lying when I said I've watched you since before I ever started this school. It's been a long time coming for me. Please. Say yes."

"See, you keep shocking me," Jace said. The visual image of Colt's muscular body and dark good looks playing in the ocean and letting all that water run down his naked flesh... Damn, Jace was freaking hard again!

"I know, just say yes. Fuck it, fuck everything. Just say yes," Colt begged.

"Yes!" he said, surprised the word flew out of his mouth so quickly.

"Great! Do you text?" Colt asked excitedly. Jace could hear some background noise on Colt's end. The call was muffled as Colt said something and came back. "Jace, do you text?"

"Somewhat," Jace said. Texting was the new thing on campus, but Jace secretly hoped that form of communication never caught on, because it was such a pain in the ass, punching all those numbers just to get the right letter to flash on the screen.

"Good. I'll text you all the info. Dates, flight times, and the address. We might not be traveling together. I'd already booked my flight when I decided to go alone." Colt's voice trailed off.

"It's okay," Jace assured him.

"Damn! I gotta go. Some of the guys on the team are here. David and Tim are on my ass, so I need to go," Colt apologized, his frustration clear from the tone of his voice.

"No problem. I'll talk to you later," Jace said, turning on his heel toward his front door.

"Yeah. And, Jace, thank you," Colt whispered.

"Thank you for what?" Jace stopped at the front door, his hand on the knob.

"Just thank you. Bye." Colt disconnected the phone.

Jace pushed open the door to his apartment. His roommates were clearly getting the party started, all dressed up and ready for the night. A row of shot glasses were lined up along the kitchen bar. There were three guys and about twenty shots ready to go. They were downing them, leaving every fourth one for Jace.

"Hey! Where have you been? We were gonna leave you a note!" Gregory said, after getting his second shot down. Every person in this apartment was at college on scholarship. The lack of money had them getting tipsy before they ever left the house. Drinks were too expensive at the bar.

"Y'all go on without me. I'll catch up later," Jace said, bypassing the group.

"You had sex!" Jonathon called out.

"You did. Lucky boy!" Gregory seconded. Jace ignored them, not even turning back, because no way could he share and they might wear him down until he told something.

"You're walking funny. You bottomed!" Gregory called out. Jace shut his bedroom door, and reached back to push the lock in, smiling when he heard them at the door.

"Details! We need details! I'm the bottom! You never bottom!" Jace couldn't tell if Jonathon or Gregory yelled at his door. They were both crazy and had zero sense of decorum. They would do or say anything.

"Way off base as usual," Jace yelled back, grabbing his iPod and shoving the earbuds in his ear, he totally ignored his roommates as he selected a playlist and stretched out on his bed, thinking about Colt.

There was a game plan to dating. Jace wondered if he'd said yes too quickly? Nobody wanted the guy who was ripe for the picking. Jace struggled with his feelings. No question, he was already falling hard for Colt. After one session in a locker room and a brief conversation on the phone, he was completely lost. What would spending days in a tropical paradise do to him? If he went through with this, he was most definitely setting himself up for heartbreak.

No way would Colt Michaels come out any time soon. Besides, if Colt did come out, he'd be the most sought after gay man on campus. He was too good-looking and drop dead sexy.

If Jace had said no to Hawaii, he might not ever get another chance to spend time with him, and he would most definitely regret that decision for the rest of his life. Fuck the rules of dating. He had to at least give them a chance, didn't he?

Colt circled the McDonald's parking lot searching for Jace through the front window of the fast food restaurant. Jace started almost every morning here, having a fruit and yogurt parfait and orange juice before his first class. This being one of the many things Colt had learned by watching Jace from afar over the years. Colt now started his day following this same routine because something about seeing Jace first thing in the morning tended to make his day a little better.

As he circled back around the side of the building, he got a glimpse of Jace's blond hair through the large plate glass window. He quickly scanned the rest of the restaurant. The place was emptier than normal, which was a good thing. Colt circled again and came up the side of the building where he spotted some of the players at the front ordering. *Damn it!* He'd have to wait before going inside, and he prayed Jace didn't finish before the others left.

Colt parked in a back spot, strategically watching the front door. After a few minutes both players left. That meant Jace was alone inside. Colt tugged his ball cap low on his head, got out of his car, and jogged across the parking lot to the front doors.

The element of surprise was on his side. Jace sat in the corner of the booth, reading the newspaper, oblivious to his entrance. He was able to make his way to Jace's table unseen. Colt slid in the booth, punching the newspaper with his hand, and got an angry look from Jace before he realized who sat across from him. Colt's heart gave a little jolt of excitement when Jace's face lit up with recognition.

"Hey you," Colt said.

"What are you doing here?" Jace asked, and then got instantly red-faced, averting his eyes, looking back down at the table. "Duh, you're getting breakfast."

"Nah, I just know this is where you usually come in the mornings, and I got your ticket. You might need this," Colt said, sliding an envelope across the table. "I tried to get us on the same flight, but everything's all booked up. I'll be arriving a few hours before you. I also got a rental car in your name. All the information's in the packet because we won't be leaving together. Now I just wish I'd let them book me two tickets when they first offered up the beach house," Colt said, keeping his casual attitude, but staring directly into Jace's eyes.

Jace picked up the envelope, opened it, doing a quick thumb through of the contents inside. The cost of the ticket was evidently still in the flight itinerary. "Colt, this was so much money, are you sure your agent's good with this?"

"I'm positive. I probably won't get to see you before we leave. I'm sorry about that, but we'll be alone on the island," Colt said, as a couple of students walked into the restaurant. They noticed Colt immediately, giving a nod before looking over at Jace. Colt caught the subtle look, but it was still a questioning glare nonetheless. "I gotta go. I just wanted to give you this and tell you thank you again for last night."

"Wait, how did you know I would be here?"

"I told you, I'm a creeper where you're concerned. I know all about you," Colt said with a laugh, but meant every word. He quickly slid out of the booth and walked away, not giving Jace a chance to respond.

# Chapter 3

*Shit!* Colt ran across the Hawaiian bungalow to the kitchen stove, sliding to a stop as he grabbed the boiling pot and pushed it off the burner. In his need to get everything just right for Jace's arrival, he'd almost overcooked their dinner. *Not good!*

Colt glanced at the large clock that hung over the brightly painted turquoise and yellow sideboard. *Shit!* Jace's plane just landed. He figured he had about twenty minutes before Jace got through baggage claim and left the airport. The drive to the beach house would take another thirty minutes. That gave Colt a little under an hour to shower, dress, and get the fire started. He also needed to put the fish he'd purchased from the restaurant over the fire to warm, and he still needed to set the table properly. In all the time Colt had to plan for Jace's arrival, he never thought he'd be this far behind. *Shit! Shit! Shit!*

Dumping the seafood in the colander at the sink, he flung the pot on the stove and ran to the bathroom. His hair would take the most time, but he desperately wanted to look his best for Jace. Because Jace always looked so fucking hot. A grin he couldn't contain spread across his face as he tore his T-shirt over his head and tossed it in the general direction of his suitcase. Excitement filled his soul. Colt was happy. Seriously, emotionally happy for the first time in a long time, maybe even ever, and didn't that just feel fan-fucking-tastic!

"Is he seriously not here?" Jace said aloud to no one as he stood at the front door to the bungalow waiting for Colt to answer his knock. The doubt that plagued him for the last few days reared its ugly head. He knocked again, this time using the side of his balled up fist to pound against the wooden door. Jace stepped back on the porch and looked at the house, before stepping forward again and sticking his ear to the door to listen inside. He saw and heard nothing. No one was home.

*Stop doubting everything. He wouldn't have fucked you, called you, texted over and over, and flown you here as some sort of sick practical joke. Right?* Jace stared at the house. Already dusk outside, the night was coming on fast and Jace palmed his phone. Maybe he had the wrong house. And he had absolutely no signal. *Great!*

So he knocked again, actually banging hard on the door this time. Five minutes later, he steeled up his spine and moved. The pending dusk was turning full night, and if this was a practical joke, it needed to go ahead and happen so everyone could get a good laugh and he could find a ride back to the airport.

This certainly wouldn't be the first time he'd been on the receiving end of a cruel prank. Nothing he hadn't endured before, many times over. Jocks, in his opinion, could be among the worst homophobes. They always tried to one up the other in some kind of sick, dick measuring contest to prove how alpha manly and hetero they were.

Jace left his bags on the front porch and walked the length of the well-kept bungalow. He stepped cautiously off the porch, through the flowerbed, careful not to step on any of the colorful blooms or mess up any of the tropical plants as he pressed his face against the dusty glass of the window to peer inside. He searched for any movement.

Disappointed there had been no sign of Colt, he made his way back to the porch where he'd left his bag. Jace stood there, his back to the door, mentally cussing himself for letting his guard so far down. Was this the big end-of-college joke for the senior football players? He didn't doubt it one bit. Going after a gay male cheerleader would provide endless hours of fun for those guys. He gave in and looked up, giving the overhang of the porch a quick scan to see if there were any cameras.

To say Jace had been made fun of quite a bit over years was an understatement. Jokes were still a daily occurrence that never seemed to get old to those playing them. Hell, Jace traveled regularly with bullying, testosterone-filled, mean-spirited jokers hiding behind the semblance of a football team. Practical jokes and sexual orientation slurs were part of daily life, but it never occurred to him Colt might have planned something like this.

Being abandoned in Hawaii… how was that even funny? Except there was no way he could afford to get home. Colt had his return ticket. Everyone knew he didn't have a dime to his name. Jace was on a straight up academic scholarship, with cheerleading footing the rest of the bill. And, for whatever reason, his heart dropped. Jace had really started to believe Colt was truly into him. What was he going to do now? *Fuck!*

Sounds other than the ocean pulled Jace's attention to the backyard. He took the stairs down, his flips flops kicking up sand as he tracked his way to the back. On guard, he took in his surroundings and noticed the next closest neighbor was still a distance away. He only knew there was a neighbor because he could see the roof of a bungalow in the distance. The properties were separated by dense tropical foliage. Jace rounded the corner to the back of the house, stopping dead in his tracks. A grin came to his lips, and he stood there for just a moment, staring.

Colt was alone in the back, lighting tiki torches that illuminated the path from the back of the house all the way down to the beach. His swim trunks hung low on his hips, and he was shirtless. Jace watched the muscles flex in Colt's back as he lifted his arm to ignite the torch. *Damn!* Jace studied Colt's profile as the guy turned and lit another wick. Intent on his task, Colt hadn't noticed him staring.

"Hey," Jace called out, his grin growing bigger as he walked toward Colt. Colt startled and spun around, almost dropping the lighter.

"Damn it! You're already here? Shit!" Jace stopped in his tracks. His smile faded instantly. Maybe this was a practical joke after all. "I wanted to meet you at the front door, surprise you with all of this. I thought I had ten more minutes!" Colt abandoned the lighting of the torches, his bare feet sinking in the sand as he headed straight toward him. He wore a big sexy smile on his face as he reached out to take Jace's duffel off his shoulder.

"Have you eaten yet?" Colt asked. Just like Jace had come to expect, Colt was the definition of random emotion, jumping from one thought to the next, never really hanging on to any one mood for too long. Colt leaned in for a quick kiss, slinging the duffel over his shoulder, and took Jace's hand as if it was the most natural move in the world.

"No, you told me not to." Jace tried to catch up with everything going on around him.

"And you listened? See, you were made for me," Colt teased. He was back to humor, now dragging Jace toward the house. Jace tried to look over the backyard, spotting a table set up close to the water. Two chairs were anchored in the sand. A lit fire pit lay close by. "Are you tired? I have this whole thing planned out here, but if you want to sleep, or something, go ahead. I can wait."

"Did you do all this?" Jace asked and realized Colt was already walking them up the steps to the back door. "Why are we going inside?"

"Well, maybe you don't listen so well after all. I'll have to remember that," Colt deadpanned. "And to think I was so proud of our progress." He pulled Jace into his arms, steps from the back door. "I made dinner for us. There's some beer out there. You like Corona, right?"

"How do you know that?" Jace asked. His attention fully on Colt's body pressed against his.

"I've traveled all over the world with you, cheer boy. I know what you drink. I know you eat almost no meat, but tons of seafood. You like fresh, raw foods as opposed to cooked. See?" Colt gave him a wink, clearly proud of his knowledge.

"How do you know that? You seriously keep shocking the hell out of me, Colt," Jace said. Colt's grin widened as he took Jace's arms and wrapped them around his waist.

"Good. Now answer me? You ready to start this vacation, or are you tired or something?" Colt asked. His expression turned thoughtful as he studied Jace's face.

"No, I'm definitely ready to start our vacation," Jace said, holding Colt tighter in his arms.

"Let's get you inside. I bought you a pair of island swim trunks. You don't have to wear them, but I thought of you when I saw them. I thought we could share a room, but if you want your own space, I can bunk in the other one," Colt said with another abrupt mood change; this time from fun and flirty to tour guide.

Colt stepped from the embrace and took Jace's hand to pull him through the bungalow to a back bedroom. Jace barely had time to absorb any of the details, they were moving so fast, but he didn't miss a beat in the bedroom. His heart picked up the pace at the thought of Colt spending so much time preparing for his arrival. Unlit candles were spread over every available surface. There was an open bottle of wine chilling in a stew pot by the bed. Wild orchids, plumeria, and hibiscus flowers were handpicked and placed all around the room, adding to the tropical decor. Colt didn't seem to notice his pause. He dumped Jace's bag in the closet without much care. On the bed was a pair of brightly-colored swim trunks, handpicked and waiting for him. The sweet gesture didn't escape him.

"Here are the swim trunks I was telling you about." Colt motioned to the bed and turned back toward him, his smile faded and his brow narrowed as he looked over to Jace. "Why are you by the door? Do you want another room?" An expression of what must have been disappointment crossed Colt's face, and there was another abrupt change in his posture. Jace was growing to love all the moods of Colt.

"Thank you for the trunks. Did you do all this?" Jace slowly stepped inside. Impressed with the visible effort and thought Colt obviously put into his arrival.

"Yeah?" he narrowed his brow again, clearly confused, and looked around the room. "You don't like it?"

"Is it for me?" Jace asked, stopping when he stood directly in front of Colt.

"Yeah." This time Colt really looked confused. "Who else…"

"Do you do this kind of stuff all the time?" Jace inquired as he turned to the bed, scooping up a bloom, bringing it to his nose. He shut his eyes, breathing in the sweet scent. For the first time since Jace arrived, chatty Colt went silent. He opened his eyes, watching Colt intently.

"Do you not want to answer that question? It's okay if you've done this before. I'm just glad you did it for me," Jace continued. He placed the flower back on one of the pillows and turned his full attention to Colt.

"I haven't ever done this before. It's probably dumb. I just wanted it special for you. You've made me happy. I always envisioned you laughing at me if I ever approached you. I can't remember ever being this content before. I just wanted to give that back to you," Colt replied quietly. He dropped his hands to the nonexistent pockets of his swim trunks, and when the movement failed to achieve the desired result, he shoved them behind his back. "I want this to happen between us. More than you know."

Jace stood in front of Colt, studying him, not missing the nervous fidget from the usually overconfident Colton Michaels. Was he worried? Surely not! Jace's attention was immediately drawn to Colt's mouth as his tongue darted out, leaving a wet trail across his lower lip, before he began to worry the lip with his teeth. God, he was gorgeous.

They were closer to the same height than Jace first thought. They fit well together, and Jace knew that for a fact. Colt's long dark lashes brushed his cheek when he blinked. When he focused those ice blue eyes on him, Jace's heart melted. Every bit of resistance he'd used to keep himself at even a small distance dissolved, and he reached up, taking Colt's face between his hands.

"No one's ever done anything like this for me before, Colt. Thank you," Jace whispered as he leaned forward initiating a kiss between them for the first time. He slanted his mouth over Colt's, trying to gain entrance. They only really kissed once in their locker room experience.

The hours they'd spent on the phone together, the dozens and dozens of text messages, combined with the effort Colt had gone to for him was better than any foreplay Jace had ever received. Colt opened, and Jace manned up, making the move to tug Colt closer to him. Their hips met, and he groaned at the contact, sliding his tongue forward at the same moment Colt snaked his arms around his waist and fused their bodies together.

It was spontaneous combustion. Colt's hips rolled into Jace. They were both hard and ready. The grinding of their cocks almost undid Jace. He thrust his tongue deeper into Colt's sweet mouth, deepening the kiss as his hands slid down Colt's perfect ass.

And then he was sucking air. A second passed before he realized Colt wasn't still in the kiss. *Wait! What?*

Colt reached forward and gave him a peck on the lips one last time before he dropped his arms, releasing Jace from their embrace, and slowly backed away, completely severing all contact between them. This was not in Jace's current game plan at all! Why was he gone? Jace looked around, completely confused. *What the hell just happened? Why aren't we in bed?*

"I want to do this right this time. You change into the trunks, if you want, and come down to the beach. I'm sorry I can't take you out on a date just yet, because… well, you know. But I can spend time with you here, be with you right now, and that's what I want. Get dressed and come outside," Colt said, now standing by the bedroom door. Jace didn't even have time to protest.

"Change! And stop looking like that. Let me do this right, Jace, baby," Colt said, and left the bedroom, Jace still completely at a loss as to why they weren't already naked with their dicks in each other's mouths. They should be having sex by now. When did that stop being the plan?

Jace gave in and adjusted his cock in his shorts. He was so hard he had to stick his hand inside the waistband to fully adjust himself. His prick vehemently protested, but he wasn't going to beg Colt to do him. Right? After reweighing that option, Jace finally turned back to the bed, eyeing the swim trunks. Colt was right; the bright floral print did suit him.

# Chapter 4

The ocean churned just feet away from where they sat. The brightness of the full moon reflected perfectly on the breaking waves causing the whitecaps to shimmer as they rolled toward the island. Colt reached over to refill Jace's wine glass as he'd done countless times over the last few hours, keeping them outside, enjoying each other's company. At least, he hoped Jace enjoyed this as much as he did.

A small radio played in the background. The station was some sort of sultry island music, local to the area. The tiki torch flames danced in the cool tropical breeze casting soft shadows across the small patio table. In Colt's mind, it whispered romance, exactly what he tried to accomplish.

All in all, Colt was proud of the time he'd spent in preparing for tonight. He really thought he'd pulled off a very seductive kind of scene. It was what he wanted most for tonight, to show Jace just how much he meant. As he placed the wine bottle back in the ice bucket, he weighed his options and decided neither of them was quite ready to give up their front row seats to nature's very own moonlit performance. They both seemed to enjoy the evening.

Colt had given up stealing sideways glances at Jace hours ago. Now he was outright staring. Nothing in the beauty of their tropical paradise held the allure of the beautiful man sitting next to him. Jace could have easily been on the cover of any fashion magazine across the country. He had those boy next door meets surfer guy good looks. His sunny blond hair and tanned six pack cut abs turned Colt on like nothing else ever had before. Jace was made for turning heads at the beach or anywhere for that matter. From the moment Colt found out about this place, he'd wanted Jace right here with him.

"Wanna swim again?" Colt asked, taking Jace's hand. They sat side by side at the table, facing the ocean.

"I'm fine right here. Unless you want to," Jace said, his chest bare, one leg crossed over his knee, and he had no problem easily entwining their fingers together as if it was the most natural thing to do. Colt liked Jace's easy familiarity.

"Nah, I'm good here, too," Colt said, finally sitting back, casting his stare out into the ocean. They swam earlier tonight, eaten a huge crab and fish dinner, and drank a lot of beer and wine. Colt felt good, and he hoped Jace did too.

"Who was supposed to be here with you this week?" Jace asked out of the blue, his eyes remaining focused on the ocean. Colt looked over at him, watched him closely. The question was the first personal thing they'd said since they been back out on the beach.

"No one, I was coming alone," Colt replied.

"But they gave you two tickets?" Jace shot back. Not necessarily an accusation, still just a question.

"I had the ticket my agent gave me, and I bought yours. They offered to buy another ticket when they told me about this place, but I didn't have anybody to bring. I almost didn't come," Colt said.

"You bought my ticket? I thought you said you had an extra ticket available," Jace asked, his eyes locked on Colt's. Jace tensed, straightening up in his chair as he started to stand.

"No, sit back. Relax like you were. I bought the ticket because I thought we could come down here, get away from everyone, and get to know each other. It's not a big deal," Colt confessed quickly. As he spoke, he reached out and pushed Jace back into the seat. No way did he want Jace bowed up tight. They were relaxed. He needed them relaxed.

"That was expensive," Jace said, alarm in his voice.

"Money's one problem I don't seem to have right now. I have one hell of a credit line all of a sudden. Jace, please sit back. It's the best money I've spent." Jace didn't listen to him. He could see Jace ticking off numbers in his head, trying to figure out how much the trip probably cost and if there was any way he could pay him back. Colt knew from all the years of watching Jace, he took every extra side job thrown his way. Colt hadn't ever heard of Jace taking handouts. If he couldn't pay, he didn't do it. "Really, Jace, sit back… I wanted you to come with me."

"Why?" Jace asked, sounding defensive.

"Do you ask all your dates why they spend time with you?" Colt questioned, trying for mischievous, but Jace just stared at him. Maybe Colt should have ended this evening a few minutes ago. The tension between them was building. Not terrible, but there nonetheless, and Jace finally seemed bolder after the alcohol, asking questions and wanting some answers.

"Man, really, relax. I wanted you here with me so I arranged it. I just feel like I've wasted a lot of time wanting you and doing nothing about it," Colt said. He forced his eyes away, starring out over the moonlit ocean. His fingers tightened around Jace's, and he could feel Jace's eyes still on him.

"You're the star of our team. You're the player most sought after by the NFL. You're gonna be a first round draft pick, and you want me to believe you're harboring some kind of true feelings for me, for apparently a long time?" Jace challenged Colt with every word he spoke. He got it; he'd have asked these same questions way before now.

"Pretty much sums it up," Colt replied, a sly grin on his face. He still hadn't looked over at Jace, but lifted their joined hands, bringing Jace's knuckles up for a kiss. "Actually, you're dead on."

"I don't believe it," Jace countered after a minute and finally relaxed back in his seat, staring straight ahead. Colt liked that much better, because now he could go back to being the watcher. "I can get you might be into fucking guys now and then. I like it, so why wouldn't you, but not the rest. And why me? I don't understand. I'm a cheerleader on scholarship, and you're, well, you. Nah, I can't see it at all."

Jace drained his wine glass.

"The first time I saw you was August of '99. We were at the stadium. It was the first community pep rally, before school even started. You tumbled across the whole field, doing all those twisty things. Your hair was shorter, you weren't as muscular, and I think you've gotten taller. You were stunning. The most beautiful guy I had ever seen. I got so hard watching you I had to walk around with my hands in my pockets, trying to hide my hard-on. The first chance I got, I went to the bathroom and jacked off. What else do you want to know?" Colt asked.

Jace turned to Colt, staring at him, not speaking, but clearly taking in his every word.

"In 2001, your dad died. You were gone for like two weeks," Colt started, but Jace cut him off.

"Don't tell me you were the one that sent that iPod to me."

"I did. I confess it was from me. I felt so bad for you. You worked so hard all the time. You always had that old Walkman with the big head phones covering your ears. Let's see, you take on every community commitment the school offers. Your grade point average is like right at a three point nine. You—"

"How do you know that?" Jace asked. The accusation was gone, but the curiosity wasn't.

"Jace, you wear a size twelve shoe. You eat fruit and yogurt every morning for breakfast. You hate the tags in the back of your T-shirts; you always cut them out. You chew the caps to your pens. You love Creed. You..." Colt was on a roll and could go on forever. He was an encyclopedia of knowledge when it came to Jace Montgomery.

"Okay, that's enough," Jace said, lifting a hand to stop Colt in mid-sentence.

"I think that might be my favorite look. It's the same look you gave me when I hit on you in the locker room," Colt chuckled.

"I don't even know what to say to that." Jace fidgeted, uncrossing his leg, and then crossing them again. He wasn't necessarily relaxed, but he wasn't about to bolt either. Colt took the chance and refilled Jace's wine glass. He poured the last of their second bottle into Jace's glass before setting the empty bottle on the table beside him. Colt pulled another bottle out of the cooler and popped the cork.

His big plan for the night was to bottom. He wanted Jace to top him. He hadn't said anything, but hoped Jace would be his first. Overall, Colt decided he probably needed to be a little more relaxed and maybe be somewhat drunk to pull it off. He didn't know what to expect. He'd only had the tip of Jace's finger breach him for an instant when they were making out in the locker room. He took a long drink straight from the third bottle.

"You could tell me you thought about me too, even if it's not true," Colt said, and took another long swig, completely abandoning his glass. Colt worried he might have freaked Jace out with his sad attempt at humor, falling short once again, because Jace hadn't laughed at his joke.

"I did think about you. Who doesn't? You're like TLU's golden child. Everyone wants to know you," Jace said as he took a sip from his refilled wine glass. "Does your dad know about this?"

"*Hell no!*" Colt choked out, quickly lowering the bottle, almost spewing the wine in his mouth all over Jace when he answered. "*Fuck no*, he can't ever know. I'm never ever gonna be old enough for him to find out I like dick. Can you imagine that? I'd cause him to have a coronary right there on the field."

"He's intense," Jace agreed.

Intense was a huge understatement in describing his father, Larry Michaels. He was an ex-professional football player who had ridden Colt's ass his entire life. He pushed Colt to excel in everything he did, especially football, and if he failed, hell rained down on his head so hard Child Protective Services had Colt's father on speed dial.

"Ya think? No, he can't ever know. My parents aren't anything like yours. My father's orchestrated my whole football career for pretty much my entire life. He's done all this for my future. He handles all the contacts and got the agents looking at me; he's my manager. He controls my life. No way would it ever be a good idea to clue him in on how much I like hot blond cheerleaders of the same sex." Colt took a big swig from the bottle after thinking about his father.

"So you're gay?" Jace asked, mercifully getting off the subject of his dad.

"I think so. I've lusted after you forever. I think about you when I'm trying to get off. Is that saying too much?" Finally, the drunk started to settle in.

"No, you don't. Really?" Jace sounded shocked.

"You know, I've seen you in the locker room over the years. It's not hard to draw that image up when needed," Colt teased, taking another long drink from the bottle.

"I jack off to you, too," Jace blurted, a shy grin on his face. Colt watched as Jace's body physically relaxed after his confession.

"Finally! You haven't given me much back in the way of encouragement, but what you just said, *that* made my day," Colt declared, his grin firmly back in place.

"Whatever! You're Colton Michaels. Your girlfriend's gonna be the next Miss America."

"I told you, she's not my girlfriend," Colt protested, lifting the bottle to his lips, taking another guzzle, close to draining it now.

"Sure fooled me."

"Nah, I really can't tell you more, but let's just say, her and I, we have a lot in common," Colt said, waggling his eyebrows.

"No fucking way! You all need to quit hiding. If everyone would quit hiding and just be who they are, I wouldn't have to be called a fucking fag every single day of my life," Jace shot back with absolutely no malice. He grinned, tightening his hand around Colt's.

"I'm not as strong as you. I wished I were, but I'm not. I'm not sure at this point if I ever will be." Colt gave up and turned his seat toward Jace, facing him now. He placed the makeshift wine bucket on the table, keeping what was left of the bottle close by. "Let me tell you what I am sure of, what I want. I want you to fuck me tonight. I want you inside me. It's my first time, but I know I liked your finger in my ass when we made out in the locker room. How do you feel about that?"

Jace grinned and rose from the chair, lifting Colt's hand to help him up. Their thighs brushed against one another as he stood. "You're finally speaking my language."

# Chapter 5

"I need a couple minutes," Colt said as they entered the bungalow's master bedroom. Jace's nerves were back in full force, and if he was any judge, he figured Colt's were too. The man had downed the last bottle of wine by himself in less than thirty minutes. Yeah, Colt was nervous, which made Jace that much more anxious.

"We don't have to do this," Jace said. Colt attempted to pull his hand free from Jace's hold, but he held on tight, keeping them in place. "I don't mind being on bottom. I love the feeling of you inside me."

"No, I just need a minute, that's all. I've thought about this night for a long time. I want this, and I want it with you." Colt kissed Jace's lips, a smile spread across his face. "I plan on doing this often. Just be gentle with me, or not. Whatever." And with that, Colt gave a devilish smirk, winked, and turned on his heel, not bothering to look back as he stepped inside the bathroom.

"Pour us some more wine," Colt called out as the door slammed shut behind him.

Jace stood in the middle of the room. The candles were there, unlit. He supposed they were there for a reason, so he found the lighter and began to light each one. It took some time, there had to be twenty-five candles placed around the room. Jace paused before lighting the last one, looking up in the dresser mirror to see his blond hair in a windblown mess. He took a second to straighten his haphazard hair before lighting the final candle.

About the same time, he heard the commode flush and the sink faucet turn off, but Colt didn't come out. Jace stood in the middle of the bedroom, looking around. He spotted the bottle of wine Colt left chilling in the stew pot by the bed. The bottle sat in cold water now, the ice in the makeshift bucket completely melted. He didn't think Colt would care as he plucked the bottle from the water and uncorked it, pouring two glasses. Colt still hadn't come out of the bathroom.

Jace looked down at himself. His swim trunks were dry, he thought he looked fine, but then he lifted an arm and took a quick sniff. Yeah, he could use a quick shower. On a whim, he grabbed his duffel and searched the house for another bathroom. He found a partial bath off the living room. No shower, but he could sponge bathe, maybe do a quick sink wash of his hair. A yawn slipped out, causing Jace to fish out his phone. Two in the morning, Kauai time, seven in the morning, Texas time. He'd been up twenty-four hours, and he switched the water to cold to help wake him up.

Jace managed everything pretty quickly. He shaved, washed his hair, cleaned his body, paying close attention to his ass, and warred with himself the entire time as to whether he should put on a clean pair of swim trunks. He loved that Colt had bought him these trunks.

As he debated, his mind slipped to the one thing he hadn't let himself consider since their time in the locker room. What in the hell was happening between them? This was like a whirlwind spinning completely out of control, making it hard to keep up. Yet somewhere tonight, Jace's heart connected, and he hadn't stopped it.

Jace stood at the mirror, looking at his reflection, his swim trunks in hand, and he finally yielded to the thoughts crossing his mind. Colt Michaels was in the other room, waiting for him to come fuck him. Never in a million years would he have seen that coming. The nagging doubt of a very well-planned practical joke didn't hold much weight anymore. Colt really seemed into him. *Colton Michaels for God's sake!* Surreal didn't begin to describe this moment.

For nothing more than a shield, Jace tugged fresh swim trucks on before he cleaned up his mess in the bathroom. By his estimation, he'd been in there about fifteen minutes. It was time to get back, face this night, and see where he and Colt were really headed in all of this.

All the lights were off in the house. Only the lit candles flickering out into the hall guided him to their room. He paused outside the bedroom door and listened. He could hear Colt breathing and maybe drinking. Drinking from the open wine bottle, if the sloshing he heard was anything to go by. Jace grinned at Colt's need for liquid courage.

Jace forced himself forward, rounded the corner, and stopped in the doorway. Colt was lying sprawled out in the middle of the bed, completely nude. *Damn!* His wet dream came true. Colt's muscular arms were propped behind his head, and he was staring intently at the ceiling, obviously lost in thought. Colt's legs were open, his left leg bent and dropped to the side, giving Jace a great view of his balls and flaccid cock.

Every one of Jace fantasies had Colt hung and apparently he didn't get it wrong. He never got the chance to gawk during the time they'd spent together in the locker room. Honestly, he couldn't remember most of what happened because he had been in such a state of blissful shock, before he spent the rest of his time bent over, hanging on for dear life.

"Why are you dressed?" Colt asked, looking over with a skittish smile. He propped up on an elbow when he noticed Jace in the doorway. His dark hair looked damp from a shower. Jace's cock swelled at the breathtaking sight of Colt staring up at him. Something flashed in Colt's eyes and his face began to cloud. "Are you having second thoughts?"

Colt was an open book, all his emotions showing right there on his face. This Colt was so different from the self-assured, cocky guy he'd watched from afar. He clearly had two very different personalities, and Jace was drawn to both.

"I wasn't sure if you needed more time," Jace responded to the first question, ignoring the second. He slipped his thumbs under his waistband, sliding his swim trucks down until they dropped to the floor. He stepped forward glad to see the approving smile spreading across Colt's upturned face as he lay fully back on the bed. Jace licked his lips, watching Colt's cock stir to life. Colt tracked his movements as he padded naked across the room toward the bed. Jace climbed slowly on the mattress until he lay on his side, propped up on his elbow, facing Colt.

"You lit the candles," Colt said, and turned the bottle up, draining the wine before setting the empty bottle back on the nightstand. He rolled back over, drawing Jace to him. "I'm pretty drunk."

"You know, at any time, you can just tell me and we can switch. We don't—"

"I want this, Jace. I want you." Colt palmed the back of his head, tugging Jace down for one of the most tender kisses of his life. Colt didn't rush. He eased himself back and pulled Jace completely over him. Jace anchored himself on his forearm, and carefully pushed his leg between Colt's spread thighs, all the while devouring his sweet mouth.

It didn't take long for Jace to slide his hand low and find Colt's balls. He held Colt's sack in the palm of his hand; his fingers circled the base of his cock. He slowly massaged Colt's balls and stroked him in the same rhythm as the kiss. His effort was rewarded by a thrust of Colt's hips, jerking forward as a low moan escaped his lips.

Jace broke free from the kiss, and Colt protested, fighting the move until he realized Jace intended to suck him. He spread his legs wider and slid his fingers into Jace's hair as he nibbled and licked his way across Colt's chest. He teased each nipple with his tongue before continuing to trail soft kisses down his stomach. Jace took his time until he reached the tip of Colt's cock. Under his inspection, a drop of pre-come formed on the tip. Jace's mouth watered at the sight. He needed to taste Colt like he needed to breathe, and his cock twitched in Jace's hand as if it had read his thoughts. Jace gripped Colt tighter and lapped at the wetness. His eyes never strayed from Colt's flawless face.

"We need condoms and lube. Did you bring any? I have some if we need them," Jace said. Colt kept his intense gaze trained on Jace. Colt didn't say a word, but lifted his hand, fumbling with something at the top of the headboard.

"I didn't want you to think I assumed this," Colt said. His voice came out deep and husky, his need very clear. Colt produced massage oil, lube, and condoms, showing them to Jace before dropping everything within easy reach. Jace reached for the bottles, but Colt stopped him, pulling Jace toward him. Colt met him halfway. The kiss was hot, intense, and full of something Jace couldn't name.

"Thank you for coming here with me." Colt kept Jace's face in his palms, his blue eyes boring holes straight into his soul as he spoke the words.

"Promise to tell me if I hurt you," Jace whispered, running his thumb across Colt's bottom lip.

"I want it to hurt a little," Colt whispered and bit at Jace's thumb. The move broke the spell of the kiss, and Jace grinned, pushing the tip of his thumb between Colt's parted lips. He wasn't disappointed with the swirl of his tongue. Colt sucked his finger in the rest of the way. He couldn't help the moan, imagining his own cock in Colt's sinful mouth.

"You're so freaking hot, Michaels. As much as I love watching you suck my thumb, I have bigger plans for you. I wanna show you how good this can be. I need to be buried balls deep inside you, and I will be, but I want you good and relaxed before we start." Jace removed his thumb and reached down to grip Colt's thick dick again. In one swift move, he slid down Colt's muscular body, engulfing him almost to his root. A hiss came from above, giving Jace a clue he'd done it right. All in all, this was where he excelled. Jace closed his eyes, opened his throat, and deep throated Colt on his second try. Colt's hands threaded in his hair, and he could taste the salty tang of Colt's orgasm already forming.

"Fuck that feels good," Colt growled. Jace lifted his gaze to see Colt's hooded eyes focused on his mouth. He made a show of swirling his tongue up and around, delving in Colt's slit before taking Colt deep again. This time he slid his fingers down Colt's crease. Colt gave a slight clench as Jace circled his rim. As much as Colt wanted this, he wasn't ready and he needed him to relax. He slid Colt back down his throat and buried his nose in Colt's dark curls. Colt's scent filled his senses.

Jace's dick throbbed at the heady smell of raw male need mingled with the fresh coconut bodywash he must have used in the shower. Jace wanted this experience to be perfect and he wanted this to last. But he knew it wouldn't by the way Colt began to buck into his mouth. He pulled his mouth from Colt's length.

"Don't stop." Colt gripped his arms as he rose.

"Shh, we're gonna do this right. Turnover." Under protest, Jace helped Colt to his stomach. Colt tried to turn back, but Jace held him in place by straddling his thighs. Jace picked up the oil, squirted some on his hands, and rubbed them together before he began to slowly massage Colt's back. The deep moans turned sensual as Jace started at the broad shoulders.

Colt was built. His muscular body tanned, fit, and now well-oiled. Jace applied pressure to Colt's back, making sure he paid special attention to his teres major and trapezius muscles as he worked his way down, slowly and methodically. Colt groaned loudly as his firm muscles began to unknot and relax, yielding under Jace's gentle persuasion. The massage turned into its own kind of foreplay as Jace took the time and ran his hands up and down every inch of Colt's body.

"I love the way you feel. I want you so bad," Jace whispered. He couldn't resist taking small nibbles of Colt's tanned skin, quickly replacing the small teasing bites with light kisses across Colt's back and down his spine. Jace shifted his straddle, causing his cock to slide against Colt's ass. Colt slightly lifted his ass higher at the contact, and Jace's cock wept with anticipation as he slipped along the crevasse.

"You're killing me," Jace whispered, forcing his body to slow down.

"Yeah? Well, I think you're a tease, cheer boy," Colt mumbled, his voice partially muffled by the pillow. Colt looked relaxed. His arms splayed out where Jace had thoroughly rubbed the tension from each one of them. Jace smoothed his hands down Colt's spine, until he finally started to massage Colt's ass. He kneaded each firm globe, and then used his thumbs to spread Colt's ass cheeks as he slowly slid his finger over Colt's rim, admiring his puckered hole. The move had Colt slightly lifting his ass, moaning at the subtle contact.

Jace tore his eyes from Colt and reached for the lube. After coating his fingers, he slowly pushed one into Colt. He was tight at first, but Jace took the time and continued to work him, pushing his finger deeper before adding another. He slowly scissored them.

"Oh, fuck! That feels so... different. Fuck, it feels real good!" Colt moved against his fingers. The time he'd taken was working. Colt relaxed and opened up to him, and he watched as Colt fucked himself on the digits.

"I wanna see you," Colt whispered into the pillow. "I wanna watch you." And he somehow managed to turn over onto his back with Jace still straddling his legs.

"You're so beautiful, Jace. I need to memorize everything about you so I can remember this moment while I'm on the road with the team and can't get home to see you." Colt's words were slightly slurred, either from the wine or the relaxing massage. He didn't respond to Colt's words. He couldn't. They said too much. Jace slid the condom in place, slicked his own dick with the lube, and coated his fingers again before sliding his knee between Colt's thighs. Colt spread his legs, and Jace moved in, pushing his fingers back into Colt, making sure Colt hadn't tightened in the turn.

"I can tell you don't believe me. I know you don't, but I mean it. I wanna figure this out between us. I want you waiting on me when I get home. I want this…" Colt's words faltered and his cock began to leak pre-come over his stomach as he experienced the pleasure of Jace's thumb rubbing his prostate.

"Fuck, that feels too good. I'm gonna come, Jace!"

"No, don't come yet." Jace reached up and gripped Colt's cock, squeezing it tight in his fist. "Hold off, baby. I want to be in your ass when you come for me." Jace stared deep into Colt's eyes, gripped his own cock, and rubbed the head against Colt's rim.

The moment was perfect. Jace pushed against the tight ring of muscle, and Colt instinctively bore down, opening for him. The time Jace had taken to prepare Colt had worked. He slid easily the rest of the way inside. He froze as his own world tilted on its axis as Colt's tight chute gripped him.

Jace wasn't exactly sure what happened. One minute he was upright, looking down into Colt's eyes, and the next, he was lying tangled in Colt's arms, resting on his chest. Colt's legs were tightly wrapped around his waist, urging him deeper. Colt's body was moving with his in a gentle, easy rhythm filled with more need than he had ever experienced in his entire life.

"You feel so good stretching me," Colt whispered and continued to roll his hips into Jace. Jace kept his eyes closed, concentrating on not blowing his load too soon. Colt's breath tickled his ear and neck, floating across his skin like a sensual touch. Jace anchored his forearms under Colt's shoulders and placed his hands under the back of Colt's head, tangling his fingers in his thick hair, all the while concentrating on carefully moving his hips.

"Am I hurting you?" Jace lowered his face to whisper in Colt's ear.

"Not in a bad way." Colt shifted his hips as he answered, pushing his head back against Jace's palms, the cords in his neck strained when he lifted his hips trying to match Jace's thrusts.

"You're so tight. I don't know if I can hold off." Seconds passed as Jace worked up the strength to move faster. He bent his knees, digging them into the mattress while pistoning his hips. Colt wasn't letting him go. He had a death grip on Jace, using both his arms and his legs to keep a tight hold. Jace managed to untangle his fingers from Colt's hair and slide his hand between their bodies to grip Colt's cock. Colt jerked his hips forward and came instantly between their bodies. Colt wasn't quiet when he came; he yelled unintelligible words as his body tensed and gripped Jace tighter. Jace couldn't hold back any longer, either. The smell and feel of Colt's release sent him quickly over the edge. Colt's ass clenched around him, milking Jace as he drove harder inside Colt, shouting his name while riding out his own orgasm.

Everything stopped for Jace in that moment. The entire world came to a standstill as Colt gripped him tighter. Colt hadn't relaxed after the orgasm; instead, he stayed tense and kept a tight grip on Jace. He had no choice but to fall back onto Colt in a heap, letting him support his entire body weight.

Neither spoke for a long time, both just lay there, panting. Colt kept him wrapped in his arms for several long minutes while they caught their breaths.

"It was perfect, thank you," Colt whispered into Jace's hair. He was limp now, but still inside Colt's body. Colt's hips were still angled up, keeping them together. "I wanna do that again."

"You'll be sore, Colt," Jace whispered, kissing Colt's neck. He tried to rise again, but Colt held him in place.

"It felt so good to have sex the right way. I don't wanna let you go. I don't ever wanna let you go, Jace," Colt said and yawned deeply. Slowly the tension began to ease from Colt's body, his arms relaxed their hold, and his legs loosened. Jace tried again to pull out of Colt. If he didn't move soon, the condom would come free, but Colt still wasn't ready to let him go.

"I won't ever forget this night, it was perfect. You were perfect," Colt whispered. Again another yawn slipped out, and Colt kissed the top of Jace's head.

"Thank you for tonight, Jace," Colt whispered again seconds before he heard a soft snore. Finally, Jace untangled himself. It took a minute. The long night, all the alcohol, and the forty-five minute massage that ended with mind-blowing sex had taken a toll. Jace smiled down sweetly at Colt as he crawled from the bed and stood.

They were a mess. There was definitely a wet spot in the bed and Colt was laying on part of it, but he didn't seem to care. He slept as peaceful as a baby, and Jace again connected to Colt in that minute. His breath hitched, his head swirled, and his heart skipped several beats. For the first time in his life, Jace knew exactly what he wanted.

No way would this end well, it couldn't. He shouldn't let his guard down and tie himself to a closeted Colt. Everyone on campus talked about Colt being a first round draft pick, and even if that didn't happen, Colt was surely going to be picked up by some professional football team. He'd have a long career in the NFL.

The NFL equaled jocks, and jocks equaled homophobes. They wouldn't be so welcoming if Colt ever decided to come out. Jace certainly couldn't help the feelings developing inside him, but his head was very clear on where all of this was headed. No matter how many times Colt told him differently, Jace lived the life of a gay man in the sports world.

The only other clear option didn't seem appealing at all. Could Jace be Colt's hidden secret? He looked down again at the sleeping Colt, before turning away. *Shit!*

# Chapter 6

Jace swiped at the annoying tickle on his nose. He tried everything in his power to stay asleep. The sun was rising, and the warmth already coated his skin. Colt's awesome sunglasses kept the brightness away. He had his own ocean wave lullaby urging him back into the comfort of his dreams. And boy, did he love his dreams. Colt was there, naked, about to suck him off again. Yeah, dreams were just the bomb.

The damn insistent fly wouldn't leave him alone. Jace carefully turned over on his stomach, keeping the suntan thing going and the sunglasses in place. Sleep came quickly, and Colt was still there waiting to take his dick back inside his mouth. Seconds before Jace was to slide back into Colt's warm mouth, the insect fluttered across his back, and then down around his ass. The small swim suit he wore gave no protection as the fly crawled down between his legs.

Jace bolted up, prepared to battle the bug to its death, only to find Colt sitting beside him laughing, using something he'd found along his early morning run to tickle him awake. "Are you gonna sleep all day?"

"Maybe. You kept me up all night," Jace lay down on his back, turning his head toward Colt.

"Okay, we can sleep if you want, or when I was in town yesterday preparing our night of love, I found a cool brochure on a sightseeing tour off the Na Pali coast on a big catamaran with dinner and drinks. I also read something about a hike that sounded pretty cool. I thought we could check it out first and then head over to the cruise. The hike looked pretty intense, but I think a cheer boy can handle it. There were waterfalls and tucked away beaches, and it's supposed to be so far above sea level you can see everything. The pictures looked cool. I was thinking we could do that today," Colt said, wiggling his eyebrows.

Jace just stared up at him.

"What?" Colt asked after several silent seconds.

"Like go out somewhere together in public?" Jace finally asked, propping up on one elbow.

"We don't have to. I can stay here and have sex with you again, and again, and again. I just thought you'd like to see the island. Give your ass a little break," Colt said, grinning. The sex idea seemed to take root. After a minute, Colt's eyes darkened and his grin turned wicked. He leaned forward, coming in for a kiss as he grazed his hand down Jace's stomach, sliding inside his Speedo.

"No, wait. What if we see someone we know?" Jace said, stopping Colt from kissing him, but not the hand sliding into his swimsuit. He wasn't stupid, and with that thought, he rolled his hips forward and lifted his leg, bending at the knee, giving Colt full access to everything he had going on down there.

"We can't go as a couple, but we can go as friends. We can just say I saw you and we decided to team up. Our dates didn't wanna do it. I like you getting hard in my hands and my mouth. Did you like that blow job I gave you this morning? It was my first. I need practice on opening up my throat like you do," Colt said, pushing Jace's swim trunks down.

"Okay, it's settled, blowjob first, sightseeing second," Jace said, spreading his legs as Colt moved to lie between his parted thighs.

"Blowjob first, fucking you second, and sightseeing third," Colt corrected, seconds before he slid the tip of Jace's cock inside his mouth. Jace lost all reason as he dropped his head back on the beach towel, savoring the warmth of the sun and the eagerness of his hot lover.

Jace sat strategically across a four top table from Colt, wishing there would have been another table open. Unfortunately, the cabin was full by the time he and Colt went through the buffet line. All the good seats were taken. He picked at the shrimp dinner he'd chosen off the buffet. They offered fish, chicken, and shrimp, and every plate came with two scoops of rice, one scoop of macaroni salad, and pineapple bars for dessert. The odd combination was something his healthy side seemed to reject, but he justified all the extra carbs because who really cared what you ate when you sat across the table from Colt Michaels.

They were late getting to the trails, but managed to spend the rest of the morning and early afternoon on the hike. They hadn't been able to hike the full Kalalau trail like they'd planned, actually what Colt thought would be a short hike surprised both of them. They only got as far as Hanakapi'ai Beach before turning back in order to make their dinner cruise in time.

Another big time destroyer was the secluded make-out session in Colt's rental car. Jace successfully fought Colt's octopus arms, keeping his clothes in place while they sat in the parking lot of the cruise line. Colt did everything he could to talk Jace out of getting on this boat and just going back home. But in Jace's far too reasonable mind, Colt had already paid for everything in advance; he spent a couple hundred dollars on the dinner cruise alone, and he felt like they needed to see it through. Besides, in Jace's estimation, they were doing a great job at pulling off the friends deal, and he really wanted to see the amazing coastline from a huge catamaran. Who knew if he would ever be back in Hawaii again?

Based on all the female attention at their table, Jace decided he might not have been wise in insisting they eat in the main cabin. The girls wouldn't leave them alone, they never got a minute's break from all the attention, and there was zero chance to look out on the Hawaiian coastline. Every available table had an obstructed view. No matter how Jace twisted or turned, he couldn't keep an eye on the island as they passed by.

From the deck, the views were gorgeous. They drew Jace in, mesmerizing coastline for as far as the eye could see. Emerald green pinnacles towered above the turquoise water, and velvet green cliffs were decorated with waterfalls that plummeted into deep, narrow valleys. The colors alone were amazing; at times the sheer sea cliffs looked as if they'd been hand painted with the red dirt of Kauai. Jace snapped hundreds of photos, wanting to remember every minute of the tour. Regretfully, none included Colt, although he seriously wanted to. He was forced to etch the memory in his brain of how handsome Colt looked leaning against the rail with the majestic coastline backdrop behind him.

Alcohol was flowing like crazy for the entire trip, and spring break had the cruise packed full of tourists. The whole experience was beyond anything Jace's lower middle class background had ever before offered. Being on a boat in the middle of the Pacific Ocean was something Jace never thought he'd get an opportunity to do, and he truly loved every minute. He just wished he could share the experience with Colt like a normal couple.

Jace didn't begrudge the flirtatious banter of the two current females parked at the table with them, or the ones who'd hiked along beside them through the trails. Much like the coastline outside, Colt just had that draw. People flocked to him like flies to honey. From the time they started the hike, until the time they were back seated in the car, people they met along the way seemed to cling and follow them everywhere. And it had nothing to do with Jace. He learned early on, his entire game plan for the day was to stay quiet, and that's pretty much what he'd done. For Colt, this seemed a big fun game, sneaking private moments and simple touches when no one was looking. To Jace, it was just incredibly stressful to hide his body's reaction from everyone around him every time Colt made one of those bold, secret moves.

Acting straight with girls flirting was another incredibly difficult thing for Jace. In no time of his life could he ever remember any girl actually coming on to him. He grew up in a small town, all his years in the same school system with the same group of friends. From the time he was a little boy, he'd loved gymnastics and dance. His very well-adjusted, stable parents knew about his sexuality before he ever did. He cheered from junior high all the way through high school. Girls were his friends, never a romantic interest, and they always just somehow knew he was gay. That same attitude lasted through college. He couldn't remember being hit on by a girl one time in his entire life, until these two at the table popped into his life.

Neither seemed to clue in on his sexual orientation or Colt's for that matter, and both looked eager for whichever one wanted the hook-up. Jace gave Colt one hundred percent of the credit. He could totally see the football guys all wanting to be Colt's wingman. Colt's good looks and fun attitude would draw the females in for the whole group of guys.

"Don't you like your drink," Colt asked from across the table. All eyes were trained on Jace, and he realized his internal dialog must have been noticeable.

"Yeah, it's fine," he said to Colt's grin and wink. Colt drained his Mai Tai and raised his hand to the waiter, motioning for another round for the table.

"I love mine… they're so good. Jace, there's a cool club close to the beach. It's fifty cent beer night. It was packed last night. You two should come!" Mandy said, grinning super big. All Jace could do was stare at her as she flashed her boobs at him. Her sheer, crisscross cover-up, with no bathing suit top underneath didn't quite cover anything. Did she know? Surely she did. But if she didn't, would she be completely mortified later? After a minute, Jace grew a spine and finally confronted the problem.

"You know, your top keeps opening," Jace whispered so as not to draw any attention. He could feel the blush on his face at his words. Colt actually rolled his eyes at Jace.

"I know! Right? They're new. A graduation gift from my parents." Mandy squealed in delight, quickly opening her cover-up, exposing her large, perfectly shaped silicone breasts for both Jace and Colt's inspection. First, she turned to Colt, and then to Jace, shaking her shoulders at him. They bounced as he stared.

"Touch them," she said, reaching out and grabbing his hand. She was fast and before he could even blink, his palm covered an exposed breast, and she squeezed his hand, encouraging him to feel her up. "They feel real, don't they?"

"That's not fair! My parents won't get me any!" Tonya spoke up, reaching across the small table to take the drink the roving waiter placed in front her. Jace had no idea what to say. His big eyes looked over at Colt who was absolutely no help. Colt laughed so hard, he was having a hard time staying in his seat. The waiter placed another Mai Tai in front of him, even though Jace hadn't drunk any of the other three sitting there, but it appeared, the waiter only had eyes for the tipsy female's breasts and never noticed he didn't need another refill.

"That's because your breasts are great, Tonya! Show them," Mandy said, encouraging her friend. Jace was horrified. His gaze flipped to Tonya, praying she wouldn't expose herself, and thank God, she didn't.

"I love them! If I could go topless, I would!" Mandy said, loosely covering herself back up when the captain walked by, giving them the eye. The problem was the captain didn't eye them in a negative way. He clearly approved of the show, grinning down at the girls. It seemed just enough incentive to have Tonya popping her bikini top up, flashing everyone in the room. Damn.

"See, I told you, you have great boobs!" Mandy said, downing the rest of her Mai Tai. Jace dropped his head to his palm. Why hadn't he listened to Colt? He was absolutely positive he was an embarrassingly bright shade of red at the moment. They should have gone back to their bungalow like Colt wanted. At least he would have had a much better reason for blushing. But no, he'd insisted on going on this little excursion and up till dinner had pretty much enjoyed himself.

"Where's that bar?" Colt asked, still laughing. They had drawn the attention of everyone on the boat. All of the sudden, the Na Pali coastline wasn't near as interesting as the pretty blonde girl exposing herself to everyone seated near them.

"It's just down the road from Polynesian Treasures. Like a few miles south of Kapa'a, it's called The Dry Dock. You can't miss it. Let me give you my number. Call me when you get in the area. We can go with you, right, Tonya?" Mandy said, running her hand up Jace's thigh. What the hell? He looked over at Tonya, and her eyes were focused on Colt. Apparently they'd made their decision between the two of them. Mandy leaned into Jace. He thought she might have tried for a whisper, but didn't pull it off at all.

"I'm a sure bet. We can just go back to your place if you want, Jacey." Mandy grinned up at him, and evidently Colt caught the action of her hand running up his thigh or maybe just the deer in headlights look that surely decorated his crimson face. Obviously the amusement couldn't be controlled, Colt burst out a laugh so hard he did finally topple from his seat.

"I... I'm here with someone," Jace offered lamely, stopping her hand from winding its way any farther up his leg.

"That's okay. I like girls too. Tonya and I do it for guys all the time. They love that shit! I bet you would, too."

"His date won't go for that. Very jealous! Give me your number. I'll call you when we come back into town." Colt saved him, and she moved closer to Colt, spouting out her phone number. Tonya followed suit because clearly, Mandy wasn't going to tread on her chosen territory.

Jace used the opportunity to escape. He stood quickly, dropping his napkin on the table. "I'm going to the restroom," he stammered, taking several steps backward as he spoke. Jace turned on his heel, heading for the door, completely unprepared for the busboy in his path. The contents of the tray went flying, crashing down around them, and just like with the breast, every eye in the cabin looked his way.

*Fuck my life!*

"That was hilarious." Colt laughed as they walked down the boat ramp. "I mean, honestly, when you ran into that waiter. Oh man!"

"Not funny, and I'm sorry if I embarrassed you. I was just so uncomfortable. And those two girls... Man! Thank God Mandy seemed into the captain; we might not have ever gotten free. This whole hiding thing makes me crazy. I'm not any good at it. I freaked myself out," Jace rambled, dropping his hands in his pockets as they walked across the parking lot to the car.

"Whooo hooo! Call me!" Mandy yelled from a car Tonya drove, speeding from the parking lot.

Jace rolled his eyes. "Is it safe for her to be driving?"

"Probably not. They said they would call a cab." Colt shrugged, his easy attitude firmly in place as he watched the car's back lights until they couldn't be seen.

"So you felt her up... huh?" Colt nudged him in the shoulder.

"Don't even say another word. You aren't funny, and give me the keys. You drank too much to drive." Colt laughed, but tossed Jace the keys and headed for the passenger side.

"Let's stay at the bungalow from now on. I think we're safer there. At least I won't be forced to feel up anyone," Jace said, as he settled into his seat. "And plus, apparently I don't like sharing. I wanted more of your attention. When you said a dinner cruise, I had something totally different in mind."

As Jace reached to start the car, Colt was on him, turning him for a deep thorough kiss. Several minutes later, when they surfaced, Colt's palms held Jace's face, staring into his eyes.

"You wanna hear something crazy?" Colt whispered.

"I don't know," Jace said, worry in his eyes. What could be crazier than the dinner they shared?

"It made me jealous when she grabbed your hand," Colt said. Jace could only stare at him. He had no idea how to respond. "I think we should stay at the beach house too, so I don't have to bitch slap a ho for touching you again! Now drive us home or find someplace to park. I want to practice my blowjob skills. Goddamn, Jace Montgomery! It turns my shit on to have you in my mouth. I love giving you a blowjob."

Jace sat there a minute, staring at Colt who leaned in, gave him a chaste kiss, and wiggled his eyebrows. Jace had to get a hold of his body in order to even remember how to drive. After a second, his brain did finally work again. He started the car, backed out of the parking space, and began to drive with Colt's head propped on his shoulder, his hand running back and forth over his thigh. Man, he wanted more of these moments.

# Chapter 7

The sun baked Jace's skin, turning his tan darker than he'd ever remembered. He was totally relaxed, lying on the beach, letting the water lap at his legs with each push of the tide. Jace loved Hawaii. The sun heating his skin, the sounds of the ocean churning in the distance, the squawk of the seagulls as they flew over the beach in search of a handout. This was the perfect place and the perfect vacation; he could easily get use to this life. Jace groaned as he rolled from his front to his back. They only had a short time left before they headed back to reality.

Jace had again abandoned his normal swim trunks, opting for a Speedo kind of deal. Once assured he was completely alone on their little slice of the beach, Jace shed those, too. He lathered his ass in sunscreen, hoping for a full body tan, not the Coppertone baby white ass he currently sported.

In the distance, he could hear the sounds of Colt's feet swishing through the wet sand. Jace was thankful he was back. Colt went for another run today, not letting a day go by without taking his five mile jog. It wasn't a bad thing, Jace loved to watch Colt's ass bounce as he ran off down the beach.

Jace turned his head and propped up on his elbow, watching Colt in the distance, running back toward him. Colt was a sweaty hot mess. He wasn't wearing a T-shirt, his chest bare, and the jogging shorts were small and tight, riding low on his hips. The sun had done wonders on Colt's skin too, creating a sun-kissed bronze, which made his dark features more pronounced and more alluring, if that were even possible. He was flawless. The most perfect thing Jace had ever seen.

Jace kept his eyes focused on Colt; his heart hammered in his chest, and his thoughts ran rampant. This vacation couldn't have been any better. He and Colt fit so well together. They laughed, joked, teased one another, and never one time did Jace feel the need for distance. He craved Colt's company, and Colt seemed to feel the same way about him. They did everything together. But this was Hawaii. What was going to happen to them when they went back to their lives? The overwhelming uncertainty made a desperate anxiety build inside Jace. A connection like this didn't just happen every day. Could they hold it? Jace prayed they could.

"You're fucking hot laying out here. I couldn't run fast enough to get back here so I could fuck you senseless," Colt chuckled breathlessly. Jace grinned, hiding behind his smile. He pushed all other thoughts out of his head, wanting to just be in this moment with Colt. Jace had had four days of Colt methodically reeling him in. He'd long since abandoned any effort at keeping his guard up. That had crumbled the very first time he pushed into Colt's body. Colt was the perfect lover, a great companion, and seemed truly into him.

Jace didn't respond; there was too much churning through him, so he kicked his leg up, splashing water on Colt as he dropped to his knees on the towel next to Jace. When Colt looked shocked, Jace kicked his other leg, splashing more water in Colt's direction before bolting up, seconds before Colt reached for him. He barely dodged Colt's grasp, but it was still a small victory. There weren't too many times he'd successfully outmaneuvered Colt over the last few days. When he got a safe distance away, Jace reached down, splashing more water in Colt's face.

"You're gonna be sorry…" Colt started, and Jace splashed him again, laughing this time as he ran out into the ocean. He was completely naked, running into the surf. He looked back over his shoulder to see Colt shedding his shorts on the beach before following close behind him. He'd need this head start and more to keep away from Colt.

Jace swam hard. He wasn't a weakling by any means. He'd lifted girls over his head and tossed them in the air for years, but Colt was faster and caught Jace easily, pulling him under by the feet. Jace broke the surface, gasping for breath. Colt grabbed him, wrenching his body forward, holding him securely in his arms. His tongue plunged inside Jace's open mouth before he could even clear the water from his eyes. Jace responded immediately by wrapping his long legs around Colt's waist and deepening the kiss. Seconds later, Colt pushed against his rim.

Between the suntan oil and the ocean, Jace was slick and ready, allowing less resistance when Colt entered him. Jace tore from the kiss, tossing his head back, gasping at the welcomed invasion. Colt pushed deep inside him in one mind-blowing thrust.

They were awkward. Neither able to get much leverage, the waves made it too difficult. Colt worked Jace, using his hands and hips. Jace wrapped himself tighter around Colt, using his thighs to help hold him against the waves. It was so freaking hot to be making love to Colt in their own little secluded spot in the Pacific Ocean. Jace grabbed Colt's face, kissing him with all the passion inside his heart.

Colt tried to keep his wits about him. There was no way he was breaking from the kiss or removing himself from Jace's ass, but he wanted Jace on the shore and that proved difficult.

Colt moved his hips, continuing to kiss Jace, all the while slowly moving them back to shore against the pull of the current. He hadn't bothered with a condom, but Jace didn't seem to notice or mind. Colt certainly didn't. Having Jace bareback again was his dream come true. Damn the consequences.

When Colt got closer to the shore, he gripped Jace's ass, balancing him as he held all of Jace's weight, and managed to keep himself buried deep inside his ass. Jace never seemed to notice they'd left the water. The look of sheer ecstasy lit his face. Jace closed his eyes, slanting his mouth over Colt's.

Colt took a few steps onto the beach before he dropped to his knees, the water still covering their legs as he pounded into Jace. He flexed his body, fucked Jace with everything he had in him. He was a man consumed, a man in love, and he needed Jace to feel how much he loved him before he spoke the words aloud.

"Goddamn, you feel good," Colt muttered, dropping his head to Jace's chest. His hips pistoned, and Jace could do little more than beg. Colt had no idea what Jace begged for. He wasn't certain Jace knew, but seconds later, Jace came, shooting creamy ribbons between their wet bodies. He hadn't even touched Jace's cock. It was such a turn-on knowing he could make Jace come without stroking him to climax.

They'd made love no less than fifteen times over the last four days, but here Jace was, eager and still ready for him. He couldn't control his release any longer. Colt came with a roar, wrapping Jace tighter in his arms as his release filled Jace's ass.

After several long minutes, well past the point of them both coming down off their orgasm, they lay in the surf, just holding one another in the wet sand. The water covered their legs, receding in intervals as the waves rolled in and then back out again.

"You're everything to me, Jace. We have to work this out when we get home. I don't want this to end." Colt finally rolled off Jace, to his side.

"Me either," Jace whispered back. This was Jace's first time to agree. Colt pushed up on his forearms and smiled down.

"It took you long enough," Colt said and kissed Jace's lips.

"I had to be sure you were serious about us," Jace replied honestly, his meaning clear in his gaze. What they shared between them was real. For Colt, it had been there for more years than he could count. Now he knew Jace returned those feeling, even if things had been left unsaid.

"Come inside with me. Let me just hold you. Tomorrow's coming too fast." Colt rose and lowered his hand to help Jace up. "Just so we're clear. I'm gonna want you with me when I get drafted. I don't know what team I'm going to yet, but if I get picked up, you're gonna have to move with me."

Colt drew Jace to him. For the first time, they both heard noises coming from down the beach. At the next closest house a couple stood on their balcony giving them a big thumbs up, whistling and cheering them on. Jace blushed, but Colt grinned at the attention and waved back. Inspired by the encouragement, Colt dropped down on one knee and kissed Jace's knuckles. The whistles grew louder and Jace looked panicked by his actions.

"I'm not gonna say it now, but I hope you see where I'm going with this. I want the promise of someday from you. That's all I'm asking, Jace." Colt stood, not waiting for the answer and gathered Jace into his arms, kissing him deeply before making his way back inside.

# Chapter 8

Even six hours after Colt's plane taxied down the tarmac and lifted off the island, the smile hadn't left Jace's face as he waited to board his flight back home. They drove to the Kauai airport together, Jace wanting to see Colt off safely. They put off the departure for as long as they could, waiting until the very last possible minute, neither wanting to miss a minute together. Colt actually held Jace's hand and kissed him before heading off to his waiting flight. Jace watched him rush down the corridor, jogging until he disappeared from sight.

The whole saying goodbye in a crowded airport was incredibly tragic in a very Shakespearian kind of way. They both teared up, making promises of forever in order to make it a little bit easier to end their secluded getaway. For the last six hours, Jace stayed put and waited for his flight home. He kept the rolling dialog going in his head, telling himself this wasn't a goodbye, but actually the first day of the rest of their lives together as melodramatic as that might sound.

Jace's grin grew, thinking about their morning. Colt worked hard to move his flight back, or push Jace's up. He used every bit of charm he possessed, but much to Colt's dismay, the last day of spring break was a heavy travel day and all the flights were booked solid. Colt was forced to board his flight, and Jace was forced to spend six hours wandering around the small airport, waiting for his flight home.

Weirdly, all this waiting hadn't bothered him. The airport was small, smaller than anything Jace had ever been in, but admittedly, he wasn't a world traveler. He wasn't even a national traveler, but sitting in this waiting area, listening to his iPod just didn't seem to bother him. Money was tight. Jace was down to his last five dollars and spent most of that in the vending machines. Colt had tried to give him money, insisted he needed to eat, but in the end, Jace refused. He'd made it on a dime for most of his life, definitely for most of his college years, and he could make do now.

Colt's argument came back to Jace, and he ducked his head, chuckling softly as he remembered the annoyed look on Colt's face as he announced they were a couple now. Going on and on about how couples shared and even told him about the eight million dollar signing bonus coming his way. Jace still refused the money. In Colt's extremely frustrated anger, he made a small scene as he declared his intention. From this point forward, Colt would be paying for their future and didn't that just completely rock!

Apparently fairytales did come true.

The whirlwind of the last week settled some for Jace. They were slowing down now, working on building a relationship together. They were past mid-terms, on the home stretch of graduation. The future all of the sudden seemed bright and shiny. Every plan Jace had made for his future flew out the window over the last four days. Apparently he'd follow Colt wherever he chose to go. Jace had fallen hard for Colt. He was a man deeply in love. Who would have had any idea things would work out like this? Certainly not him.

This relationship wasn't without problems. Jace was signing on for discretion. Without question, he'd be hiding, even though he'd never hid one day in his life. His well-adjusted outlook on being a gay man was all out the window. Colt's world wasn't ready for them, and that seemed okay, too. Regardless of the display he just put on in the airport, Colt wasn't ready to come out just yet, but Jace would be right there, holding his hand when he made the decision.

Reasoning everything through, feeling all those happy, in love feelings made Jace strong and secure. He truly believed he could handle anything, at least until Colt signed on to a team. He'd even hide longer, if that's what it took, waiting until Colt could establish himself as a star on the professional field, just like on the college field.

If all the rumors were true, Colt would sign with New York. Based on their commitments to one another last night, Jace would be moving there in May. He had agreed to follow Colt anywhere while Colt had been moving slowly inside his body. The strategy was tricky, but one that seemed to work perfectly. Colt made him affirm the promise both last night and again today before he boarded the plane.

By now Jace had a full blown, toothy grin lighting his face. Just thinking about a future with Colt made him so happy. Moving to New York, wow, that was a big step. Living in New York had always seemed like a cool thing to do, but living there with Colt made the thought even sweeter.

Before this week, Jace's big future plans were to go back to Dallas, get a job with whoever hired him and open a gymnastics center somewhere around the area. The National Cheerleaders Association was huge in Dallas and it seemed like a good plan, but living in New York with the man of your dreams blew that idea right out of the water! If they stayed in New York, maybe he could open his gym there instead. Maybe he could go on to graduate school, and secure his future so he could help support Colt when he retired from playing ball.

"Flight two thirty-seven to Austin is now boarding." Jace could hear the overhead speaker and looked up, pulling the earbuds from his ears as he read the sign. The vacation of a lifetime was coming to an end. His suntan had grown darker from the hours he'd laid on the beach, his hair blonder, and his future brighter. The island was hard to leave, but at the same time he was ready for what life had in store for him. Jace rose, squared his shoulders, and slung his old, ratty backpack over his arm.

His phone beeped, signaling a text, and he pulled the cell from his pocket. The text was from Colt; he planned to pick him up at the airport tonight. He wanted to get a room close to the airport. Colt didn't want their vacation to end. And somehow that thought alone had him grinning like the Cheshire cat all over again. He'd always known Colt was a decent guy, but who would have known how caring and kind he really was?

Jace returned the text with a quick 'boarding' and dropped the phone back in his pocket. He stepped forward, fishing for the earbud when he got shoved against the shoulder. The push was hard enough to cause him to stumble several steps. Less than a second later, Jace got an angrily whispered, "*Get out of the way, fag.*" Where had that come from? Jace frowned and looked around, but he only got a glimpse of the guy's retreating back. He was big, clean cut, and Jace had never seen him before. How had he picked that up? Jace glanced down at his T-shirt and shorts. Nothing about him or his clothing stood out as gay, so how had a stranger known?

"Final call for flight two thirty-seven." Those words got Jace moving. The perpetual smile of the last few days faltered. What if Colt had been there with him when something like that happened? Colt wasn't experienced in those kinds of moments, and for the first time in days, Jace thought about Colt's dad. No way was he ever going to be okay with Colt being gay. They'd have to hide forever from Colt's family. His dad was a brutal, angry kind of guy, the direct opposite of Colt. No way they could ever tell him.

Some of the confidence Jace gained while being on this island seeped away as he walked down the jet bridge to the airplane. Was he crazy for thinking this could work? Jace forced the thoughts from his mind and palmed his iPod, turning the wheel to his favorite playlist. He wasn't thinking about this right now. Colt said they could work, and he'd believe him. It was what his heart told him to do.

## Chapter 9

Somehow, being in downtown Austin at eight-thirty on a Monday morning, the day after spring break, wasn't terrible. Colt sat happily in the waiting area just outside his agent's twenty-seventh floor, impressive corner office. It had been hinted to him on several occasions that the corner office, with the amazing view, was just one of the few perks of being high up on the professional sports management food chain—whatever that meant.

His agent, Johnny Bench, was a legend in this industry. His clients were local sports heroes. Colt had been told many times how lucky he was to have Johnny on his side. He'd only gotten the chance because of the connection Johnny shared with his father. They had played professional football together over twenty years ago. Colt had known Uncle Johnny his entire life. He was even Colt's godfather.

The agent's secretary, Mrs. O'Rielly, sat at the front desk, right outside his office. She was a little bit of a woman, and older. Maybe even in her seventies, but she'd been in this office every time Colt had come since he was a little boy. She had always been kind.

When he was a kid, he remembered how he loved to stop by when his father would visit. She always had suckers and candy, with drawers full of coloring books and crayons. She'd sometimes even let him play on her computer. But not today, that friendly attitude vanished. She sat there stoned-faced, staring at her computer screen, ignoring Colt completely. Maybe there was too much spring break for everyone.

From Colt's perspective, it wasn't a bad thing to be ignored. He was totally exhausted. He didn't much feel like carrying on a conversation about the weather. An unexpected jaw cracking yawn tore free, and he realized his eyes were drooping closed as he sat there waiting. If he wasn't careful, he'd be asleep soon. He didn't think that was how professionals handled themselves, and he sat up straighter in his chair, forcing his eyes wide open.

He wasn't a kid anymore. He was an adult with responsibilities and commitments. One being the super-hot boyfriend he'd just committed himself to, and didn't that feel great? Colt was head over heels in love with Jace Montgomery. And everything inside him wanted to take care of Jace for the rest of their lives. Thank God Jace felt the same way.

Colt had the entire nine hour flight to plan. When he arrived back home, he got them a room at a nearby hotel, planned room service, and then just hung out at the airport waiting for Jace's plane to arrive. When Jace walked off the jet bridge and into the terminal, Colt's heart was set right.

He took Jace back to the room, fed him, made love to him, and slept with him in his arms. Funny how Colt resisted the idea of them going back to their old lives; he wanted more from Jace than a secret relationship. Jace deserved more. Hell, Jace deserved everything.

Colt made Jace promise again to stay with him no matter where he lived. With this trip to Hawaii, Colt had solidly opened the closet door and was about to step out. There was no way he was ever going back to being that scared, hiding guy again. Jace made him whole, and he couldn't wait to share this with the world. Jace was his everything, just like he'd always been, but now Jace returned the feelings, and didn't that feel fan-fucking-tastic?

As Colt drove to the office today, he made the decision he wasn't hiding Jace. It wasn't fair to ask Jace to keep their relationship a secret. Fuck anyone who wanted him to hide. He could manage whatever was thrown his way as long as Jace stood by his side.

"He's ready to see you," Mrs. O'Rielly said. She never looked his way. She didn't show him to the door like she normally did. Instead, she got up from her desk, and walked a wide circle around him, closing the main door to this part of the corporate office. Colt eyed her as he made his way to his agent's office. Her actions were confusing, but he didn't question them. Nothing was going to interrupt his high now that he was a man in full-fledged love. Damn, his future was so bright, he might need to stop and buy some new sunglasses before picking Jace up and going back to school!

Colt looked down at his feet and grinned as he opened the door, trying to make his face a little more passive. He hadn't said the words to Jace, but he did love him. They were young, just starting their lives, but with all his heart, Colt loved Jace Montgomery. Regardless of what anyone might think, this wasn't an instant love kind of deal. Colt had four years of gradually falling head over heels. His future began and ended in Jace's caring hands. Colt just needed Jace to catch up, and he planned to focus on that over the next few months until they moved to whatever team picked him up.

The right hook came out of nowhere. Pain shot through his jaw as Colt's head snapped to the left, forcing first his head, and then his entire body, around. He struggled to stand as stars filled his vision. *What the hell?* Colt slumped against what he thought was a wall. But it turned out what held him up wasn't a wall after all, but a brawny man that now had Colt locked in his arms. He tried to fight against the hold, swinging blindly. Was he being robbed?

Everything happened so fast, his mind wouldn't work except to register the secretary hurriedly shutting the office door behind him seconds before Colt was stuck again. Maybe not. Shit! The guy lost his hold; Colt slumped forward and was jerked up by his T-shirt. His father's face came into focus, anger contorted his features as his big fist connected with Colt's gut over and over again.

*Fuck, he already knew.*

"Larry, stop it! Stop it! You're gonna kill him!" Johnny yelled from somewhere behind his father. Minutes later, after another solid round of the beating, Johnny had a hold of his father, pulling him off Colt.

"I don't give a fuck. I brought him into this world, and by God, I can take him out! No son of mine's a fuckin' cocksucker!" His father was a big man, an ex-NFL linebacker, and the agent struggled to hold him as Colt slid down the body holding him in place. His face was bloodied and the pain unbearable. He was losing his vision. His left eye was already swollen shut and blood flowed freely, dripping down his face. He might not be able to focus his eyes, but he saw what was going on very clearly. His father had somehow found out about Jace.

Everything in the room came in double vision, and he realized a second too late that he was going to throw up. The bile rose in his gut. His father wasn't the type of man to let things go. Without a doubt this wouldn't stop with just him; he would go after Jace. Fuck, he had to protect Jace!

Colt struggled to stand, but his legs gave way, and he crumbled back to the floor. Whoever else was in the room had to still be behind him because a boot connected with his throat, holding him in place against the thick carpeted floor.

"Larry, sit down! Stop it! That's enough!" Johnny screamed as a pair of brass knuckles fell to the floor in front of Colt. No wonder his father's punches crippled him so completely. Colt managed to look up at the same moment his father spit in his face.

"You make me sick, you queer piece of shit. I've guided your whole fucking career, laid everything out perfectly for you. And I'm not about to let some little cocksucking faggot fuck it all up for me!" His father had broken free of Johnny's hold and barreled back down on Colt, his fists pounding while the boot held him on the ground crushing his throat.

"This is what happens to faggots, and it'll do you good to remember it." He heard his father yelling as he struggled to get free, but something or someone else was holding his legs. He hadn't been double teamed, but triple teamed. *Fuck!*

Colt's intake of air was being dramatically restricted, and at this point, if he didn't do something, he wouldn't live through the next few minutes. Darkness came, seeping in from all sides and there was nothing he could do to stop it. The pain of his father's steel-toed boots connecting with his already worked over rib cage was the last thing Colt remembered before he vomited on himself and passed out.

"You're alive, boy, but barely." There was contempt in Johnny's voice, and Colt groaned, trying to open his eyes. His body hurt, and he couldn't get his left eye to cooperate, but his right finally fluttered open enough to see his agent standing over him with an ice pack in his hand.

"Your father's..." Those words had Colt jerking forward, recoiling from any pending attack. He instinctively tried to prepare for whatever might be coming, but the sudden movement caused unbearable pain to shoot throughout his body and settle in his ribs. His mind rejected everything except the need to flee. He had to get out of this place. Colt struggled to stand until his agent grabbed him and pushed him back down on the sofa.

"He's gone, Colt. Settle down, son, and listen to me. He's gone!" The agent kept saying while pushing him back down on the sofa. His body ached so badly. He fought to stand, but couldn't manage to get his feet underneath himself. Why was his body betraying him? He had no choice but to lie back down.

"Drink this. It'll help."

A cool glass was placed between his lips, he opened slightly and straight whisky was poured down his throat. Colt choked and gagged on the disgusting liquid blazing a flame down to his stomach. He could feel the excess running down his cheeks and his neck as he was forced to consume everything put to his lips. Johnny laid an ice pack on his face as someone entered the office.

"What happened?" There was concern in the unfamiliar voice. Colt prayed that meant help had arrived.

"I don't know. He came in like this," Johnny lied. Colt could see him turned toward the door, but couldn't see who else was in the room.

"How'd he get here like this?" The voice was getting closer, and Colt tried hard to focus. He groaned, and tried to speak. He wanted to say who'd done this to him, but his throat hurt, and the sounds coming out didn't form any of the words he wanted to say.

"He stumbled in like this." Colt looked up to see an older gray-haired man standing over him, looking concerned. He must have looked as bad as he felt with that much concern on the guy's face.

"Son, I'm Dr. Patterson. Who did this to you?" the doctor asked. The look on the doctor's face made it clear he wasn't buying Johnny's story, but the agent wasn't giving.

"I think he's broken some ribs, maybe most of them and you need to look at his face. It might be a broken jaw. Check his cheekbone, too. His nose is shattered," the agent butted in. Colt focused his only good eye from the doctor to the agent who gave him a very unmistakable 'keep your fucking mouth shut' look.

"We need to get him to the hospital." The medical professional was gone from his eyesight and then came back into view. Colt could feel his gentle hand on his body, and he closed his eyes in relief.

"No, it needs to be done here. This is Colt Michaels. We don't need the press."

"No shit? He's a good kid. Seriously, John, what happened to him?" The gentle touch faltered, and Colt hissed as the T-shirt was stripped from his body.

"He's pissed off the wrong people, apparently." That was the closest thing to the truth Johnny had said since Dr. Patterson walked in the room. Colt kept his eyes closed and concentrated on breathing through the pain. Minutes felt like hours, and Colt thought he may have passed out again, until another glass of whiskey was forced down his throat.

"Drink this. They're bringing more people up to work on you. Stay quiet, do you understand me? You don't know what happened. You were attacked last night. Got it? Dr. Patterson will bandage you up, and we'll talk more when he leaves. Got it?"

Colt nodded; it was all he could do. He was scared, alone, and broken. Who would believe him anyway? Opening his mouth, he took another drink of the offered whiskey, this time the harsh liquid didn't burn a trail down his throat, instead it soothed him. He kept his eyes closed and let sleep take him.

Colt sat slowly, wincing through the pain. His ribs were bandaged, he was careful of them as he eased up on the sofa. Colt happened to catch his partial reflection in the mirror hanging over the dark leather chair across from him. His face was cleaned, stitched back together, looking better than he'd thought it would after the beating he'd just suffered. Nothing hid the intense swelling or bruising, but remarkably, his father hadn't broken anything too badly. He would heal. "How did you find out?"

"It's a small airport and you were too public. I knew before you left the island."

"You didn't have to tell my dad."

"Of course I did." Johnny watched him intently, his regular scotch and soda in one hand. He tossed the drink back, downing the contents in one swallow before hitting the mini bar in the corner of the room for a refill.

"No, you didn't. I'm an adult. This should have been just between us," Colt said in little more than a whisper. The alcohol seemed to have a sedating effect on his nerves, which he welcomed. Colt looked down at his hands. The pinky on his left hand was jammed. He held out his left arm, taking note of his injuries. His left arm was already turning black and blue, but this wasn't his throwing arm, was it? God forbid that. Colt looked over his right arm and sneered. Finding exactly what he expected, his father was always protective of his right arm. Not a scratch to be seen.

"Colton, he's my best friend and your manager. He's worked your career since you were five years old. He had a right to know you were making the worst mistake of your life," Johnny said. He placed a drink in front of Colt and sat across from him in a leather side chair.

"I think I'm gay." Even after being beat with an inch of his life, Colt wasn't willing to let Jace go.

"No, you aren't, son," Johnny said and drank his drink down in two big gulps.

"I love him." Colt hung on to Jace even if the words were said with shaken confidence.

"No, you don't. This thing you're going through is normal. It's nothing more than hormones, a rebellious kind of deal. We all go through it at your age." Johnny was back up, refilling his glass. Colt chuckled, which pulled at his stomach muscles. He immediately regretted the action when he sucked in a breath and pain shot from his cracked ribs.

"Don't laugh, it's true." Johnny's glass was filled to the rim this time when he took his seat across from Colt. Johnny looked so casual sitting there, so sure of himself.

"So, you're saying you fucked guys when you were twenty-two years old?" Colt stared at Johnny who wouldn't look him in the eyes. Instead, he took another long drink. It sure looked like he was weighing each answer before he spoke.

"No, I didn't do that, but I did other things. The difference was I always kept my future first in my mind. It's what you need to do, son."

"Don't son me. You let him beat the shit out of me," Colt said. He finally lifted his drink, taking a sip. He wasn't sure it was a good idea to mix the pain medicine the doctor had given him with alcohol. But if Johnny needed the liquid courage to finish this conversation, he supposed he might too. No way was he giving up Jace, even after having his ass handed to him. He loved him. Jace was moving away with him; they had it all planned out. And he was the happiest he'd ever been.

"I stopped it, didn't I?"

"Not soon enough," Colt shot back. Johnny leaned forward, placing his elbows on his knees, and stared at Colt for several long seconds until he finally stopped playing cat and mouse and started talking honestly.

"There's no way this is gonna be acceptable to the NFL. Your father has too much ridin' on you. He's not gonna let this just slide by, you know that. When we heard what was goin' on in Hawaii, your dad went fuckin' nuts. He wanted to go after that boy."

"Jace knows we have to hide." Colt didn't know the time, and he carefully turned his head to look out the window. It was dark outside. Shit, he'd been here all day, and he'd told Jace to wait at the hotel for him.

"Son, you can't hide well enough. Look what just happened."

"Were you watching me?" Colt asked. He searched his shorts, looking for his phone. It wasn't there.

"None of that matters. You just got the shit beat out of you by your family. Wait until you get on the field. You'll be more of a target than you'll ever understand. No team's gonna pick you up and watch their quarterback be targeted. Ain't gonna happen, son. Homosexuality's frowned upon in the sports world." Johnny drained his glass but didn't move. He sat there staring at Colt. All Colt cared about was his phone. It wasn't on him. He looked around the couch and then around the floor to see if it fell out when his dad attacked.

Colt started to ask, but the agent interrupted him.

"Son, you aren't hearing me. Listen to me closely. When we first found out, your own father was ready to take the cheerleader out of the equation... Do you get my meaning?" That caused Colt to stop searching and stare at Johnny. His heart panicked at the words. To have his father put this kind of whoop ass on Jace. *God please no...*

"His name's Jace Montgomery. I think that's the name on the report. It took about thirty seconds to find out who you were with. Colton, this isn't just about you, it's not gonna be good for him, either. What happened to you is nothing compared to what will happen to him. Your daddy loves you. Imagine if he paid someone to go after Jace. And it would be all your fault. You'll be painting a big red target right on his back."

"No, no, not Jace," Colt shook his head as dread filled him. Where was Jace now? Colt stood, the room started to spin around him. He was weak, but he had to go find Jace and warn him. Colt was wobbly on his feet, and he stumbled until the agent stood in front of him, blocking him, and forced him back down on the couch.

"Calm down, I stopped your dad. The boy isn't going to be touched, at least not right now, but if you don't stop this, I can't protect him or you. You know how your dad is, and he's serious. You're throwing away too much by keeping this going." Anger shot through Colt, and he fisted Johnny's dress shirt, drawing him in closer. Colt wasn't in any condition to make this show of brute force, but that didn't stop the fear from building rage inside him.

"Yeah, you're right to be concerned, that boy's life rests in your hands." Somewhere in the back of Colt's mind, he knew Johnny was playing him, but the dread was already taking up residence in his gut. This couldn't be happening. Jace was too beautiful of a person to go through something like this. Johnny held his position, right there in Colt's face, letting Colt keep a hold of him even though he could have easily broken away.

"Your family's name has too much ridin' on you right now. And remember they love you. Let some unsuspecting team sign you and find out you're gay. You won't be able to keep either of you safe. Is it worth that risk? I wouldn't let the person I care for go through that."

Colt was silent for several minutes. He released his hold as his heart shattered, now becoming the most painful part of his battered and broken body. All his hopes and dreams of starting a new life with Jace crumbled down around him. Colt picked up the glass, staring down at the amber liquid, thinking things over. He was so confused, what was he going to do? He wanted Jace. Colt drained the glass. Another glass appeared in front of him, along with the bottle. He downed the whisky in a few gulps and poured another. An undetermined amount of time passed as Colt sat there warring with himself.

"I love him, I love him so much," Colt said in defeat.

"Then protect him. You need to take the high road and be what you need to be at this stage in your life, unattached and focused on your future. It'll save his life."

"He's not gonna understand. There has to be a way," Colt said, emotion clogging his throat.

"Clean break, Colton. I'm not supposed to tell you, but your father's havin' you followed. The cheerleader will be followed, too. He's prepared to do whatever it takes to keep you from makin' this mistake. I hope you understand what I'm gettin' at."

"Fuck it," Colt said and bypassed the glass, opting for the bottle.

"End it, now, before this ends him, and I promise it will end him."

Colt couldn't let Jace be hurt. He had to protect him, no matter how badly his heart broke. Jace was too good for this, too perfect for Colt's world. He gripped the crystal glass, fighting the conflicting emotions pouring through him. The glass went flying across the room, shattering against the farthest wall. Colt watched the broken pieces fall to the floor, along with his dreams of a life with Jace.

# Chapter 10

Early Wednesday morning, Colt sat slumped in a chair at the Shaggy Dawg, a local bar targeting athletes. Country music played in the background. Little female barflies sat like groupies ripe for the picking. This place was like a home to him. Colt spent more time here over the last four years than anywhere else, including the football field.

His teammates and buddies were all there, hanging out at his table. Colt had stayed drunk pretty much since leaving Johnny's office, and the drinks hadn't stopped flowing all night long. They dulled the ache of his body, but not so much the one in his heart. His one good eye focused on the clock against the back wall of the bar. Already close to two o'clock in the morning—closing time. And that scared the shit out of him. Did he have enough alcohol at his apartment to get through the night?

"I still can't fuckin' believe you got fuckin' jumped. What's this damn town comin' to?" Hank Wilson asked. He was a redneck country boy from Kansas who'd played ball with Colt since their freshman year. They were friends, although Hank's days were numbered. He didn't make the cut for the draft.

"Yeah, it sucks, man. If I'd've fuckin' been there, this would be a way different deal." Paul Moon slurred his words while slamming a drunken fist down on the small round table in front of him. He was another four-year player, and he reached across the table, giving Hank an angry fist bump.

"Damn straight, it'd be a different fuckin' deal. We should be out lookin' for those mother fuckers. It's such bullshit, man!" Hank agreed, his words said on a slur as spit flew out across the table. They were all completely trashed. So much for studies! Colt was the only one who was in line to end his college years with a degree. Now, it sure was looking like that wouldn't be happening. He didn't see any of his professors allowing him to come to class drunk, and he didn't ever plan to be sober again.

"Nah, calm down, I handled it," Colt said, and drained his Jack and Coke, lifting his hand for another. The tail his dad had on him sat perched at the bar, drinking water, and every so often looking over to check on him. They were easy to spot, and he wondered if they were just an intimidation tactic. Hell, it worked. Colt was intimidated, and the guy served as a constant reminder he needed to protect Jace at all cost.

"You're being shady fuckin' quiet about this, Colt. What's the deal?" Hank said, leaning almost across the table to get closer to Colt. The spit never slowed as Hank eyed him closely.

"You never drink this much," a cute blonde said to him. She stood just to the right of Colt, concern on her pretty downturned face. "Are you okay?"

"He'd be better if you sucked him off right now," Paul said to the cheers of Hank, both were now focused on the girl who shot them a hateful look.

"Don't be rude," the girl shot back, before turning to Colt. "You don't look good, Colt. Let me call Magda. You don't belong here like this…" She was cut off in mid-sentence, and from out of nowhere, her body was shoved down against Colt's. The girl lost her footing and slammed into him. Pain shot the length of his body, momentarily robbing his brain of function. He shoved back in his chair, but hit the wall as her face made contact with his crotch.

The guys at the table where hooting and hollering, carrying on as Hank shoved her head down. He held her firmly in place, pressing her face against Colt's blue jean covered groin. The girl let out a scream and pushed against Colt's stomach and ribs.

"Goddammit, Hank!" Colt yelled, but he wasn't heard. He focused on controlling her hands, which pushed her farther into his lap. Jace appeared in front of him, pulling the girl from Hank's hold.

Jace walked through the streets of Austin worried sick about Colt for two solid days. He had waited for hours at the hotel, well past the time of check out. Somewhere around six o'clock in the evening Jace finally sent one single text message asking if Colt was okay. He never heard anything back. He waited at the hotel until about nine that night before he finally called Gregory for a ride home.

Jace missed class the next day, waiting for Colt to call. He'd also missed his classes on Tuesday worried sick, waiting by his phone, the television on, hoping to hear something, anything, from Colt. Jace couldn't figure out what possibly could have happened. Surely if something terrible happened, the local news would cover the story. Colt was as big a celebrity in their small town as just about anyone. When he hadn't heard anything, Jace started scouting out Colt's townhome complex, and then pacing the halls in front of his classes.

By midnight Wednesday, Jace did the girl thing and called all the hospitals. When that effort turned up nothing, he again walked past Colt's place about thirty times before deciding to head into town. He had no plan, except to search for anyone who might know something about Colt. Funny how the thought never occurred to him Colt might have abandoned him at the hotel. It still didn't as he walked past the bar where all the football guys hung out. Jace glanced through the big open window at the front of the bar, and his heart seized in his chest when he saw Colt sitting at the table with his friends. *What the hell?*

From where he stood, Jace could see Colt had been beaten up. As he gazed in the window, Jace's worst fears materialized as he looked closer at the side of Colt's bruised face and body. Jace pulled out his phone and texted Colt while standing there staring in through the window. He'd never entered this bar before. The Shaggy Dawg was restricted domain, a guy's guy kind of place. Every player that had ever given him a hard time hung out at the Shaggy Dawg. Jace waited and watched, but Colt never searched out his phone.

The thought occurred to Jace, maybe Colt had been mugged and they had taken his phone. Maybe? But it was Colt slightly turning in his chair, giving Jace a better angle of his torn up face that made him throw caution to the wind and enter. Jace pushed through the front door, stepping inside, ignoring everything going on around him. He wound his way directly back to Colt's table. All the while he tried to calm his pounding heart. He needed to play this cool and yet somehow get some answers.

As Jace got closer, he saw a girl at Colt's table. She spoke directly to Colt. Jace recognized the girl from her years of hanging out with the guys. He got close enough to see her being shoved down by the head toward Colt. To Colt's credit, he recoiled at the touch, pain clear on his face. It wasn't within Jace to ignore such a violent act, and he instinctively intervened when Hank wouldn't let her go.

No question, everyone at the table was drunk off their asses. Jace helped the girl up as he focused on Colt. He got right in his face with panic filling his heart at what he saw. The entire left side of Colt's face was contorted, swollen, and bruised.

"What happened? Are you all right?" Jace asked, the girl he'd helped all but forgotten. Seconds later, Jace was ripped away from Colt. Hank was in his face, pushing him backward.

"What the fuck are you doing here, fag?" Hank stayed on Jace with each step he took, his big beefy hands shoving against Jace's chest. Paul came out of nowhere and pushed at Jace, too. They worked together, caused Jace to lose his footing and slam back against a crowded table. He toppled drinks and sent the table sliding until finally dumping over. Jace fell with it. Everyone sitting at the table got angry and involved, all focused on Jace. Hank was standing over him, pulling him up by the collar, only to push him backward again. This time, Jace stumbled back several steps until he landed on his knees.

Where was Colt? Why was he letting this happen?

"No one wants you here, faggot." Hank didn't spit on him, but every drunken word that came out of his mouth was followed by its own round of spit. The bartender jumped over the bar, and the bouncer appeared out of nowhere, grabbing him around his waist, separating Jace from the angry crowd. They abruptly lifted Jace and began dragging him to the front door. Jace couldn't help but turn toward Colt who sat there staring at a man at the bar. Only for a brief second, did Colt look his way. That's when Jace saw pain, resolve, hurt, and something else… a clear decision. Colt wasn't going to get involved in stopping this brutal manhandling. His heart broke in that moment.

"Find your fuckin' dick someplace else, fag," the bouncer called out as Jace was shoved out the front door. He lost his footing again and landed on his ass on the sidewalk. This time the spit had purpose and landed on his chest. The window of the bar was filled with patrons cheering the bouncer on. A few of them stood sneering through the glass. Jace got to his feet, dusted himself off, and searched for anything to wipe the blob of spit off his shirt. He found nothing and carefully tugged the shirt over his head and tossed it in the trash. He'd wear his undershirt home.

As the crowd dispersed, the window cleared out, and Jace stayed back, hiding in the shadows, watching. Colt was still sitting in the same spot, his eyes focused on his cell phone for several long moments. He willed Colt to text him. Nothing came. Colt never moved and didn't return the text, but his eyes were back on the man at the bar. Jace's sensible side begged him to turn and leave, but his heart rejected his head. Colt had held him, made love to him, and romanced him like no one ever had before. Colt was for real, he had to be.

"You need to get the fuck out of here. Are you here tryin' to start fuckin' problems? Your kind isn't welcome here. And I'm not gonna stop them if they beat the shit out of you, bitch!" The guy Colt had been staring at yelled at him from the front door. Jace still took a second to look at Colt one last time, praying he would get up and come outside.

"Get the fuck outta here, fag," someone said from behind him. Jace hadn't even known he was back there. The guy at the front door started advancing on Jace. That got him moving. Jace wasn't sure how, but he jogged all the way from the bar to his apartment four miles away. As he hit his front door, the pain of everything finally settled in, becoming almost too much to bear. His heart went into survival mode.

Jace had broken the rules tonight and gone into Colt's world. He shouldn't have ever stepped foot inside the bar. Since he had met Colt, he'd allowed his heart to control his emotions, not his head.

When he saw Colt had been beaten, he'd simply reacted. He knew better than to approach Colt when he was surrounded by his teammates. Colt wasn't out. Surely that's why he sat there. This whole night was Jace's fault, he shouldn't have gone there. Surely if he had been in any real danger, Colt would have gotten involved, right? This wasn't the time for a broken heart. Colt had been hurt, that's why he hadn't called, right?

"Hey, are you okay?" Gregory asked.

"Yeah." Jace didn't say another word. He went straight to his room, praying Colt would find some way to make this okay.

# Chapter 11

*April 2003 (six weeks later)*

The April sun shone brightly as most of Austin, Texas, turned out for the NFL football draft. It was early, a little before eight in the morning, and the university football stadium was packed full. This was Jace's final cheerleading performance before graduation. The university had multiple players in the draft this year and most were suspected to be picked up by a team. For a town with no professional teams, this was the Super Bowl, World Series, and NBA Playoffs all rolled into one.

A stage was set up in the middle of the field. Huge television screens were installed and sat in every corner of the stadium. Although all the picks were important, Colton Michaels held everyone's attention. He was widely reported to be this year's number one, first round draft pick. The anticipation hanging in the air was almost tangible, and yet, Jace tried hard not to care.

Since all the cheerleaders were required to be here, he'd picked the first shift. There were enough of them to have two sets of stunt groups on the field for three hours at a time. If he was lucky, he could get in, entertain the crowd, and get out before the draft even started. If he wasn't lucky, he'd be watching Colt accept his offer live for national television. Jace prayed for lucky.

Jace stretched on the sidelines with the rest of his teammates. Haley, his stunt partner was beside him, pulling her leg back and up to her head, loosening her muscles.

"Are you doing all right, Jace?" she asked, dropping down into the splits. Haley had been with the team for four years. She was an awesome cheerleader and his only stunt partner since the beginning. They were effortless together.

"Yeah, why?" Jace said absently, stretching out his back.

"You know why. You haven't been yourself for weeks now." Haley bent over, touching her toes. It's like all the bones in her body disappeared when she began to stunt.

"I'm fine," Jace said, lifting his arms above his head, stretching out his shoulders.

"Are you over it?" she asked, turning her head up toward him.

"Over what?" Jace bent down and touched his toes, hanging there for a second, letting his back muscles get a good stretch.

"Whoever dumped you?" Haley jumped up and down, shaking her legs and arms out before doing a standing back tuck, landing solidly with both feet on the turf.

"How did you know?" Jace didn't evade the question. Unlike his roommates, Haley was safe, and she just rolled her eyes.

"Hello? I'm a girl. I know heartbreak. I've been worried about you." Haley grabbed their bags and ran them the few feet away, sitting them against the stadium wall.

"I'm fine. We need to get started," Jace said to her as the music began to play.

"And that was a total guy response. It just takes time, Jace. I promise it'll get better." Jace stayed quiet, like he'd done for six long weeks. He'd never heard from or seen Colt after the brief encounter at the bar. His heart still ached. How had those few days of spring break changed everything about Jace? He shook it off and joined the others at the front of the field. He plastered the smile on his face and began his long signature tumbling pass to the excited cheers of the crowd.

Two and a half hours later, Jace lifted Haley in a one-man stunt right as the screens abruptly changed. The actual draft was starting, not just the fanfare of the event. Years of training had him keeping Haley solidly in the air. He tossed her up, catching her easily in his arms as the draft began. All the cheerleaders ran to the stage and dropped to their knees to watch the first round pick. If Colt made it, Jace and his team were required to cheer after Colt received his new jersey.

Ten minutes later, Colt was announced as the number one, first round pick. New York Panthers, under major televised fanfare, selected Colt as their first choice. Colt, his father, and agent, along with Colt's newest girlfriend, all walked out on stage. Colt held her hand and it was all Jace could concentrate on. Colt accepted the offer and received his jersey. The crowd went wild. They reported a multi-million dollar signing bonus came along with the offer, more than Colt had even anticipated. Well, good for him.

The town's local hero had done well, following in even bigger footsteps than his father's. The stadium went wild, his teammates were already up, leading chants, but Jace couldn't find it in him to cheer. He stood frozen in place as shot after shot of Colt flashed across the oversized television screen. Pain lanced through his heart, crippling him, and he couldn't breathe. Jace's heart ripped from his chest.

He never imagined seeing Colt could hurt as bad as this. Colt was obviously excited. Colt's father was extremely proud, accepting handshakes from everyone involved. The blonde on Colt's arm leaned in, giving him a celebratory kiss. And with that Jace was done. He left the stage, headed down the field to grab his gear, not bothering to say goodbye to anyone on the way out. He left the stadium and never looked back. He had finals to study for. The need to finish this semester and close this chapter in his life was the most pressing emotion pouring through him as he walked across the empty campus to his apartment.

# Chapter 12

*June 2012*

A slap across the face jolted Colt awake. He laid there in his booze-induced haze, a dull ache beginning to form in his head. The start of another fucking day, yippee! Colt struggled to clear the fog clouding his brain.

Fully awake now, he needed up. Colt tried to turn to his right. The body lying on top of him wouldn't allow the movement. He struggled unsuccessfully to dislodge from the hold until something hard scrapped against his stomach when the female on top of him flopped around. Long strands of hair fell across his face.

Colt brushed away the offending strands and opened his gritty eyes, rubbing at the film covering them. Thankfully God had mercy on him. Even though the small rays of sunlight peeked in from all sides of the heavy curtain, the room was still dark.

Maryia lay across him, her arm tucked around him. A movement on his other side caught his attention. Colt turned his head, groaning when his eyes landed on Clint, his driver, who was snoring next to him. Pain shot through Colt's head as he sat up, the dull ache now becoming a full blown headache. He glanced across Clint's sleeping form to see another woman sleeping nude.

Fuck, had they had a four-way again last night? He couldn't remember. Just another in a long string of nights and days that ran together in one big fucked up giant mess. He wondered if they remembered condoms this time. Probably not.

Colt lowered his head back to the pillow, staying there for several minutes, trying to regroup. His head pounded, but not so terribly he couldn't deal with the throbbing. He'd drunk himself into oblivion last night, which wasn't much different than he'd been doing for the last nine years. His life had become nothing more than a drug and alcohol induced blur, with moments of playing football mixed in between.

He remembered forcing himself to throw up last night. That seemed to help the intensity of the next day hangover. This morning, his body already craved his morning Bloody Mary to help ease the pain. What was the old saying about hangovers... hair of the dog?

Maryia mumbled, and her hand came up. Something scrapped Colt across the face. He lifted a hand to his stinging cheek and it came back bloody. The scratch came from Maryia's engagement ring. Reality came crashing down on him.

He was an engaged man. *Fuck!*

Ignoring his aching body, Colt dislodged from Maryia, and apparently Clint, who had his legs tangled up with Colt's. He pulled himself up, working his way to the end of the bed. Colt placed his feet on the floor and pushed himself into a standing position. *Shit!* The pounding in his head was making him nauseous, fighting to keep the contents of his stomach down. He padded to the restroom, determined if he were going to throw up, it would be there and not his bedroom.

The bile churning in his belly had nothing to do with the alcohol he'd consumed and everything to do with the situation he let himself get involved in. Colt had agreed, or rather, had been coerced, into marrying a conniving, manipulative bitch, which seemed to be a metaphor for his entire adult life. *Fuck my life!*

Colt doubled over the commode, purging everything in his belly. He didn't fight it, staying right there through all the dry heaves, never forcing himself up. He had allowed himself last night to have the pity party to end all pity parties.

He always heard a person needed to experience every possible crappy outcome of their partying ways and hit rock bottom before they underwent detox. For Colt, rock bottom already happened nine years ago. Something seriously needed to give. He heard rehab sucked shit, but for him, nothing could suck as much as this miserable, fucked up existence he called a life.

Colt didn't know firsthand, but he assumed it was going to be difficult to just stop drinking. Alcohol was something he'd drank every single day since the meeting in Johnny's office where he'd been forced to give up Jace. If only his heart would have let go, too.

Actually, Colt had done a lot more than drink for much of the last nine years, trying to fill the void of Jace Montgomery. He'd stayed drunk because drinking numbed the pain and helped him forget. His few patches of sobriety centered on football games and working out, but honestly, he'd been pretty messed up for most of those, too.

Alcohol was the second most important thing in his life. Like always, when he thought about the situation like that, the first most important thing came to mind. Colt cut his eyes to his closet door. The scene of the crime and the only reason for his impeding nuptials. Fuck, the evidence was still lying all over the floor.

The contents littered across his closet were the only thing that enticed Colt into getting off the tiled floor in front of the toilet and cleaning himself up. It was just better all-around for him to ignore the image greeting him in the mirror. He looked like hell, and who wanted to see that? Instead, he brushed his teeth, washed his hands—because they smelled like ass—and splashed water on his face. After drying himself off, he finally made an attempt to deal with the chaos in his closet.

Colt hadn't bothered to dress; he could do that later. He forced himself to enter the closet and clean up the mess Maryia had made. Bitterness rose. How could she? There lay his most precious possessions in the world. His heart sank as he got a closer look at what that bitch had done to them. Anger at Maryia gripped him, but the pain and hurt of his past forced him to his knees. Almost a decade's worth of his collection dumped all over the floor. Many of the pictures and articles were crumpled, some were ripped up, but as Colt looked them over, he saw some had managed to survive her wrath. He smiled. Relief hit him strong as he looked down at the photo lying on the floor in front of his knees; Jace's sweet face stared up at him.

Colt slowly picked up the photo, his gaze centering on Jace's eyes. He liked this picture the most because Jace had looked right at the camera. The eyes seemed as if they looked right through him, seeing straight into to his soul. If Colt moved to the right, the eyes in the picture followed him. God, how he wished his life were different right now. He wished he'd never walked into Johnny's office that day after spring break.

Colt began methodically making two piles. One pile collected all the salvageable pictures and articles Colt had found on Jace throughout the years. He organized them as he went, starting with college and working his way to the last few months. Jace had done well with his life. He'd opened a cheerleading gym in Dallas and had done great over the years.

The next pile held the pictures and news stories he'd have to replace. The ones Maryia shredded in his face when she'd blackmailed him yesterday. Colt didn't know what pissed him off more. The fact Maryia had dared to touch his secret collection or that she'd used Jace to extort him into marrying her. Both set fire to his soul, adding to the long list of vile names that came to mind when describing the gold-digging, scheming Russian whore, better known as his fiancée.

Yesterday's battle had been epic. Maryia was strung out on meth. He had been in his normal drunken state, and it shocked the shit out of him that he'd refrained from putting his hands on her. He'd never hit a woman before in his life, but when he came in and found her going through his pictures, threatening to expose him if he didn't do exactly what she wanted him to do... yeah, he'd almost punched her right where she stood. Instead, the closet door took the brunt of his anger. And it now lay broken to pieces just feet away.

How had she even found these? He'd kept them hidden, tucked away in a shoebox at the bottom of his closet. No one ever found them. She had to be searching for something—something to use against him. His little Russian, up and coming supermodel was arm candy, nothing more. She drank too much, popped too many pills, and had moved into the serious drugs sometime last year. He didn't give a shit about her one way or another. Her only benefit, the only true reason he'd kept her around was that she seemed to like to watch him fuck guys. And he liked to fuck guys, but she didn't need to know that.

Watching him with other men turned her on. The guys always let Colt fuck them in order to get their hands on her. Win-win for everybody. He'd always known she was using him for his fame. He was definitely using her to hide behind, but somehow, he'd missed the conniving bitch part of her personality. Colt was just her ticket to becoming a United States resident. Apparently, her visas were all denied because of the multiple drug charges she'd faced over the last couple of years. A marriage to him solved those problems.

Colt sat back on his ass and lifted another picture of Jace. This one was a side shot, and he ran a fingertip down the length of Jace's body. Jace was thicker now, not the lean guy he remembered. His legs and arms were bulky, heavy with muscle, and his blond hair was longer. He'd turned into a man. Being thirty-two years old would do that to you. In the picture, Jace's jaw was set as he looked at one of his winning teams, and to Colt, Jace was still the most gorgeous man he'd ever seen. This was one of Colt's favorites. Maryia hadn't messed it up either. *Thank God!* Colt carefully laid the picture aside and moved deeper into the closet to finish getting Jace all picked up.

# Chapter 13

Jace rose from his bed and searched the floor for his athletic shorts. He found them in a pile of clothing, not all his, and slid them on before grabbing his old iPod off the nightstand. The alarm clocks dim light showed three o'clock in the morning, and his date still slept in his bed. That was kind of new. He usually didn't bring guys home, and if he did, they certainly didn't end up sleeping in his bed for the night.

Jace refused to consider how much he didn't like having someone in his bed or how he hadn't gotten remotely close to getting off last night. Neither thought needed his immediate attention, so he pushed them aside.

Absently, Jace grabbed his tank from the lampshade and quietly shut the door as he slipped on the shirt, making his way to the kitchen. He anchored the earbuds in his ears and quickly and efficiently picked one of the hundreds of playlist in the iPod. This one was this year's Nationals music, along with his top secret mixes for Worlds. He hadn't listened to either one all the way through, even though he had teams performing in every division.

Jace grabbed a can of guava juice from the refrigerator. Brushing a stray piece of his long hair behind his ears, he took a seat at his kitchen table. The music in his iPod thumped to life as he unrolled blueprints and spread them across the table. A grin slid across his face, the music all but forgotten as he looked at the front page of the final plans for his new cheerleading gym.

He had no idea how much time passed as he went through the blueprints, page by page. He watched for every correction they had talked about, and from the best he could tell, they were all there. Jace had also decided on a general contractor. He didn't go local, nor did he go with the cheapest bid, instead he chose Layne Construction out of Chicago. Their reputation was the best, and his cheerleaders deserved the best practice facility money could buy.

"Babe, come back to bed." Jace tensed as arms slid around his shoulders and full blown morning breath hit his face. Jace automatically tugged the earbuds from his ear, as the bold guy lifted his tank from the bottom, pulling the shirt up and over his head. "You're built like a brick house. Don't cover it up, baby."

On a score of one to ten, this guy was a ten when it came to the come-ons. That being the main reason Jace had finally gone out with him. About thirty minutes into the date, Jace remembered come-ons only lasted a minute and the guy had nothing else to back him up. They had fallen almost immediately into gratuitous sex and even that had failed. Again, not something he cared to think about right now.

Jace grabbed the shirt and rose, getting out from under the bad breath. He walked around the table, the opposite direction of the guy, and tugged his shirt back on.

"I've been waiting for you to wake. I need to get to the gym," Jace said, walking into the bedroom. He scanned the floor and found all his date's clothing, laying them out on the bed. Bad breath came up behind him, evidently not taking the hint, and wrapped an arm around him, kissing his back.

"Don't send me off yet. You were incredible last night. I want you to do me again."

Jace cringed at the thought, narrowing his brow. It was almost comical the way his body physically recoiled at the idea of fucking this guy again. Bad breath wasn't bad looking; probably younger, maybe in his early twenties, short, and had a nice tight body... but his nose looked too wide for his face. Jace broke from the hold.

"I'll call you, but I gotta go. I'm gonna be late."

"I don't believe you." Bad breath had his hands on his hips and a pout on his lips.

*Really?*

Jace had no idea what to say, so he didn't bother with words. He bypassed the guy, placed his earbud back in his ear and returned to his seat at the kitchen table, reading over the contractor's report. The guy never uttered another sound, but the front door of his condo slammed shut. A strong indication that bad breath left angry.

Jace grabbed the report and the juice and plopped down on the sofa, praying he might get an hour or two of sleep before he needed to be at the gym. Reaching for the remote, he turned the television to ESPN, hoping to catch the highlights of the missed Dallas Mavericks playoff game last night. He wished he'd gone to the game instead of on the date. What did that say about him? Jace ignored that question, too and looked down at the report in his hand.

Everything with the contractor's proposal looked in order. They would begin breaking ground in about a month, and by football season, the cheer gym should be ready for a grand opening. Layne Construction was known for staying on schedule. Which would be critical in the timing of his move. A beeping sound caught his attention as a breaking news report popped up across the bottom of the screen. At last, something about the game. Jace turned up the volume, but nothing could have prepared him for the image of Colton Michaels that flashed across the screen. Jace's bare feet landed with a thud on the hardwood floor when he leaned forward as though being closer to the television would make the information come more quickly. His heart reeled before it fell from his chest as he watched images of Colt and his latest girlfriend out on the town. The girlfriend flashing her ring in front of the cameras. Reports claimed they just got engaged last night.

Jace sat frozen in place. The realization Colt planned to marry punched through his already fragmented heart, ripping open old wounds. Jace never got over the pain of Colt's rejection, of his complete abandonment. Even today, he still wanted to know why Colt had left him without so much as a goodbye.

How could he still have a devastatingly broken heart over a guy he'd spent five days with? Anger shot through him, but not enough to stop him from hitting the play back option on his remote control and replaying the footage. Colt didn't look happy. He actually didn't look anything. He played no part in delivering the statement; the girl did the talking, and she was clearly drunk or on something, perhaps both.

Well, good for him. Colt landed himself a party girl. They fit together perfectly.

Jace, by no choice of his own, had inadvertently kept up with Colt's career. All the tabloids and gossip magazines kept his picture plastered on the front page, all claiming in big bold print that Colt Michaels was America's Sweetheart Party Boy.

The obstacle came in reconciling the Colt of today with the boy he'd known all those years before. The famous, party-at-all-cost, living-on-the-edge-of-trouble guy of today wasn't the self-assured, easy-going Colt he'd watched through college and certainly wasn't the man he'd spent five days with in Hawaii.

Even when derogatory news began filtering out about Colt a few years ago, nothing dissuaded Jace from the deep down goodness of the young man he'd been given the brief opportunity to know. Yes, Colt had totally played him, but the iPod in his hand proved he also had a big heart. And also proved Jace still wasn't over their brief fling almost ten years ago. Damn, he thought he'd resolved these feelings a long time ago.

Jace punched off the television, tossing the remote back to the side before he grabbed the laptop off the coffee table. His gym had been invited to perform at the Dallas Broncos-New York Panthers football season opener. He hadn't responded to the invitation. Instead, he let the email sit. The only concern he had over the invitation centered on his personal doubts about being in the same circles as Colt. Jace cleared his head and forced himself to think from a business perspective. Performing at the season opener was too big a deal to pass up. Jace booted up his email and replied to the offer. He'd be happy to prepare a routine and send one of his teams for the halftime entertainment. The opportunity would be cool and exciting for the kids in his gym, but Jace wouldn't be attending with them. He'd send Haley, give her a bonus or commission or something as an incentive to take that many kids across country by herself. He placed the resolve firmly back in his heart. Although clearly, he'd always love Colt and that would never change, their relationship happened almost ten years ago. The man he loved wasn't the man Colt had become. End of story.

Jace finished his email and clicked send before he could change his mind. He'd already stalled too long. He took the minute and sent his coaches a message to add this to their calendar of events for the upcoming year. When done, Jace closed the computer and shoved away the crazy pain the few unguarded seconds watching the television had caused. He forced positive, productive thoughts back into his soul.

No way could he sleep now. He stood, stretching out his long body. Colt always wound him up tight. That being one of the biggest reasons his gym performed in so many competitions during football season. They would keep Jace too busy to think about the professional quarterback.

Since his lifelong strategic plan focused on staying busy and ignoring memories, Jace decided the time had come to get to the gym. If only this newest round of pain in his heart would ease up some. On a sigh, he headed for the shower.

Hung over and hurting, Colt showered, dressed, and forced himself to put aside his craving for liquor. He began carefully going through his apartment, tossing everything party-related in the trash. He wasted no time draining the bottles of liquor and flushing all the drugs he could find down the toilet. Everyone in his bed stayed sleeping as he made his way through his bedroom and bathroom, cleaning out those rooms too. He personally took everything he found downstairs to the dumpster, making sure nothing was left behind inside his apartment to tempt him.

On the way back upstairs, Colt palmed his phone and made the first of three planned phone calls. He started with the easiest one, which just confirmed how complicated his life had become.

Dr. Knox, the New York Panthers head physician, answered his call on the first ring. "Hey, Doc, it's Colt."

"I know who it is, son. To what do I owe this pleasure?" Dr. Knox was an older man, well into his seventies, and he'd counseled Colt on more than one occasion about the quantities of liquor he consumed.

"I'm ready," Colt said. The words didn't come out as strong as the resolve he'd thought he'd had this morning.

"I'm relieved, son. It's a good decision. It'll be hard, but I'll be there with you every step of the way," Dr. Knox said, the relief evident in his voice.

"Thank you. Do I make the arrangements?" Colt asked. He stopped at his front door and leaned back against the wall. The best he could tell, he stood alone in the hall. As dangerous as this conversation might be to have in a public setting, the results would be worse if everyone was awake inside his apartment.

"No, don't worry about that, I'll make them. The place I have planned for you is in Utah, tucked away in the mountains. You'll be there ten days, under an assumed name. We'll get you detoxed, cleaned up, and back here for the rest of the treatments. The support group here is just as discrete, but you know all that. We've talked about it before."

"Yes, sir. And thank you. I can leave today. I want to start right away," Colt said.

"Good. I'll take you there myself. Let me get the flights booked now."

"Thanks again. I better call Coach Atkins and let him know."

"Colt, this is going to change your life, son. I'm proud of you." Colt nodded at no one. The emotion of the words clogged his throat. How long had it been since anyone had been proud of him, including himself?

"I'll call you back within the hour," Dr. Knox assured him.

"Thank you." Colt was truly grateful. The words broke as he said them. Dr. Knox disconnected the call.

Colt didn't wait. He dialed Coach Atkins as he entered his apartment, relieved the place was still quiet. As the phone rang, he walked to the guest bedroom and quietly shut the door. Coach Atkins answered on the fifth ring.

"This better be good and make it quick. I'm in cooking class." Colt grinned. In what world did a head coach of a professional football team find his relaxation by taking cooking classes?

"Coach, I'm gonna be MIA for about ten days," Colt said. He plopped down on the bed and dropped his head between his shoulders, waiting for the coach's response.

"Is Dr. Knox gonna be MIA, too?"

"Yes, sir, he said he'd be going with me." After another lengthy pause, with nothing said between them, Colt could almost see the coach doing the math in his mind. Spring training camp was just a few weeks away.

"I want regular reports," Coach said.

"Yes, sir," Colt agreed and released the pent up breath he'd been holding.

"Did something happen, Michaels? Do I need to get public relations in on this?" Coach asked.

"I'm getting married, but I'll announce that myself when I get back, if it hasn't already been said. I honestly don't remember."

"To who?" From the sound of the coach's voice, the man had trouble thinking of anyone in Colt's life suitable to marry. Hell, he completely agreed.

"Sir, I don't wanna talk about it. I'll tell Doc to keep you updated. Go back to your class. I'll call you when I'm back."

"Colton, you need this. Get sober. Do whatever it takes to beat this addiction. We have a championship to win this year."

"Yes, sir." The call disconnected. Now, on to his third and final call. The one he absolutely didn't want to make. He struggled with himself. The need for a drink made his tongue thick and his palms sweaty. Instead of calling his dad, he called his agent. The decision was lame, but they were really like talking to the same person. When one knew something, so did the other. Besides, this was Saturday morning. Maybe they'd be on the golf course and he'd get voice mail.

"Hey, Colt, how's it going, buddy?" Johnny answered on the first ring. *Damn!*

"Johnny, I'm going into rehab. I'll be heading to Utah in the next couple of hours. Will you tell my dad?" He bit the bullet, refusing to beat around the bush.

"What? You don't need rehab!" Johnny's financial concern drove him to say that, certainly not any care for Colt himself.

"Yeah, I do. I'm also getting married. Tell my dad that, too." Colt stood. His nerves had him pacing. He left the guest bedroom, heading straight for the small living room. A muffled noise came from his bedroom, and Colt cut his eyes in that direction, watching for the bedroom door to open as he lowered his voice. "I gotta go. They're coming to pick me up. I'll be gone ten days."

"Wait! Don't do this. Your dad's here with me. Talk to him." Just as Colt figured, they were together. Why had Johnny answered the phone?

"No, tell him for me. I'm leaving now." He prayed that would stop his dad from coming over. Colt didn't wait, but disconnected the call and dropped his phone on the coffee table. He ignored the immediate ring back from the phone. He had all his photos and articles of Jace sitting out on his desk. He needed to put those away. Colt stacked them carefully on top of each other and went to his wall safe. He should have kept them there from the beginning. He just liked having faster access to them.

Colt worked quickly, keeping an eye on the bedroom door. Maryia didn't know about the wall safe. And if she did, there was no way she knew the combination sequence. He opened the safe and carefully placed the photos inside. He shut the door, twisted the handle, and spun the combination, before hanging the picture back in place. Relief replaced the overwhelming need to drink that had plagued him since he'd spoken to his agent. His memories of Jace should be safe inside there. Colt would always protect Jace from anything else in his world reaching out and fucking up his life.

Jace was the motivation behind this stab at sobriety. Maryia was a cold-hearted bitch. She had sworn to out Colt, but worse than that, she had threatened Jace. She would do whatever it took to destroy him, and he had inadvertently given her an arsenal of information about Jace's life. She vowed to make up horrific rumors and leak them if he didn't do exactly what she wanted. That's why he would never pick up another drink again. Jace needed to be protected. Colt had failed once, but never again.

A crash came from the bedroom, and then a round of laughter had Colt looking over at the closed door. He cringed. No telling what was going on in there. He slowly made his way to the door, pausing before he entered. He needed to pack a few things before he left, but they were all awake now. He'd cleaned out as much of their stash as he could find. All the noise probably came from them looking for a hit.

Colt manned up and opened the door.

The site greeting him shocked his almost-sober mind. He recoiled at the thought of being in the middle of them last night. They all turned to look as he stepped inside the room. Maryia straddled his driver. Her hair hung in a long tangled mess and her silicone breasts bounced in Clint's face. The other female was equally as naked and lay there taking a hit from a pipe. Apparently he hadn't found it all.

"Join us, man," Clint said, gripping Maryia's ass with his hands, spreading her for his view. "She likes you in her ass while I'm fucking her."

Maryia giggled and gripped Clint's dick, sinking right down on top of him. All conversation stopped as the female on the bed moved to join them. Colt turned away and went straight to the bathroom, locking the door behind him. Maryia might be controlling him right now, but when he got back, none of that would ever be happening again. He was a determined man.

Thirty minutes later, Colt opened the bathroom door with his duffel bag slung over his shoulder. They were still going at it on the bed. No surprise there, those were usually hours' long sessions. Colt planned to be long gone before they realized he was no longer in the house. A note should suffice his bride-to-be. He certainly didn't think she would curtail any of her activities in his absence. Clint seemed to be her latest object of desire, and the guy had no problem doing her bidding, whatever that might be.

Colt walked into the bedroom, keeping his head down and his eyes averted until it registered there was an additional person in the room. Colt looked up to see Maryia and the other female making out on the bed. His father sat spellbound on the side of the bed, watching the two naked women kiss while Clint moved to join them. His father's hand disappeared inside his golf shorts, a look of depravity in his eyes as he leered at the women. His dad was a sixty-eight-year-old perv, watching his future daughter in-law fuck a woman and another man. His father sat so entranced by the scene before him he hadn't yet noticed Colt's exit from the bathroom.

Colt weighed his options and decided he'd try to make it out unnoticed. His dad disgusted him. Colt lived the life his father made for him. How fucked up was that? It took Colt years to realize his father hadn't done all this just for him, but instead for himself. Larry Michaels lived the high life on Colt's dime, and they had never gotten past the ass whoopin' his father had given him in Johnny's office all those years ago. His father controlled him by never letting him forget how easily he had kicked his ass that day.

A few years ago, Colt had finally grown some balls and fired his father as his manager. It took finding out his financial status had him somewhere close to flat broke, even after signing a multi-million dollar contract for the second time in his career. His father's spending habits had Colt on the verge of bankruptcy. For the last two years, he tried hard to shake the old man loose, but he hung on like a leech, sucking the very life out of Colt.

There would definitely be restrictions on his old man after he got back from rehab. Thank God his mother hadn't lived long enough to witness that dirty old man jacking off to a twenty-five-year-old whore. The moment somehow built Colt's resolve. He was cleaning up his act, forever. He'd never allow himself to become like Larry Michaels.

Colt stayed close to the wall and moved slowly across the bedroom to avoid attracting attention; he made it to the hallway undetected, and breathed a sigh of relief as he stepped into the living room. Colt grabbed his phone off the table and placed it in his pocket. He did a quick check for his wallet and keys before heading toward the door. He'd wait for Dr. Knox at the man's office. He couldn't stand being anywhere near this place or those people. He didn't want this life another minute longer.

# Chapter 14

*February 2013*

Silently counting off to the beat of the music blaring overhead, Jace stood at the front of the spring floor mat, watching each stunt group lift their flyer into the air simultaneously. Frustration narrowed his brow. This was his cream of the crop coed team, reigning world champions for four years in a row, national champions for even longer. The ones every other cheerleading gym in the world aspired to beat. And for some reason, they couldn't hold their stunts five days before Nationals. *Not good.*

Jace let the young coaching staff continue to count out loud and the cheerleaders continue in their routine for about thirty seconds longer, then he lifted his eyes to the sound room above. At his cue, the music came to an abrupt end and so did the cheerleading routine. Silence filled the large gym, and everyone turned their gaze toward him, waiting for Jace to speak.

"NCA Nationals is in five days; therefore, it's going to be a long night ladies and gentlemen. Take five and call your parents. We aren't leaving until we get it right!" Jace called out from the edge of the mat. He continued to stand rooted in the spot with his muscular arms crossed over his broad chest and his feet spread apart. When he heard the mumbled protest from some outspoken members of the team, he looked up, daring them to test his patience any further. He watched the cheerleaders for several seconds, contemplating his options. The young coaches for this team came to stand in front of him.

"We'll get it. I promise." One coach started to speak, but Jace lifted his hand to stop the flow of excuses.

"I want Tina, the front flyer, moved to the back. I want Autumn moved to center. Collin is no longer the point for the triple toe back. Move Robert there, instead. Nikki and Laureen need to swap places. I think if they switch positions it may help in some of the chaos running back and forth, also in some of the attitude I'm seeing while they're performing. I also want Ally and Amanda's group to show the team what a switch kick double basket toss should look like. Work them for about an hour more and then let them go. I'll take their class tomorrow night myself." Jace never paused for a response, but turned to the next team standing to the side, waiting to take center mat. With a motion of his hand, they moved forward to take their position.

While the new team took their spot on the floor, Jace looked around his gym. He moved his teams into this building a couple of months ago, and he was proud of this new facility. It still needed work, there was always room for improvement, but he ran six hundred ninety cheerleaders through here every week. Never turning anyone away, yet still winning something in every competition for the past ten years. The trophies were three rows deep and had been placed on shelves running around the top of the thirty thousand square foot building after the gym ran out of room in the trophy cases. Championship banners lined the walls and hung from every beam in the huge facility.

All six hundred ninety cheerleaders were in the gym today, watching this showcase. It was a mandatory practice. They sat and stood in every available space, either waiting for their team to perform, or once finished, there for moral support.

The team he had just called to the mat was his junior prep team, level six, the highest level achievable in cheerleading. They were his top junior team. The other nine junior teams in his gym sat in order behind him, quietly waiting for their turn on the mat. The transition took no more than three minutes, and the girls stood in position, ready and waiting. Their coaches looked nervous. *Good.* He lifted his eyes to the sound room once again.

The music blared overhead, signaling the girls to begin their routine. The coaches counted loudly, trying to help keep everyone synchronized. After they nailed the first round of stunts, the entire gym busted out cheering the girls on. They were flawless all the way through. Jace stood there watching in the same manner he'd observed his elite senior team before. Watching closely for the mistakes and catching them just as the judges would this weekend.

Haley placed her hand on his shoulder and leaned in from behind. His five foot two inch tall assistant lifted on her tiptoes, still only hitting about his shoulders, requiring him to bend his head slightly to the side as she whispered in his ear. "ESPN's here. They're setting up in your office. The video cameraman's over in the corner. He looks like a dad. The reporter's standing directly behind you in the viewing window of your office." Jace kept his eyes trained on the routine in front of him and only straightened his head, not giving any indication he'd heard Haley.

Jace continued to stand in the exact same position as before, brawny arms crossed over an expansive chest, for several moments after the team finished their routine. The music ended, plunging the gym into silent hopeful tension. The girls stood, trying to catch their breath, obviously excited they'd nailed their three minutes of fast-moving tumbling, dancing, and stunting. But they needed to hear from Jace before they gave in to the excitement.

Jace just stood there, thinking over what he saw wrong. This team was close to perfect, or as close to perfect as they could get. They had been together since they were all about five years old. Now, at twelve, they were a well-oiled machine. Finally, Jace gave them a nod and a smile. The coaches and girls jumped up and down, screaming, running over to him. His bad, mean reputation fell short with this group of girls clinging all over him.

"Just because I nodded doesn't mean you don't continue to work the rest of the week. It needs to be perfect. Alesha, your counts were off on the triple toe back. Kennedy, your double needs tighter rotation. And for God's sake, keep it clean. Point those toes. No bobbles and I saw some. You know who you are." The girls listened, hugging each other, and him, while the camera's captured the entire moment.

*So much for trying to be a hard ass.* Jace wedged his way from the group of excited giggling girls.

"Haley, watch the next team. I'll be in my office," Jace said, and for the first time, looked toward the window where the reporter stood. He gave a single nod of his head, lifting one finger, asking for an extra minute. She nodded back, smiling.

"Yes, sir! Ladies, next team on the mat please, pronto," Haley called out, but Jace didn't listen any further. He made his way through a back side door, which lead to his personal office space and the full bathroom that lay strategically hidden behind his office. The reporter waited just on the other side of the bathroom door. The music would drown out any noise he might make. He figured the reporter would still be standing at the floor to ceiling windows of his office, mesmerized by the teams' practice session. Whether flying through the air or tumbling across the floor, his teams were some of the best in the world. They worked hard and it showed.

Standing at the simple sink, Jace washed his hands and splashed water on his face. The week before Nationals always meant longer hours. He felt the fatigue already beginning to set in and wished for a strong cup of coffee right about now. With a sweep of his eyes, Jace checked his appearance in the small mirror. He removed the small leather strap holding his short ponytail back. His hair stylist trimmed his chin length hair a little too short this time, causing some front pieces to escape the band and fall to his face. The summer blond streaks he asked her to add made him look more naturally blond than the light brown his hair had become as he'd aged, and the tanning bed turned his normally fair skin into a golden brown. Jace hoped he appeared a little healthier looking for the camera.

ESPN co-sponsored this year's National Cheerleaders Association's Competition. His gym was being spotlighted for some of the breakout sessions, giving the station something to run during the down times of the competition. Jace usually didn't go to these extremes to look good, but this week he needed to represent as best he could.

He took a step back from the sink, looking over his clothing. Jace pulled at the clinging, tight fabric of his gym shorts. His thighs were thick from years of tumbling and lifting girls in the air, and the material clung to his legs, making his muscular thighs look massive. The fabric stretched as he pulled a little free room in the material. The double XL company logo T-shirt he wore stretched tightly over his upper chest and arms. He pulled on that material too, trying to gain a little extra room before tucking the shirt into his shorts.

At the last minute, he decided to let his hair hang loose, running a brush through the strands before tucking it behind his ears. Then he smiled, looking into his own green eyes, before lowering his gaze, making sure nothing from dinner had been left behind in his teeth. Giving himself one last look in the mirror, he decided he looked as good as he could and left the bathroom, walking directly into his office.

"Hello, I'm Jace Montgomery," he said immediately to the two women standing together. The makeup artist came straight to him, ignoring his out stretched hand. Instead, she began to examine his face before ushering him to his chair.

"Hi, Jace, I'm Sandra Hamilton. It's a pleasure to finally meet you. I feel like I know you already with the amount of time we've spent together on the phone." Sandra stuck out her hand, shaking Jace's in quick, aggressive motions. "This is Candy, our makeup designer. She's a bit no-nonsense as you might be able to see." Candy smiled at him.

"I don't need to do much. You're extraordinarily handsome. Your skin tone's perfect as it is. Let me just get the eyes a little more pronounced. Have you ever modeled before?" Candy started right in, aiming her makeup brushes at his face. She worked quickly and efficiently, never taking her eyes from her work.

"No, I haven't," Jace said quietly, trying not to move his facial features as she worked on him. He hoped she hadn't notice the blush creeping up his cheeks. He wasn't shy by any means, but Jace hated being on the receiving end of compliments about his looks. It made him feel a little awkward, never really sure what he was supposed to say. On the other hand, someone could compliment him on the gym or cheer teams all day long; those were easier to respond to because of the hard work and dedication it took from all involved. And he was extremely proud of all the time and effort his kids and coaching staff put in at the gym. All of that diligent work was exactly the reason he was sitting in a chair blushing while chatty Candy fussed over his makeup.

"You should. The camera's gonna love you!" Candy stepped back, examining him again before having him sit up straighter in the chair and adjusting his clothing. "Here, lift this sleeve up a little. Yes, perfect. It shows your bulked-up arms, and let's pull the shirt back some. Yes, perfect, it outlines your chest, defines you more.

Your legs look great. Just make sure you keep your foot on the bar of the chair. It keeps your leg muscles flexed."

The whirlwind of directions slowed and Candy finally stepped back. The producer and cameraman were now in the office, setting up the camera while the producer began talking over their game plan for the interview. There would be a fifteen minute interview leading into a tour of the building showing some of the trophies and awards received. Jace had redecorated his office specifically for this interview. They sat in director style chairs in front of the large floor to ceiling window with a view of the teams behind them as they continued to perform. Sandra took her chair, and Candy now gave her the touch-up she insisted she needed before the cameras started.

"We have coffee mugs here full of water. If your mouth gets dry, just take a drink and keep going." Jace glanced toward the deep voice and gave a nod to the young male producer while he pinned a microphone to his collar. On the producer's order, all the activity came to a sudden halt and the reporter started the interview. And just like every single time, Jace's stomach filled with butterflies and his palms grew clammy. He never got used to being on television or doing these interviews, but the exposure was great for the gym. After the interviews ran, he always had an influx of new members. He tried to recall all the instructions given to him earlier and prayed he didn't say the wrong things. Taking a deep breath, he sat up straight, making sure his foot was on the bar of the chair and his muscles were flexed, just the way Candy had instructed him.

"I'm Sandra Hamilton, here today with Jace Montgomery, owner operator of Cheer Dynasty in Dallas, Texas. Many in the world of cheerleading credit Jace Montgomery for creating the phenomenon known as all-star cheerleading. His top senior team is the reigning, unprecedented four-year champion in the Worlds division. His gym is the largest in the world, competing with twenty-four teams this year, here in Dallas, at the national cheerleading competition. Jace, I'm going to jump right in. I've spent most of the evening talking with your team members. They just love you. Both the children and their parents adore you. How do you accomplish this level of rapport in such a strictly disciplined environment?" The cameras swept around them during the introduction until they finally moved in on Sandra and then over to Jace.

"Sometimes they like me, when I say the things they like to hear. The team before the one you watched wasn't quite so happy with me. They might not have such glowing words right now." Sandra gave a chuckle while Jace just smiled. She didn't pause before asking her next question.

"So you have earned your reputation?"

"I don't know. What's my reputation?" The question was somewhat of a lie. Jace knew how the cheerleading community thought of him. He worked hard to come off as a big jerk most of the time. He learned early on that his easy-going, light-hearted attitude toward life would be run over in the real world of business. A few well-placed hard stares and moments of silence had the cheerleading world considering him a serious business man, intent on making a name for himself.

"Well, I've heard your competitors call you a hard-nosed business man who's just in it for the money. Your coaches call you a tough workaholic who never stops pushing. Your cheerleaders call you brilliant, and the industry as a whole says you have single-handedly changed cheerleading into a world-wide revolution. You've created athletes out of this sport."

Jace stayed quiet, just looking at the reporter. He didn't feel like any of that described him at all. Okay, maybe the workaholic described him the best. He did work all the time, mainly to avoid the other parts of his life. He decided he wasn't really sure where the question lay in what the reporter asked. Jace just stared at her, giving a little smile before saying, "I'm sorry. I don't really understand your question."

The reporter's eyes met his, and she gave a small giggle before leaning in toward him, her body language visually changing. After a brief pause, she closed her eyes and shook her head. "I have also been told, over and over, what a charming, nice-looking man you are. I see it and can easily say throughout our conversations over the last few weeks, I believe your reputation has been very well earned on every level. Let's move this forward, tell me about a day in the life of Jace Montgomery. Is it true you're a vegetarian?"

"Yes, absolutely. I'm a complete vegan."

"Why did you become a vegan?"

"I did it several years ago. I liked the health effects. The gym was taking off. I was tired all the time. I needed to make some changes."

"And you work out every day. You still tumble and keep up your skill level?" As the reporter spoke, the camera focused on Jace. He was still incredibly nervous, trying hard to hide his sweaty palms and shaking knees, but he kept the smile on his face and hoped no one would be the wiser. He had been watching the reporter, keeping her as his anchor in his sea of nerves when she looked down over his chest and lower to his stomach and then lower to his lap. It caused a heat to rush to his cheeks and those anxious nerves to skyrocket under her scrutiny.

*What? Did she just check me out?* The little smile she gave made him stumble just a little in answering this question.

"I think it's only fair that if I'm asking my kids to be their best, I need to be at my very best as well. I certainly can't ask anyone to do something I can't do myself." The reporter's eyes stayed settled on his lap while he answered, and her smile grew a little broader before she lifted her gaze to meet his. Seconds later the camera turned back to her. Did that mean they didn't catch her checking him out? He prayed so. Parents wouldn't trust their children with him if they thought he put this kind of thing in front of them.

"Is it true the average cheerleader spends about twenty hours a week here in this gym?" she asked.

"Yes, I believe that's probably true. Well, let me rephrase that. Not every one of the cheerleaders commit full time and it's certainly not required, but we hold two or three open gyms a week to work on their skill levels. We also have tumbling, jump, and technique classes. Many of them take advantage of those."

"What do you say to those who feel that's a bit excessive on a child's schedule?"

"I would say this probably isn't the place for them then," Jace said with a wink. The reporter laughed, leaning in a little closer.

"I've been told you're here all day, every day. Do you ever get a break?" she asked, anchoring her elbow on the arm of the director chair she sat in.

"Of course, when I feel like I need one, I get away," Jace replied, confused as to how the interview had taken such a personal turn. He didn't want to talk about his personal life to her or anyone else for that matter. None of these questions were sent over as possible choices in the pre-interview lineup. He wondered if the woman sitting across from him realized he was a completely, one hundred percent gay man. Her body language sure didn't seem like she got the memo.

"When was your last vacation?" she asked, her smile still on her lips.

"Hmmm." Jace could only grin, thinking over the question. She had totally called his bluff. In ten years, he'd never vacationed one time. "Okay, I don't vacation much. Probably my last year in college, I took a long trip to the beach. It was a good time. Some of us from college went. Those were good days. I do have something planned after Nationals this month. I've got a vacation planned in Hawaii."

"You've bought a home there, I understand?" she asked. He lifted his brow, realizing she had done her homework. No one should have known of the house he'd just bought on Kauai.

"Yes. It's been ten years since I've seen it. I'll be going there for the first time in the next couple of weeks."

"You bought it and haven't seen it in ten years?" she asked, lifting a perfectly arched eyebrow, sounding a little disbelieving.

"Yes, it's actually where I vacationed my senior year in college. And I happened across it on a real estate site. It was a very good trip." The reporter laughed at his response, and thankfully finished the interview, turning back to the professional. She asked all the questions he was prepped for, and his nerves settled the more they got through the Q&A session. He was much more comfortable talking about the world of cheerleading than anything to do with his personal life. They ended the interview with a formal walk-through of the facility.

Jace's cheer gym measured the largest in the world and housed state of the art equipment throughout. They toured the long halls to the locker rooms, gym entrance, and trampoline areas. They walked the length of the banner and trophy case wall. His public relations firm had enlarged several pictures highlighting the gym's last ten years and placed them all over the facility. Jace and the reporter walked slowly past each one, with the cameraman filming the entire time. She continued asking him questions along the way. Finally, they came to the end of the tour where one of his college pictures hung. It had been taken at the Rose Bowl game. The picture showed him and his stunt partner in a tight, perfectly executed full up cupie.

In this particular picture, Colt stood in the background staring in the general direction of the camera.

"I forgot Colton Michaels went to school at Texas Longhorn University. You cheered those years he played there?" Sandra stopped walking and stood in front of the picture. Jace could almost see her mind working, hoping to get some scoop on the world famous athlete from back in the day.

"Yes, we graduated the same year," Jace said, trying to move away from the picture, but Sandra wouldn't budge. She stayed rooted right in front of the picture, moving to the side so the camera could get a good shot.

"Wow, did you know him?"

"No, not really, just in passing. We were at the Rose Bowl for this shot. We all traveled together quite a bit, the cheerleaders and football players that is. But no, I wouldn't say I knew him. He wouldn't remember me, now, anyway. I'm sure of it. He went on to a huge career in the NFL." Jace stared at the picture a second longer, looking at the youthful, devilishly gorgeous Colt, wishing he'd caught this picture before it was hung so he could have prevented it.

"He's getting married next week. His fiancée is Maryia Cherchesov, the Russian supermodel. I wondered if you could tell me what he was like back in college? Theirs is the wedding of the century. It would be great to have something on him that no one knows."

Jace stayed quiet, turning back to the picture. His heart filled with a small ache as he remembered their short time together. Even after all this time, he still hadn't gotten over those few days they'd shared. What could he say? This year's MVP, Super Bowl winning quarterback loved to bottom? Even thinking such a thing had betrayal knotting in his stomach, pain nudging at his heart.

Jace had never breathed a word to anyone of their special time together, nor would he ever. But looking at this picture now, he knew the truth as to why he planned to leave for vacation. The wedding coverage of the man he still stupidly and deeply loved would be too hard to watch. The complete truth about super athlete Colton Michaels? He was the man who in five short days set the bar too high for anyone else to ever live up too. *God, I'm too old to be this pathetic!*

"Like I said, I didn't really know him at all. I can't speak on him, except to say he was loved on campus and seemed to be a good guy. The school spirit was high the day of his first round draft pick. Those were great days. I wish him the best, always have."

# Chapter 15

"Goddammit, Colt, stop throwing my coke away! That shit costs money. The money you keep throwing fucking fits over. Get a clue, ass. I'm spending it over and over again because you *keep flushing my shit away!*" Maryia screamed at Colt. He ignored her anger as he stood in the kitchen, making a turkey sandwich. He needed to amend that thought. He stood in his brand new, way overpriced kitchen in a downtown New York City penthouse.

"I'll throw it away every fucking time I find it. The tequila's gone, too. You look like shit, you need to eat something," Colt said, taking a big bite in front of her. He made a delicious moaning sound and rolled his eyes to the heavens. Colt loved to tease her about food, because the woman refused to eat.

"I hate you! Do you understand that? I *hate* you!" Maryia screamed, whirling from the counter, banging open the swinging kitchen doors as she barreled from the room.

"Feelings mutual, bitch. You know the way to get rid of me!" Colt hollered back at her and took another bite, counting off in his head. On the count of three, tropical storm Maryia barreled back through the kitchen, leaning over the granite countertop, trying to get in his face.

"I'm not ever leaving you, *gay boy!* You'll never be rid of me!" She screeched the words and he took another bite, although he'd completely lost his appetite. The perfectly made sandwich tasted like sawdust, and he knew he had to get out of the house fast. She was in such a rage, Jace's name would be flying from her lips soon and someday he wouldn't be able to stop himself from shutting her hateful, nasty mouth. It was remarkable he hadn't already.

"I'm going to a meeting, don't wait up." He grabbed his plate and walked from the kitchen, trying so hard to at least appear unaffected. If she ever knew she got to him, she'd pour salt on that wound every chance she got. "The wedding planner called, she needs to talk to you. She's been trying to reach you for days."

"You're such a fucking pussy for going to those meetings every day. You're a drunk, Colt. You're never gonna make it. You're just doing it now to piss me off!" Maryia stayed right on his heels, yelling at him as he wound his way to the entry.

"What, meth head? I'm sorry, I think you're confusing yourself. Jonesing for another bump already? Makes you crazy inside to watch me eat food?" She hated anything to do with the wedding plans and food. Out of spite, he took another bite and she slapped the sandwich out of his hand. The pieces sent flying every which way. She reared back and slapped his face. He just barely moved away before the pointy toe of her hot pink Christian Louboutin pump made contact with his shin.

"I hate you!" Her nails were drawn, and she was ready to fight. Colt went quickly for the door. Scratch marks took forever to heal.

"Feeling's mutual, sweetheart! Maybe our children will get your sunny disposition." Colt went through the front door, barely making it out before she slammed the door and turned the lock from behind. She was ridiculous. He didn't let the anxiety show until he stood alone inside the elevator. He fought against his need to drink. One thing he realized for certain… he was a complete alcoholic. His need to drink centered into his need to escape his fucked up, out of control life.

As the floors ticked downward, Colt thought back over the famous quarterbacks of his childhood. Did those guys really have this kind of life, hidden behind all the smoke screens of fame? How could anyone want this kind of life?

Unlocking the front doors of the gym, Jace glanced at the intricate window etching of his gym's paw print logo and made his way to the security system, quickly disarming the device. Every morning since moving into this facility, he would smile with pride at those front doors. He loved the large tiger paw etched into the glass. It cost a bundle to create, but had been worth every dime. That large paw always put him in a better mood and set his day right just looking at the etched glass. Something about those hand-made doors made him feel more successful than anything else around him.

Now, with his attitude ranking somewhere between bad and just shit, Jace only focused on it being four thirty in the morning and still completely dark outside. He had left late the night before, probably close to midnight, but he really didn't know for sure. Flipping the switch under the security system, the overhead lights came to life, forcing him to squint under their bright glare. Jace gave a jaw-cracking yawn while turning back to lock the front doors. He started every morning the same way, with a good hour-long workout before showering and beginning his work day.

February, even in Texas, meant cold weather outside. Winding his way to the locker room, he stepped inside and pulled off his sweats. Jace changed quickly into a pair of athletic shorts and a T-shirt. With his running shoes in hand, he went into the workout room. This room was available to any member of the team over the age of sixteen, and looked like any other gym's workout room. Floor to ceiling mirrors ran all along the back wall. Drop down flat screens from the ceiling were positioned in the four corners of the room. Several treadmills, bicycles, and ellipticals were lined across one wall. The other side held assorted weight benches and free-weight stands filled with every kind of weight available on the market. Jace started one of the treadmills, letting it warm-up, while popping his iPod's earbuds in place.

Sitting on a random weight bench, he slid on his running shoes. He ran a finger over the iPod's screen, going through several playlists. This morning seemed to be more of a Linkin Park or Rage Against the Machine kind of day, he picked *New Divide* to start with, turning the volume up loudly. As the song rang through the earbuds,

Jace jumped on the treadmill, began with a warm up, which quickly led to a five mile full out run.

Sweat poured from him with each mile he ran. The hard-edged music blared through his headphones. The long days of hard work and little sleep were beginning to take their toll. Jace stayed exhausted, but no matter what he did this time, no matter how he manipulated himself, nothing took his mind off Colt.

The interview happened five days earlier, and every minute since he'd looked at that stupid picture of his college days, Colt had haunted his thoughts. What the hell was wrong with him? It had been so long ago but the hurt and loss still messed with him. What happened to the strategically placed resolve he'd thought he had?

Things finally broke in his mind. The memories he barred came flooding back, crashing through the barriers he'd erected in his mind. He remembered the first full day they were in Hawaii together. He was lying on the beach, eyes closed, letting the soothing hot rays of the sun bake his body. He could still recall the sound of the ocean and the smell of coconut suntan lotion mixed with the salt water carried on the tropical breeze. Colton had called out to him from a distance. Jace propped himself up on one elbow, shielding his eyes from the sun's bright glare, and watched Colt run along the water's edge toward him.

Colt was stunning in every way. His muscular, well-trained, athletic body flexed and teased Jace's senses as he ran. His short black hair, piercing blue eyes, and easy-going, charismatic smile reached straight out to Jace's heart and stole it, right then and there. Every feeling toward Colt that he'd tried to regulate went into frenzied overdrive. That day on the beach in Kauai, Jace willingly gave his heart and soul over to Colt; they were no longer his.

His heart had jumped from his body and landed squarely in Colt's hands. Colt seemed to know. He dropped down in the sand next to Jace, took his face between his strong palms, and captured his mouth in a devastatingly tender kiss. He couldn't forget the way Colt made the sweetest love to him right there on the beach.

Today, Jace remained completely disgusted with himself. He thought all these feelings were buried and gone, never to return. Fuck, Colt had taken and stomped all over his heart. He should be completely done. Instead, even after all these years, the deep hurt and deep love still remained. Jace was that schoolboy wishing his crush would have picked him. Nothing had changed. Not in ten long years had his feelings lessened for Colt, and the revelation totally pissed him off. Why couldn't he let Colt go?

Last night, when Jace couldn't sleep, he got up and broke several of his long standing rules. Jace allowed himself to give in to curiosity and Googled images of Colt and his beautiful bride-to-be. He sat there for what must have been hours looking at picture after picture of the happy, beautiful couple, until his heart couldn't take another minute. It finally broke in two, and Jace cried while berating his stupid computer.

"Hey, you! What time did you get here? It's almost seven in the morning, did you oversleep?" Haley came through the workout room door carrying a venti Starbucks coffee in her hand.

"It's seven?" Jace pulled his earbuds free so he could hear Haley better. His legs finally gave out. Punching the treadmill's off button, he slid off the back of the belt, landing in a thump against the wall behind the machine. The last time he looked at the digital read out on the top of the machine, it read mile five. Now he was at mile eleven. Jace lost track of six miles thinking over how hot Colt looked these days. Yeah, wasn't that just pathetic? Years later and he couldn't let it go, Colt was getting married and Jace couldn't move on. *Wasn't that pathetic?* Running his hand over his face, he finally responded to Haley. "Damn, I lost track of time."

"And I don't even understand how you do that working out. Every other person on the planet watches the clock all throughout their workout, begging the minutes to pass faster, but not you. You lose yourself. I think that's called weird," Haley said, grabbing a towel from a stack on her way over.

"We have a day. I need to shower. Then, let's go over the entry forms. We also need to make sure the music for the competition is complete and ready to go. I want extra CDs this time. Do we have any uniform issues? Also what about the coaches meeting? I don't remember seeing it on the schedule this morning." Jace leaned against the back wall as he spoke. His legs were shaking, and he tried to catch his breath from the full out run. He ran the towel over his face and through his dripping hair.

"Whoa, slow down there, mister! Jace, I know I'm your employee, but I like to think we're also friends. I'm worried about you, something isn't right. I'm here if you need to talk." Haley stood in front of him, staring at him with deep concern. Jace did appreciate the thought and did consider them friends, but no way would he let her in on what was currently going on inside his head. After all, what could he really say that wouldn't make him come off as a complete freak?

"I appreciate it very much, but I'm fine. And we are friends. I'm just looking forward to my vacation, that's it." Jace pushed away from the wall, relieved he remained upright on both feet. He pulled his wet T-shirt over his head and his shorts hung low on his waist as he walked toward the men's locker room.

"I know that's a lie, but I'm a girl enough to be distracted watching you walk away. And since we're friends, I'm gonna go ahead and say those wet shorts don't leave much to the imagination," Haley called out after him.

"You're a lesbian, Haley. You don't like boys." Jace chuckled, tossing his T-shirt and the towel into the laundry bin by the door.

"I think you just turned me bi," Haley added, causing them both to laugh.

"I'm going to shower. Meet me in my office in twenty minutes. Let's get started. I also wanna hear all about your date last night. I hope at least one of us is having some kind of life outside of this place." With a look over his shoulder and a wink, he pushed open the locker room door, and disappeared inside.

# Chapter 16

Tossing his drunk, passed out bride-to-be down on the bed, Colt glared at her for a couple of long minutes, completely disgusted. Nothing could be worth enduring any length of a marriage to her.

"Why the fuck am I doing this again? Oh yeah, you're the nosey little bitch who found my pictures of Jace. The ones I had buried away in the back of my closet in the farthest shoebox in the row with other boxes stacked on top of them. And then you threatened to expose us in a web of fucking lies. Who does that? I fucking hate you," Colt said through clenched teeth. His voice had slowly risen with each word, and he lowered himself until their faces were only about an inch or so apart. It didn't matter, she didn't wake or move. That was what eight shots of tequila, four cosmos, and a couple of bars of something, probably Xanax, did for you.

He stood and stuck a finger in his knotted tie, pulling the silk material free. Colt was tired of this game. Tired of the cameras following him everywhere he went and way past tired of his life.

Leaving the blackmailing little bitch on the bed, Colt walked to his closet. The expensive tie dropped carelessly on his brand new, grossly overpriced, handpicked by his awful fiancée, dresser. Colt flung his suit jacket in the general direction of the armoire and toed his shoes off. A gnawing feeling ate at him.

He hated what he'd become, and what he was being forced to do. He swore the cancerous pit in his stomach grew larger every day, and for the first time in months, he seriously reevaluated his plan to stay sober. Colt had been sober for two hundred and seventy-eight days. With each day passing, he grew to hate his life a little bit more. How had he let things get this out of control? Yeah, Colt knew the answer. He'd drank from sun up to sun up every day for the last ten years of his life.

Shockingly, Colt had finally kicked his alcohol habit, yet played some of the best football of his life. Who would have ever thought that could be possible? It was the only positive in his life.

Clearly, Colt remembered all too well the circumstances surrounding the moment he took his last drink. Correction, he took his last drink the following day. That night he drank until he became stupid drunk in order to fuck Maryia and her friend like she wanted. When he got drunk, he didn't care who he fucked, just as long as he got to fuck. Colt got to the point where he drank to wake up from the hellish hangovers, and he drank to escape the pain in his heart at being so deep in the closest he couldn't see his way out. Alcohol could be a sneaky little bastard. It made him truly believe he'd kicked his homosexual tendency. How stupid was that?

One interesting point he now realized, Jace Montgomery still starred in every single major event of his life. It took the chance of Jace being hurt again to make him see what he really had become. Not the multiple You Tube videos of him drunk, acting an ass, or being the cocky jerk he became when he drank. There were also You Tube videos of him being arrested for public intoxication. But none of those sobered him up like Maryia threatening what he held most precious in his life.

Being sober and being forced to be honest with himself, he knew Jace Montgomery was the man he loved above all others. The first time he'd laid eyes on Jace was before school even started. The tall blond cheerleader stood on the sidelines, looking hot as hell in his snug fitting uniform, but it was the smile he wore that melted Colt.

The memories soothed Colt as he undressed. Jace was clean-cut and unspoiled. He'd somehow managed to escape all the hate and bitterness so many gay men hung on to. Running his hands through his short-cropped dark hair, Colt let out a sigh. He shed his pants and his shirt, thinking over their first time together. Colt stayed late one afternoon, conditioning in the gym like he always did when he needed to clear his mind. He noticed Jace in a connecting gym. He couldn't keep his eyes off him.

Jace worked a cheer clinic for tryouts, and like normal, Colt knew everything there was to know about the guy and his schedule. Colt knew Jace had an easygoing attitude. Jace laughed easily, and when he did, his eyes lit up, which made Colt's heart race.

Colt observed Jace's entire session that day, admiring him for staying late to help a new potential cheerleader master some skill. But when the session ended, he watched Jace enter the locker room alone. Colt waited a few minutes before he picked his towel up off the bench and followed. Like a perv, he stood with his arm propped against the tile wall, quietly watching Jace in the shower. Jace was beautifully made. Tall with a hard athletic body, his muscles tensed and flexed as he ran the soap over his tanned skin. His sun-streaked blond hair transformed to dark when wet. He longed to run his fingers through those dripping strands and take Jace's mouth in a drowning kiss.

Jace looked so very good and fucking hot as hell. His perfectly cut dick hung temptingly between his legs as the water poured over his body. When Jace turned to soap his back, his ass could only be described as mouthwatering. He was such a turn on to watch that Colt's hands had clenched into fists, aching to grip that tight ass.

Instinct more than anything pushed Colt to approach Jace, cornering him at his locker. Jace seemed so confused at first, but their kiss set everything right. Their sex was magical. It surprised Colt when Jace seemed to want him as badly as he wanted Jace. Colt stood slightly taller than Jace and a little more muscular. He dominated Jace, fucking him hard without a condom, right there for anyone to walk in and see.

Now, walking through his condo to the living room, Colt didn't bother with clothing. He preferred to stay nude. There were no drapes or window blinds, but he lived on the top floor of the high-rise. And he honestly just didn't give a shit anymore. Every time Colt allowed the memories of Jace to surface, he couldn't rid himself of the nagging guilt that twisted his stomach as he recalled the pain he'd put in Jace's eyes. Colt would never forget the look etched on Jace's face, the betrayal in Jace's eyes, when his football buddies shoved him through the bar.

Colt sat there and let it all happen, not saying a word to stop their vicious attack. He just stared down at the dirty floor as their hurtful words echoed through his mind, and the tails his father hired watched both his and Jace's every move. Colt hated himself for being a coward, for not standing up and stopping them. Most of all, he had hated knowing he was just as much a *fag* as Jace and too afraid to speak up.

God, Colt regretted his actions. The pain in Jace's eyes still haunted him to this day. He'd been wrong to end their relationship the way he had, but at the time, he'd feared his father would go after Jace like he had his own son. Colt had no choice but to put separation between them. After Hawaii, after all the deep love crap he'd confessed, he needed to distance himself to keep them safe and to keep his career going, like his fucking father dictated.

In some ways, his father had been right. No way was the professional sports world ready for a public display of a homosexual relationship. Back then, Colt had been touted as a star in the making; his potential was the best of the best. He would have ruined everything if he'd come out. Lots of money and notoriety had followed being number one. Lots of money in which his agent pocketed a hefty commission and his dad pocketed an even larger salary. Hell, Colt had made his agent and his father millions of dollars over the last ten years. If he had come out, they would have had to kiss it all goodbye!

From where he stood today, Colt couldn't say he'd made the correct decision. Actually, Colt knew for certain he hadn't made the right choice. Nothing could be worth hurting Jace and continuing on in this shell of a life he lived. Without question, Jace would never believe he had truly fallen in love with him or that he still loved him today. He loathed himself for what he'd done... or rather didn't do. It was in Johnny's office after his beating that he discovered Jack Daniels helped numb the pain, but it was the night his friends hurt Jace that Colt firmly resolved to drink with serious intent.

Jace never again tried to contact Colt. It only took once. Colt tried hard to make himself believe that if Jace truly loved him, he would be back. Once wouldn't have stopped *him*, but he knew Jace better than anyone. Jace would never put himself where he wasn't wanted. He just wasn't that guy.

Picking up the remote control from the coffee table, Colt brought the recording guide up and selected the ESPN cheerleading special. Seven years ago, Colt accidentally stumbled across Jace's face during a cheerleading competition. Since then, Colt followed the competitions and Jace's company as best as he could. Colt even went so far as to talk his professional football team's cheerleading coach into bringing Jace's gym out to perform at last year's season opener. He footed the entire bill, but Jace didn't accompany his team. Colt didn't even rate high enough in Jace's past to warrant an overnight trip to New York.

The remote control's fast forward allowed him to skip the competition, just pick the breakout sessions. Colt selected the interview in the Cheer Dynasty gym and brought Jace up, pausing the screen to stare at his handsome face. Colt's flaccid cock began to swell just looking into those green eyes.

After a couple of minutes, he pushed play, watching the entire interview. Pride consumed his heart at seeing everything Jace had created. Colt followed along while they talked and then toured the gym. He watched all the national championship banners and trophies pass by. Then they landed on the enlarged photo of Jace cheering in college. Colt remembered that day, their last game together. In the interview, Jace stood by the photo, looking down with the reporter close by. Jace's body had been leaner back in school, his hair shorter. Colt pressed pause on the remote, thinking over which way he liked Jace's hair better. The longer hair accented Jace's strong jaw, but the short hair looked more like the beautiful man he had fallen in love with all those years ago.

Unable to decide which looked better, Colt clicked play and the reporter continued the interview. Hearing his name, Colt slowed the picture down, watching Jace closely as they spoke. Jace never gave anything up, but Colt laughed out loud when Jace said he didn't think Colt would remember him. Looking down at his rock hard erection, he laughed again and spoke directly to the screen. "Yeah, babe, I have no problem remembering everything about you. My problem is I can't forget you." Looking back up at the screen, still chuckling, Colt saw the moment—the very brief, almost-not-there look Jace held in his eyes when he stared back at the picture on the wall.

Colt paused the interview on the screen and then pushed rewind. He watched the look again and again, before going to the television and bending down in front of the screen, watching Jace for the third time. Sadness filled Jace's eyes. He didn't see hate, instead there was sadness, maybe even longing? Could Jace be longing for him? Surely not... After ten years, surely this must be one-sided; Colt had hurt Jace too badly.

Moving back to his sofa, Colt rewound the whole interview and watched from the beginning. He listened to every part, word for word. Colt looked for any sign in Jace of what Colt felt in his own heart. This time around, he focused on Jace's announcement that he'd bought a place in Hawaii. He'd missed that key bit of information before. Jace had purchased their vacation spot of ten years ago. Fast forwarding the interview, Colt replayed over and over the expression on Jace's face as he looked at his photo. His heart pounded in his chest; Colt wanted that look he swore flashed in Jace's eyes to be real. Could he just be seeing the lights casting shadows and playing a cruel joke?

After a while, Colt scanned through the entire competition, watching for signs of Jace. Pride hit him again at how well all of Jace's teams did during the competition. Eighteen out of the twenty-four teams took first place. Jace's interviews played repeatedly during the breakout session. The other cheerleading gyms highlighted had nothing on Jace's gym. The place looked spectacular. Clearly Jace made money in the sport, but he put it back into his kids, giving them a badass facility to practice in.

Hours passed as Colt watched, never getting tired of what he saw. Jace appeared again on the screen and each time he saw the handsome male, he pushed the button and paused it. At the end, there was a shot that focused on Jace with his team surrounding him. They'd just won their fifth national championship. Colt stopped the recording and zoomed in on Jace's beautiful face, enlarging his image, taking in one last look before bed. Jace would star in his dreams tonight ensuring a good night's sleep.

"Goddammit! Eww, you're so fucking *gross*! You're jacking off to that guy on TV." A drunk Maryia whined, startling him from his pleasant thoughts. Her Russian accent more pronounced and filled with disgust and hateful accusations. Colt slowly turned his head toward the annoying voice. Maryia stood naked, leering at him from the living room door.

"You're such a pussy. Come fuck me, goddammit!" She swayed on her feet, her hair a tangled mess, all matted around her head like a giant rat's nest. Her makeup from the night before smeared across her angular face, and her mascara ran down her cheeks in thick black streaks.

"Go to bed. I'm not fucking you tonight, or any night," Colt said, turning back to the television. He quickly changed the channel. Jace was too perfect for his drunken whore of a fiancée to look at.

"You're a pussy! You won't let your driver fuck me anymore, and you won't fuck me because you're queer. I'm fucking tired of this goddamn *shit*! I'm going out!" Turning to the door, Maryia tried to open it, but Colt darted over the sofa, barely getting to her before she could get the door unlocked.

"You aren't going out naked and this drunk. We don't need any more bad press. Go back to bed, Maryia." Colt put both his hands on her shoulders, turning her toward the bedroom. She went nuts in his arms, fighting and kicking while screaming at him.

"Don't put your hands on me, you faggot mother fucker!" Maryia screeched at Colt, stumbling backward, finally falling on her ass. "Don't you touch me! I'll call the police again. They'll arrest you and put you back in jail! Oh, but wait, that's where you want to be, locked away with a bunch of men to fuck you in your ass. You're pathetic and I hate you. Why won't you fuck me?" Tears started to roll down her cheeks, and she fell back on the floor; passed out in a drug-induced haze.

Colt didn't bother to move her but did take the throw from the sofa, tossing it in her general direction. Grabbing the remote from the sofa, Colt removed all the traces of what he'd watched and turned off the television. He didn't want Maryia to find Jace and threaten to draw him into their mess again. Placing the remote on the coffee table, Colt walked to his bedroom. If Maryia slept on the floor, he could have the stupidly expensive, but very comfortable bed in his bedroom for the night. He stepped over his so called fiancée lying passed out in the middle of the floor, and the moment wasn't lost on him; he just truly didn't give a shit anymore.

# Chapter 17

He seriously needed to get a life. Jace sat behind his desk at the gym, getting everything in order for his two week vacation. Time was running out. His flight left in about an hour and a half. His intention was to only spend about an hour here before he drove to the airport, which would give him plenty of time to navigate DFW International Airport. Now he was pushing it. Haley stood in the doorway to his office, looking at her watch.

"Come on, if we don't leave now, Jace, we're gonna be late," Haley scolded, tapping her finger to her watch.

"Haley, please keep this office locked. All the kid's personal information—"

"I will, Jace. Come on… please, stop worrying." She cut him off. He could tell she was growing impatient with him.

"I have my cell, but that's it," he said, placing a file in his top desk drawer. He closed the drawer, locked it, and began to straighten the rest of the papers on his desk. He switched off his computer and printer before glancing over his list one last time.

"So text if I need anything. Got it. FYI, the gym's closed for two weeks. Remember? I'm really not planning on being here either," she added with a huff.

"Yes. Security scheduled?" He looked up from his desk, waiting for her answer. All right, he would admit he was always the constant worrier. He couldn't help it.

"Yes, no one will be here unattended. Jace Montgomery, now! Get your ass moving, we're late!" Haley clapped her hands, stepping back from the door. Jace grinned and grabbed his backpack, slinging it over his shoulder. He searched his walking shorts and found his phone, iPod, and keys. He pulled the keys from his pocket to lock his office door.

"Are you seriously leaving for two weeks with just this backpack?" Haley questioned, the disbelief clear in her voice.

"Yeah, I'll buy whatever I need when I get there." He couldn't believe he was seriously leaving for a vacation. A trickle of excitement began to replace the nerves of leaving.

"Jace, are you sure it's safe to go there alone?" Haley asked as Jace set the security system.

"We've had this conversation," Jace replied, dismissing Haley's question. They had thirty seconds to get out the door before the alarm went off, so they hustled out the front.

"Just make sure you text me so I don't worry. Okay?" It took Haley a second to remember she was driving and finally stopped following Jace. She pushed past him and started toward her car so that he now followed her.

Jace didn't say another word about it. Haley acted like his own personal mama bear. She'd become as close to him as family, and right now she was alarmingly close to being an annoying little sister... who was also doing something super nice, like driving him to the airport. Okay, he'd forgive her hovering because he hated figuring out the airport on his own.

Lihue Airport was shockingly similar to what he remembered. Jace bypassed baggage claim, the benefit of the single backpack, and headed straight for the car rental. It only took a few minutes, and he was off, his smart phone guiding him to his new home. The anxiety of seeing the place finally settled in. It was funny how that hadn't occurred to him when he'd bought the place, but now, as he drove the back roads to the house, the memories of when he'd first arrived here ten years ago played through his mind.

Wow, the emotion of the moment caused him to let off the gas as he remembered how Colt had been out back when he'd arrived. Jace actually thought he'd been pranked. Maybe it would have been better all the way around if it had been a cruel joke. That steeled Jace's heart.

"No, you aren't doing this. You're here to make new memories, not continue living in the past for one more day. Colt's gonna be a married man in a few days. The past is done, it's over... gone. No more pining. It's getting seriously old." Jace nodded his head to affirm the resolve and ignored his heart. Once his heart had the new memories to hold on to, those old ones would be long gone. He was certain.

Jace turned on the sand-covered road and drove the quarter of a mile down to his property. The street was exactly as he remembered it. So was the house. Not necessarily in a good way. Jace parked the car right out front and looked the property over through the windshield of his Prius. He slowly got out of the car, his eyes still glued to the house, and he stood there, flabbergasted.

The vacation home of his dreams, the place he thought was the most majestic, perfect place on the planet was a run down, uncared for piece of crap. *Great!* He should have negotiated a better deal.

# Chapter 18

Sober turned out to be such a different way to live life. Colt looked himself over in the floor length mirror of his overpriced spacious bathroom. Funny how every time he thought about this stupid condo, all he could think was how ridiculously expensive it had been. But the supermodel insisted he buy this place and threw a god-awful fit in front of the agent until he had no choice but to agree. She only ever got so far before she would toss the ever-present *gay boy* into the fight. Perhaps today the buyer's remorse was a little worse, because after all, this was his wedding day.

Maryia selected a traditional style Armani black tuxedo for him to wear, since he'd refused any involvement in the plans for the day. As he stood in front of the mirror, he had to give her credit; she did know something about fashion and had chosen the perfect tux for him. Colt's blue eyes popped against the stark black and white of what he wore. The puffy circles under his eyes, the ones he'd worn for much of the last ten years were now gone. His skin looked healthy, clean, and tanned. He turned in the mirror, looking at himself closely. Surprisingly, Colt thought he looked pretty good today, all things considered.

Maryia chose to sleep away from the condo last night. Claiming she wanted everything just right, including the tradition of not seeing the groom on the wedding day. She claimed something about turning over a new leaf in their relationship. Colt noticed his driver conspicuously absent until just about an hour ago. Colt didn't care about their late night hook-ups. Actually, more like their secret late night, mid-morning, and after lunch hook-ups. He'd only ever told the driver to stop in order to piss Maryia off.

Once he realized their frequency, Colt paid special attention to the situation. He could tell his driver resented him being in the picture. Hell, he resented himself for being involved with whole thing. So Colt had a one-on-one with Clint. Explaining they needed to be discreet and stay out of the line of cameras that always followed her around. He even point blank offered to pay Clint to marry her. They were clearly completely taken with each other, but the money grubbing bitch wanted Colt's fame to boost her career. She refused to follow her heart's desire and allow him in return to follow his. Goddamn, how he hated her!

SportsCenter played in the background from the television in the bedroom. Colt still had an hour or so before he needed to be at the wedding hall. He took his time, dressed slowly, and sat on the arm of the loveseat, listening again to the interview he'd given just a few days ago. Pictures of Maryia and Colt were on the screen. Funny how they were such a train wreck of a couple, yet considered an international superstar pairing. Colt couldn't see the appeal at all while looking at the two of them on screen. Not one of the dozen or so photos shown had either one of them touching the other, unless of course Maryia was drunk and he was forced to care for her or keep her standing.

It also never ceased to fascinate how no one ever seemed to notice Maryia couldn't keep her eyes open. They called her look sultry, exotic, and foreign. She was considered a rare beauty across the world, but Colt knew the truth. Maryia spent much of the time stoned out of her mind.

The SportsCenter interview wound to an end with the reporter finally talking about his career. After all, ESPN prided itself on their sports coverage, not the entertainment report this interview had turned out to be. The reporter bullet pointed the highlights of his football career. Ran quickly over the three Super Bowl rings he'd earned. The six years he was asked to play in the Pro Bowl. Colt's number one quarterback ranking and this year's MVP of the big game, all awarded to him by the NFL.

None of that mattered to the world or this interviewer—they only cared about the hype of his marriage to the blackmailing little slut. Maryia sat beside him in the interview. Colt slowed the program down to catch the little yawn she gave as they talked about his life, not hers. He laughed every single time he watched the program. She claimed to be exhausted from jet lag, but you had to be on a jet, flying, in order to get *jet* lag.

Colt's alarm buzzed, reminding him of the time. At the same instant, the replay of the cheerleading competition began. Jace, hugging his last performing team, flashed across the screen. The image of him in that moment struck Colt hard and tears came to his eyes. In his heart of hearts, Colt wished this day was being spent with Jace, where he prepared to marry his Jace and no one else.

He closed his eyes and thought about how good he would feel standing proudly at the altar, Jace dressed in his tuxedo, offering his hand to accept Colt's ring. He let himself dwell on that image for several minutes before his heart started the slow steady pound, remembering the longing he thought he saw in Jace's expression while he looked down at their picture. This day was wrong. Marrying Maryia was all wrong.

He'd played the interview enough to know Jace planned to be in Hawaii this week. Goose bumps sprang up on his arms, his chest tightened. He took a deep breath to steady his pounding heart. If he allowed himself another second to think his decision through, he might change his mind, so Colt flew solely on emotion. He rushed to his closet and threw open the door. Colt jerked his duffel bag off the top shelf and tossed a couple of pairs of shorts, T-shirts, flip flops, and a few of his toiletries inside. He pulled a random ball cap down off a shelf, grabbed the duffel and shut the closet door behind him.

Colt decided to throw all caution to the wind and follow his heart this time, something he'd never had the courage to do before. He'd always told himself he protected Jace when he allowed his father to control so much of his life. Marrying Maryia was essentially the same, only trading one controlling leech for another. He refused another minute of giving that bitch control of his life. If he didn't take this opportunity now and go after the man he'd always loved, he might never have another chance. His stomach knotted with excitement as he strode across the room to grab his wallet, sunglasses, and cell phone from his dresser. Colt didn't leave a note. He needed time to get out of town.

Never looking back, he took the elevator down, acknowledging all the well wishes along the way. His driver stood ready by his Bentley, pulling the car door open as he walked out. Bypassing the opened back door, Colt rounded the hood, walking to the driver's side.

"Shut the door, buddy. I'll drive myself to the church. Catch you later, man. Wish me luck!" The driver looked confused as Colt got inside the car and pulled away from the curb, leaving him standing there alone. Colt told the lie easily, hoping Clint didn't wait there too long. Colt needed time to get out of the city. He drove straight to the airport, leaving his car running while parked in fifteen minute parking. He removed the tie and jacket, tossing them in the backseat of the car, and placed the ball cap on along with the sunglasses. He booked the first flight taking him in the general direction of Hawaii. He had fifteen minutes to board. *Perfect!*

Forty-five minutes after leaving his apartment, Colt sat in coach with the airplane charging down the runway, heading to Los Angeles. With his iPhone, he booked the connecting flight to arrive in Hawaii before morning. Colt refused to allow himself the luxury of thinking this through; too afraid he would chicken out if he had second thoughts.

Once the plane got in the air, he did a quick change. He kept his head down and his eyes averted, but when recognized, he used his natural deep southern accent to throw people off. Colt wanted one person and one person only. There would be no more waiting. Regardless of how Jace might respond—and that thought did give him a moment of intense anxiety—he planned to see this through. If Jace didn't want to have anything to do with him, at least he'd tried. Then Colt would know for sure and he could apologize for the pain he'd caused years ago.

# Chapter 19

The end of the lounger sat perched along the beach where the water came forward meeting the sand in a frothy swirl. The waves kept the water coming and going, back and forth. Jace loved the feel of the wet sand and water between his toes. A cooler sat to the right of his chair, anchored deep into the sand and filled with alcohol, all cold and ready for him to drink. The trash bucket collecting the empty bottles sat to his left. Jace lay in the low reclining chair, staring out into the retreating sun, sizzling its way back into the ocean. The evening was beautiful. The balmy breeze slid across his skin like a soothing caress. Jace sat there in what had become his regular wardrobe for the island: loud, colorful swim trunks and nothing more.

As the sun dropped over the horizon, day five of his fourteen day vacation came to an end. Jace was now one hundred percent certain buying this house sight unseen hadn't been the best idea. The inside turned out to need more repair than the outside. Clearly, no one bothered with maintenance on this place in all the years since he'd last been here.

Jace spent the first few days securing the flooring back in place, both inside and out. He would never consider himself a handyman, but those first few years of getting his gym up and running required he do a lot of repair work himself. Apparently he'd learned reasonably well. The last two days he built a larger deck around the front and back of his new home. He hoped he made the steps not quite so treacherous getting inside the elevated beach house.

Sleep still wasn't coming easily. Jace hadn't hooked up any of the televisions or internet devices and kept his phone internet turned off most of the time. It stayed quiet in the house, only turning on an old AM/FM radio when he felt like he needed company. The island had lots of oldies stations which were absolutely the best to listen and sing along to. The memories still lingered. When he first walked through the front door, they'd rushed back and struck him hard, reminding him of his and Colt's time here. Memories so vivid they caused him to reconsider even being here. The old stove top, refrigerator, and table were still in the kitchen, the same sofa still in the living room. Each one of those held a strong memory of something the two of them shared together. He and Colt had made love in every room in this house.

Jace warred with himself, and he'd almost bolted, but resolve finally pushed to the forefront. He would make new memories here—it was always the plan. He would force himself to look back on the old ones with nothing more than the nostalgia of good times shared. Jace reasoned with himself, long and hard, for the rest of that entire first day. All these feelings were only because the man he once loved was marrying another, when he couldn't even find anyone interesting to date. He had managed to bury these feelings once, and he would do it again.

Jace spent much of the first day making a list of needed repairs and then gathering supplies in town. Everything went faster than anticipated. Tomorrow, he would begin the roof repairs and then the paint job. He bought buckets and buckets of paint for the inside and out. The plumbers and electricians would be here in the next couple of days. By the time he left, he hoped the house would be complete for his future visits. And he planned many future visits.

For tonight though, Jace took time off. He'd driven into town a couple of hours ago to purchase more alcohol than he'd drank in the last five years, including half a case of Longboard Island Lagers and a bottle of Malibu coconut rum. He picked up two veggie sushi rolls, an order of pineapple fried rice, and a bottle of white willow bark for the morning. The sushi rolls were long since gone, and he'd made a solid dent in the alcohol. A glance toward the trash bucket and he counted eight empty bottles of Longboards, with one open in his hand right now. Jace felt pretty good, assessing his current state somewhere between pretty buzzed but not quite a solidly drunk yet.

Looking out into the sunset, he watched the light of the sun dip below the horizon. The sunset turned the sky from deep orange and pink to a dark purple. Full on night would be here soon. He wondered what Colt might look like in his wedding tuxedo. With all his dark good looks, a black on black tuxedo would probably look the best. Colt's sapphire eyes would stand out against the black and sparkle like crown jewels. At least that's what he would want Colt to wear if they were getting married. The contrast of Colt's deep, dark tan, jet black hair, and black tuxedo would make him by far the best looking man in the room. Colt probably wouldn't have gotten more than five feet down the aisle before Jace tackled him to the ground, having his way with him right there.

Honestly, Colt could wear anything and he'd look good. A smile slid across Jace's lips thinking about how hot Colt always used to look. He made football interesting to watch. Pain sliced through his heart at those thoughts. Running a hand over his face, he reclined against the chair, forcing his thoughts back on the house and the paint color scheme he'd chosen. He could have no room for thoughts of a married man in his mind. A sting skidded across his heart again in a fast sweeping motion just like before. Paint colors and cheerleading routines were all he would allow inside his mind for the rest of the night. Hopefully with any luck, he could pull this off for the rest of his life.

A flight delay, then problems with the rental car, made Colt's trip longer than expected. He followed the headline news on his phone and listened to the radio news stories closely, but surprisingly no one called. As best he could tell, the authorities weren't involved and out looking for him. Those were good, yet surprising, signs.

Colt used his driver's license and credit cards to buy the airline tickets and rent this car. If the authorities were involved, they would see all his activities, he hadn't hidden anything. Maryia's publicist had put out a statement of false starts, and the couple sneaking off for a private affair, asking for privacy, but nothing more. That did make Colt laugh. No way would Maryia do anything without the cameras trained on her. The wedding alone would have been a financial gain of almost three million dollars, all going directly to her.

What Colt couldn't figure out… why hadn't his father or Johnny called?

Deciding he'd dodged the first wave of the storm, and for some reason the second wave wasn't hitting him quite yet, Colt concentrated on driving the stretch of road from the airport to Jace. It must be somewhere around two in the morning. Exhausted from the time change and the travel, he pressed on, refusing to wait another minute.

Colt pulled in the long drive of Jace's bungalow, parking next to a Prius and killed the engine. He sat staring at the house. Jace was there. His only reason for living was just inside the quaint little cottage. Would Jace reject him after all this time? Turn him away?

"God, I hope not." Colt sighed. With apprehension, he forced himself out of the car. Anxiety filled his soul, his palms were sweaty and his heart began to race. Funny, he hadn't been really scared or nervous until he got within a few feet of his past.

A broken down sidewalk began from the gravel driveway. He wound his way to the porch steps leading to the front door. For the first time since leaving New York, he realized Jace might be here with another man. Why hadn't that occurred to him before? *Shit!*

The thought stopped Colt in his tracks. Jace didn't wear a ring, but had Colt banked everything on the absence of that ring? Texas wasn't a gay marriage state. Jace may not have the ring but might be in a committed relationship.

The pain and fear of that thought almost sent Colt to his knees. Then envy filled his soul. Jace was his, no one else's. Jace always belonged to him from the first moment he'd laid eyes on him. Colt had claimed Jace then and never truly let him go! Those primal thoughts came to an abrupt end just as they started. Regardless of what might be going on inside this house, Colt would apologize. He would be honest, tell Jace everything, and if he left without Jace, at least he'd tried. Colt would set the record straight. Tonight, he would have his answer, one way or another.

Reaching forward, Colt gently knocked on the front door. Waiting a minute, he used more force, this time banging with his fist. After a few minutes more, he gripped the metal knocker, rapping urgently against the weather-stained door. When nothing came from the house, he pressed his ear to the door. He heard nothing inside.

Stepping back, he went to a window and peered inside. There he could see a light on, somewhere toward the rear of the bungalow. Colt walked the length of the wraparound porch, following it to the back. The porch was new; apparently Jace had been busy.

He looked out over the water. The ocean looked calm and quiet. The clouds covered the moon, casting a silver glow, but not providing much in the way of light. Scanning the beach, he found the embers of a dying fire and made out the shape of a chair close by. Colt took the back porch steps down to the sand. The farther he walked from the light of the house, the more his eyes adjusted to the dark. He could make out the form of a man lying on an outstretched lounger, close to the surf. Colt's heart lurched, realizing Jace slept there alone. For all his claims of not being primal, Colt would have been hard-pressed in keeping his calm and not attacking if there had been someone with his Jace right now.

Colt slowed his pace as he walked tentatively to the chair. He took in the cooler on one side and the trash on the other. The smell of alcohol hit him hard, and for the first time in his adult life, he wasn't drawn to taking a drink. Instead, he reached the chair, looked closer into the trash, lowering a finger inside to quietly lift a couple of bottles to count what Jace might have consumed. Colt counted twelve bottles. That wasn't too much for one person. Hell he could drink a thirty pack in one sitting, but he looked up at the house. Still no movement from inside.

Bending to his knee, he squatted down and studied Jace's face. He slept quietly, a long towel draped over his body. It wasn't quite long enough, causing Jace to curl his legs up to get his entire body covered. Jace's long hair fell forward with wisps covering his face. Jace looked so beautiful, so peaceful.

Colt had lazed on this very beach ten years ago, watching this gorgeous man sleep just like he did now. He remembered the night so clearly. He had decided right there that he wanted to spend the rest of his life with Jace. Now, while lifting his finger to move a piece of hair from Jace's face, Colt again experienced the rush of those deep feelings of everlasting love. Jace's eyes fluttered open.

"I should have drunk more. Shit. Leave me alone. Not tonight... not..." Jace turned over on the chair and got comfortable again, tucking his body back under the towel. Colt chuckled, but stayed there. Jace was still sleeping and perhaps a little drunk.

"It feels so natural to touch you. I missed this." Lifting a hand, he stroked Jace's hair on the back of his head. Jace slowly turned toward Colt, a groan coming from his throat. His eyes were little more than slits. "Hi, handsome, are you alone here?" Colt asked with a small smile.

"What?" Jace opened his eyes a little wider, but still really nothing more than slits, and Colt could see he began to finally wake up.

"Are you alone here? Is there anyone here with you?"

"Yes, I mean, no... I mean, yes." Jace turned away from him, rolling onto his back, stretching out his long body. After a brief moment, Jace's eyes fluttered closed, his long lashes briefly brushing his cheeks before the smile on his lips relaxed again. Alcohol had a way of putting you back to sleep, allowing you the privilege of not dealing with whatever woke you. Colt knew the effects well.

"Well, which one is it?"

Jace's head darted back in his direction, his eyes fully opened now. "You're here? What? Fuck."

"I'm here. We need to talk, Jace. Are you here alone? Can you go inside the house with me?" Colt kept his voice quiet, somewhat amused. Jace's movements were shaky, a little sloppy. Colt knew all the signs, Jace was still drunk, but trying hard to sober up and just too stunned to pull himself together.

"Are you honeymooning here? Fuck. That never fuckin' occurred to me. Of course, you would come here. You loved it here. *Fuck!*" Jace pushed himself up to a sitting position and dropped his legs on each side of the chair while scrubbing his hands over his face. Jace leaned over the edge of the chair, scooped up some water from the cooler, splashing his face before turning back as if to see if Colt were still there. "Fuck! What are you doing here with me? Where's your wife?"

Even to Colt, when Jace said the word wife, he sneered and for some reason that gave him hope. "I didn't get married, Jace. I'm not here on my honeymoon. Please answer my question. Are you alone? Can we go inside?"

"Why do you wanna go inside?" Jace rose, brushing his hair off his face, and he stumbled a little on his feet. "Fuck, I never drink. It's because of you that I'm even in this state. Go away," Jace shouted and turned, heading toward the house, but turned quickly back around. Colt took a couple of steps in his direction, stopping in midstride as Jace spun around, and faced him.

"Why are you here?" His love yelled, clearly angry, but stunningly beautiful in his irritated state. The moon escaped the clouds and shone brightly down on Jace. He stood tall and strong with his swim trunks riding low on his hips, the dark line of Jace's treasure trail drew Colt's attention, making his mouth water. Jace was perfectly sculpted from head to toe, and a sight to behold, even completely annoyed.

"I'm here to talk to you, Jace."

"What could you possibly have to say to me?"

Colt stayed quiet. The speech he came up with on the plane escaped him. Jace seemed so angry, and he just didn't know where to start. After a moment, he decided the end would be the best place to begin. "I'm sorry, Jace. I'm sorry… I…"

Jace didn't listen to him. Instead, he stormed back the few feet between them, reaching for Colt's head and aggressively pulled him in for a hard, demanding kiss. Jace thrust his tongue forward giving Colt no choice but to open to him. *Yes!*

Jace wrapped one brawny arm tightly around Colt's lower back, pulling him head to toe against Jace's body. Every bit of longing Colt felt deep in his heart smoldered inside this kiss they shared. Just as abruptly, Jace ended the kiss and the contact, pushing him away.

"That's all I'm interested in from you, and I know that's not why you're here." Turning, Jace took a step away before jogging up to the house.

A smile burst across Colt's lips. Relief flooded his heart. If Jace were with someone, he wouldn't have just kissed him on the beach. After several long moments of watching Jace run to the house, he whispered, before he followed. "That's exactly why I'm here, cheer boy."

# Chapter 20

Water ran freely from the bathroom sink faucet. Jace brushed his teeth and splashed water once again over his face, trying to sober up. What the hell was Colt doing here? For a minute on the beach he thought his drunken mind played tricks on him. It was the reason he'd forced himself on Colt. Surely to God his mind couldn't have created the spicy, sweet musk of Colt's delicious scent or those spine tingling feelings when their bodies touched. *Right?*

Apparently, Jace's raging hard-on sure thought this was all very real. And he splashed his face again with cold water before reaching for a towel.

Looking himself over in the mirror, Jace picked up the brush and pushed it through the tangles of his hair and away from his face. The long ends fell forward again, until he shoved them behind his ears. Jace stared at himself in the mirror. "Sober up. Sober up now. You need your wits about you. What the fuck is he doing here and not with his wife? Sober up, now! He's married. Colton is a married to a *woman*! Sober up, Jace Montgomery!"

Jace racked his brain, but still couldn't come up with anything to help make sense of this. This couldn't be possible. And hiding in the bathroom wasn't going to make Colt go away. Unless he dreamed this and Colt hadn't really come here. Could Jace have finally snapped? Maybe Colt and the all too real kiss only happened inside the confines of his alcohol-clouded mind?

Opening the door to the bathroom, Jace looked out and saw nothing. Poking his head around the door, he listened and heard nothing. A small amount of relief filled him, but the yearning for Colt gripped his heart, and the ache of that loss followed quickly behind. Could he be so past the point of normal behavior that he could have imagined touching Colt? Walking slowly down the hall, he caught a shadow and his heart did a small leap. Taking the corner into the living room, Jace stopped mid-step. Colt was there, hands tucked into the pockets of his shorts, his feet spread apart, and his gaze focused directly at him. They both simply remained frozen in place, staring at one another. Neither said a word. Jace's heart began to race in his chest. He could feel the tears threatening to fall. Colt was everything he remembered and so much more.

Ten years ago, Colt stood in that very same position, waiting for him to go swim in the ocean. Jace desperately wanted to relive that moment. Not moving, afraid his legs would fail him, he finally spoke. His voice cracked at the emotion pouring through him, but he forced the entire sentence out.

"Why are you here?"

"I couldn't keep living this lie for a minute more. I've been sober for two hundred and eighty-three days. My sobriety requires me to apologize to you, but my heart can't take another day without you knowing how much I still love you, and how deeply sorry I am for the pain I've caused you." Colt didn't move as he spoke, his deep blue eyes pinned and held Jace where he stood. Hope and longing rushed through his body stealing Jace's breath and voice.

Jace managed to lift a hand to steady himself against the doorframe. He thought about what Colt said, and after replaying the words in his mind, things didn't add up. "You're a married man, Colton. I'm not sure what you want from me. You can't come here and say things like this. It isn't fair."

"Jace." Colt took a step forward, but Jace stopped him with a lift of his hand.

"No, it's wrong of you to show up here like this. If you need to apologize, then consider it done, but don't say those other things to me. It's too hard to hear."

"Baby, I'm not married. I couldn't do it, I never loved her, hell, I never even liked her." Colt finally moved from the spot where he stood and walked slowly toward Jace. He kept his hands in his pockets as he came to a stop directly in front of Jace.

"Maryia blackmailed me into marrying her. She needed to stay in the country. Jace, I'm so very sorry. My life's shit and it's been that way since the morning I left you in that hotel room. When I showed up to my agent's office, I was gonna tell him about us. Tell him how badly I wanted a future with you. Let him know you would be going with me. God, you were all I ever wanted, Jace, I swear. But my dad was there. They somehow found out about our trip. He beat the crap out of me, and told me there was no way the NFL would take me being gay. Even then I wasn't gonna let you go. I told them I loved you. But then he threatened you. My dad planned the same beating for you, and even worse. I couldn't let him… It scared me…" Colt finally took a breath, his voice broke, and he shook his head, clearing his throat.

"You've always meant everything to me. I was broken, I had to sever all contact, they told me they would be watching me and you. I left my agent's office that day drunk, and I'm not sure I stopped drinking until ten months ago. Maryia found my pictures of you and threatened to expose us. I couldn't risk you being hurt by my actions again."

"Colt, I don't understand." Confusion clouded his mind. Jace's hands were shaking and he wrapped his arms around his chest to try to hold himself together. "You had pictures of me?"

"Yes," Colt said, a small grin lit his face. He stayed about an arm's length away, hands still shoved deep in his pockets. "I got alerts anytime your name was mentioned on the internet or television. I printed every picture. I followed your career. I've watched every time your gym performed, just hoping I would see you. I have years' worth of video coverage on your gym. I love you, Jace. I always have, and through all my mistakes, I wanted you to know I've never said that to anyone else. Only you."

When words failed him, Jace brought his palm to his mouth. They both held their ground for a minute or two, observing each other. "Am I too late? Have you moved on? If you give me another chance, I promise to do everything in my power to never hurt you again."

Jace didn't say a word, he couldn't. All the pain, hurt, and doubt he'd tried so desperately to bury came rushing forward, overwhelming him. He closed his eyes at the magnitude of emotion pouring through his body. He finally had the answers ten long years in the making, and Colt said he loved him. He still loved him after all this time. Colt didn't get married. The tears forming spilled over and ran down his cheeks. Colt reached out for him, and his hands felt like heaven.

"Baby, why are you crying?" Jace allowed himself to be wrapped in the firm comfort of Colt's strong arms, exactly where he was meant to be.

"No matter how I tried, I've never stopped loving you. I missed you so bad." Jace lifted his face and leaned in, bringing his palms up to Colt's face. "You're really here." A smile spread across his face, before he pressed their lips together.

The moment their lips met all the intense feelings Jace tried so desperately to push from his heart came crashing back. Jace deepened the kiss, sliding his tongue forward into the warmth and sweetness of Colt's parted lips. Their tongues collided in a frenzied dance of heat and passion. He poured ten years of longing into the kiss and feasted on Colt's mouth. Colt slid his hands up Jace's back to cup his head, opening his mouth for more of the kiss. Jace melted against Colt and his cock swelled in his shorts.

"I need you so bad," Jace whispered as he tore his mouth free. He ignored the spinning room, no doubt a lingering effect of the alcohol, and lost himself in the depth of emotion pouring through him. Both emotionally and physically, Jace needed Colt back in his life. For the first time in a long time, he felt complete wrapped in Colt's arms. The extension of himself was back. He had his heart back in his arms. Jace leaned his head back, closing his eyes, letting Colt nibbled hungrily along his jaw.

"I need you too, baby. I've missed you," Colt said, untangling his fingers from Jace's thick hair. Colt lifted his gaze to Jace's face. Love and deep regret reflected in Colt's eyes. The look melted more of Jace's heart. As Colt spoke, he ran his fingertips down Jace's neck to his shoulders.

"God, you smell so good, just like I remember. I was so afraid you wouldn't want me, you wouldn't forgive me, but I had to come here, at least try." Colt's fingers lightly traced the dips and curves of

Jace's broad chest, stopping to circle his hardened nipple with the tip of his finger. Jace did nothing to stop Colt's exploration of his body. He loved seeing and feeling Colt's hands touching him again. Colt hesitated, but finally reached out, teasing and rolling the tightening bud, before his strong fingers slid down the front of Jace's body.

"I've only ever wanted you. You're the only person I've ever made love to." Colt bit his lip as he spoke the sweet words.

"You're all I've ever wanted. No one could ever fill your shoes," Jace whispered the words, sucking in his breath when Colt's hand skimmed across his hardened cock. His other hand moved up to Jace's face, his knuckles ran softly along his cheek, and then came to rest under his chin. Colt used his finger to tip his face up, making Jace look directly at him.

"I only let myself think about this moment one time on the way here. I told myself if you gave me another chance, I would take this slow and somehow prove to you that you're the only one that ever mattered to me. I'm willing to spend the rest of my life showing you how much you mean to me. I'll work every single day to be the man you deserve, but let me make love to you tonight. Let me know what it's like to feel you again. Please." As Colt spoke, he gently massaged Jace's cock and drew him in until their foreheads touched. Jace leaned forward and kissed Colt's lips.

"I'm going to be really pissed off in the morning if this turns out to be a dream," Jace said, his lips remaining against Colt's. His hips rolled into Colt's hand.

"Come on, let me end any doubt right here, right now." Colt turned Jace in his arms and guided him to the master bedroom.

The overhead light was on and Colt flipped the switch, allowing the moonlight to cast a perfect glow through the bedroom window as he urged Jace to the edge of the bed. The moment was perfect. Jace's warmth pressed along his body, he loved the feeling and wanted so desperately to make tonight count. Too many years had passed since Colt tried to make something special for any one. Actually nine years and ten months since he stood right in this same place letting the moon guide his path. This room, with this man, was the last time he'd cared about who he had sex with. He'd gone full circle and Jace had accepted him back. Colt sighed on a slow grin as relief hit him.

"You had me by the balls and didn't make me beg," Colt whispered, turning Jace around, keeping him in the circle of his arms.

"Should I have?" Concern filled Jace's voice, doubt flashed across his face. Colt hated knowing he caused that doubt.

"I would have done anything to get you back," Colt confessed, gathering Jace tighter in his arms. Colt slanted his mouth over Jace's. He willingly opened to accept the deep, demanding kiss. On a swirl of tongue and teeth, Colt slowly and instinctively relaxed into Jace. *Oh, yeah... so right!*

The deep tender kiss built into an impassioned frenzy between them. Jace closed his eyes, and tilted his head into the kiss. His insistent tongue explored the far reaches of Colt's mouth, and he eagerly returned the favor. How long had it been since he had kissed anyone with this much passion? He knew the answer and delved deeper into Jace's mouth.

A steady chant started in Colt's mind. *Slow, keep it slow.* But his dick had other plans, and he ground himself against Jace, rubbing his cock against Jace's bulge until he swore he would spontaneously combust. He couldn't hold off another minute, Jace's mouth and tongue were driving him over the edge. He ripped free of the kiss and lowered to Jace's neck, flicking his tongue against his skin, tasting and teasing him.

"I haven't had sex with anyone since I've been sober," Colt whispered when his mouth reached Jace's ear. "I'm gonna try to do this right, but you feel too good. I'm having trouble controlling myself and we've barely started."

Jace leaned back and held Colt with a lust-filled gaze. A playful grin spread slowly across his handsome features. "It's been a while for me too. I actually thought it was broken until just a few minutes ago."

The words surprised Colt, but he went with them, tucking them away, hoping for an expanded explanation later. There were more important things to consider right now, like testing Jace's broken dick theory. Colt reached down and loosened the drawstring of Jace's swim trunks. He pushed the brightly colored shorts down his thighs until gravity took them to the floor. Jace's perfectly cut cock sprang forward, and he moaned at the sight of the pre-come beading at the tip. Nope, Jace's prick certainly looked to be in fine working order. His mouth watered as he took in all that hard flesh demanding his attention.

Shit, was this really happening? He couldn't believe Jace was in his arms again and so readily allowing him a second chance. Ten years of their lives taken, stolen by his avaricious father. Colt pushed the anger down, none of that mattered now, because he had finally done what he should have done ten years ago—he stood up to his father and went after the man he loved.

"I wanna taste you... it's been too long." Colt dropped to his knees and sampled that small potent drop of need. His own cock twitched at the salty tang that was uniquely Jace, and he shoved his hand in his shorts to ease his ache. A small gasp from Jace caught his attention. A sweet sound that Colt wanted to hear more. He needed more.

Colt opened his mouth, sliding Jace's rigid prick against his tongue. He licked the bulbous head and traced the large veins running along its length. Jace's fingers tangled in his hair and his nails dug into his scalp, but he didn't care, he savored the sting. He loved Jace and everything about him. Jace let out another approving groan as he sealed his lips tightly around him, sucking him down the back of his throat.

"God, yes, Colt," Jace panted and used short measured thrusts to fuck his mouth. He teased Jace's balls and felt them draw up in his palm as a burst of pre-come hit his tongue. There was no doubt Jace was close. With one last swipe of his tongue, he pulled Jace from his mouth. The need to have Jace come unglued while buried deep inside his body overwhelmed him. Colt kissed his way up Jace's chest. He licked across his collarbone and ground his body against Jace's while going in for another kiss. Jace rewarded him with a moan.

Instinctively, they lowered together onto the bed and feasted on each other's mouths. Colt tugged his T-shirt up, only breaking from the kiss to get the shirt completely over his head. He toed off his shoes while urging Jace up farther onto the bed. Jace worked Colt's shorts down. He kicked them off and relaxed between Jace's parted thighs. He rested his chest against his lover's, causing their heavy cocks to rub together as he settled into position.

Most of his weight was held by his forearms as he kissed up Jace's chest and neck, making him squirm. Colt anchored his body as Jace wrapped around him. Their legs tangled together. Jace slid his arms tightly around Colt's back, opening for another kiss. Colt ran his fingers through Jace's long strands, before roughly palming the back of his head, his fingers tangling in the silkiness as he deepened the kiss. Thrusting his tongue deep, Colt made love to Jace's mouth, rolling his hips forward, pushing his cock between their bodies.

"I want you in me," Jace gasp, and rolled his dick hard against Colt's. He pulled back from the kiss, fighting Colt's hold on his head, and sucked in a deep breath. "Please. The condoms are in the nightstand."

Jace arched forward and met Colt, thrust for rolling thrust, clear in both word and action that he wanted to move this along. Colt leaned over, reaching for the drawer. When his arms weren't quite long enough, he tried to push up to his knees, but Jace went with him, keeping a tight hold of Colt's chest. The awkward move surprised Colt, and he looked down at Jace's face, confused.

Jace smiled up at him.

"I'm not letting you go. I don't want you to vanish," he whispered and began sucking on Colt's neck. The sweet words and Jace's mouth on him had Colt on his knees and scooting faster toward the drawer. He hurriedly pulled the condoms and lube out. Colt didn't bother to move them back to the middle of the bed. He stayed right there and took Jace's mouth hard and fast, driving his tongue forward. Jace took over, devouring his mouth, turning the kiss into a mind-blowing mouth-fuck as Colt tried to work his hands between their bodies.

He couldn't make it work. Jace held him too tight.

"Babe, let up some. I can't reach." Jace responded by driving his tongue into Colt's ear. His hand slid down to Colt's ass, teasing along his crack. He felt Jace's fingers knead his ass, spread his cheeks, and a warm fingertip ran over his rim. Colt shivered. It felt so good, too damn good. He wanted to push back against Jace's fingers and feel them open his ass. He fought his need to have Jace fill him... that would be happening soon, but not right now. Colt bucked his hips until he wrenched himself from Jace's hold and sat up. Jace followed right behind; his hands running along every inch of Colt's skin. The touch turned possessive, Jace's hands proclaimed their ownership. He craved Jace's insistent touch, even though it took longer to condom up.

"I need to get you ready," Colt said softly. He sat back with his legs folded under him, Jace's thighs laying over his. Jace had somehow managed to straddle him. Jace's arms were still wrapped tightly around him and he was busy placing kisses eagerly along Colt's shoulder and chest.

"I'm very ready," Jace whispered, his tongue leaving a wet path up Colt's neck to his jaw.

"We have time. I'm not going anywhere," Colt said, lifting Jace's face to look at him.

"You've said that before." The honest, uncensored response got both their attention. Jace stopped the rub his hands were giving along Colt's ass and released his grip as he lay back against the bed, never breaking eye contact. His thighs remained spread over Colt's.

The position was right, but not the reason.

"I deserve that. I was such a coward. I hurt us both, and I'm very sorry." Jace lay there for a moment, unblinking. A wanton smile grew on his lips as he walked his fingertips up Colt's inner thigh.

"I don't wanna talk about it right now. Just want to feel you."

The words touched Colt's heart like a tender caress. Jace's heavy gaze filled with lust. Colt loved this man. He ran a finger over Jace's rim, circling his tight pucker before he lightly dipped into Jace's warmth. He found he wanted Jace back up there with him, all in his way. "Lift back up, babe. Help me with the lube."

Jace pushed up on his elbows. Colt added the condom, and Jace poured the slick liquid onto his fingers. Jace's body tensed and he let out a long groan as Colt added a second finger. Only a moment passed before he was writhing on Colt's fingers. Colt watched, mesmerized at the sight of his fingers working Jace open, pressing and scissoring inside his ass. Jace's eyes widened, his breath hitched and his hips arched off the bed when Colt's fingers brushed over his gland, letting Colt know he was hitting the spot just right.

"Yeah, that's right, fuck my fingers, Jace." Jace angled his hips, ground his feet into the mattress, and let out a loud moan as he rode Colt's fingers. *Fuck!* He was so turned on, and his dick jerked at the sight. Jace was so hot working against his fingers that he could come from that sight alone. Colt didn't add the third finger, but reached for the bottle and poured the contents directly on his dick, stroking his length a few times to spread the lubricant.

"I'm gonna fuck you so good." Colt peered down at Jace, withdrawing his fingers slowly.

"Please…" Jace whimpered. Colt gripped his cock and teased Jace's hole, circling the rim, before slightly pressing in till the resistance gave way. When he pushed deep into Jace's ass, they both gasped.

"Oh fuck!*"* Jace's ass tightened around him, threatening to send him over the edge before they even started. Colt closed his eyes, gritted his teeth, and dropped forward into Jace's waiting arms.

"It's so perfect," Jace whispered into his ear. His hot breath sent chills down Colt's already overly sensitized body. Colt couldn't speak. He barely managed a nod. He wasn't sure how long they stayed like that, but they both let out a breath at the same time. Colt melted as Jace's breath slid across his skin. Jace recovered first and tilted his ass up, forcing Colt to bottom out.

"Yesss!" Colt ground out as Jace began moving and working himself on Colt's cock. Colt rolled his hips to the rhythm Jace set. Their eyes locked as he slid in and out of Jace's body. The moment was too much; emotion flooded Colt. He'd dreamed of this for so long, yet the experience was somehow so much sweeter than he'd ever hoped. Colt wrapped his arms around Jace and took over the thrusts. Colt slowly began to push deeper and faster, building a delicious momentum until his hips were pistoning, slamming into Jace.

"Ah, harder… need to feel you," Jace panted. Colt drove himself in and out of Jace's ass. He barely got his hand between their bodies, sliding his palm up and down Jace's hard length.

"Yes, Colt… yes!" Jace yelled out his name, and he felt the hot, warm burst of Jace's seed shooting between their bodies. Colt moaned and sunk his fingers into Jace's shoulder, holding him in place while he bucked his hips with purpose, driving himself deep into Jace's clenching ass. His balls churned with the need to come, the feeling grew in his spine.

"Gonna come, baby... you're so good." It didn't take long until his world exploded and he came on a shudder of ecstasy, filling the condom in Jace's ass.

Jace lay underneath him, his chest heaving as he gasped for air. Colt's arms gave out and he collapsed on top of him. It took several minutes for the world to settle back, and Colt smiled into Jace's sweat-covered skin, breathing in his scent. Colt pushed up on his forearms and placed a soft kiss in Jace's hair. Jace lifted his face, turning to capture Colt's mouth to deepen the kiss, enfolding Colt tighter in his arms.

"I love you," Colt declared against Jace's lips. He truly meant those three little words. There had never been any doubt in his mind Jace was the only man for him.

"I love you, too." Jace made Colt smile. He'd waited so long to hear those words from this man. Too long.

"Thank you for taking me back." Colt kissed the tip of Jace's nose. He held the end of the rubber as he slid from Jace's body before rising. Jace made a little sound of protest, but rolled to his side.

"Thank you for finding me," Jace mumbled into the pillow on a deep yawn. "I need to sleep. Be here when I wake up."

"I'm here for as long as you want me." Colt swore he heard Jace snoring before he finished the sentence. A smile touched his lips as he glanced down and found a soundly sleeping Jace.

"I promise I'll be here when you wake, Jace," he whispered and pressed a kiss to Jace's furrowed brow. "Every day... for the rest of our lives."

# Chapter 21

Colt rose from the bed and padded to the bathroom, disposing of the used condom. As he turned toward the sink, he caught a glimpse of his reflection in the mirror. His dark hair stood out in every direction, and the sight made him laugh. To say he was happy would be an understatement. He was giddy. Giddy? Did guys even get giddy?

The faucet squeaked when turned on. That was something else they would have to see to, something else to fix together. Colt always dreamed they could be together again, and now here they were in the same tropical island paradise with Jace's scent all over his skin. This run down bungalow was quite possibly the best house in the entire world.

Opening the cabinet door, first his eyes, and then his heart connected with the red and white stripped washcloths along with a soft terry towel. Funny the things he remembered. Jace used these towels to clean him the first time he'd ever bottomed. The tender love and care Jace used when wiping him off had stayed with Colt all these years. No one ever came close to caring for him like Jace had. How had he ever let him go?

Colt grabbed two washcloths and sat the towel on the cabinet. He ran the washcloth under the now warm water. Colt used one of the cloths to clean the drying come off his chest. He ran the other under the hot spray, before picking up the towel. Colt made his way back to Jace, gently climbing on the bed and tenderly washing his lover. He took care not to wake him, but to be as gentle as Jace had once been with him.

Finishing, he dropped everything to the side of the bed and moved in behind Jace, pulling the covers across them. After a while, the sound of his phone vibrating in his shorts pocket pulled him from his blissful state. He ignored the call, refusing to allow the anxiety of whoever was on the other end to get to him anymore. Whoever called could wait. The only person he wanted to talk to lay right here in his arms.

Colt tugged Jace across him, wanting Jace as close to him as possible. He'd lost too many moments like this. Jace woke briefly as Colt hauled him up, and he gave the sweetest crooked smile.

"You're still here," Jace whispered in a sleepy voice.

"I'm here until you don't want me anymore." Colt pressed a kiss to Jace's forehead. Jace made a sound of approval and wrapped himself around Colt, finally settling on his chest. Nothing else was said as Jace fell back asleep. These few hours with Jace were the most perfect moments of his life. Way better than spending his honeymoon with a drugged up, drunken wife. His phone began the insistent vibration again, and he rolled his eyes.

Colt laid there for what seemed like hours, lightly stroking his fingers up and down Jace's back, taking in the scent and warmth of his lover. Jace slept soundly. Colt never knew he snored or drooled until now. Colt kept Jace lulled into deep sleep with the light massage on his back. Slumber never came for Colt.

As daylight began to peak through the curtains, Colt's stomach let out a loud rumble. The noise caused Jace to stir and drew Colt from his thoughts. He hadn't slept now for twenty-four hours, but somehow he wasn't tired. He also hadn't eaten since breakfast yesterday morning. That looked like it might become a problem as a full blown growl erupted from his stomach.

After a short time, Colt very carefully slid from Jace's hold. The process took several minutes to untangle himself, before tucking pillows in against Jace so he could manage leaving the bed without waking his sleeping beauty. The thought brought a smile to his lips. He stared down at Jace's closed eyes and slightly parted full lips. He was so perfect. Jace was his and apparently always had been. Colt's smile widened, turning into a grin as his heart filled with unbelievable pride.

He'd cook Jace breakfast in bed. His prince would be served breakfast by his hand. A perfect plan!

Colt grabbed his shorts and the T-shirt he'd worn yesterday and quietly made his way from the bedroom. On a thought, he turned back and looked over the door's hinges, trying to decide if they would squeak if he closed the door. Taking a chance, Colt slowly shut the bedroom door, which moved without a sound. The goofy smile never left his face. His life was looking up. What a difference twenty-four hours made.

Colt pulled on his shorts and buttoned them as his phone went off again. He tugged on his T-shirt and pulled his phone out of his pocket, manning up enough to look down at the screen. Seventy-two missed calls. Damn! The secrecy of the trip had apparently ended; from the looks of things, his life actively searched for him.

With seventy-two missed calls, his phone must have rung all through the night. Yeah, he was certain everyone wondered where he'd disappeared to. Colt silenced his phone, turning off the vibration, and dropped the phone on the turquoise painted cabinet— he remembered that from before, too. The calls could wait. He had other priorities now. First on his list, coffee. Colt looked around the way outdated kitchen. There wasn't a coffee maker sitting out on the counter. Did that mean Jace didn't drink coffee? Everyone drank coffee. *Right?*

Colt began quietly opening cabinets, going through drawers, and finally searched the refrigerator. He knew Jace was a health nut, but seriously? Carrot juice, guava juice, tofu, a huge bag of mixed nuts, whole wheat pasta, and celery… What the hell? Who ate that?

And what kind of man didn't drink coffee? Running his fingers through his hair, Colt decided a trip to the grocery store wouldn't qualify as not being here when Jace woke up, especially if he hurried. Colt felt around in his pockets. He had his rental key and his wallet. Swiping his phone from the cabinet, he dropped it back inside his pocket before going to the drawer where he remembered seeing a pen. Colt searched for paper and finally opted to write on a paper towel, just in case Jace woke while he was gone.

He also needed to grow some balls and call his coach and doctor to let him know he was okay. If his spine held, he might even call his dad on his way to the grocery store. Anxiety immediately hit. He might wait making that call to his old man.

Colt turned on his GPS and picked the closest grocery store he could find. He carefully drove the back roads, following the directions into town. Before yesterday, Colt hadn't driven a lot in the past few years, especially not after his last DUI charge. He hired a driver to take care of those things. As Colt got his bearings and the roads slowly came back to him, he palmed his phone and dialed Dr. Knox.

"Son, you sure know how to stir a pot, don't you? You all right?" Dr. Knox bypassed the standard greeting and cut straight to the point.

"I'm great. Better than great actually. I haven't heard anything, but my phone's lighting up. What're you hearing?" Colt asked.

"First, how are you holding up?" Colt knew exactly what the doctor asked and didn't try to hide from it. It was the reason he'd chosen Dr. Knox to talk to first.

"I haven't had a drink." The truth was he hadn't even thought about having a drink since he boarded the plane.

"Good! That's real good. Do you need a meeting wherever you are?" The concern in the doctor's voice came across loud and clear.

"I might, but right now I'm fine. I haven't even wanted a drink since I left New York." Jace made him stronger, made him want to be a better man.

"That says a lot, Colt." The words were said quietly.

"It's due to the person I'm with," Colt confessed just as quietly.

"Son, I'm here for you, no matter what. Off the record, I'm glad you've made the decision to stay sober, for whatever the reason."

"At the time I made that decision, I was protecting someone. I'd give my life to protect him. I'm glad it didn't come to that..." Colt stopped in midsentence, realizing what he'd just said. Even through all their days of rehab, of the support groups, of Dr. Knox being Colt's sponsor, he'd never brought up Jace's identity.

"I've been worried about you keeping your secret. I hoped you'd make the right decision, but you were still hiding. To recover fully, you can't hide. But just so you know, until you're ready to go public, your secret's safe with me."

Colt actually got emotional. He let out the pent up breath he held and stayed quiet for several long moments. Dr. Knox accepted him. Damn, it felt good.

"Did I lose you?"

"No, sir. I was just wishing you were my dad. He's not gonna be okay with this." His throat clogged as he said those words.

"No, I don't suspect so, but you're a grown man now, Colt. He needs to lead his life, you need to lead yours. Just because you're family, doesn't mean you owe him anything. You've been an incredible son to him. Let that be enough." The words were candid and clear. Dr. Knox didn't walk the fence this time like he normally did, and Colt stayed quiet again.

"You do need to call Coach Atkins. He's called all night long asking if I've heard from you."

"I'll call him now. Thanks, Doc. I'm in Hawaii, Kauai actually, so I'll have to look for a meeting, just in case I need it. I hope I don't need it."

"Let me take care of that for you, I'll look  right now and send you a message. Take care, Colt. Call me if you need me." The phone disconnected and Colt paused before making the next call. He'd actually said the word 'him' and the world hadn't imploded around him. As Colt pulled his car into the grocery store parking lot, he made the call to his coach.

"Colton Michaels answering service, what the fuck do you want?" Colt laughed; he needed that laugh. His coach was in a joking mood this morning.

"Did I interrupt cooking class?" Colt asked.

"Fuck you very much. Next time you ditch a wedding, text me. I sat in that fuckin' church in a fuckin' suit and tie for two fuckin' hours."

"I'm sorry about that."

"I think you don't give a shit."

"I kind of do," Colt said and laughed at the huff he got. "So where does everyone stand?"

"As far as the team, our official statement is that we're as curious as everyone else. After I heard from you, we're moving it to, we stand behind you and the decisions you make. Is that what we need to say?"

"I guess so."

"All right, I'll have PR make contact with you in the next twenty-four hours. I suggest you lay low for the next few days. By the way, your bride-to-be has told me that you have forty-eight hours to make this right. That was fifteen hours ago."

"I don't give a fuck what that conniving bitch says about anything," Colt blasted back.

"I thought so. It's why I started the conversation with our plan, not hers." Colt was silent for a minute. The coach was quiet as well. There was one thing, or person rather, left unsaid. When the coach didn't automatically say it, Colt finally asked.

"My dad...?"

"Yeah, he's a concern. Did you know he's dating a friend of Maryia's?" Coach Atkins dropped that little bomb so solidly it took him a minute to replay the words in his mind.

"What?"

"They were hot and heavy last night. I wondered if you knew," Coach Atkins said on a chuckle.

"Goddamn. There's gotta be a fifty fuckin' year age difference between them." Colt sat in the front seat of his car, staring at the grocery store, seeing nothing. He couldn't have been more shocked.

"Forty-seven years, per her. They're in love. I think you'll be calling her Mom soon." His coach gave a full-fledged laugh on that one.

"Damn, which one is she?" Colt asked, praying he hadn't had sex with her.

"Super skinny blonde, big boobs... Elena, or Helen. Who the fuck knows? While we were sitting in that church for two hours last night, Knox and I decided we were double teaming you on this. You've been good to that old man, and I'm not sure he can say the same when it comes to the way he's treated you. Look, I'll have PR call you. The way things stand right now, we're behind you. Call Knox, he's worried."

"I spoke to him a minute ago," Colt said. Nothing would have changed, but knowing these two stood behind him gave him courage like nothing he had ever experienced before.

"Good. Stay low. Call if you need us," Coach Atkins said.

"Thank you."

"And fuckin' call me before I put the damn tie on next time." The phone disconnected. Colt sat in front of the grocery store, completely relieved. At least his paycheck wasn't angry over this decision. Thank God! The relief was pretty staggering until he remembered he needed to call his dad. And what the hell was up with him dating Maryia's friend? Which friend? Skinny blonde described just about every one of them he had met. Images of his father stroking off in his bedroom came back to mind, and he dropped his head to the steering wheel. Surely not! That made his decision; he'd wait to call his father.

On a deep sigh, Colt pulled the internet up on his phone and Googled what vegans ate for breakfast. Colt had a lot to learn, really quickly.

Colt grabbed a cart and followed the ingredients list on his phone. He grabbed every possible fresh fruit he could find. A corner aisle shelf held coconut water so he grabbed a case. Peanut butter, oatmeal, grained breads, muffins, soy crumbles. Colt looked down at the foods, studying them all closely, and somehow, none appealed to him. He walked to the other end of the store and found the eggs, butter, and bacon. Bacon! Colt loved bacon.

He warred with the bacon. Did vegans hate all things animal food related? Colt put the bacon back. Then he realized the eggs came from a chicken. Did that mean no eggs? Certainly not! Colt put the eggs back, but then a sound came from across the aisle. He looked quickly over his shoulder. The bacon was actually calling his name. Colt palmed his phone and again Googled information on being a vegan.

Did vegans have a card carrying membership to PETA?

Colt stood there several minutes reading everything he could find on a strictly vegan diet. Did Jace eat cheese? The more Colt thought about it, the more confused he got. He decided he'd get the bacon and the eggs. If Jace didn't like them in the house, he'd remove them immediately and swear to never bring them in his presence again.

On the way out, Colt grabbed a box of Hawaiian coconut cakes and a boxed coffee cake. Surely there weren't any meat products in either of those delicacies. As he strolled to the front of the store, he saw an aisle of health food. He didn't pay any attention to what he was getting, because to him it all looked terrible. Colt loaded the cart down, put a couple of extra cases of protein drinks on the bottom. He worried how Jace got his protein. He pushed the buggy to the only checkout line open and waited his turn.

The woman checking the groceries would probably know where he could take Jace for a night on the town. When he got to the front of the line, he began asking her questions about this particular part of the island.

"Where's the best place to take my partner dancing?" Colt asked, hoping he'd said enough about Jace and what he was looking for. The woman looked up, but never stopped the movement of her hand over the scanner, letting the beeps sound off every few seconds.

"The Reef," she said, and Colt immediately started typing in his phone.

"What about a nice dinner?"

"Seafood or steak?"

"Both?" Did vegans eat seafood? Probably not. Colt looked down at the tofu and gave a small groan. Did this mean he signed on to be a vegan?

"There's a bar in the restaurant. Very good. It's at the end of town. Right down this street. No reservations. Tell them Tilly sent you. You'll have a good time." She winked at him, and he hoped that wink meant what he thought it might.

"Cool, thanks." Colt quickly entered the information into his phone. She worked fast, and he was bagged up and out the door in less than thirty minutes of arriving. Could he be lucky enough that

Jace might not have woken yet? Maybe! Things definitely seemed to be going his way right now.

Colt backed out of the parking space with every intention of calling his father when he got on the road. What the hell was wrong with his old man? Maryia's slutty friends had to be less than twenty-five years old, and every bit the money grubbing whore Maryia turned out to be. No way whoever his dad dated would get her hands on his money. He was done wasting what he had. He'd put limits to his father's spending a long time ago. What did she think she was getting?

Completely disgusted, Colt dropped the phone in the cup holder, deciding he'd make that call later. He'd call Maryia too. His gut churned at the thought, but he ignored the feeling; it didn't matter. Jace had accepted him back and hadn't made him grovel. Everyone in Colt's life manipulated and used him. Jace had done neither. However, he had doubted Colt's presence at first and that made Colt smile. Then Jace kissed him and made love to him, without ever questioning his integrity. That just fucking rocked.

Another huge revelation from last night, sober sex was great sex! Okay, well perhaps it had nothing to do with sobriety and everything to do with Jace. Sex with Jace always amazed, but last night just topped every fantasy he'd ever had. Definitely the best sex of his life. Colt never wanted to leave Jace's side again. He would prove himself, show Jace he meant every word he said. He'd work hard to be a man fit to walk beside Jace. Someone Jace would be proud to have next to him. Colt wanted to be a proper partner in every sense of the word. Forever and always, and those thoughts had Colt grinning ear to ear.

Jace hadn't made him beg. Exactly a Jace thing to do.

Colt drove the fifteen minutes home and pulled to the front of the house. Funny how he hadn't noticed how run-down the place looked last night or this morning. The porch appeared new. There were stacks of lumber and shingles on the side of the house. Large buckets of paint sat right beside the steps leading up to the front door. Colt had missed most of those last night. He wondered if Jace hired the work out or planned on doing it himself.

After parking his car, he grabbed the groceries from the back and juggled them all in his hands. Colt hated unloading groceries, always had. No matter how he tried, he couldn't manage the cases of protein drinks and decided he'd have to make a second trip after all. Colt banged through the front door and turned to the kitchen right as Jace came through the other side door. His hair was a mess. He wore his swim trunks from last night, pulled down low, and he looked hungover. To Colt, Jace was about the best looking man he'd ever laid eyes on, and he couldn't contain the grin he felt plastered back on his face.

"Oh, I wanted to have breakfast ready—" Colt started to say as Jace stopped in midstride, looking Colt over.

"You're really here," Jace said, in the same moment, and Colt chuckled.

"You don't normally drink very much do you?" Jace stood there as Colt managed to get the groceries to a random counter before dropping them on top. He kept his eyes on Jace, anxious now. Would Jace still want him this morning? How had the thought never occurred to him in all the planning he had just done?

"No, not at all. I won't be doing it again either." Jace bypassed Colt and went straight for a can of guava juice in the refrigerator. Colt spotted the bottle of white willow bark in Jace's hand and lifted a brow.

"Headache," Jace mumbled, popping open the cap. Colt got it. He knew all too well exactly how Jace's body felt right now. He turned, resting his weight against the counter, pushed his sunglasses up on his head, and crossed his arms over his chest.

"You can change your mind about me being here," Colt finally said. He tried to keep his face from giving away his true feelings, terrified of what Jace might say now that he'd sobered up. As he waited, his heart pounded so hard in his chest he wasn't sure he would be able to hear the response.

"My ass is a little sore." Jace gave him a grin and leaned back against the counter, popping the pills in his mouth. He swallowed them down in one gulp. Colt barked out a laugh. The words calmed him in the way Jace always seemed to do.

"I wanted to make you breakfast in bed. I know it's kind of lame, but it's what I wanted to do. I'm sorry I didn't get back here quick enough to surprise you." Colt pushed himself off the counter, and stepped forward, moving closer to Jace. He stopped as he got within a foot of him.

"We're gonna need to hit the high points again. Why you're here, what happened, how long you're going to stay. I think I got it down, but I'm not a hundred percent sure."

"All right, whatever you need." Colt stood there in front of Jace, concentrating on not reaching out to touch him. Jace needed to make their next move on his own.

"Okay, I'm going back to bed. My head's killing me." Jace left the kitchen without touching him, but he also hadn't kicked him out either. That had to be a good sign, right?

"A Bloody Mary would help that hangover." That earned him a loud groan and Colt laughed.

"You don't have to make me breakfast."

"It'll help. And I want to," Colt yelled back. He still stood rooted in the same spot in the kitchen. Jace didn't say anything more, but he heard the mattress strain as Jace lay down. Okay, he wasn't kicked out. Things were still good. After Colt put the groceries away, he started preparing their breakfast. Solid game plan—*break*! Colt clapped his hands and started to work.

# Chapter 22

Jace laid there, watching the ceiling fan rotate, waiting for the white willow bark to work. He didn't move a muscle. His body hurt, his head was killing him, and he still had cotton mouth even though he'd drunk two big glasses of water and downed the full can of guava juice. Please God, let the pills kick in soon.

He found if he didn't move, his head wouldn't throb, and he could think. So he was sprawled across the bed, not moving a muscle, listening to Colt banging pots and pans around in his kitchen. The kitchen of the house he'd just bought. The one he and Colt had vacationed in ten years ago. *What the fuck?*

The smell of bacon frying hit Jace and his stomach rolled. Colt didn't know he was a vegetarian. Of course he didn't know. How would he know something like that? And why was that the first question Jace thought of lying here in this bed? Better questions were like, what happened to make Colt leave his wedding? Why had he thought to come here? Did Colt come here to be with him or was it an accident? Nostalgia of old times and Jace just happened to be here.

This whole thing made no sense. And his eyes cut over to the nightstand to see if they had used the condoms he stored there when he arrived. Relief was staggering as he saw the box opened, laying on its side. At least they'd been safe last night, but why did he have to have a hangover at such an inopportune time? Jace needed to get his ass up. Forget the hangover and take a shower. He needed to get his wits about him. He needed perspective and better clothing. After a minute more of letting the white willow bark take hold, Jace forced himself from the bed and headed straight for the bathroom. He needed to face Colt, clean and clear. Without question, he knew he could accomplish at least one of those things.

Jace showered, washed, and dried his hair, brushed his teeth, plucked a couple of stray hairs and dressed in a pair of khaki shorts and a button down. He'd bought both after he had arrived on the island. He looked the best he could. Certainly not power clothes, but also not swim trunks. He looked himself over in the mirror one more time and pushed his freshly dried hair behind his ears, instead of tying it back.

Okay, he had this... maybe.

Jace slowly opened the door and saw Colt lying across the bed, a tray covered in food sat at the end of the mattress. Colt ate a piece of bacon, looking about as hot as Jace had ever seen him. The five o'clock shadow in the early stages of forming, the stubble outlined Colt's perfect lips. Images of Colt's lips wrapped around his dick immediately sprang to mind, and Jace had to shove those thoughts aside. *Not now*! He mentally scolded himself. Colt looked up at him and stopped in mid-bite, chewing it down quickly before taking a gulp of his coffee.

"Is it okay that I eat bacon? I can toss it out if you don't want it here?" That confused Jace, and he looked closer at the contents of the tray, moving slower toward the bed. The tray was loaded with oatmeal, toasted bread with peanut butter, island jellies, waffles, pancakes, macadamia muffins, and every kind of sliced fruit Jace could think of. A protein drink sat next to a can of guava juice that sat next to a bottle of orange juice. To the side of all the food was a small plate of bacon, eggs, and toast.

"How did you know?" Jace asked, lifting a piece of dry toast. Could his stomach handle food? He sniffed at the toast before taking a small bite.

"Know what?" Colt placed a paper napkin over his plate, lifting it from the tray as he moved off the bed.

"Where are you going?" Jace asked, again confused. Were they having breakfast separately?

"I battled with myself about bringing this in here. I know you're a vegan, and I'm a carnivore. I'll ditch it. Hang on." Jace stopped Colt as he stepped around him.

"How did you know what I eat?" Jace stared straight into Colt's eyes, still very confused, operating six steps behind in everything between them this morning. There was too much at stake for him to be this far off his A game.

"I told you last night, I've followed your life. I've read every interview, everything written about you," Colt said with a shrug of his shoulder. The words seemed honest and sincere. They stood there, looking at each other, but neither spoke, and Jace realized they were both back to being nervous. He didn't like that.

"You can eat meat. I don't care." Jace forced a chuckle, trying to lighten the mood, but the chuckle turned real at the look of relief on Colt's face.

"Thank God! I thought you were going to make me eat this." Colt looked down at the tray and cut his eyes back up. "No offense."

"None taken. I'm not a PETA activist. I just like to eat like this. It's better for me or at least I feel better," Jace said, and Colt nodded, but made no move to sit back down. Colt picked up a piece of bacon from his plate and took a bite off the end; his eyes never strayed from Jace.

"Can we go to the kitchen table?" Jace asked after what felt like a lifetime of standing there silently. "I think it would be easier to talk there."

"Of course." Colt placed his plate back on the tray and lifted it, motioning for Jace to go in front of him with a sweep of his hand. They walked in silence until right before they arrived at the table.

"Your ass is still perfect," Colt mumbled. Jace's cheeks heated in a blush at the words. For some reason the warmth crawling up his cheeks, along with the hot shower and perhaps the white willow bark made him feel better, but he had a hunch it was more Colt's words than anything else. He grinned at Colt and took a seat, eating another bite of the toast. Colt put all but the plate of eggs and bacon in front of him, then sat down and started picking at his food.

Jace weighed his questions and ate until the sheer volume of food Colt made for him resonated in his mind. He grinned again and picked up a bite of pineapple. "I think I got most of it down. Tell me if I'm wrong. You left your bride at the altar and came here. Did you know I was here?"

Colt nodded. "Yes, I did. I watched the ESPN special."

"So you came here for me?" Jace asked the question, but regretted it immediately, wishing he could take it back.

"I did."

Jace's mind was still solidly on wanting to take back his words, and it took several seconds to absorb what he heard and let it take hold in his mind.

"Why?" he finally asked.

"Because I love you, Jace. Don't you remember anything I said last night?" Colt placed his fork by his plate.

"I think so," Jace said. All the delicious food Colt cooked for breakfast was forgotten as he rose from his seat and moved to Jace and dropped down to balance on the balls of his feet. He took Jace's hands and kissed each one.

"I've never gotten over you. Ever. Not one day passed that I didn't think about you. For me, you're the love of my life. Wherever you are is exactly where I want to be," Colt said, the sincerity in his eyes filling Jace's heart with hope for the first time since he woke. All the unanswered questions fell away and nothing else mattered in this moment. Only this beautiful man in front of him who was willing to throw his bacon away if meat offended him. What a sweet gesture.

"So, you aren't thinking a night, or even a week?" Jace needed to be sure.

"I've wasted too much time already. I don't want to waste another single day without you. I want a future with you," Colt said, looking perhaps a little insecure.

"I want that, too." Jace pulled his fingers free of Colt's hold and palmed his face. Truly, his entire world rested in those pleading eyes staring up at him. Jace drew Colt in enough to reach his lips and placed a small, sweet, lingering kiss there.

"Without your father," Jace added with a whisper, looking straight in Colt's eyes.

"Definitely without my father. I swear I'll never let him hurt us again. I promise." Colt smiled and kissed Jace again before he stood, picking up his plate and the oatmeal, taking both to the microwave for a warm up.

"Are you doing this repair work yourself or did you hire people?" Colt asked from the kitchen.

"Me mostly," Jace said, braving the jam on a slice of toast with peanut butter, hoping this didn't test his stomach's limits. Did all this make sense in his mind? Not really. Okay, not at all, but his heart desperately wanted it to be true and real.

"And we're here another week before we head back to life?" Colt called out as the microwave dinged. Jace stayed quiet until Colt pushed the oatmeal in front of him, handing him a spoon. Colt stared at Jace, clearly waiting for an answer.

"Won't you be missed before then?" Jace finally asked. He warily took a bite of the oatmeal and reached for his toast. Too many complicating factors were competing for his attention. Couple that with the dull ache in his head and it became impossible to think straight. His heart took the win and fluttered each time Colt's gaze connected with his.

"Nah, I talked to everyone I needed to. I have a couple more calls to make, but they don't matter," Colt said as he ate his breakfast in earnest now. "So what's on the list for today? I saw shingles and paint. What's first?"

"I'd planned to work on the roof today," Jace said and took a bite of his toast, chasing it down with a bit of guava juice. The battle going on inside him gave. The bottom line, just like always, he belonged to Colt for however long he was wanted. Did that make him pathetic? Probably.

"The roof it is. Maybe tomorrow or the next night we can go out, go dancing. I talked to a local woman, and she gave me the name of a place she thought we'd like. I need some clothes too; this is about all I brought." Colt finished off his plate and drained his coffee, rising for another cup. "Do you need anything?"

"No, I'm good. I usually drink a protein shake for breakfast," Jace said, realizing Colt had just described them going out together in public. Like on a date... his heart liked that a lot, tallying up more points against his head's reserve.

"I got lots of those, too. I didn't know. I need to learn these things about you." Colt's voice trailed off when he disappeared into the kitchen. Jace nodded in affirmation and finally smiled. He tried so hard to keep the nagging doubt at bay. He reached down, pinched himself, and winced at how hard. Why did he always pinch himself too hard? When would he learn that lesson?

Okay, so he wasn't dreaming anymore, but did this fall into same song second verse? He would just have to play this out and see what happened.

The day passed in a blur of manual labor and an in-town shopping trip. The roof was complete. Together, they worked not much more than a few hours hammering shingles back in place and fixing a few problem areas. Jace perked up pretty quick and got past the hangover that plagued him most of the morning. They decided tomorrow's big master plan would be to start the painting.

Colt drove them into town and loaded up on beach wear, sandals, and toiletries. They also stopped back by the grocery store, grabbing a couple pounds of shrimp, crab legs, potatoes, and ears of corn for a crab bake. Jace went into fits of ecstasy over the grocery store's salad options. Colt watched Jace glazing over at the look of all the exotic fruits and vegetables on display. Jace looked so happy Colt took a second glance around the produce department because clearly he must have missed something special.

Jace gave the same reaction again on the salad dressing and seasoning aisle. Colt stood at the end of the aisle and actually got a good solid hard-on watching Jace excitedly explain why there were so many rare treats at this particular grocery store. Colt ended up buying just about everything Jace showed him, because he found Jace gave small kisses of delight each time something special was put inside the cart. This was a new side to Jace, one he hadn't seen before, and the more Colt saw, the more he wanted a repeat any chance he got.

Colt's only concern with their outing came at the times they actually ate together. He was amazed by Jace's very strict and disciplined eating habits. After watching Jace load his hot dog bun down with the cooked vegetables from the street vendor, Colt couldn't understand how Jace wasn't starving to death. No way man could live without meat or animal products. Only the fragile new steps of their relationship had Colt backing off, not voicing his concern. He decided he was absolutely going to have to look at this vegan thing more closely. He wanted Jace strong and healthy for his whole life. If that meant he needed to eat meat, Jace was eventually going to have to put some in his mouth. Colt went so far as to even put a note in his phone to contact the team dietitian as soon as they got back home.

For a man who'd hidden who he was all his life, Colt didn't hesitate to take Jace's hand, wrap an arm around his waist, or give him a simple peck in public. Colt wore his ball cap and sunglasses, but in his master plan, he wanted them out, around people, acting like a couple. At least while they were on this island. He wanted to give Jace as many moments like this as possible to help make up for all his mistakes in the past. Jace went along with it, never questioning him or denying a touch. After a bit, Jace even initiated some handholding, and in those moments, Colt felt like the king of the world, even getting cocky when they passed people. Jace belonged to him and no one else.

They developed a balance between them. Colt was thankful Jace seemed just as eager to make this happen as he did. Neither of them spoke of the past, although the pain of their lives was still there between them every single time Colt's phone vibrated uncontrollably. The tension of the missed calls weighed between them. After about the first two dozen times, Colt finally got the clue and turned the phone off.

"You're completely on the wagon?" Jace asked, washing the vegetables at the sink as Colt shelled all the shrimp, standing right beside him. As dusk fell outside, Colt had piled all the drift wood and discarded wood from the house into a pit, ready for a fire. Lounge chairs were in place, bottles of water, tea, and guava juice chilled.

"I haven't had a drink in ten months. I haven't even wanted one since I got here," Colt said.

"I'm proud of you. That's a big deal," Jace said, looking over and bumping Colt in the shoulder.

"It's day by day, but you help more than you know." Colt leaned in, puckering his lips. Jace didn't deny him and kissed him quickly.

"You should call whoever keeps calling you," Jace urged, still looking at Colt. His face changed some. Colt couldn't be sure, but he thought he may have seen one of those protective walls sliding in place, surrounding Jace. He didn't like what he saw, and tried for funny, to ease the tension away.

"Yeah, and you need to bend over like you did on the roof today. Damn that ass of yours." Colt waggled his eyebrows and bumped Jace in the shoulder.

"I'm serious, Colt. You need to deal with them before too much more happens here," Jace said, his tone serious. Colt could tell Jace didn't want to be a downer, but the nagging doubt was there. Jace wore the concern in his eyes. Colt pushed Jace so hard to commit, but the big elephant in the room was the man who drove them apart last time. Colt had to deal with him to prove to Jace he was past his father. Overall, the logic made sense, but damn that call would suck to make.

"I deserve that. Only time's gonna show you that what you're thinking about me's wrong."

"Then deal with the rest of them. Come to me open and honest," Jace said quietly, his eyes were on his hands as he washed vegetables he'd already washed. They still worked at the sink, but those walls Colt had speculated on were now solidly between them, and Colt didn't like that one bit.

"Babe, don't do this," Colt started but Jace cut him off.

"Part of me wants to take you for however long you plan to stay. I like you here. I feel more alive than I have in a long time. I've been lonely for you. I just know what it's like to have to deal with a heart broken by you…" Jace said quietly, looking over at Colt with deep, unguarded pain in his eyes. God, he hated that look.

"All right, I'll take care of it right now. I need some privacy. I'm not hiding anything from you; they're just really crappy people.

I don't want that around you." Colt moved the seafood and washed his hands in the sink, thinking over his best approach with his father. Not one scenario he ran through his mind played out without a god-awful, ugly scene.

"Colt, you treat me like I'm in a bubble…" Jace started, but Colt cut him off. He wanted a new life with Jace, but he was well aware his old life needed to be laid to rest first. He had tried hard to set everything in motion.

"I'm serious, Jace. Please, just let me do this alone. I'll meet you outside, okay?" Colt asked, drying his hands with a dish towel. He was steeling his spine, taking the final steps to becoming the man he truly wanted to be.

"Okay." Jace gathered their things, dumped all the food in the big pot of water sitting in the kitchen sink then turned to leave the kitchen.

"Please, don't be mad," Colt pleaded, reaching out to grasp Jace's arm, stopping him from leaving the kitchen.

"I'm not," Jace said, but Colt didn't believe him.

"Then don't act like you're pissed at me. It scares me. It won't take me long." Colt stepped in closer, releasing his arm. "Please, I need to do this alone. Do you think you can start the water boiling?" Colt asked with only inches separating their faces. Jace nodded, worry in his eyes, and Colt kissed him. "I love you, Jace."

"I love you, too."

Jace said the words he needed to hear most. Those words buoyed him, gave him strength, and Colt kissed him, again. Jace left the kitchen, and Colt tracked him until he was out the door, walking to the fire pit. Colt shut the big sliding doors and palmed his phone, dialing. He could feel his facial features hardening as the phone began to ring. Colt kept his eyes on Jace to give him perspective as his father answered the phone.

"You're a goddamn pussy, leaving me here to clean up your motherfucking mess like always." Those were the first words out of Larry Michaels's mouth when he answered Colt's call. Did no one say hello anymore?

"Dad, I'm fucking tired of your fucked up bullshit. I've given you my whole life. I've done every fucking thing you've ever asked. You need to back the fuck off." Colt needed to take the upper hand from the beginning, not that he had ever accomplished that before, but he needed to try. As he spoke, he began to pace the small living room, but his interest stayed focused on Jace.

"You're with that cocksucker, aren't you?" his father bellowed.

"Leave him out of this, Dad. It's a different game now. If you take one fucking step toward him, I promise, it'll be your last," Colt avowed. Malice filled his words, and he allowed his voice to carry a warning that sounded deadly, even to him. Colt closed his eyes and tried to control his breathing. Every muscle in his body tensed, ready to fight when his father mentioned Jace. The old wounds his father had inflicted on him, the ones he thought were buried so deep they were surely forgotten, all surfaced again.

"A goddamn queer. My only son is a goddamn piece of shit queer. You're throwing everything away for some piece of ass with a dick?"

"Dad, I haven't thrown anything away. I've talked to the team…"

"You told them you like to fuck guys?" his dad shouted back.

"Dad," Colt started again.

"I didn't think so. It was only Helena that stopped Maryia from exposing you. She was ready, going to the press, and Helena stopped her. I don't know how long she can keep hold of her. You have to leave your butt fuckin' and get your queer ass back here. Take care of this mess like a man, not some pussy, slinking off like the slug you've turned out to be. You disgust me. You get back here, beg Maryia back. Do whatever it takes to get that precious woman back. You need to marry a goddamn woman, Colton. It isn't right to leave this on Helena's shoulders."

"Dad, you're almost sixty-eight years old," Colt started.

"Fuck you. I love her, she loves me," his dad stated in no uncertain terms. This whole situation was so fucked up that Colt laughed into the phone.

"She loves my money. And she didn't keep Maryia from doing shit. Dad, you do understand your Helena fucked me the night before you met her, right?"

"Don't you dare speak of my future wife like that again, you little butt licker. I swear to God, when I get my hands on you. You think I kicked your ass once before, you ain't seen nothin', boy."

Colt was quiet. The anger wasn't worth the frustration. Jace was less than twenty feet from him, waiting. Colt changed the way the conversation was headed. He'd had enough, and he wouldn't allow his father to do this again. He was finished hiding, and he was taking his life back, simple as that.

"I love him, that won't ever change. You stopped this one time before, and I won't let you interfere again. If you expose me, you risk your livelihood. If you let Maryia out me, then you risk it again. I'll handle it, old man. Back the fuck off. You don't control me anymore. Never again, it's done." Colt disconnected the call and dialed Maryia. His driver answered on the third ring.

"She's not well," Clint said, and Colt barked out a laugh at that one. Translated, it meant she was more likely stoned or so drunk off her ass that she couldn't talk.

"You should be thanking me," Colt said.

"Fuck you, you hurt her," Clint shot back.

"Impressive and very gallant. When she wakes, tell her I'll give her the downtown penthouse and ten million cash. It's honestly all I have left that she hasn't spent. It's all hers. I'll have my attorneys draw up the papers and have them delivered tomorrow. The only contingency is she never breathes a word about what she found. She does, it's all off, and I'll bury her," Colt said.

"Don't you dare threaten her."

"You're bold when you're off the payroll," Colt said, assuming Clint understood that he was now fired.

"Fuck you," Clint shot back.

"Tell her. She has until tomorrow night to sign the papers. She knows the right decision, and it's why she hasn't outted me yet. FYI, you two were video recorded the days leading up to my wedding. Time stamped and dated, I'm not a fool. Poor me, my bride cheated on me with my own employee. The papers will be there tomorrow." Colt grinned at the bluff and disconnected the call. How had that not ever occurred to him before now. He almost high-fived himself thinking about the clear proof his apartment building would have of all their coming and goings. Hell, they had had sex in his bed. He could have certainly recorded them together. They didn't need to know he hadn't.

Before he stepped outside, he left a voicemail with his attorney outlining his instructions. Once he hung up, he took a deep breath and rolled his shoulders, trying to remove the tension those two short phone calls caused him. Ironically, for the second time in ten years, he was close to flat broke. He hoped Jace would understand and give him time to recover. Sliding open the back door, Colt realized he was done. Everyone was handled, dealt with, and Jace was right, he did feel better, actually much better. Colt took the porch steps down, heading straight for Jace.

Chapter 23

Jace kept a close eye on the fire pit, watching as the crab came to a boil. He timed it, trying for just right. Per the seasoning packet instructions, the contents needed to sit in order to let the seasoning do its job. It didn't go unnoticed that he was cooking meat or trying to get it perfect for Colt. It also wasn't too big a surprise to realize, ten years of longing meant nothing. He was already back to doing just about anything to please his lover, who was currently inside, making the phone calls Jace had asked him to make.

Jace removed the oversize pot from the rack and anchored it in the sand next to their lounge chairs. Ignoring the chairs, he took the time to spread out a large terry cloth bath sheet they'd found in town today, hoping for a romantic setting in the sand, a more intimate place to sit, eat, and watch the moonrise. Maybe like a midnight picnic? Anything to soothe the tension he'd formed between them. Jace dropped down on the towel, anchoring his arms around his knees, dropping his head between his shoulders. Why had he insisted Colt make those calls?

He warred with himself, completely uncertain if this was the right move to force Colt to call his dad. He liked things so much better when he'd had the hangover this morning. His head hurt too bad to fight with his heart. Now, as the battle raged between the smart thing to do versus what his emotional needs were, Jace scrubbed a hand down over his face and through his hair. Each minute that ticked by made him more desperate, convincing him this hadn't been a good idea to push Colt into settling his past life.

What if Colt didn't come outside? What if he worked out whatever caused him to leave in the first place? Colt could have taken off straight from the phone call, without so much as even a goodbye. Surely to God Colt wouldn't do something like that... again. No, he wouldn't, not after the day they'd shared.

Colt had easily held his hand today, accepted and gave quick pecks. Those things didn't go unnoticed. Jace had been surprised they were already out around town as a couple. After the newness of the touches wore off, Jace realized Colt made conscience choices to do those things, and he was proud of him trying. It couldn't have been easy to hide yourself all your life, and then just put who you really were out there, but Colt had in order to prove he was serious about their pairing. Right? At least that's the conclusion he'd come to while they were shopping today.

Jace sighed, pushing himself to his feet, and walked to the end of the surf, standing with his feet at the water's edge. He stared out at the night. Could he handle another Colt Michaels heartbreak? He wasn't so certain he could. He actually knew he couldn't.

Somewhere in the back of Jace's mind, he felt Colt's approach way before he ever heard him walking up. Relief staggered. He closed his eyes and said a simple prayer, asking God to please not let this be a goodbye. He was already so in tune to Colt, he felt his presence before Colt reached him. Jace gave an inward groan, pushing his inner negativity away. He needed to hope for the best, and he dropped his hands into the pockets of his shorts. Colt came to stand beside him, mimicking his stance. They were close, but not touching, and both looked out into the night, watching the lure of the ocean.

"It's so calming out here," Colt said after a minute. His mind was clearly elsewhere, and Jace didn't look over at him. He just waited to hear what Colt had to say.

"I called my dad, and I called Maryia," Colt said and inclined his head toward Jace. He still wouldn't look at Colt; he just stood there, waiting.

"My father's not happy, but he'll get over it. He needs the allowance I give him. And Maryia... well, I should know something tomorrow, but I think she'll bend. You shouldn't be mentioned." That caught Jace's attention, and he turned his head in question, unsure whether he'd heard correctly.

"Oh right, you were drunk." Jace rolled his eyes at Colt's comment and got a chuckle from Colt. "I told you she found my stash of your pictures. I had this collection of articles and pictures, and she found it. She had your name and threatened to expose you. Said she would ruin you, start rumors about you being a child molester. I couldn't risk her hurting you. That's how it all started with us getting engaged." Jace stared at Colt for several moments, and then nodded. He didn't remember that from the night before. For about the twentieth time today, Jace had wished he'd been in his right mind to remember everything between them last night.

"I wouldn't recover from something like that, no matter how big a lie it was. Parents wouldn't ever trust their kids with me again," Jace said quietly.

"I know. It's why everything went down the way it did," Colt said. They were both back to staring out into the ocean.

"So where does this leave you?" The magnitude of the situation settled on Jace. If Colt had truly taken care of his life, then everything sounded good, he guessed. Maybe. Jace wasn't sure.

"It leaves me right here with you, but you keep giving off this vibe that I might not be welcomed. Jace, am I welcomed here?" Colt asked, without looking at him.

"Yes. I'm sorry. I just…" He turned completely toward Colt.

"No, I get it. Look, either Maryia's going to expose us or take the money. My gut says she's gonna take the money. I think she has the fame she needed to boost herself up, especially if she's the bride left at the altar. She'll use that pity and work it to her advantage. My dad's a non-factor anymore. He destroyed us once, but he can't touch us anymore. Besides, apparently he's getting married to one of Maryia's friends." That caused Jace's jaw to drop. He was dumbfounded, and he could only stare at Colt.

"Yeah, that's pretty much how I felt about it."

Jace shook his head. "Unbelievable, Colt. And this is the man who beat the shit out of you?"

"Yeah, I don't like to think about that. Except he's apparently still thinking he can kick my ass again if need be. My only defense for what I did ten years ago is that I was scared for both of us. He had such a tight grip on me back then. I knew he'd come after you and hurt you. I couldn't let that happen. He's such a bad man. I had those same feelings when Maryia attacked you. It just paralyzed me. It took me a solid ten months to realize I held the cards to my life." Colt ran his fingers through his hair.

"Oh, and I'll be near broke. Is that a problem for you?" Colt added, lifting a brow. He tried to lighten the mood.

"No. I'm not broke. Far from it, in fact," Jace said, and now he was grinning. Colt didn't touch him, but moved closer.

"I'm honestly exhausted, both emotionally and physically, but I haven't wanted a drink since I left New York. You can trust that's a first for me. You've been kind to me. I would've groveled and begged. I was all set to do anything to get you back. I can't erase the doubt that I put between us, but I'm here, and I'll spend the rest of my life doing what it takes to keep us together."

"I'm trying to go with it, trying to understand," Jace said, stepping into Colt who wrapped him in his arms and finally kissed him softly.

"Thank you. I don't even deserve that much." Colt took Jace's hand and pulled him down to the beach towel, and he kept Jace right there in the circle of his arms through the entire meal.

"What made you grow your hair out?" Colt asked, leaning against the doorframe of the bathroom. He watched as Jace primped for their big date night.

"You don't like it?" Jace asked, looking directly at Colt through the small mirror above the sink. Jace left his hair down, flipping the ends under with a hairdryer, but now, as Colt asked the question, he started brushing the strands back, digging in the drawers for the leather strap he used as a tie-back.

"Hey, I didn't say that. I like it fine. You're fuckin' hot as hell. I just wondered, that's all. When I watched the cheerleading competition, I kept pausing the screen, looking at you now and then back at the picture of you in college. I like both looks." Colt immediately back pedaled, moving into the bathroom as Jace worked his hair from his face. Jace went from painstakingly styling it to pulling his hair into a tight ponytail.

"Wear it down. What are you doing putting it up? I wasn't saying I didn't like it. Seriously stop, I like it down. I like to play with the ends," Colt said, placing his hand on top of Jace's, stopping him before he could complete his task.

"Are you sure?" Jace asked, and Colt grinned at how easily Jace tried to please him. How had he ever let this go?

"Of course, I'm sure. It was just a question over a part in your life I missed. I have lots of questions. Another one is why didn't you come to the season opener with your cheerleaders? I was so disappointed you weren't there." Colt handed the brush back to Jace and took the leather strap from his hand, dropping it back in the drawer and closing it with a decidedly hard shove. End of issue.

"You know why I wasn't there," Jace said, brushing his hair back in place. He bypassed Colt still standing next to him and walked into the bedroom. Jace was wearing new blue jeans and a violet purple button down, untucked with the sleeves rolled up. He stood at the dresser, adding a string of island shells around his neck and a braided leather strap around his wrist. He dug through his shoes to find anything appropriate for dancing.

"I don't know why you didn't come, except for maybe you didn't wanna see me," Colt said, waiting now. He was ready to leave fifteen minutes ago.

"I didn't. I wouldn't have been able to stand seeing you and not being able to do anything about it," Jace said, sliding his feet into a pair of sandals. They weren't really dancing shoes, but it was all he had. As he worked the strap onto the back of his heel, Colt arms slid around him from behind, and he kissed his neck.

"I wanted you there so you could see me and fall hopelessly back in love with me, to confess your life was shit without me, and I planned to do the same," Colt whispered against his skin.

"It's probably what I would have done and exactly why I didn't go." Jace stood, turning his head for a kiss. Colt's lips found his, and Jace pressed back into Colt's hold.

"We could always stay in tonight. I think you're way too hot to share. Some island guy might try and steal you away from me," Colt whispered and ground his cock into Jace's ass. Jace turned in Colt's arms, allowing him the opportunity to slide his hands down to Jace's ass. Shifting his hips, he brought their jean covered erections together and wiggled his eyebrows.

"Dinner out was your idea to celebrate your ex-almost wife agreeing to your terms, but if we stay here, we should finish painting…" Jace didn't have time to finish the sentence. Colt had him by the hand, pulling him from the bedroom.

"Dinner out it is!" Jace laughed as Colt hurriedly tugged him from the house to his rental in less than a minute. They had painted half the house today, and out of all the repairs, it was absolutely the worst thing he'd done yet.

Hours later, the dance floor was packed, but neither paid any attention. This moment only existed for the two of them. "You were made for me, Jace Montgomery."

Colt held Jace in the tight circle of his embrace. So far the night was turning out pretty perfect. For dinner, they enjoyed a large salad and grilled vegetables. Colt hadn't ordered any meat with his meal, hoping to impress Jace, and he was surprisingly stuffed. It made him feel much better about Jace's long term health, even though Jace scoffed a little at his too fatty—per Jace and definitely not Colt's perspective—Caesar dressing. Colt responded very clearly that a man could only give so much.

It hadn't taken long for Colt to lure Jace out on the dance floor. These weren't baby steps at all. Instead, Colt again pushed away his lifelong need to hide and stepped way out of his comfort zone by dancing intimately with a man. Once Jace agreed to dance with him, Colt immediately drew their bodies together. Jace grinned at him, and slid right in, meshing them together. For every bold move Colt made, Jace made another. These moments were incredibly freeing to Colt's soul, allowing him bolder moves as the night progressed.

They swayed together for a couple of hours, only pausing for water or bathroom breaks. Colt had even encouraged Jace to drink alcohol tonight if he wanted. Colt would absolutely be okay being the designated, but Jace scoffed that off. Not because of Colt and his alcoholism, but because he'd sworn off drinking three nights ago, claiming he never wanted another hangover as long as he lived. They were a match made in heaven.

A local band played the rhythms of the island. The restaurant turned out to be the perfect place, just like Tilly said. The club was intimately small, not large like the dance clubs back home. It seemed designed more for the locals, not the usual tourist trap. Colt would classify the place more of a grill with a dance floor that cozily opened to the outside and overlooked the ocean. It was dark, very romantic, and lit only with flickering tiki torches.

A cooling breeze blew inside, keeping the dance floor a perfect temperature, even though his body was past hot and bothered. Colt loved the foreplay of dancing. He slid his hands up and under Jace's shirt, letting his fingers strum across the bare skin of his back. Goose bumps sprung along Jace's back and arms, and Colt grinned. "I love dancing with you."

"You were never this bold before," Jace said close to Colt's ear. His eyes were closed. He moved instinctively as Colt led, and Jace slid his hands down along Colt's ass, gripping him, pulling him tighter against his body.

"I made love to you on the beach in broad daylight," Colt said, turning his face toward Jace. It was something he'd done before when they were younger, but would absolutely repeat today. He was forced to lean back a little so he could kiss Jace's lips. Jace kissed him back but never really lifted his head from Colt's shoulder. Jace was about the sexiest thing he had ever seen.

"You make me feel like we're a couple," Jace said and pulled Colt's polo from his jeans to run his hands over the exposed skin. The move was bold, and there was no mistaking Jace's intent as he lowered his hands to the waistband and slid his fingers down as far as he could go.

"We are a couple," Colt said, welding Jace to his chest.

"The island's so much freer with things. Everyone seems more open here. I'm gonna miss this when we go back," Jace sighed and raised his head to kiss Colt's neck, nibbling his way to Colt's ear.

"Fuck, you're making me crazy," Colt growled and leaned his head back farther to give Jace better access.

"Good. Me, too. Let's go home," Jace whispered.

"I want you to feel wined and dined. I'm trying to impress you with dinner and dancing," Colt teased, not letting Jace move from his hold.

"Let me show you how glad I am that you came back to me," Jace whispered, staying pressed against his body, as he slid his right hand inside the back of Colt's jeans and trailed a finger down his ass crack. "I need to be inside you again. It's been way too long."

"Oh, fuck yeah. I've missed that," Colt groaned and tilted his ass to accommodate Jace's seeking finger. Jace pulled back and gave him a strange look.

"What does that mean?" Jace withdrew his hand from Colt's jeans.

"The feeling of having you in me... you know. You're the only one that's breached that surface. No one else," Colt explained. He would rather have Jace's hands back on him, and he tightened his grip on Jace, leaning in to nibble on his neck. He couldn't even understand why they were talking right now and flicked his tongue out, licking his way straight up to Jace's ear.

"I thought you fucked guys?" Jace's voice carried, and they came to a stop on the dance floor.

"Yeah, I fucked them. I didn't let them fuck me. Don't stop dancing," Colt whispered. He was bolder, but not ready for everyone around them to know his sexual history. He used his body to try and sway Jace, nudging to get him moving again, but the stunned Jace wouldn't have any of it and remained stiff as a board. Okay, maybe they were having this conversation right now after all.

"But you liked that so much," Jace said, or maybe asked, Colt wasn't sure.

"I liked it with you," Colt responded, telling the truth. No one had ever known him like Jace, and as far as he was concerned, no one ever would.

"Let's go home," Jace finally said after looking at Colt for several long seconds.

"Let me get our tab." Hot damn! All of the sudden it was okay they weren't swaying together any longer. He was about to get some, which technically shouldn't have made him so happy. Jace turned out to be a safe bet. They had been pretty much like newlyweds over the last two days, but as Colt eagerly pulled Jace from the dance floor and grabbed their check, the intense look on Jace's face broke, and he gave a crooked grin.

"You're officially broke. I'll get our tab."

# Chapter 24

Colt drove, keeping Jace as close to him as the car and console would allow. He kept their fingers entwined, lifting Jace's hand every now and then to place small kisses on his knuckles.

"I'm glad we're back together," Colt said, winding through the curves of the dark road. He drove slowly, staying under the speed limit, hoping he was doing an adequate job at building anticipation. Jace didn't respond, but reached over and kissed his cheek. Colt turned his head quickly, trying in vain to capture those lips with his. Jace stayed inches away, still right in his face, grinning until he bent in, giving another quick kiss to his lips.

"I know a lot about you. I kept up with you, but there were like two or three years after we finished college, before your gym hit it big, that I have no idea about. Tell me about it," Colt said. He brought Jace's hand to his lips for another kiss and then rested their entangled fingers on his thigh, slowly stroking his thumb over Jace's palm.

"I… it took me some time to get over you. I was so into you by the time we got back, our breakup tore me up pretty good. I didn't do so well when I first got out of college. I kind of let my mom down some. That first year, I moved back home and took a job telemarketing. How lame is that?" Jace asked; he kept his gaze directed out the front window. Colt could feel Jace's pain as he told the story. He hated he was responsible for putting the ache in Jace's words.

"I'm sorry. If it helps any, I never got over you." Colt kissed Jace's hand again, trying to draw him back. He wanted Jace's eyes on him, not focused outside. "We can talk about something else."

"It's okay. All that turned out for the best. I was working at the telemarketing company overnight, and one of the director's daughters was trying out for cheerleader. He paid me to train her. She had no clue what she was doing, and I had to spend a lot of time getting her ready. I actually made more money training than I did answering the phones. It got me thinking, so I bought a couple of mats, and I put an ad in the paper. I started training kids. All the kids I worked with made cheerleader. Word of mouth spread. Haley, my stunt partner in college, became my assistant, and we grew from there. Anyway, so yeah, that's about it." Jace held him with his jade stare. Colt melted at the sadness he found in Jace's eyes. He'd done that, he put the pain there. Colt silently berated himself. He should have thought of something else to talk about.

"You really hurt me. Even when I got kicked out of that bar, I told myself you'd call. That what we had was too real between us and all you needed was time. You said you loved me, and I believed you. It took me a while to realize you weren't ever gonna call, you were done with me. I blamed myself for getting shoved out of that bar." Jace laughed, but the tone was bitter.

"As it turned out, it was my fault you were beat up. You know, I considered that. I wondered if you were beat up because we were seen together, but I thought you would have told me, so I let it go." Jace's lip trembled, and he quickly adjusted his seatbelt.

"It was my dad's fault I got beat up, Jace, no one else's. He scared the shit out of me by beating me so bad, and then threatening you. Hell, you saw his handiwork that night at the bar, and I'm his son. Even after he beat me, I was still gonna be with you, and then Johnny said my dad planned that beating for you, not me. He made me fear for your life. I was so scared. I did whatever they told me to do, no matter what it was, just to try and protect you." Colt stopped talking and stared out at the night, thinking about those few years.

"I'm sorry I hurt you. I was wrong. I hate I did it. My dad said he was having us followed, he'd know if I talked to you. I was such a fucking coward, and too young to know the difference," Colt said. He'd come to a stop sign on the road leading to Jace's place. He cut his eyes to Jace, who was watching him intently. Deep emotion etched the lines of his face, but Colt couldn't read it.

"I thought you hated me. I carried all these feelings for you all these years, and I really thought you hated me," Colt whispered.

"I've carried them, too," Jace said as he leaned across the console and kissed him. Colt reached up and threaded his fingers through Jace's hair, keeping him close, not letting him move back to his seat.

"You took me back without degrading me. Everyone tries to degrade me, but you. You never have. I hate the doubt I see in your eyes," Colt whispered.

"I'm trying hard to just go with this," Jace whispered back.

"You always have. I love that part of your personality." Colt lifted his eyes back up to meet Jace's. "I've loved you since I first laid eyes on you."

"It was slower for me," Jace said. "But it's forever for me."

"It's forever for me, too. There was never any doubt about that." Lights filled the car from behind seconds before a horn sounded, interrupting their moment. Jace was still leaning across the console, almost in Colt's seat. Colt reluctantly let go and started to drive.

"I wanted us to be home by now. We should be in bed with you fucking me like you mean it, Montgomery." Colt quickly stole a glance over at Jace, and just as he suspected, the use of his last name had Jace grinning as he sat back in his seat. The tension of the moment eased.

"When I was being interviewed, they wanted to know a secret about you. The first thing that came to mind was that the big strong quarterback liked to bottom. I'm thinking I should have just said it, Michaels." Jace laughed as Colt pulled up the driveway. Jace flung open the passenger side door and jumped out, not waiting for Colt who moved a little slower. He got out, shut the door, and started up the walkway. Jace rounded the hood of the car, jogged up alongside Colt, and patted him on the ass, before shoving his hand between Colt's thighs, giving his balls a playful squeeze. .

"Last one in bed has to clean us up afterward," Jace called out after he got a few steps in front of Colt, and he took off running. Colt picked up his pace, following close behind. They were shedding clothes as they fought to be the first one to enter the house. Jace was the clear winner, but Colt was having none of it. He had always been a sore loser and jumped squarely on Jace's back as he entered the bedroom. Jace stumbled under his weight, but recovered quickly and hurried to the bed, trying to toss Colt off. As soon as they neared the bed, Jace fell forward, both of them landing with a bounce. Since Jace was under Colt, he technically got to bed first.

"Dammit! I'm never gonna get to sleep after sex!"

"Shut up, Michaels, and kiss me." Jace wiggled, trying to flip to his back. No matter what Jace did, he couldn't get the upper hand and twist around. In that, Colt finally won.

"My pleasure." The playfulness quickly turned to passion. Colt descended as Jace angled his head backward, and their mouths met in a heated kiss.

The way Jace's lips moved against his was so fucking sweet he couldn't get enough of that mouth. Now, Colt tried to turn Jace over, but he fought the move, pushing back at Colt, until he lay flat on his back. The kiss never broke as Jace came down on top of him, straddling Colt's waist.

The kiss deepened as Jace showed Colt exactly what was about to happen. Jace made love to Colt. Only the need to breathe had Colt pulling away, moving his head to expose his neck, urging Jace to him.

"I've missed you so much. I've needed you, I've needed us. I missed this…" Colt declared, grinding his hips up, rubbing their cocks together. Jace answered by anchoring his knees into the mattress, nipping and sucking his neck before running his lips and tongue down the taught muscles of Colt's shoulder, chest, and stomach. Impatiently his fingers began tugging at the waistband of Colt's underwear, the only thing not discarded on their race into the house.

Jace rose to shove Colt's underwear down. Colt pushed at them, helping to work them off before Jace centered himself between Colt's spread thighs and nudged his legs farther apart. Colt lifted his head, looking down, and groaned loudly at the sight of Jace on his knees in front of him. Jace's cock sprang forward under his appraisal, jerking in anticipation. Jace watched Colt as he watched him. His cock wept as Jace slowly ran his fingertips up Colt's thighs.

The sensation sent a shiver throughout Colt's entire body only to intensify when Jace's rough hand palmed his sac.

"I've missed you. Your smell, your taste, everything about you. I've dreamed about this, and I swear I'll never let you go again. I promise," Colt declared seconds before his eyes rolled to the back of his head and he dropped back on the mattress as Jace engulfed his cock to the root.

Jace's technique was perfect. Colt's tip nudged the back of Jace's throat on the first try. Colt groaned as Jace swallowed around him. *Fuck!* His balls ached with the need to come. Colt was most definitely taking a plunge off the edge with this one. Jace's grip tightened at the base of his dick, and he said a silent prayer begging for endurance. He only had a few seconds to recover, and Jace was back on him, his mouth moving proficiently up and down his cock, licking and lapping, teasing the underside of his sensitive tip before flicking his warm tongue into the slit.

"Dammit, I've missed your mouth." Colt bucked into that hot mouth and tenderly ran his fingertips through Jace's hair, sliding down until they lingered on Jace's moving jaw. He was lost to the feel of Jace's skillful mouth consuming him. Jace worked him back and forth, the constant motion creating a seductive rhythm, causing Colt to slowly roll his hips to match Jace move for move.

Colt lifted his hand, threading his fingers into Jace's long, silky hair. His hips rolled forward until he began fucking Jace's obliging mouth with purpose. Colt's moan turned primal when Jace hollowed his cheeks to suck Colt's dick deeper into his mouth.

"Goddamn, don't ever fuckin' stop this." Jace drove him crazy, threatening to undo him too quickly. Jace moaned around him and continued teasing his sensitive head, not showing any signs of slowing. Colt lifted his head, his eyes glued to Jace's full lips wrapped around his cock. He couldn't stop watching, and his hips never stopped thrusting.

"Fuck, Jace, I'm gonna come..." Colt panted, dropping his head back down on the cotton duvet. Jace deep throated him again before pulling free and gripping Colt's cock with his fist. His brain took a second to register Jace wasn't sucking him anymore.

"Don't stop!" Colt opened his eyes to see Jace coming into his line of vision.

"I'm just getting started, football boy." Jace waggled his eyebrows and Colton groaned at the old endearment. He could tell he was in for a long, torture-filled night.

"You don't know what you're doing to me!"

"I don't want this to ever end," Jace said, climbing up Colt's body. He leaned in for a kiss. Colt met him, pushing his tongue greedily into his mouth, immediately deepening the contact. Jace's hands slid around Colt's head, turning him until their mouth's welded perfectly together. They tasted, probed, and mingled together until Colt finally slowed in sweet surrender. Jace won the battle for dominance. Colt ground his hips against Jace, urging him to continue. Jace's eyes swept down Colt's body, and he felt the heat behind the gaze burning him from the inside out.

"I'm having such a hard time believing you're real. I'm afraid I'm going to wake up and this is all gonna be a dream," Jace said, becoming a man possessed. He ended the statement in a growl as he again gripped Colt's cock, wrapping his fingers around the firm length, and stroked from tip to base. Colt shuddered under the move, every muscle in his body twitched and rippled as he reached up, turning Jace's head to look at him. He wasn't opposed to begging.

"I want you in me, Jace… I want you to fuck me hard, just like you did before, remember?" Colt barely got the words out before Jace pushed back on his knees and slid his hand between Colt's ass cheeks.

"Oh, yeah, like that." Colt remembered this. *Fuck yeah!* He wanted more; he loved Jace's clever fingers, slowly, carefully, and thoroughly massaging his rim, urging him open. He hadn't been able to push the memory from his mind. It had haunted him and was every bit as good as he remembered.

The little sounds coming from Colt were the best foreplay on the planet. Jace fought a losing battle, but kept going as Colt bucked up into his hand. He tightened his grip on Colt's cock, making him thrust his hips harder. The effect was a hot sexy Colton Michaels squirming under his hold. Colt lifted his head and looked at him from under deeply hooded lids.

"You're beautiful. You've grown into a gorgeous man," Jace said and placed his hand on Colt's splayed knees, pushing the muscular legs back toward his chest. The movement tilted his ass up, leaving Colt open for his viewing pleasure. Jace grinned wickedly as he looked down at the hottest ass he had ever seen.

"Damn, you're sexy as hell. Do I suck you again till you beg or do I give you what you want and fuck you nice and hard, Michaels?" Colt's dick jumped and his eyes darkened at Jace's words.

"Jace, stop teasing me. I wanna feel you moving in me... please." Colt squirmed against the bed and lifted his hips. Jace kept his grip tight on Colt's rock hard cock, giving a long slow stroke. Jace licked the bead of pre-come building at Colt's plump tip.

"Fuck... baby!" Colt groaned, his body trembled as Jace swallowed him. "God, yes, Jace. Yes!" Colton's hips bucked forcefully. Jace pulled Colt's cock from his mouth, trailing his tongue along the underside before nibbling at the soft skin of his sac.

Jace reached over, pulling condoms and lubricant off the headboard, laying them within easy reach, and then turned his attention back to his man. He lowered and traced Colt's rim with his tongue. The move he loved most. Colt's taste and scent had him so turned on his dick wept with desire. Jace kneaded Colt's ass, spreading him wide. He teased his rim with long slow swipes and little flicks before delving in and fucking him with his tongue. He'd waited so long for this, so long to have Colt writhing and moaning just for him. Jace took care, massaging the tender globes in Colt's sack as he devoured Colt's ass.

"Goddammit, you're fuckin' killing me," Colt hissed. He was holding his own cock now, gripping tight, trying to keep the orgasm at bay. "Fuck me, end this, Jace, fuck me," Colt begged louder now. God, he prayed Colt meant every word he'd said, because he wanted nothing more than to spend the rest of his life with this man, doing this very thing as often as humanly possible.

As Jace glanced up, Colt lifted his head from the pillow and looked down at him. The heat and need burning in Colt's eyes almost slayed him. He broke their gaze and let his eyes wander. Colt's hard dick lay against his tight abdomen, perfectly cut, thick and slightly curved. Colt had a gorgeous cock.

He couldn't help it—Jace lifted, reaching again for Colt's length and swallowed him; he tasted the salty pre-come and sucked harder, ignoring Colt's pleas, ignoring everything but his own determination to show Colt everything he'd been missing.

"Your mouth... my dreams... fuck, you feel so good."

Jace moaned at Colt's words as his fingers fumbled for the lube. He popped the cap easily, managing with one hand. Jace coated his fingers, flipping the bottle cap closed. He brought his hand back to Colt's ass and trailed his finger around his rim, massaging, taking his time before he pushed a slick finger inside. Pulling Colt's cock from his mouth, Jace watched as Colt ground his hips, pushing back against the invading finger. He eased another digit into Colt's tight passage, again watching Colt's expression of pleasure as his fingers found and grazed the sweet spot in Colt's ass. Colt pushed harder against his palm rolling his hips in pleasure, begging Jace for more.

"Fuck me, Jace ... I can't take this... I need you in me," Colt whispered breathlessly, grinding against Jace's hand until he lifted his ass, drawing his legs up, hugging them to his chest, opening more for Jace.

"You're still tight, Colton. Relax for me. I've missed having you like this. We don't have to rush it," Jace said, slipping a third finger inside Colt. Jace ignored Colt's pleas along with the insistent ache in his own cock and took the needed time stretching Colt, relaxing him, making sure there would be no pain.

Finally, Jace grabbed the condom and ripped the package with his teeth. He rolled the condom on with one hand, pouring more lube directly to the tip, giving his dick a few coating strokes. Jace aimed, circling Colt's entrance with his tip, making this the moment of truth. Everything Colt said he wanted. Jace lifted his eyes and connected with Colt's gaze. His heart raced so fast the only sound he heard was the pounding in his ears. They stared at one another as Jace pushed against his tight ring of muscle. Colt slowly gave him a wicked grin, his dark lashes fluttering as his eyes rolled back into his head when Jace entered him. Everything fell in place, making this so right and so perfect that Jace had no idea which one of them let out a sexy groan as he slipped deeper inside Colt's tight heat. He was home.

"Oh, yeah... that's right. Just like that, cheer boy." Colt's words punctuated the silence, proving Jace *could* hear over the pounding of his heart after all. Who knew?

"You can count on it, Michaels!" Jace growled his response, inching deeper, pushing his hips forward. The strain of keeping control had Jace gritting his teeth. Every muscle in his neck, shoulders, back, and chest tensed. Jace slowly, but completely buried himself in Colt in one long deeply gratifying thrust. Colt dropped his head back, gripping the bedspread with his fist.

"I love this," Colt moaned. Jace anchored his arms under Colt's knees, lifting him to keep him in the perfect position as he began the slow, steady rhythm of sliding in and out of Colt's tight passage.

Colt relaxed back against the soft bedding, his cock bounced against his stomach leaving spots of sticky wetness dotting his skin with each thrust of Jace's hips. He groaned at the feel of their bodies coming together, of Jace filling him, completing him. He loved to bottom with Jace, he always had. This was the one thing he'd managed to keep just between them. Colt glanced up at Jace's face, watching him, seeing the waves of pleasure cross his stunning features.

"Oh god, you're tight." Jace adjusted his position on his knees, gripped his hands on the back of Colt's thighs and began moving faster. Overwhelming emotion flooded Colt's heart as he watched the gorgeous Jace above him.

"God, you're hot," Colt groaned the words as Jace pistoned his hips, hitting Colt's spot over and over. Every single thrust sent electricity coursing through his body, robbing him of his sanity. Jace managed to grab his bobbing cock and stroke in rhythm to his hips. How did he do that?

"I can't hold back. Not now. You feel so fucking good," Jace said, biting his bottom lip, pumping harder into Colt's body. He was stunning to watch. Jace still held a leg locked against his chest, his muscles tensed and rippled with each thrust and the look on Jace's face proved he enjoyed every single second of his assault. Somehow watching Jace's delight made the entire experience more intense.

"Why hold back?" Colt encouraged and tore his leg free of Jace's hold, grinding his heels into the mattress. He kept a steady rhythm going as he bucked his hips, matching Jace move for move.

Jace's eyes were shut, his breath coming in pants. Concentration was now the most dominant feature on his face. God, his Jace was unbelievably sexy as sweat trickled down the side of his face.

"Because, I don't want it to end… I wanna fuck you all night, Colton," Jace gasped, fisting the silk sheet as he thrust harder. The tendons in Jace's neck bulged under his restraint.

Colt changed their position, wrapping his legs around Jace, toppling him down across his chest, and pulled his lover to his mouth. Jace's lips parted for Colt. His tongue was met with a wet velvet stroke that quickly became an erotic dance of lips, teeth, and tongue. He was so close. They were both close.

"I love you," Colt said, wrenching his mouth from Jace. His body was on fire. Liquid heat flooded his balls, the pressure growing in his spine as Jace continued to nudge against his prostate, sending him into oblivion. Sweat rolled down his torso his breathing became erratic, and his heart pounded wildly in his chest. Though Jace was wrapped solidly in his arms and legs, he somehow managed to pound him harder. This moment was perfection.

"Baby, now, come for me now," Colt begged, dropping his head back. He wanted to feel Jace lose control; he needed Jace to claim him, mark him as his. Colt's balls tightened at the thought. The need to come grew, and he flexed his ass and felt Jace's thrust falter.

"Ah, oh, God, yes!" Pushing deeper, Jace came with a yell.

"That's it, baby, make me yours," Colton growled and tilted his hips up so he could feel every delicious spasm of Jace's thick cock filling his ass. He squeezed his eyes shut and ground himself against Jace. He let go of his pleasure in wave after wave of sweet surrender, shooting milky ribbons in thick spurts across his chest and stomach. When Jace finally collapsed on top of him, Colt wrapped him tightly in his arms and held them there together.

# Chapter 25

"I love you," Jace gasped, trying to suck air into his searing lungs. After several minutes, Jace pulled from Colt's embrace and rolled to the side of the bed, still trying to catch his breath. It took a second more for him to slide the condom off his sated cock. "I don't think I'll ever get enough of you," Jace said, turning his head to give Colt a kiss on the shoulder. Colt lay there, catching his breath, and smiled at Jace's words.

"I know I won't ever have my fill of you." Colt reached for Jace, but got denied. Jace rolled from bed, reaching for the condom and the wrapper, before heading to the bathroom. Colt only chuckled at his move.

"I knew you would do that, my sexy clean freak. Regardless of you winning the race, you'd never wait for me to do it. When I'd dream of us being together, you always got up to clean us like you did before," Colt said to Jace's retreating back.

"Mmmmm… You remembered and dreamed of that, did you?" Jace disposed of the condom and grabbed a towel, wetting the end before heading back to Colt. His heart nearly stopped at the sight greeting him. He just couldn't get over how beautiful Colt looked lying in his bed. After they made love, Colt's cheeks and body flushed, somehow making him even better looking. On a quick silent prayer of thanks, Jace turned off the overhead light and flipped on the only lamp in the room before crawling back into bed. He scrubbed the towel over Colt's stomach before curling in around him. "That was pretty good."

"Better than I remember. I wish we could stay right here forever and never leave this house," Colt whispered, lightly running his fingers through Jace's long hair.

"It's good for my heart to hear you say those things," Jace said and buried his head in Colt's neck, kissing him.

Colt lifted and pulled the bedspread up, covering them as Jace tucked himself back against Colt.

Colt ran his fingers up and down Jace's back, something Colt did every night. The tender, sweet move usually lulled Jace to sleep. He was beginning to understand these caresses weren't reassurance to Jace, but instead to Colt. Touching Jace seemed to calm him, and Jace gave a sleepy grin at the thought of all these touches coming his way over the next few years.

"I missed this," Colt muttered and pulled him closer. Colt lay on his back, pillows tucked under his head. Jace lay sprawled across him, wrapped tightly in his arms. They were in the early morning hours. Jace had drug their sex out longer than he even realized. Both should be fast asleep by now, but like what had become their new normal, neither seemed to want the minutes apart that sleep brought.

"Missed what?" Jace asked, a yawn forming. He was a drowning man. Not too much more time would pass, before he'd be back to a man who seemed to live, eat, and breathe Colt Michaels. Jace was even now forgetting why he considered that a cautious thing, and his heart lurched at the protectionary thought his mind tried to insert into his musings.

"This right here, what we're doing now. You here with me, lying in my arms, I like sleeping like this with you."

"Hmm… I like it too." He stayed like he was, not moving, his head on the warm pillow of Colt's chest, breathing in his scent. Colt made sweat smell so sexy. Self-preservation had Jace finally bridging some of the gaps they hadn't discussed. He turned his head and placed a simple kiss on Colt's chest, flicking his tongue across the damp skin before laying his head back down. "What's going to happen now? There was so much coverage about your wedding. It's not gonna just die down if people are poking around to see what happened."

"I honestly don't know. Maryia signed the agreement so she has to stay quiet to get the payments over the next five years. If she doesn't, everything's coming back to me. She might sell me out, get a better payday, but I doubt it. The team's publicity people are coming up with something to say. Hell, they might have already said something, I don't know. You're tired, Jace, we need to sleep. I kept you up all night." Colt reached down, placing a kiss on the top of his head, hugging him tighter to his body.

"I will," Jace said, turning his head again to press a small kiss on Colt's chest, close to his heart. Something wasn't sitting exactly right with him. He couldn't quite place it, but it kept him from sleep now that he'd started down this road. After a minute more, Jace finally asked the million dollar question, the one he'd avoided from the beginning. "What's our future, Colt?"

"Forever, I hope," Colt replied instantly. Jace lifted his head at the answer, a smile tugging at the corners of his mouth. He kissed Colt, who kissed him back lightly on the lips, before giving a giant yawn.

"I meant more immediate. What're our next few steps?" Jace laid his head back down, listening to the beating of Colt's heart.

"Well, I guess off the top of my head, I'm thinking I have about five years left in the NFL. And if we could just keep this on the down low for a little while, I can finish up my career. I need to recover some financially, so I'm guessing I should probably take every endorsement deal I can get. Maybe we could live together in Texas while I'm in off season? We would have to be careful. I could probably buy a few hundred acres out somewhere like in Anna or Melissa, or maybe down around Cleburne, but that would mean you'd have to drive in to work every day. Whatever, we can figure it out and be discreet. No one really recognizes me unless I'm in New York. I'll live there during the season until I can retire. Hey, that's a pretty good plan for just off the cuff!" Jace's eyes closed as he listened to Colt. His heart ached with each of the words he heard, but he tried hard to keep a level head, thinking through everything carefully.

"So you're saying we wouldn't be a real couple for a few years?" Jace asked several minutes later.

"No, I'm saying we're a couple, but just hiding us a little longer. I don't wanna be with anyone else, and I sure as hell don't want you to be with anyone else. It's just I think the NFL will cut me. I'll be targeted or benched, and they'll find a way out of my contract if I come out right now. I've caused them a lot of bullshit over the years." Colt wrapped Jace snugger in his arms, and Jace let Colt pull him against his warmth. He made no move to leave the embrace.

"Why are you quiet?" Colt asked.

"Just thinking everything over," Jace answered, hurt and maybe a little surprised at Colt's plan. He'd hoped after everything they'd been through, Colt would come out and stop all his hiding. It didn't seem too much to ask, especially with how out they had been around the island. The ins and outs of the plan kept circling around in Jace's mind. Colt kissed the top of his head, but he didn't rise to meet the kiss this time.

"I love you," Colt whispered.

"I love you, too," Jace replied, hoping he hid the ache clouding his heart.

"Then lift up and give me a kiss." Jace schooled his features and did as Colt requested. Colt kept him there with a finger tucked under his chin, his gaze penetrating his soul. He reeled from the pain of hearing Colt's plan for their future. His heart couldn't take this. As he stared back at Colt, he realized they weren't really getting back together. They were just another island fling, and somehow he'd known this from the beginning, even if Colt hadn't. Jace felt his eyes tearing up so he forced the kiss and lay back down.

"It's gonna be hard to spend all that time away from you during football season. If we make the playoffs, it's gonna be like seven months out of the year," Colt said and gave a jaw cracking yawn. Jace didn't move, didn't want Colt to know how badly he'd hurt him again. He rubbed his eyes and faked a yawn, trying to keep the tears from rolling down his cheeks as Colt's words replayed in his head.

"Maybe we can arrange a weekend here or there so you don't look for someone to fill my cleats while I'm gone." Jace never said another word as he listened to Colt slowly fall asleep. The pit in his stomach grew with each passing minute. The reality of their relationship wasn't any different than before, except now Colt wanted him to be his regular fuck buddy. They wouldn't be together seven months out of every year. The other five months, Colt would have Jace hidden away from the world. No dating, no dinners, Colt could never be seen in the gym or at any of his competitions.

Hours passed as Jace lay there awake, trying to talk himself through Colt's plan. Surely to God, Colt only had another five more years to play ball. They were thirty-two years old. That would make Colt thirty-seven, how long did those careers last? Hell, that Green Bay Packer quarterback was forty years old and still playing, and Colt was a better player. What if five years turned to ten? That was ten years from right now, and Colt would still be a young man at forty-two. What if Colt went on to coach? Or worse, became a television broadcaster after he retired? Would five years turn to twenty or thirty more years? Would he be waiting and worrying about Colt for his entire life? Were alcoholics supposed to do things like hide the truth?

Those thoughts caused all new levels of pain to cripple his heart. Jace had walked this walk already. There was no way Colt could stay strong under all the stress of the life he'd just fled from. He'd buckle under the strain. His father and agent would target him every day. No, they might not physically beat him up, but they would emotionally destroy Colt in order to keep their meal ticket from walking out the door.

The thought enraged him and had Jace already wanting to tear them up, but he'd never be able to protect Colt tucked away from everyone. If Jace agreed to this, Colt would eventually do it again. Not come home after one of those extended leaves. Jace closed his eyes and let the pain of the possibility slice open his heart.

Jace had bought this place and moved the cheer gym into a state of the art facility all in an attempt to move his life forward. If he followed the path Colt outlined, he would be taking them back to where they were ten years ago. What would happen if one of Colt's football buddies caught them together, would he let them assume the worst and hurl slurs at him again? Probably, because being hidden only worked when the object hidden stayed removed from everyone at all cost.

What were his choices? The idea of leaving Colt broke his heart, and he tightened his hold on Colt's chest. These last few days were some of the best of Jace's life. They taught him he'd never stopped loving Colt, and the reality was he never would, but that didn't mean they were meant to be. A tear welled and slipped from Jace's eye, rolling down his cheek and fell silently on Colt's chest. He wiped at the wetness on Colt's skin. He wasn't a kid anymore. He knew the decision he needed to make.

Slowly Jace began untangling himself from a sleeping Colt's arms. Colt instinctively tightened his hold as Jace rose. "Shh... Sleep, I'm going to the bathroom."

Colt seemed good with the excuse; he turned over, pulling his pillow to his body. Jace quietly grabbed his clothes and watched the bed for any sign of movement. He picked up his shoes and softly walked across the house to the kitchen. It took a second to dress, before he looked around for something to write on and a pen. Jace refused to allow himself to think with anything other than his head, and that turned out to be a trick, because his heart hurt on a level he'd never, ever experienced before in his life. Did this really feel worse than ten years ago?

*Yes*!

Slowly Jace closed his eyes and forced himself to calm. It allowed him to think, and after a moment of silent meditation, he opened his eyes and penned the note. Easily finding the words.

*Colton,*

*I've lived this life with you before. Loving you from afar, never letting anyone know how I feel. I can't do it again, I won't do it again. Five minutes is too long to hide what we share. I certainly can't do five years. Take your time here. Stay as long as you need. I'm flying home today. Please don't contact me again. It will just make it all harder.*

*Jace*

Jace sat his keys, phone, iPod, and sandals on the entry room table before he silently padded back across the house, and even more quietly checked on Colt, who had turned, but was still sound asleep. Jace allowed himself one last look before he placed the note on the nightstand and left the room.

He grabbed his keys and iPod, dropped his phone in his pocket and slid his feet into his sandals as he opened the front door. Everything else could stay. Nothing mattered more than the distance he needed to place between them.

*"It can't work, let him go,"* he repeated over and over to himself to help his mind stay strong even as his heart begged him not to take another step away from the house. Jace put his earbuds in his ears, rounded the hood of his rental, and slid inside. He didn't even look as he used his thumbs to start whatever the next song might be. The car's engine revved, and Jace backed out of the drive, more desperate than he'd ever been in his life. He prayed he could find some flight leaving immediately. He'd go anywhere in order to get out of here.

He tugged the pillow closer to his face to hide the smile as Jace came back into the room dressed. Colt kept his eyes almost closed, barely seeing enough to know that Jace didn't plan to come back to bed, instead Colt assumed he planned to surprise him. Maybe breakfast? And he had almost blown the whole thing with the grin he gave, thinking how Jace might try to cook some bacon and serve him breakfast in bed.

He'd have to give Jace credit, he was quiet, but after so many days, Colt's body wouldn't rest unless Jace was right there in his arms. Who did he try to kid even thinking he could live without Jace for seven months? Colt couldn't seem to go seven *minutes* without going to find Jace, just to be in his presence. Jace had the gym, but he would just have to give in and come to New York. They could fly back and forth all the time. Besides, Colt was too proud, he wouldn't be able to keep Jace hidden. They'd be seen and Colt wouldn't be able to deny him. Fuck anyone who had anything negative to say. The bottom line, and what Colt didn't want Jace to worry about right now, was that he would probably have to find a new career and that seemed all right too. Colt's grin grew as the front door clicked softly shut.

Colt rose and reached for Jace's note, lifting it first to his nose. Jace's cologne lingered, and Colt smiled, knowing he'd absolutely lose his man card for such a girlie act as smelling the paper, but still he couldn't help himself. Colt rolled over, sitting up on the side of the bed and started to read the note. Disbelief seized his heart and pain nearly pushed it from his chest. He got as far as *I can't* before he bolted from the room, weaving through the house and hitting the front door within seconds of leaving the bed.

Still naked from the night before, Colt saw Jace backing out of the drive. Jace's face was turned away from him. Colt made it down one step before he jumped off the front porch in a dead run across the yard, trying to get to the street before Jace could pull away. Colt ran as fast and as hard as he ever had in any game, sprinting to the street as Jace put the car in drive and started forward.

Colt threw his hands out as the car accelerated seconds before the brakes screeched. There was no time to react. Colt squeezed his eyes shut, bracing himself for the impact. The front fender bumped him above his knee. Colt slowly opened his eyes, his heart rate rocketing from the adrenaline coursing through his body. Colt stood with his hands out, the note gripped tight in his right hand, afraid to move from the hood of the car for fear Jace would drive off without talking to him. Jace glared back at him through the windshield, wide-eyed, and clearly shocked by Colt's actions. The look of determination that soon settled on Jace's face caused fear and dread to coil in Colt's gut.

"Don't leave!" Colt yelled, panicked worse than any other time in his life. His heart began to stutter violently in his chest, not from the run or the near miss with the car, but from the look of sheer hopelessness in Jace's eyes. They begged him to make this right. Jace continued to stare at him while he removed the earbuds from his ears.

"Please, talk to me. Don't leave me like this." Colt rested his hands on the hood, refusing to move from his spot. The note crunched in his hand when Jace shook his head no. The sun was just coming up and struck the car at the worst possible angle, but Colt thought he saw tears in Jace's eyes. The panic turned to heartbreak, and Colt slowly, carefully moved off the hood and around the car to the driver's side.

"You have to talk to me. Please, Jace. If we can't work it out, I won't stop you from leaving, but please give us a chance," Colt begged, knowing the words he spoke were one hundred percent a lie. He'd never let Jace leave. He would absolutely do or say anything to keep Jace with him. Colt moved around the car and hastily gripped the gap in driver's side window. If Jace left, he was dragging Colt with him. Jace rolled the window down.

Colt waited as the window lowered before he reached across Jace and turned the car off. Jace kept him from pulling the keys out of the ignition, but the car wasn't running and gave Colt the minute he needed to try and talk Jace out of the car.

"Why are you leaving me?"

"You're naked, Colt. Go back inside."

"Not without you," Colt said, gripping the windowsill, trying to keep from touching Jace. "Come back inside, Jace. Explain this to me. Let me try to make it right. Whatever it is, I'll do whatever. Please, don't leave me," Colt pleaded, pulling the door open from the inside until he could step around and get closer to Jace. He took Jace's hands, and on a deep breath started again. "Baby, why are you leaving me?"

"I can't do what you're asking of me. Not anymore. I can't hide. I've never hidden who I am. And if we go with your plan, not only will I be hiding, you will only be my partner for a few months out of the year." Jace stopped talking and shook his head, looking away from Colt. "I can't. You can't. It'll be too much."

"Okay, then we won't hide. When I was lying there, I didn't think I had it in me to be away from you that long. I'll figure something else out that keeps us together. I'll find a way to retire if I have to. Now come back inside," Colt said, pulling Jace from the car. He wouldn't be happy until Jace was in the house and the car parked back in the driveway.

"Lookin' good, old man!" A truck full of teenagers rounded the corner and drove past them, slowing way down to get a better look. Clearly they were coming home from a long night of partying and Colt ignored them as the hoots and hollers continued.

"Go inside, Colt. I'll come back in, but go inside," Jace said.

"No." Colt finally tugged Jace hard enough to get him out of the car, and he slid in the driver's seat. "I'll meet you inside. I can't risk you leaving me."

Colt pushed Jace back, shut the door, and parked the car back in the driveway, right behind his car. He jumped out, his eyes on Jace who walked slowly back to the front door, and Colt clicked the locks to the car. He resisted throwing the keys out into the ocean. The throw would be a distance, but Colt thought he had it in him to reach that far, anything to keep Jace from leaving.

Instead, he watched Jace take the stairs back up to the house and go inside. He found a random beach towel hanging over the rail on the porch and covered himself as he followed. All of the sudden his feet hurt, the dried grass and rocks he'd ran full force over only minutes before were like nails and glass under his tender soles, so he tiptoed his way back inside.

He opened the front door and entered. Jace stood right in the middle of the entryway. Colt kept a tight hold on the keys and faced off with him. Now that Jace was back inside, the immediate panic had subsided and Colt wanted the problems out and solved. There would be no more future talk of leaving and apparently that needed to be discussed too.

"Put some clothes on," Jace said, motioning at him, before crossing his arms over his chest.

"Why? You haven't had a problem with my nudity since I arrived," Colt shot back. He kept a tight grip on Jace's keys, but moved around him, going to the bedroom to grab his blue jeans from the night before. "If I walk away, are you going to try and leave again?"

Colt meant the words as more of a dig, but he didn't stay in the bedroom long just in case Jace really did try to run off again. He grabbed the jeans off the floor and tugged them up while walking back into the living room. Jace was standing in the same spot, like a statue, cold and unmoving. Colt stopped long enough to raise his zipper, while carefully avoiding any possible pinches or hair pulling.

Jace glowered at him, expressionless, not saying a word. The near miss, combined with Jace's clearly indifferent attitude had anger coursing through his veins.

"Goddamn, Jace. You won't fuckin' talk to me. I try to get you involved, and you just fuckin' stand there, in stoned silence. But you have the nerve to fuckin' leave me while I'm sleeping? It's bullshit. If you have something on your mind, you need to fuckin' tell me. I can't fix what I don't fuckin' know about." Colt was angry now. He circled Jace as he raged. His shoulders rolled, his body tensed, and he actually yelled the last few sentences. When Colt came back around to stand in front of Jace, he threw his hands in the air. "See? You don't communicate with me. You leave it to me, and if I don't fuckin' get it right, you leave me. That shit ain't right, Jace."

"We don't operate on the same page," Jace finally said, his voice calm and low. Lifting his head, he pinned Colt with his stare and stepped forward until they stood toe to toe. His lip quivered, but he stood his ground.

"Then put me on your page. I'll stay there," Colt shot back. They stood face to face, staring at each other. Colt wasn't willing to move back even an inch. He was going to stay in Jace's personal space until this got resolved.

"I'm always gonna be afraid for your safety as long as you keep your life in New York. If you're there for months at a time, I can't see you not breaking. Your dad's gonna stay on you, your agent too. You'll fall off of the wagon sooner or later just under the sheer magnitude of pressure they put on you. And football isn't just going to accept you if you come out gay. I can't see how it's gonna work, how we will work, Colt."

"So you were leaving me, instead of talking this through?" Colt couldn't let it go.

Jace sighed, closing his eyes, dropping his head back between his shoulders.

"If it helps you not worry, I'll figure out a way to retire. Do you love me? Am I it for you?"

"Colt, you can't retire. You're at the height of your career. No way will they let you out of your contract." Jace was back to squaring off with him and adamant as hell.

"Do you honestly think I'm the only gay guy in all of the NFL? I mean really. Do you think I'm the only gay on my team? I'm not. It doesn't have to be a big deal. We can work it out."

"I'd like you to be able to be at my gym. And attend all the things that are important to me," Jace said.

"Me too. Done! See how easy that was?" Colt threw his hands in the air, shaking his head, trying to make Jace feel ridiculous, even though he wasn't, and they both knew it.

"Don't trivialize my concerns, or act like you would have so willingly listened to me before." Jace finally moved away, walking across the living room to the back sliding glass doors. He stared out at the ocean. Colt followed behind him at a slower pace.

"We won't know because you've never given me that chance," Colt said, his anger fading quickly, needing to better assess where they were in this argument. "Look, I don't know the answers. We'll have to work it out as we go. I understand now where your concern is, but you have to fuckin' tell me when I'm steppin' outside of your expectations."

Colt hesitantly took the steps and closed the distance, coming to stand behind Jace. When he didn't move away, Colt slowly slid his arms around Jace's waist. Jace finally leaned back against him in a small move of giving some in their argument. Colt tightened his hold, tugging Jace firmly against his chest.

"You're it for me. Am I it for you, Jace?" Colt buried his face in the crook of Jace's neck and closed his eyes, breathing in his scent. Forever was what he wanted, and he prayed Jace wanted the same life he so desperately craved. Jace lifted his hand and cupped the back of Colt's head, his fingertips grazed across Colt's scalp and sent chills down his spine as they threaded through his hair.

"You're it for me," Jace whispered. Colt turned him in his arms and drew him back against his body.

"I love you. Now, say it back." Colt needed to hear those three little words, needed Jace to ease his fear.

"I love you, too. But I'm scared." After all these days, Jace finally gave some hint as to where his head really was in this whole deal.

"I put that doubt in you, and I'm sorry. I'll carry the burden of knowing I hurt you for the rest of my life. But I can't make us right if you keep your feelings all bottled up inside." Colt placed a kiss on Jace's lips. "So well figure out what's next. What's right for us as we go. I'll always put you first, above anyone and anything, Jace. I've learned that lesson. I've lived a life without you, and I'm not going back there. You're my future. Now, tell me you're staying with me."

Jace nodded. His eyes held only a hint of apprehension, but exhaustion was clearly dominant on his face. Colt didn't press him more.

"You need to sleep," Colt said. "I can't see where you had any last night."

"I'm sorry for doubting you."

"I get it. Just talk to me before you leave again. Now, come lay down. I'll be standing guard to make sure you don't try and bolt again." Colt grinned and took Jace by the hand, pulling him back to the bedroom. Jace undressed and slid back in bed. He made a halfhearted attempt to pull Colt down with him, but he fought the move. That would lead to sex, and that needed to wait. This was one of those times in a relationship that other things needed to be worked out before anything else happened. Jace was asleep within seconds of hitting the sheets.

Colt decided he was awake for the day, adrenaline still pumping after his near miss. How had he almost lost Jace, again? What would he have done if Jace had gotten on a plane? The answer came quickly, he'd have gone after him and he wouldn't have stopped pursuing him until he had him back in his arms. Jace was the right road for him. He'd been forced off this road ten years ago and where had it got him? Nothing but a screwed up life filled with pain and heartache. Never again.

Colt showered and dressed, quietly shutting the door behind him as he left Jace sleeping in the bedroom. He padded into the kitchen, made coffee, and started to pull the bacon and eggs from the refrigerator only to find he'd eaten them all.

He did a quick scan and realized Jace was out of his morning guava juice too. That wouldn't do. His decision made, Colt grabbed Jace's keys and went for the front door. He'd get a few groceries and be back way before Jace woke. A grin tore across Colt's face as he sat in the driver's seat, settling in behind the steering wheel. Through all the drama of the morning, he hadn't let himself remember the reason for the ache in his ass.

# Chapter 26

Colt drove to town with the windows of the Prius rolled down and the radio cranked up. The early morning air was crisp and sultry against his skin. He took the long way into town, choosing the scenic route, through the hills. The rising sun and ocean made a picturesque backdrop. He could see for miles and miles, being so far above sea level. He wound his way through the small roads, thinking about how much he wanted to bring Jace out here tomorrow morning. He had to see the island from this perspective. The view calmed his haggard soul.

A fallen rock tumbled out onto the road. Colt dodged it, making a wide sweep to the right. Two things happened simultaneously. First, his brakes faltered. He stomped on the pedal when he swerved to miss the rock. The soft brakes gave way and his foot went to the floor. Colt did a couple of quick stomps and got nothing in return. He had no brakes.

Second, an old pickup truck came out of nowhere, following too close behind him. He tried to signal to the driver he was having problems. A second passed for him to realize the other driver wouldn't understand his hand signals, but he panicked and didn't know what else to do.

Colt gripped the steering wheel, weaving through the curves as the car descended down a hill, picking up speed with each turn of the wheel. Colt kept his eyes trained on the road in front of him, praying no one pulled out from a side road because he couldn't stop. He took a second and glanced in his rearview mirror, but the other driver stayed on him, not doing anything to acknowledge he had even seen Colt's hand waving franticly out the window.

His car was picking up too much speed, he needed to slow down. He ignored the motherfucker on his ass and carefully lifted the emergency brake. He hadn't lifted the brake more than an inch, but the vehicle started to slow.

Relief hit his panicked heart. Colt slowly lifted the brake lever, slowing the car down when the truck slammed him from behind. *What the hell?* His eyes shot back up to the rearview mirror and then down the street. Not a quarter of a mile away was a sharp curve. Colt was going forty-five and the curve allowed for twenty-five. Colt ignored the truck and again pulled up on the emergency brake. The truck rammed him from behind and this time stayed on his bumper, pushing him forward. Colt turned the wheel to the right, the truck followed. He pumped the brakes, nothing.

The truck's engine roared and they lurched forward, gaining speed. *Fuck no!* The truck had them both barreling down the small road at full throttle. Colt had no choice but to navigate the sharp turn at his current rate of speed.

What the fuck?

Colt tightened his grip on the steering wheel, preparing to take the curve at sixty miles an hour, and for the briefest of seconds, he looked back in the rearview mirror. The truck was pulling up along his side, attempting to pass him. From out of nowhere, the truck swerved to the right, hitting him full force on the left side of Jace's little rental, driving him toward the edge of the road. When his tires hit the loose gravel on the side of the road, the car slid into a tailspin, and Colt fought for control. The force of gravity took the little Prius off the shoulder and down the steep embankment.

Colt didn't register anything as his world turned upside down. The sickening sound of twisting metal and shattering glass filled his ears as the roof collapsed and the car smashed in around him. His legs were crushed as the car rolled over and over. Seconds felt like hours before the car finally came to a jolting stop. Pain rocketed through his brain as Colt screamed for help, fighting to keep conscious. He tried to move his arm and push himself from the smoking vehicle, but he couldn't get his body to comply with his brain. He tried desperately to move his legs away from the heat, but he was wedged between the metal. He didn't have the strength to do anything more. Excruciating pain shot though his body with every gasp of breath he took. The darkness he fought closed in around him. His last thoughts turned to Jace and how much he loved that man.

Jace was startled awake by the sound of the doorbell and then the heavy pounding on his front door. After a second round of banging, Jace registered Colt wasn't getting the door. He smiled. Colt must have locked himself outside. Jace thought about making him wait, but decided against it. He rose quickly, looking over at the alarm clock. He'd apparently slept the entire morning and half the afternoon away. He hadn't had this much sleep since Colt arrived, and his head took a second to clear from the sleep-induced fog clinging to his brain.

"Hang on! I'm coming," Jace yelled to the front door and grabbed his jeans, putting them on as he made his way to the entrance. Smiling, he reached over to unlock the door, but the lock wasn't set. His smile instantly faded as he opened the door to see two island police officers standing on his front porch.

"I'm Officer Kahala and this is Officer Laemoa, we're looking for anyone connected to Jace Montgomery." Two men stood at his front door. Officer Kahala was about Jace's height; Officer Laemoa was much shorter, and a lot more muscular.

"That's me," Jace said, confused.

"Sir, how are you related to him?" Officer Kahala asked. They were no nonsense, and made Jace's nerves a little frantic.

"I'm Jace Montgomery." That seemed to throw them off. He watched as they exchanged looks with one another, then in unison they turned back to Jace.

"Did you rent a blue 2012 Toyota Prius?" Officer Laemoa asked.

"Yes, sir," Jace affirmed.

"Is there another Jace Montgomery traveling with you?" the other officer asked.

"No sir, what's this about?" Jace asked.

"Sir, your car's been in an accident. The driver's in critical condition at Island Memorial. Your wallet was in the car. We were operating under the assumption this individual was you. Do you know who had your car?" The officer held out Jace's identification and his heart seized. He couldn't decide if it was pounding out his chest or had stop beating all together. His brain froze, and he turned his head toward the sliding glass door, praying Colt was outside on the back deck. When he saw no one there, he closed his eyes, letting the weight of the world center into him. This couldn't be happening, his knees threatened to give under his weight.

"I'm here with a friend. I've been asleep. Let me see if I can find him." Jace left the officers and went through the house searching room by room, the panic intensifying with every step he took. Colt wasn't in the house. Jace hit the back door, searching the back of the house. Colt loved to go running. Maybe he was jogging along the beach. Jace lifted his hand to his brow to block the sun's glare and frantically scanned the distance both on shore and off shore. He saw nothing.

"Sir, who was traveling with you?" an officer said from behind Jace.

"Colton Michaels." His hand remained in place, shielding his eyes from the sun as he kept them trained down the beach, praying Colt would magically appear before him.

"And he's not here?" Officer Kahala finally asked.

"Not that I can see." He took a second more to admit the obvious.

"Sir, we're going to need you to come with us." For some reason, those words cemented everything for Jace. His heart already knew and his head finally gave in. All the fear settled in his gut. Colt must have had an accident. Jace went straight for the house.

"How bad of a condition is he in?" he said, walking straight inside.

"We're not at liberty to discuss that, sir," Officer Kahala said. Jace grabbed a T-shirt and sandals from his bedroom, tugged the shirt on as he went for the kitchen and grabbed his cell phone. His iPod was right beside them. Colt had given him that iPod ten years ago. It meant something, and he palmed it too. Jace didn't ask another question. He was dressed and in the squad car in less than five minutes.

# Chapter 27

Jace walked silently through the halls of the hospital following the two officers. With every step, dread coiled in his stomach. How had this happened? What had Colt been thinking? From the time they entered, curious faces kept looking his way as he kept pace with the men in uniform. The officers seemed to know everyone and were met with friendly greetings as they sauntered through the building in long slow strides. Jace's fearful heart desperately wanted them to move a little faster. It didn't work. Instead the steps from the front door to the ICU folded in around him as if he were taking his last walk down death row. The cold sterile halls and dull monotone color led him straight toward the death chamber.

He didn't want this to be Colt in the car accident, but his every instinct prepared him for the worst. Jace's heart thumped wildly in his chest with each excruciatingly slow step they took. The officers needed no direction; they seemed to know exactly where they were going. They walked past the nurse's station and no one stopped them as they rounded the corner, heading straight to a back room.

The hospital rooms had large windows placed partially across the front of each room and all had the doors open. Jace had no problem seeing each patient lying in their beds. Jace supposed the windows and wide open doors were a way for the nurses to keep watch over their critical patients. For some reason the thought seemed to make matters that much worse, and he forced his gaze straight head, focusing on the back of one of the officer's heads.

There were two rooms at the end of the corridor, and both looked to have the same setup as the rest of the rooms in this part of the building. As the officers veered to one side, Jace strained so hard he got tunnel vision, trying to see through the windows at the end of the hall. He had to see if Colt was lying in one of those beds.

His heart struggled fiercely with his head. He still couldn't wrap his mind around the whole situation. His head told him without question Colt would be in one of these rooms. There had been no note at the house, and he wouldn't have been gone this long, but his heart desperately wanted Colt safe, tucked away at home, waiting for him to return.

They entered the hospital room and the harsh smell of the astringent overwhelmed him. His focus trained on who was in the bed, but all Jace could see were the many machines pushed close by. The machines beeped every few seconds, dozens of tubes ran from the machines down to the person lying on the bed. Jace could only see covered legs. Nothing to give away their identity. The officers came to a complete stop in front of him, blocking his view. It was a frustrating minute as Jace pivoted on his heels and snaked around the two. A dark-headed nurse in happy pink flowered scrubs worked on a chart at the head of the bed, Jace couldn't see around her.

Jace walked to the bed, his eyes slowly moving up the legs then torso. Panic filled him. *Please, God, let this be anyone but Colt. Oh, God!* His heart stuttered, agony gripped him like a vice threatening to squeeze the life from him. He couldn't breathe, couldn't pull enough air into his lungs. Jace reached out for the bed to steady himself, his knees weren't doing the job.

Everything he'd been fighting since the officers stood at his front door came crashing down around him. All those walls he had immediately constructed to protect himself fell away as he saw Colt's right arm strapped down in some sort of a semi-cast, and a left arm in about the same condition. A stark white sheet covered part of Colt's chest, and from what he could see, there was very little left unmarked. Dark ugly bruises marked Colt from his chest leading all the way up to his face.

Everything around Jace slowed, centering straight into the two of them. Every beep of the machine was more pronounced as he stared at Colt's swollen and badly bruised face. The nurse who stood at the front of the bed took a step back, and Jace moved up, taking her place. The moment wrenched his soul and his prayer instantly changed. *Please, God, don't let him die.*

Bandages and tape covered a large portion of Colt's head, with the exposed half, puffy, black and blue, and covered with cuts. Part of Colt's hair was pushed back off his face, tangled and matted together. Jace could see the bruising went up into his scalp. *Shit.*

"Is it him?" Jace reached out to touch Colt, but he stopped for fear of hurting him more.

"Yes," Jace whispered. A silent tear slid down his cheek. "What happened?"

"He was in an automobile accident. We believe he was found right away, but aren't completely certain until we get the doctor's report. We don't know who hit him." Jace had no idea where the cops were standing behind him, but he could barely hear their voices over the sound of his own heartbeat. He never took his eyes off Colt. *I need you, please don't die.*

"It was a hit? Someone hit him," Jace said after the words had time to sink in.

"Yes, sir. Could you step outside, please?" Again, an undeterminable amount of time passed before Jace reluctantly left Colt's side, only to walk to the front of the hospital room. He refused to walk out that door.

"Someone hit and left him?" Jace asked in a hushed tone. Confusion set in, the processing part of his brain wasn't working right no matter how hard he tried to focus. Somewhere in the back of his mind, he knew the investigation was important. Yet the simplest thoughts seemed to be too much, and he cut his eyes back to the bed. Anguish filled his soul. Jace moved slightly to the left where he could keep his eyes on Colt. It took a full minute for Jace to realize the officers were trying to get him to understand something, without actually saying the words.

Officer Laemoa kept watching him closely, while Officer Kahala nodded his head.

"Like this was done on purpose?" Jace asked. He'd apparently gotten to where they needed him to be. Reality came crashing down, and right then, Jace remembered he was in a tricky spot. He wasn't family. He couldn't make these decisions for Colt. He technically shouldn't even be in this room right now, but they needed information from him. Panic set in for real this time. Colt's only family was his father. His father. *Fuck!*

"Who do you know would want to cause him or you harm?" Officer Kahala asked. The other officer just continued to stare at him. They also asked a very loaded question, too loaded. How should he answer? *Think, Montgomery!* His brain went in overdrive, trying to remember who helped Colt during his alcohol rehab. *Think!* His eyes cut back to Colt, and dread filled him when nothing came to mind. Jace just wasn't the type of person to hide things.

"I think his father would do this. I need to call his team. I think the team physician should be involved in this," Jace said. Still struggling with what to say and what not to say, he turned back to the two officers. "Wait, how do you know it was done on purpose?"

"It's still under investigation, but we believe the brake lines were cut. We'll know more soon." Officer Kahala responded in a matter-of-fact tone.

"He was in my car." Jace crossed his arms over his chest and took a deep breath in an unsuccessful attempt to calm his racing mind. Whoever did this, didn't want them together, but to hate enough to try to kill one of them? Damn, what an incredibly sobering thought that changed everything.

"It appears that way."

"Then whatever they had planned was aimed at me," Jace concluded. Colt had driven his car because he had parked right behind his this morning. Colt wasn't the intended target. Jace would have been without brakes driving to the airport this morning. His attention moved back to Colt, and right then, he desperately wished he was lying in that bed, not Colt. Colt didn't deserve any of this. Hell neither of them did. For what, loving each other? Jace didn't have any enemies, not like this.

"You believe his father would want to harm you?" Jace looked straight at the officer.

"Absolutely. He's already done something like this before," Jace whispered the words. "To keep us apart," he said as an afterthought. Fuck what should or shouldn't he say? Colt's father had taken this too far. A woman walked in, distracting the officers, but Jace could think of little more than how in the world he could protect Colt from a crazed lunatic who was technically his next of kin.

"Officers," she said.

"Dr. Nguyen," they both acknowledged in unison. Her serious gaze focused on Jace as she extended a hand. "Are you his family?" She had a warm smile and inviting tone. The comfort she so easily extended had all the questions Jace held back since entering the room tumbling out.

"How is he?" Jace asked and turned away from the officers, following the doctor back the few steps to Colt's bed. His spine slowly began to buck up. What would happen if Colt's father got involved? He truly was Colt's next of kin. Jace had to figure out how to stop this somehow. The truth seemed the only way he could see. Could court injunctions stop his father's involvement until the investigation could prove he'd done this?

"He's in critical, but stable condition," she said. Jace surveyed Colt's body and chose his left side to stand by.

"What exactly are his injuries?" Jace asked, gently picking up Colt's hand and lacing their fingers together. He made sure not to move any part of Colt's strapped down arm as he rubbed his thumb softly back and forth across Colt's knuckles.

"What is his name?" she asked, offering him the same kind smile.

"Colt Michaels," Jace said.

"Mr. Michaels has three fractured ribs and a punctured lung. He has a femoral fracture of his left leg and suffered substantial blood loss due most likely to the severity of the compound fractures he sustained to both his legs as well as his right arm. All required immediate surgery. He seems to have handled the surgery like a pro. Everything's set, with the exception of his right arm. It has breaks at the wrist, his upper arm, and forearm. Our goal was to get him stable before we look at those options. He's under heavy sedation to help the multiple..." She efficiently ticked off a laundry list of injuries. After the first dozen, Jace lost count, and his attention settled back on Colt's face. *Please don't die.*

"He's a quarterback for the New York Panthers," Jace said lamely when she finally stopped talking, wondering how Colt could ever recover if he did live.

"Colton Michaels, MVP. I knew I knew the guy!" Officer Laemoa finally spoke. His island accent more pronounced as he said the unguarded words.

"I need to make a phone call," Jace announced quietly as the attitude in the room changed with the recognition of what they were dealing with formed.

"Mr. Montgomery, what are your plans, sir? It would be better for everyone involved if you stayed put," Officer Laemoa advised.

"I don't plan on leaving," Jace said. Officer Kahala began writing in earnest on his note pad. The other officer picked up his hand-held as he nodded at Jace. He left the room with the doctor. Jace palmed his phone, keeping hold of Colt's fingers. His only contact in Colt's life was the cheerleading coach who'd worked with him when his teams were invited to perform in New York. Jace scrolled through his contacts, selecting her name, or what he hoped was her and pressed call. Shelly answered on the first ring.

"Hey, you."

"Hi, Shelly, I need help," Jace said, clearing his throat as he tried to use a normal tone of voice.

"You don't sound very good," she said, her normal bubbly tone now bordering on concerned as she identified the fear in Jace's tone. Damn, he hadn't hidden the worry like he'd hoped.

"I'm not good. I need to get in touch with your team's head physician. I don't know his name, but the one over everything," Jace said.

"That would be Dr. Knox," she said.

"Yes, him! Can you reach him?" he asked. That was the name Colt used, Dr. Knox. Please don't let Dr. Knox suck!

"I can try," Shelly hesitated.

"Shelly, I need him right away. It's urgent," Jace said.

"Do I tell him anything?" Jace paused at her question. Did he dare say anything? Shit, they were back to hiding. He didn't even understand this hiding world. Fuck, he hated this.

"I… I can't," he stammered.

"Jace, let me see what I can do."

"Thanks, Shelly," Jace said, relieved. He disconnected the call and looked around the small room. For the first time since he stepped foot inside this room, they were alone. He assumed they left to give him privacy for his call. Jace didn't care why he was alone, just that he was, and he moved closer to Colt, leaning down till his face was only inches from the man he loved. He took in every bump, bruise, and cut on his lover's battered face. His tears welled, spilling over. He couldn't hold back his emotions any longer.

"I love you, and I'm so sorry. It should've been me, not you. You have to pull through this, Colt, you just have to." Tears fell on Colt's bruised cheek, and he gently used his thumb to wipe them away.

"I'm here. I'll be right here. I'm not leaving your side, baby. I'm gonna figure this out and keep anyone from hurting you more than they already have." Jace never let go of Colt's hand, but extended an arm and pulled the hospital chair next to the bed. The chair made a loud scrape across the floor, and he looked toward the door to see if anyone noticed. It wasn't minutes since he hung up with Shelly before his phone rang, and he answered on the first ring. His eyes stayed glued to Colt.

"This is Dr. Knox. I've been given this number."

"Sir, I'm Jace Montgomery, and I'm here with Colton Michaels."

"I'm listening," the doctor said. He could hear concern, but he gave nothing away, and yet, somehow gave him hope. Jace prayed he'd gotten this right.

"Sir, he's been in an accident. It was actually a hit and run. A purposeful hit and run, at least that's what they gathered from the scene. They're still investigating and should know more in a few days."

"How is he?" Dr. Knox asked.

"Not good. I mean real bad. I couldn't remember exactly who helped him in his rehab. I thought it was you," Jace said.

"I did. Where are you?" Dr. Knox asked. Jace wasn't ready to answer that particular question yet.

"Doctor, he's messed up. They say the brake lines might have been cut. They don't know who did it." That got nothing but silence, and again Jace was forced to continue without encouragement. "It was in my car. He took my car, and I don't know who to call. His father beat him once before over me. I didn't know if you knew about that or not. And honestly, I'm really not sure his dad should be told about this." Jace finally got to the bottom line, dumping everything out there.

"I heard something about that in one of the sessions with his therapist. I'm going to be frank. Colt has battled too many demons where that man's concerned. And I had honestly hoped he'd gone to find you. Jace, I need you to stay put. Do they have security on you?"

"The local police are involved, but there isn't any security." The relief was staggering. He hadn't made any of this worse by calling. Jace closed his eyes and leaned down to kiss Colt's hand.

"I need to make some phone calls, but stay right there with him. Tell me where you are."

"We're at Island Memorial, in Kapa'a. I'm worried. He's not good. His throwing arm's in bad shape, I'm really worried."

"Stay right there. I'll call my son, he'll know exactly what to do. I promise we'll get this sorted, son. Don't leave him, Colt needs you," Dr. Knox said.

"I won't. I'm not going anywhere." Dr. Knox barely waited to hear Jace's response before the phone went dead.

# Chapter 28

Mitch sat at the keyboard in his one-room dump of a motel in Mexico City, pecking out an email to his supervisor. It wasn't coming easy. How the fuck did he explain to the United States Justice Department that their top field deputies had failed to apprehend their target? Which was bad enough in its own right, even before you factored in the United States military had beat them to the mark.

How the hell did that even happen?

None of his intelligence showed they had a clue about the guy's existence, yet from out of nowhere, the military swooped in and stole him right out from under their noses. His entire field operation went to shit in a matter of an hour.

He pushed his well-worn ball cap back on his head as he scrubbed a calloused hand down over his face. He was frustrated. Actually past frustrated, he was straight up angry. Somehow he had to back that off and let the tone of the email convey a passive, completely in control senior Deputy US Marshal, and didn't that just piss him off that much more? He hated the politics of this job.

Technically, his supervisors should just be happy the slime of the earth was in custody, but it didn't work that way. In today's economic times, every department was held accountable and expected to show their worth. Mitch and his team were under constant pressure to perform. And his latest fugitive was as big as it got for a department who specialized in finding and apprehending sick mother fuckers who sexually targeted children. The asshole had sold more children into sex-trafficking than any other person or group of people the department had ever come across. He was a real bad dude. Fuck! How had the military found him before Mitch's team could get him out of that mission?

Worse than all of that, the current political climate demanded he be socially conscience to the extreme. To fire off an email saying, *those goddamn motherfuckers came out of nowhere and took my fuckin' guy, that I really wanted to get my hands on for a few fucking minutes before I turned him over.* Yeah, no. Saying something like that would be seriously frowned upon. Not only frowned upon, but he was absolutely certain they would require him to take some kind of sensitivity training which was completely out of the question. Sensitivity training because he offended the senses of those dealing with a child predator. *Fuck, this sucks!*

Hunkering down, Mitch pulled his ball cap low, narrowed his brow and stared at the screen as he began to type. He wasn't three sentences in before his phone began to ring. He jerked the cell up, ready to answer on a curse when he saw the number.

Okay, no way this call could be good.

"Mitch Knox," he said, sitting back in the desk chair, the laptop and email completely forgotten.

"Hello, son." Mitch could hear the strain in his father's voice.

"What's wrong?" Mitch asked. He swiveled out of his chair, ignoring all the squeaking as he stood immediately. He didn't know why he chose to stand, maybe it had to do with the momentary silence that came from his usually no-nonsense father. His eyes scanned all the surfaces in the room looking for his car keys. He touched his weapon holstered to his body. He reached lower, his keys jingled in his athletic shorts.

"Is Mom okay?" Mitch asked into the silence when his dad didn't immediately answer. Mitch was the youngest of four children and his birth had been a surprise at that. He tried hard to remember if any of his brothers and sisters had been sick when he saw them last. Mitch's thoughts shifted as he realized the last time he'd made time for his family was over three years ago. Maybe this was a *come see us* call. The pent-up breath he held released as he plopped back in the chair with a thud.

"She's fine. Missing her youngest. You should make time for her more often." Mitch nodded and lifted a hand, giving himself an invisible tally mark. He'd got it right. Score one for the home team.

"I might be forced into some time off after the email I send tonight. Is that all you called to say?" Mitch asked, a smile spreading across his face. His father had retired ten years ago from practicing medicine. His retirement had consisted of taking a head physician's assignment for the New York Panthers. His pop worked harder at seventy-five years old than most people worked their entire lives.

But his father never called to chat. No, definitely not a chatter, so Mitch waited for him to get to the point.

"Forced time off, is something wrong?" he asked.

"You know I can't talk about it," Mitch said.

"Son, I need a favor." His dad went straight to the point, not wasting another second beating around the bush. Mitch's smile faded. His dad didn't chat and never asked for favors.

"Anything, Pop. What's goin' on?" Mitch asked.

"One of my player's has had a mishap. He's in Hawaii, the island of Kauai. From what I've gathered, it wasn't an accident."

"All right, want me to make some calls?" Mitch asked.

"This one's more important to me, Mitch. Can you get someone over there to help them?" Dr. Knox asked.

"All right. I guess I can," Mitch said, trying to remember who was onsite in their Hawaiian field office and what favor he'd have to give back for getting them involved.

"Son, it's Colt Michaels. He needs us."

"Whoa. What happened?" Michaels was a big one. Mitch had instant visions of drug problems and prostitutes. Something he'd need to get swept under the rug before the press could do too much damage to the team.

"I'll fill you in, but it's sensitive. And I'm afraid neither of those boys are safe at this point." Okay the prostitutes weren't girls, but boys. Mitch got that. Even saluted it.

To a gay professional man that said enough.

"I can head out tonight. I'm not too far from there. Send over the details. Are they in a position to have security?" Mitch asked. He was standing again, shutting down his laptop, already in the process of packing.

"Only the local police as best as I can tell. They're at Island Memorial Hospital in Kapa'a. Do you know about the place?"

"It's small, but certainly not the worst," Mitch said, thinking of where to land closest to the hospital. "I'll change security forces when we hang up. I'll call you when I arrive."

"Thank you, son. I'm flying to Hawaii in the morning. It's the earliest I can get out," his father said.

"The team isn't flying you there?" Mitch pushed his toiletries in his bag and zipped with the phone perched to his ear.

"They don't know yet. No one knows, Mitchell. Colt's been hurt bad and the list of reasons as to why runs pretty deep."

"So he's your special case Mom kept talking about last year?" Mitch asked, pausing as he tossed the travel bag in his suitcase.

"What you might not see in the background information you'll pull, but what I've made clear to the hospital was those two were married in New York last week, honeymooning on the island. It's not common knowledge, and whatever you can do to make that paperwork happen will be appreciated. I'll see you tomorrow afternoon." It was all his dad had to say on the subject.

"All right…" Did that mean he wasn't with a prostitute? Wait, more importantly, his father never lied. He sounded believable. Were they married last week? "I'll have someone pick you up at the airport."

"Thank you, son," Dr. Knox said. Mitch had his bags packed. He dropped his phone in his pocket, checked his weapon again, this time paying closer attention to the chamber. The benefit of being a US Marshal meant he could hitch a ride on any jet, anytime. It made everyone feel safer with him on board.

Funny how his father turned out to be a perfect diversion!

The island hospital didn't look so bad from the outside, but still could have been in every horror flick Mitch had ever seen. He hated hospitals, always had. There was just something creepy about them. He walked through the front doors of the quiet, dark hospital in the early morning hours, way before the sun came up. The pungent smell of the hospital hit him like a ton of bricks. Hospitals always reeked of something. Just exactly what, he couldn't put his finger on, but they all had that same smell, every last one of them, and he would never get used to it as long as he lived. For the purpose of this moment, he put the smell off to formaldehyde and death and chuckled at the thought.

His adrenaline junkie side had him secretly begging a decomposed zombie to jump out of a darkened corner, thereby forcing the start of the ever anticipated *Zombie Apocalypse*. In Mitch's mind, he'd be Marcus from *State of Decay*, battling those zombies, saving the world, keeping his people safe. Seriously, wouldn't that be completely badass?

Mitch trained every single day for that life-altering event, knowing in his heart it would never truly come, because, after all, video games weren't real, but whatever. If he found his motivation through Xbox and he kept everything all inside his own head, never breathing a single word out loud, who really cared?

The Justice Department shrinks would probably care, but that fell strongly in the category to never breathe that thought out loud, period. A senior Deputy US Marshal shouldn't be having flights of fantasy while on duty—well, actually, never, but definitely not while on duty! He hid the grin and rolled his shoulders, flexing his neck and back muscles, preparing for the attack as he ate up the distance from the front doors to ICU.

His long legs and booted feet resonated with each step. His beloved ball cap was in his back pocket, since as an afterthought, he'd decided not to leave the hat in the rental parked out front. The island was known for petty thievery. Funny how he hadn't had that same thought about his laptop.

With a pop of his wrist, he flashed his badge at the nurse's station, never stopping as he went to the back rooms. He knew which room John Doe aka Colt Michaels was listed in and he also knew which room Colt was actually in. He didn't need his agents stationed out front to clue him in.

Mitch strolled forward, exchanging a quick look with the agent by the door. He'd worked with the fresh-from-college agent while on his last case. The look they gave one another made it clear nothing had bothered the two people just beyond the door. Which meant everything was running right as planned. Damn, Mitch liked that so much more than the chaos that ended his last case.

Except, this wasn't a case; this was a favor for his father, and he'd had to call in a few favors of his own to get a security detail. It didn't matter; he'd do anything for his old man.

The blinds on the room's window to the hallway were drawn tight. Another good sign, and he gently pushed open the hospital room door, slowing his roll as he entered. He didn't suspect any zombies to breach these walls. Not with the four armed agents on this floor.

The sight that greeted him was expected, yet somehow still took him off his emotional guard. The tactical information gave him the who, what, when, and where. So the scene shouldn't have been a surprise with Jace Montgomery stationed in a hospital chair as close to Colt's gurney as he could get. His eyes were focused forward on Colt's face and their fingers entwined. Clearly Jace had no problem being out. Mitch respected that. Something he'd also accepted many years ago about himself.

Jace turned red-rimmed, exhausted eyes toward him, and his expression changed when he realized Mitch wasn't a hospital staff member.

"I'm Deputy Knox, US Marshal for the United States Justice Department. Please call me Mitch. My father, Dr. Knox, sent me," he said, walking around to the side of the bed where Jace sat. Jace was reluctant to let go of Colt's hand, but did, and for whatever reason, Mitch found it incredibly endearing.

"Jace Montgomery, thank you for coming." He could see the cringe in Jace's response. Years of doing this job had him guessing the cringe was the innate understanding that Mitch was about to ask all the same questions Jace had already answered, probably about a hundred times since entering this room. Mitch decided not to do that to the guy. The time would come when he had to ask questions, but not now. The police reports were enough.

Based on what he'd seen so far, Montgomery's answers never changed. He had no idea who did this, except to say Colt's father would never agree to their relationship. Mitch had also moved Jace over on the list. He was no longer a suspect, regardless of what the local authorities thought. Mitch had seen the grief in Jace's eyes. The look wasn't guilt, but straight up grief, and you didn't have that deep down sorrow if you caused the accident.

Enough said there.

"These are my guys out front. No one comes or goes without their approval. My father's on his way, he should be here in a couple of hours," Mitch said, standing behind Jace's chair, tucking his hands in his blue jean pockets.

"I noticed a couple of hours ago they went from being uniformed police to guys in suits. Thank you," Jace said, briefly glancing at him, before turning his attention back to Colt, stroking and holding the other man's hand.

"It's not a problem. What're they saying about him?" Mitch asked, nodding toward Colt.

"He needs another surgery. He's got some internal swelling. I guess it's your father they're waiting on. His doctors seem to have all changed too, but I'm not exactly sure." Mitch looked Colt over. He wasn't the worst he'd seen, but still pretty damn bad. Then he reexamined that thought. Those others he'd seen hadn't survived, and for whatever reason, Colt had. Some strong incentive had to have kept him alive under that badly abused body.

"It's hard getting answers, isn't it?"

"You have no idea," Jace said, looking back over his shoulder. There was a slight grin there, and Mitch watched Jace closer. He was an incredibly attractive man. Mitch felt sure the five o'clock shadow wasn't normally there. Jace's long, a little past the chin length blond hair looked disheveled, absently tied back with pieces shoved behind his ears. There was clearly a muscular sculpted body underneath those wrinkled clothes.

That kind of bulk took training. He himself spent hours a day in the gym to make his body hard. He could see why Colton Michaels might risk everything to be with the guy. Actually, he could see why Colt was fighting to stay alive, if their relationship was a love match like they seemed.

"I wanted to stop by and introduce myself before I head to the local police station. We've exercised our rights in this case, and based on its sensitive nature, everyone is under strict orders to stay quiet. We'll see how long that last."

"Good, thank you. I know Colt will appreciate the discretion."

"Hmmm," Mitch grunted. "We'll see." Usually wherever the leak came from, you could eventually find the perpetrator. The bad guys rarely kept these kinds of things quiet for long—bragging rights and all that. Mitch dug out his billfold and produced a business card. He handed it over Jace's shoulder. As the man took the card, Mitch placed a hand on his shoulder.

"You're as safe as you can be for now. Your whole concentration should be getting him well. My dad's top of the line, but if you need a second opinion, I can arrange that, too." Jace looked up again and smiled softly as their gazes connected and Mitch was once more taken a little aback by the look in Jace's eyes.

"You're gay?" Jace asked.

"I am," Mitch confirmed. Jace nodded, and those green eyes moved back to Colt, releasing Mitch from their intense grip.

"Good. He needs someone sympathetic on his side. He's just barely out."

"I figured. I'll be back in touch in a few hours. Take care, Jace," Mitch said, already making his way to the door.

"Thank you, Deputy Knox."

Thoughts of killing zombies didn't cross his mind as he left the hospital. Instead, his heart connected with the intense love he picked up inside the room. He never really thought love existed for people like him; at least, he hadn't ever experienced anything even remotely close.

In a matter of a few brief moments this went from a case of helping his dad out to wanting to help these two men. *Interesting.*

## Chapter 29

Jace sat perched on the chair, observing every single person who came through the room. He watched everything done and rarely asked any questions. There was a method to their maddening routine. It seemed to proceed like clockwork, only changing when the shift changed. If there was any foul play going on, Jace couldn't identify it.

Somewhere in the back of his mind, he let himself go, thinking all the terrible thoughts. He'd tried to keep those hidden, not letting them be seen by the staff. Jace needed to hold himself together for Colt. So thinking things like, *what if the next person in this room came back to finish Colt off* or *what if they came back to finish them both off*, couldn't be productive. Surely Colt's dad wouldn't be that aggressive, but as the minutes turned into hours, and the hours almost equaled a full day, reason lost some of its draw to Jace's overactive imagination.

Jace released the pent-up breath he held and started up again on the rolling dialog he performed when they were alone in the room. It kept the crazy thoughts buried and consisted of three things.

*Please get better.*

*Open your eyes.*

*Don't leave me.*

Realistically Jace understood Colt was heavily sedated. No way could he open his eyes even if he wanted too. But that didn't stop the insanity from spilling over, or his heart's desires to be said aloud. If Colt would open those eyes, Jace would know everything would be okay. Right?

The hospital room door opened. The smell of a new cologne caused Jace to look up, his gritty, tired eyes landed on a portly, older man. Not much more than five-six, maybe five-seven.

"I'm Dr. Knox, you must be Jace," the doctor said, already dressed in scrubs. He came to his side of the bed. Jace rose. He assumed the visible relief showed on his face as the doctor took his hand and reached around to pat Jace's back.

"Thank you for coming."

"This guy's come to mean a lot to me. I'm glad you called," Dr. Knox said. He rounded the bed again and did a small exam, looking Colt over.

"Your son stopped by," Jace blurted, filling the silence in the room as he closely watched each move the doctor made.

"I spoke to him while I was downstairs. I've been here a little while, reviewing his charts. I'm encouraged by what I'm seeing. I'm worried about the possibility of Compartment syndrome, though. He's got a small amount of swelling in this arm that's a bit of a concern from a nerve damage standpoint. He needs surgery, but it shouldn't take along. They're prepping now. With your approval, we'll be transporting him back to the mainland as soon as he's stable." The doctor never looked at Jace as he bent his head, surveying Colt's right arm.

"Do you think that's a good idea?" It made him nervous to have Colt on the same ground as his father.

"I'm encouraged, but concerned. His legs and right arm are pretty battered. It's going to take a lot to get him back on his feet. He needs the best care possible," Dr. Knox said, finally looking back up at Jace.

Jace nodded, knowing from a career standpoint none of this was good, but they weren't there yet. Colt's protection was Jace's first priority. Back in the states his father could easily step in and push them all away.

"I understand why you're worried. We've been working behind the scenes, taken significant steps to ensure both your safety. My son has committed to this case. It shouldn't take long for him to track the people down who did this. Mitch is cocky, but excellent at what he does. I promise we won't make one move until we've gone through him."

He still wasn't feeling any better about this, and he scrubbed a hand over his face.

"Son, at this point there are three people who know about this: you, me, and Mitch. The team hasn't been told. There are two very distinctly important issues. One, the two of you and your safety, and two, to get Colt the best possible care as quickly as possible. I made a call to a friend in Dallas. He's top in his field of orthopedic medicine and at hiding public figures. Colt will do well there." Dr. Knox didn't invite anymore questions. The man looked down at Colt's face. Something sad crossed the doctor's features before he turned to leave the room.

"Oh, by the way, you might not be aware that I've told them you two were married in New York last week. You're his legal guardian for the time being." The afterthought was said so casually, Jace had to rethink the words before they snuck in and relief staggered him. Those few simple words were exactly what they needed to fend Colt's father off.

"I need to go. I'm observing this surgery. I think Colt might want that; it's a sensitive procedure. I'll get him back to you as soon as possible. I promise to be with him the entire time." Dr. Knox left to be replaced by a frenzy of activity as a hospital gurney was pushed in the room, followed by several hospital staffers.

The new gurney was pushed to Colt's side and locked into place. The medical professionals worked like a well-oiled machine, but lifting Colt properly required all of them. They unhooked some of the machines while leaving others going and connected to Colt. They gently tugged and carefully pulled Colt until he slid from one bed to another. His arms and legs treated with the utmost care. Jace jumped in to help, working Colt over onto the gurney by supporting his feet.

He trailed along behind the crew, down the hospital corridor as long as he could. The minute came where he had to let Colt go to the operating room beyond the closed doors. They stopped momentarily, and he stole the moment to lean over and kiss Colt's lips.

"I'll be waiting on you," Jace whispered. He stood there, watching them bump open the swinging doors and disappear inside. As the doors swung closed, he got a glimpse of Dr. Knox scrubbed up and ready for the operating room. Good. Colt wouldn't be alone. Jace turned and found the ever present agents close by. They quietly followed him back to Colt's room to wait.

"It's definitely a cut. It looks like the locals did a pretty good sweep," Tommy Wagner said, clicking off his pen flashlight and rolling out from under the wrecked Prius. Tommy was head of the Crash Data Retrieval Department for US Marshal's Hawaiian field office. Mitch had worked with him for years. He knew his stuff, and if anything differed from what was reported, he'd find what no one else could. "It's professional and planned."

"It's what I thought, too. Either route to town would have had the brakes going at the worst possible time. Someone local has to be involved."

"It's hard to see, but the safety on this frame had to give before he rolled. I'd say he was hit from the driver's side of the vehicle. A precise hit, very intentional," Tommy said. His head was inside the vehicle now, his body arched through the small opening in the side window. The pen light flashed on, his eyes scanned the roof. Tommy didn't mention the dried blood on the door's frame and maneuvered his body farther inside. "Once it gave, it allowed the hood to give a little easier. The safety on the left side held. Interesting…"

"That's what the skid marks in the road show. I'd say someone sideswiped him at a high rate of speed. There was also evidence he was hit from behind."

"And he lived through this?" The pen light clicked off, and Tommy worked his body out of the window.

"Yeah. He's pretty fucked up, but yeah," Mitch said, standing back, watching Tommy work.

"Surprising."

"Tell me," Mitch said. When Tommy looked done, Mitch pulled his notepad out of his pocket and jotted down a few notes.

"Yeah, this is a professional. It was executed with precision," Tommy added, surveying the damage from outside the car. "Damn."

"Yeah. Who do you know around here that would do this?" The question didn't hurt to ask. He knew the answer, but maybe if he asked enough people, the answers might change.

"It could be any of them. Gangs, cartel, any trained mechanic that needed cash, shit, just pick one. Better question is who would have the money to pay someone to do this?" Tommy asked, playing the twenty questions game with skill. "Someone's pulling purse strings, somewhere."

"The best I can tell, about fifty percent of the trash in his life could pay with Colt's own money and would."

"Nice. Makes for a great family reunion. What's your next step?" Tommy asked, turning to Mitch.

"The locals are running everything through their database. They've assured me they're on it, interviewing and all that bullshit. I got some feelers out there, but no one's talking which at this point is pretty damn weird. Somebody's got to be bragging somewhere." Mitch flipped the small notepad over and tucked it back in his pocket.

"Unless it's cartel."

"Right."

"He had to have a pretty big mark on his head. Could this guy be on the island for reasons other than the standard vacay?" Mitch had wondered the same question himself and dug a little deeper, looking to see if Colt could be a seller, but he found nothing. Besides, the car was Jace Montgomery's rental, not Colt's. As crappy as Colt's human leech baggage looked, they didn't come off as killers. And from what he could find, Jace was squeaky clean. He ran a legit business dealing with children, and he seemed to take it seriously. Jace's bank accounts were loaded, his pockets past full grown, and his savings was huge. He didn't spend his money. Nothing in his background pinned this to him.

Besides, Mitch's gut told him this was some sort of hate crime. "I see that brain of yours ticking. I'll write this up using the name

John Doe. Let me know if you need anything else," Tommy said as he reached down, loading his toolbox.

"They have a second vehicle at their house. You might check it out when you have time," Mitch commented absently.

"Sure thing. Address on the report?" Tommy asked, standing and lugging his toolbox up with him.

"Yeah, thanks, Tommy," Mitch said.

"No problem, man." Tommy took off, but Mitch stayed right there, staring down at the mangled car. From this side, you couldn't even tell what kind of car Colt had driven. How did he survive this accident? At the very least, how had there been no severe brain damage? The roof crushed in around him. Mitch found his heart connected again. Damn, that never happened. Fuck! Two men finally found happiness and to have someone try to tear them apart so tragically. How much more would they have to endure? He guessed as much as it took. And they were dealt a shit load right here.

Pivoting on his heels, he walked to his truck, forcing the emotion out. He needed to help these guys. This wasn't just about his father anymore, but damn his dad had a way of finding the neediest ones to attach himself to, he was such a freaking do-gooder. That caused Mitch to grin. It was actually what made his father such a great man to him.

# Chapter 30

Exhaustion made everything that much more difficult. Jace rose from the hard plastic recliner and paced the small ICU room. He stretched his body, lifting his hands high in the air, feeling the tension cracking and popping before he bent over, reaching low. He let his head hang and closed his eyes. The stretch did wonders for his sore muscles. Jace lifted and rolled his shoulders, brushing his hair back off his face, retying the strands with the rubber band he'd swiped off the chart this morning. They were in day two, almost day three, of their hospital getaway, and Jace had barely left the room for more than a minute since he'd arrived. He could smell the days old stench on his body. He needed a shower and bad.

Jace's eyes lifted to the large clock above the hospital bed. He'd only burned about four minutes in his stretch. Damn. Jace's eyes landed back on Colt's battered face. None of the swelling had gone down. It was hard to look at him without wincing at what he must have gone through. He wondered if Colt had been afraid, or had his adrenaline pumped too fast to do much more than just experience the moment?

Colt needed to wake up and answer those questions. They were almost twelve hours from being taken off the heavy sedation medications and Colt hadn't budged. Jace had no idea what to expect, but he prayed for miracles. He wanted Colt to wake up. He wanted Colt to be difficult and ornery, insist he had this and try to get out of the hospital bed. It didn't happen that way. So now they waited. Much like every minute since he'd arrived, Jace waited and forced all his positive energy to Colt, willing him to wake.

In Jace's reasonable mind, he understood Colt should sleep, but if he could get even just a second of Colt looking at him, telling him everything would be okay... That was all he needed, because this waiting thing was hell, and the idea of starting day three sent panicked shivers springing up on his arms.

"I need a shower," Jace said to Colt. "Really bad, I stink to high heaven." He'd kept a steady stream of communication going between them. Jace's normal demeanor kept him generally quiet, rolling with whatever came his way. Not in this. He'd probably talked more in the last three days than he had in the last twenty years.

"I need you to wake up, Colt. I can't shower with you in this bed like this. Please wake up," Jace pleaded, swinging his arms back and forth, side to side, walking closer to the bed.

"If you'll wake up, we can rethink your idea about the future. I know your doctor's making plans for you. I don't know exactly what they are, but whatever he decides will be okay. If you have to go back to New York for your care, I'll be there if you want me to, or I can stay in Texas. We'll figure it out. I'll be wherever you want me. Just wake up. Please, wake up." Jace walked up to Colt's right side, the most broken and battered side of his body. He didn't touch Colt, didn't jostle the bed, but leaned over the gurney and placed a simple kiss on Colt's lips.

"Please wake up, Colton. I need you." There was nothing, not even a twitch of his eye, and Jace sighed before saying another prayer. *Please God, get him through this.*

Hours later Dr. Knox entered the room, Mitch following right behind him. Jace pushed himself out of the chair and shoved the fallen pieces of his hair behind his ear. He vowed right then he was cutting his hair as soon as possible.

"He hasn't come around, yet," Jace said as he made his way to the end of the bed. There were no polite pleasantries, no coddling. The panic Jace felt prickled at him. He needed answers.

"It's normal. These things take time. We've arranged to have Colt transported to Dallas." Dr. Knox said, not letting Jace fire off all the questions he had.

"Are you certain that's a good idea?" Jace crossed his arms over his chest, narrowing his eyes at the doctor. Dallas was better than New York, but still close enough for his father to try to intervene.

"I believe it's our best option for now," Dr. Knox answered. Mitch was all but forgotten as he stood a couple of feet behind his father, listening to the conversation, not participating. "The orthopedic surgeon in Dallas happens to be a close friend of mine. He's the best in his field and my preferred choice for Colt's care," Dr. Knox said.

"Thank you for everything you've done for him." He battled with this decision. No matter how Jace played it out in his mind, he worried about Colt's father, but on the other hand, he was grateful to know Colt would at least be close to him while he recovered.

"Does that mean there's no word on who did this?" Jace questioned, his gaze shooting up to Mitch's. He stood tall, and solidly built much like an immovable object he so clearly put out into the world. His dark eyes and deeply tanned handsome face bore straight into Jace as he spoke.

"No, nothing, and on an island this size, if anyone knew anything, they'd be bragging by now. There hasn't been a peep. Colt's rental at the house hasn't been touched. All the ground work has led us to a big, fat nothing. We're gonna have to restart an investigation when we get back to the mainland. There's no choice," Mitch said. He stayed back, spoke quietly, and matched Jace's stance.

"If you do that, won't it draw attention to Colt?" Jace asked. He glanced over to the bed before shifting his focus to the doctor. How could they protect him on the mainland if they didn't know who was responsible?

"As the team physician, it's within our rights to direct his care, but Mitch's pulled some strings." Mitch stepped closer to Jace and handed him a grocery sack. Jace took an envelope out of a Wal-Mart shopping bag. He juggled the bag, until he dropped it and opened the manila envelope, pulling out several documents, one being a New York State marriage license. It took Jace a minute to understand both his and Colt's name were signed across the bottom.

"I've looked into Colt's background. He needs you to be involved in his care, Jace. There's nothing but backstabbing, money grubbing sons of bitches everywhere he turns. It could have been anyone in his camp. They're all shady," Mitch said as he bent and picked up the shopping bag, pulling out a new pair of athletic shorts and T-shirt.

"How's he gonna feel about this?" Jace asked the first question that came to mind. He held a marriage license, tying Colt to him, and the paper looked authentic as hell.

"Once he wakes, he can make his own decisions. For now, this protects him." Dr. Knox smiled and inclined his head in Colt's direction.

"I also brought you a change of clothes. You need to go shower and find something solid to eat. Now go, everything will be okay." Mitch reached out and hugged him, giving him a couple of pats on the back. "I'll watch things in—" Mitch was cut off.

"He's mine. And as soo…" A gruff voice hissed in a breath. Surprised, they all turned toward Colt. He was staring at them, his eyes were open, not much more than slits, but they were open. "Fuck! Soon as I get my body moving, I'm kickin' your ass." Colt finally managed to get the words out between labored breaths. His voice was hoarse and weak. Also about the sexiest thing Jace had ever heard, and he was the first one to Colt's bedside.

"You're awake," Jace said, a smile broke across his face as he moved closer to the bed, grinning down at Colt.

"I can't move to kick his ass," Colt muttered, his eyes on Jace. "Help me get up."

"You have to stop moving and lay still. You've been in an accident. You're hurt," Jace warned. Colt didn't listen and kept struggling, so he carefully placed his hand on Colt's chest to keep him still.

"Colton, stop moving, son," Dr. Knox scolded, his deep voice held authority. That caught Colt's attention, and he stopped fighting, turning his head toward the doctor.

"Where am I?" Colt's voice cracked, along with his lips, and he tried to swipe his tongue across them, but it was too dry to do much.

"You're in a hospital in Hawaii. You had an automobile accident," Dr. Knox said. Jace grabbed the cup with a straw. Colt took a couple of solid pulls from the straw and gave another loud groan.

"That explains why my head hurts so fuckin' bad," Colt said and took another sip when Jace put the straw back in his mouth.

Colt's eyes landed on Mitch. He pushed the straw out of his mouth and narrowed his brow. Okay, maybe he didn't narrow his brow. It was hard to tell with the condition of his face.

"I'm kickin' your ass."

"I welcome the opportunity," Mitch grinned at Colt and remained standing at the foot of the bed.

"Colt, this is my son, Mitch. He's a Deputy US Marshal over the investigation of your accident."

"Shit," Colt began but didn't finish. His eyes closed and he was back asleep in a matter of seconds. As they all registered he'd truly fallen asleep, Colt woke suddenly again, his eyes connecting with Jace's before he closed them again to sleep. The strain of the last few days lifted. Jace gently took Colt's hand, being careful to keep his arm still, just like he'd done so many times over the last few days. The exhaustion of moments ago already faded as he looked down at his battered, bruised Colt. The injuries just seemed so much better with Colt responding.

"I'll get the nurse," Mitch said, leaving them. Jace looked over at the doctor. He seemed visibly relieved too. *Thank you, God!*

## Chapter 31

Colt lay in the hospital bed, his eyes glued to Jace. He'd been moved from ICU to his own private room, and from what he'd been told, he had a really nice view of the ocean. Not that it did Colt any good. On the positive side, at least his visitors didn't have to stare at boring white walls. He based that on his new glass half full attitude he'd taken on since he realized he couldn't even scratch his own ass without help. Not good. Accept on the positive side, Jace planned to scratch Colt's ass for him, and really now, could that be considered a bad thing?

Besides his obvious problems, Colt only had limited options available to keep his mind occupied. Another half full deal, Jace provided enough entertainment to occupy him for hours. Currently, Jace prattled on about something, who knew what, like he'd done pretty much since Colt first woke. After a minute more of pretending to listen, Colt put his lips together and blew, trying to make a helicopter sound. Score! He totally caught Jace off guard. He glanced up, confused.

"What?" Jace stopped, tucking the sheet around Colt's newly casted legs and looked up at him.

"You're hovering," Colt said, lifting an eyebrow. It was a challenge. One he hoped might get Jace back to the top of the bed, kissing him, and telling him how worried he'd been.

"I'm not hovering. I'm taking care of you. Big difference." Jace huffed and went back to his task of making sure Colt was all tucked in and wasn't too cold. Then would come the task of making sure Colt wasn't thirsty, then hungry, and then back to being too cold.

"I don't need taking care of," Colt retorted, laughing at the look Jace gave him. He did have to admit he needed some tender, loving, care, but what he needed and wanted were two different things. Jace still hadn't moved closer to kiss Colt, and damn he'd become a girl, but he wanted all those whispered sweet love words said to him while he was awake. Not just sleeping, like Jace seemed to do.

"I could use a kiss," Colt suggested and puckered his wet lips.

"You're trying to divert me," Jace said, picking up the small cup of ice water, anchoring the straw in just the right position against his lips. Colt took a sip and pushed the straw out of his mouth before he pursed his lips again. The corners of Jace's mouth curled into a smile. He relented and leaned across Colt, giving him a quick kiss. Jace looked deeply in his eyes, gave a small smile, and ran the pad of his thumb down Colt's cheek in a soft caress. Colt loved that move the most. His heart stirred. No wondered he'd turned into such a love-sick girl, his prince was just too perfect.

"We need to figure out what Mitch needs to do to reverse the marriage certificate. You can make your own decisions now," Jace said absently, carefully sitting on the side of the bed, a bowl of broth balanced in his hand. He lifted a spoonful to Colt's mouth. He had no choice but to open for the cold chicken soup.

"Why do we need to change it?" Colt asked after swallowing the first spoonful. Jace wasted no time in bringing a second spoonful to Colt's lips. He immediately opened. He learned earlier, when he'd tried not opening for Jace he ended up wearing the soup. Jace would then go nuts, trying to clean him up without causing pain, which was pretty impossible to do.

Apparently, his question earned him silence from his now chatty Jace. So much so things turned slightly awkward between them. What did that mean?

"We can leave it like it is, right?" Colt tried approaching the subject again before opening his mouth wide, encouraging Jace to participate in the feeding. Jace continued to sit there, staring at him. After a minute, Jace mechanically lifted the spoon and put the broth to his lips. Colt forced the bland liquid down. Cold chicken broth wasn't on his list of favorite culinary delights and tasted worse when his boyfriend didn't want to stay married to him. Damn.

"Isn't a commitment what you wanted when you were leaving me?" Colt asked and tried to shift his position so he could see Jace's face without straining his neck.

"I wasn't leaving you," Jace said.

"Really? I definitely think notes of goodbye forever and don't contact me again constitute as leaving me," Colt said, arching his brow. Jace scoffed, and Colt couldn't help the chuckle or the immediate curse when his ribs made sure he knew how much they disliked the movement the laughter caused.

"You deserve that, mister." Jace smiled and continued watching him closely. "I guess I'd prefer a marriage not to be decided for you. You were forced into it," Jace said, placing the bowl back on the tray and lifting the water glass back to his mouth. Jace angled the straw between his lips. Again, he was given no choice but to drink.

"Bring the hospital chaplain in. I'll marry you right now," Colt shot back, and just like he'd done about twenty-five times already today, Jace stood and began re-tucking the sheet back around Colt's body.

"You're not thinking right. You had a major traumatic accident four days ago. Your mind's clouded and medicated, and you're basing your decisions on events, not emotion," Jace explained, reasonably.

Colt watched him for a couple of long moments. He hated he couldn't get up and shake some sense into Jace. Even more frustrating, he needed to have this conversation face to face, not while lying flat on his back.

The doctor cast both his legs and his left arm earlier this morning, but his right arm was still wrapped and immobilized in a semi-cast. More surgeries were needed before the actual cast could be set. The gravity of the breaks to his throwing arm seemed to become a dark cloud looming over everyone who entered the hospital room. It didn't weigh on Colt, though. He knew the odds were stacked solidly against being ready for football season this year, and if he wasn't ready, he wouldn't have to leave Jace for all those months. Colt couldn't convince himself that was a bad thing.

"Babe, look at me," Colt said. Jace kept his head turned away, obviously pretending to busy himself. "Jace, I'm serious, look at me," Colt tried again.

Jace finally stopped, rose from fixing the sheets, and looked over at Colt. The raw emotion pouring from Jace's gaze caught Colt by surprise. The clear sentiment reflected in his eyes caused Colt to take a sharp breath. They were exactly on the same page. Just as Colt's heart lurched, so did his ribs, making him instantly regret the extra draw of air. Jace came back to the front of the bed, concerned about his discomfort, and the sweet gesture sealed the deal for Colt.

"Baby, it's not spur of the moment, and I'm thinking just fine. I've loved you since the first time I laid eyes on you. We've already wasted too much time. Jace Montgomery, be mine forever. Marry me on our terms before we leave this island," Colt implored. He couldn't pull Jace to him, he couldn't even get out of this damn bed and fall on one knee and ask Jace properly. All he could hope was that Jace would see the sincerity in his eyes and believe him.

"Just say yes. If I could move, I'd hold you, kiss you, beg you to say yes. Please, go find the chaplain and let's do this thing, right now. I don't want to destroy that marriage certificate. I want it to be real. I want to marry you. I want to say the words 'I do' in front of witnesses."

"If you get back to the states and want out, I won't hold it against you," Jace replied softly, still right up in his face, exactly where Colt wanted him to be.

"Noted, now go get the chaplain, please. Tell him we have the marriage license, and now we want a ceremony. And call the nurse in here for me. Fuck! I hate being so useless," Colt cursed his predicament. He'd gotten his agreement. Now all he needed was a little help from someone other than Jace, and he stared helplessly at the call button, willing the device to ring the nurse. Clearly his mental telepathy needed fine-tuning. He finally lifted his heavily casted left arm, intent on reaching out for the button.

"What do you think you're doing?" Jace was right on him, pushing the button and tucking the covers back in around him.

"You go find the chaplain. I want the nurse to help me with my hair. I don't wanna marry you with bed head." That had Jace stopping in his tracks and glancing in his direction. The look on Jace's face was comical.

"You look fine to me, pretty boy," Jace responded with wink.

"Go, you're stalling," Colt barked and then gave him a grin. The nurse came through the door as Jace started to exit.

"Did you call?" The nurse looked from one to the other while carrying a small tray of his medicines into the room.

"I did. Jace, go!" Colt waited until Jace left the room before filling the nurse in on everything he had in mind. Her eager expression meant it might all actually work out!

Colt was barely cleaned and medicated before Jace came back through the hospital room door. He was smiling, talking, and laughing out loud at something someone behind him must have said. The last twenty-four hours of strain had magically faded away, leaving Jace looking years younger and devastatingly handsome. Colt was instantly taken with Jace, but again, Jace had always captured him body and soul. Colt couldn't take his eyes off the man he loved. He was drawn to that smile, and even through the haze of medication, he felt his heart connect and his body stir. He loved Jace more than life itself. It was turning out to be a great day for a wedding.

Colt realized right then he'd give up everything, give his own life, to keep Jace safe. Thank God, he'd been in that car instead of Jace. The relief was staggering. He struggled to breathe even considering he may not have made it to Jace before he left the house that morning. The panic of the thought resolved his body's stirring problem with a large dose of reality. Another big thank God! It wouldn't do to have the hospital sheet tenting with a minister in the room.

"So this is who had me stopping everything to come to this room? He told me you were dying; you needed your last rites. You don't look like you're knocking on death's door." The minister's voice boomed, and he chuckled at his own joke. His smile was equally as big as Jace's, and he walked around Jace to the right side of Colt's bed. Jace took his usual spot on the left. This time Colt reached out to take Jace's hand in his own.

"Is it safe for you to be up like this?" Jace asked, worry creasing his brow. Colt's nurse had lifted the head of his bed at a better angle, not quite sitting, but up more, positioning his arms carefully under layers of pillows.

"Jace hovers," Colt deadpanned to the minister.

"He needs to hover. You were badly injured," the minister said. Colt could tell the minister wanted to reach out and pat him, but he stopped in mid-motion, rejecting the idea.

Colt had gotten his hair tamed and his teeth brushed, but the bruising was still dominant. He knew he was a sight, but what else could he do? He couldn't help the yawn that slipped out, either. He was exhausted and the medication the nurse had given him made it even worse.

"He was injured badly, and he overdoes." Jace seemed to clutch on to the ministers words, gave Colt a look, and nodded, no doubt in total agreement with the minister. Jace was such a mother hen. Colt made a show of rolling his eyes.

"I understand I'm needed to perform a marriage ceremony. Is that right?" The chaplain broke the silence.

"Yes, sir," Colt said. His voice was strong, clear, and decisive. He hoped Jace heard it that way.

"And you were married before this? You understand this is not a legal ceremony?" the minster asked, looking between Jace and Colt. He was serious now.

"Yes, sir," they both answered in unison. There was a knock at the door and the nurse came through the doorway, followed by others from ICU, all holding bouquets of flowers.

"Perfect timing," Colt grinned, tightening his hold on Jace's hand. "It wasn't much, but I asked her to buy whatever was appropriate from the gift store." The nurses placed the flowers everywhere. Happy faces regarded him curiously, including Jace's. No one looked like they wanted to leave.

"Thank you," Jace leaned in and gave Colt a soft peck in front of others. Colt beamed like a man in love, which technically hit the mark.

"You're our favorite patient," one of the ICU nurses said, shrugging, taking a step back, clearly ready to watch the ceremony.

"I'm good with you staying. Are you good with it?" Colt asked, glancing at Jace.

"I am," Jace said.

"Well, that's good, because you didn't see us asking, did you?" That caused a laugh and the chaplain wasted no more time. It took about five minutes of happy emotional overload before Colt got to say his "I do" and have Jace say the words back, and then he got to kiss his groom. The clapping only penetrated after Colt slid his tongue over Jace's lips, gained entrance, and was retreating. Jace pulled away with a blush while Colt grinned ear to ear.

"My husband," Colt sighed, his focus fixed on only one person in the room. Yeah, like he was ever going to be able to hide Jace away from anyone. What had he even been thinking saying something as dumb as that. Besides, regardless of Colt's past, he believed in the sanctity of the union and planned to stay married to Jace for the rest of his life. Thank God Dr. Knox intervened in his life again. "I love saying those words."

"I love hearing those words." Jace leaned down and brushed his lips softly across his. The cheering started again as everyone congratulated them. Over the next few hours, Colt thought the entire hospital staff might have stopped by. Dinner consisted of two fully packed cafeteria trays, with two large pieces of white cake for each of them.

While they ate dinner Mitch stopped by. He came as part of the investigation, doing a full question and answer session with Colt. He wanted every detail of the accident, but Colt wasn't a huge help. Most of the accident was just still too blurry to remember. He knew there had been a male in the truck who drove him off the road, but he couldn't identify the face in his mind. Mitch never pushed him or got frustrated and truly believed the information would all come back to Colt in time. He seemed willing to wait. Mitch sat there, quietly talking to them when his father entered the room sometime later.

"Everyone's buzzing about this room," Dr. Knox said from the door. He walked to the bedside, grinning.

"He married me," Colt said, stifling a yawn. He was tired, exhausted really, and the yawn won out. Hearing a noise in the hallway, Colt turned his attention toward the open doorway and groaned when he spotted another nurse entering his room, carrying a tray full of medicine.

"Here we go," she said cheerfully, going through the motions of entering his medicines into a computer as she handed each one to him.

"I'm glad for you two, but I think you overdid today," Dr. Knox said as he started to examine Colt. The doctor pulled a pen light from his pocket and shined it in Colt's eyes.

"He did!" both the nurse and Jace said in agreement.

"Hey," Colt started, but the nurse shoved the last pill in his mouth, silencing him.

"You'll be asleep soon with that one, sweetie," she said with a smile. Colt could almost see her and Jace doing a mental high five.

"Good, he needs to sleep," Jace piped in. "I keep trying to remind Mr. Hardhead that he was just in a really bad automobile accident."

"You should go home to sleep," Colt said, ignoring them all as he looked over at Jace and gave him a nod to affirm his statement, before giving in to another yawn.

"I'm not going home," Jace protested, shaking his head.

"I'm with Colt on this one, Jace. We have a flight scheduled at six in the morning," Dr. Knox said.

"Did you talk to the team?" Colt asked, changing the subject.

"I did. I've spent most of the day on the phone with them and the medical staff in Dallas, preparing for your arrival."

"How did they take it?" Colt asked. He wasn't near as concerned about his medical care as he was the attitude. He needed to know what faced him when he returned to the mainland.

"As well as expected," Dr. Knox said, leaving everything right there, not offering anything more. For Jace's worrywart sake, Colt didn't ask further. He could read between those lines. The owners of the team couldn't have been pleased with any of this, especially the impending investigation of Colt's accident, all right after their big Super Bowl win. Colt figured they questioned whether his alcoholism played a part in the crash. It had to be assumed he'd been drunk driving during the accident. Damn, why hadn't he considered that before now? Colt didn't voice any of his concerns, instead he turned toward Jace.

"Doc, tell him to go home and get some rest," he said, tightening his grip on Jace's hand, but Jace wouldn't look at him.

"Jace, I'm not going to tell you what to do, but I did take the liberty to ask Mitch to arrange secured transportation for you to go home, pack, close up your beach house. I can stay with Colt while you're gone," Dr. Knox offered.

"That's a great point. We don't know when we'll be back. And you could sleep a few hours," Colt suggested again. He could feel his eyes already drooping, the drugs taking effect. It had been a big day. A wonderful day, probably too big for his injuries, but he'd married the man of his dreams.

"It would be easier if we could leave from here in the morning," Dr. Knox offered. Colt nodded and his eyes slipped closed. After a minute, he managed to pop them open again.

"Sleep, Colt. If you're certain you can stay, I'll go get our stuff together and lock up the house, but I'll be back soon." Jace leaned in for a kiss and tenderly brushed a strand of hair off Colt's forehead; Jace held his position and remained right in his face. "I love you."

"I love you." Colt kissed Jace again and then grinned. "My husband," he whispered. He tried to put up a valiant fight, but he couldn't hold his eyes open any longer.

"I wanted Mitch to destroy the marriage license," Jace said immediately to both of them while he covered Colt up.

"I didn't think he'd do it," Dr. Knox said, taking a seat on the long sofa Jace had called home since they had arrived in this room.

"No, but he's not thinking right. I won't hold him to it," Jace said, busying himself with cleaning up their dinner plates. He wouldn't make eye contact with either Mitch or Dr. Knox. There were too many conflicting emotions rolling through him, and he pushed them all aside. This wasn't about him, only about Colt. Nothing mattered in how he felt about anything. At this point, they were all about Colt and his recovery. No way would he do anything to cause resentment between them, yet if he forced this marriage, it most definitely would.

"I think he's done with that other world, without you it holds nothing for him. He loves you. And he knows the deal, and he seems fine with it," Mitch quietly said, rising, fishing the keys out of his jeans.

"What's that deal?" Jace asked, and for the first time, turned to Dr. Knox.

"It would be speculating at this point," Dr. Knox said, staring him directly in the eyes.

"Please speculate then. I need to know what to prepare for. Colt certainly won't tell me until it's gotten too out of hand," Jace said, moving to stand in front of Dr. Knox.

"Well, I'm sure New York's already been on the phone with their second string quarterback, going through everything trying to find an angle to take on someone new. Public relations is already on overload with his drinking and partying, not to mention his last highly televised relationship. Public records will show him married to you for a couple of weeks now. So he's a recovering alcoholic with a sorted past and now a homosexual," Dr. Knox said, finally rising to stand in front of Jace. Mitch came to his side. All of them spoke in hushed tones so not to bother Colt.

"This investigation will filter through every part of their organization. I'm taking this personal, and I don't have any filters. It's gonna be a lot for Colt to bounce back from. They'll stand by him for a while, Jace. Maybe indefinitely if he keeps his nose clean and does what he is supposed to do," Mitch said.

"And if he doesn't, they'll do away with him? Get rid of the *drunken fag* in other words?" Jace scoffed.

"We aren't there yet. Nowhere even remotely close, and if we get there, it won't be his sexual preferences that remove him from the team," Dr. Knox said, and Jace just stared at the doctor. He hadn't considered any of this.

"Come on. Let's get your shit. The sooner we go, the sooner you'll be back," Mitch said.

"I won't be gone long," Jace said to the doctor. He felt around in his jeans, found his keys and phone as he followed Mitch out of the hospital room. For the first time since arriving, he remembered the gym and mentally chastised himself.

"What's today?" Jace asked. He palmed his phone, opened the screen, and scrolled to Haley's number.

"It's Sunday," Mitch answered, keeping his pace beside Jace as they left the hospital.

"He has me all messed up," Jace said, sending a quick message to Haley. The gym was back open tomorrow for business. She'd be handling the classes and cheerleaders by herself. How had he not thought to let her know?

"Newly married men usually feel that way," Mitch said and bumped Jace in the shoulder. "I think I should look into a side business of selling marriage licenses to partners of unsuspecting men. I bet I'd make a killing."

"It didn't happen that way," Jace said, looking up panicked.

"I'm just giving you a hard time, man." Mitch chuckled and hit the outside doors to the hospital, opening them for Jace. All the teasing stopped right then. Mitch went from easygoing guy to deputy in the blink of an eye. Jace felt safer than he had in his entire life.

# Chapter 32

Nothing about the flight back to the mainland was easy, mainly because Jace fretted over everything, worse than any mother hen Colt had ever seen. As a matter of fact, his normally level-headed, quiet, roll with whatever's tossed his way Jace wouldn't settle down for a minute. Jace only took his seat and buckled in after the flight attendant's third most stern look. Even then, Jace kept his eyes on Colt the entire time, from takeoff till landing.

Almost from the time he had opened his eyes after having this accident, Colt learned to hide any discomfort from Jace. If his brow lowered a centimeter, Jace was right there, stopping everyone from their duties until he could see for himself that Colt was okay. A really sweet gesture. Sort of.

Turning less sweet with each mile that passed. There were two sides to how Colt felt about his overprotective honey. One, he'd never been so completely cared for in his life. Jace took care of him like he'd always wanted someone too. He was attentive, and considerate, on top of his medicine and every one of his needs. The other side had Colt wanting to cuss up a streak.

His pain levels were at an all-time high and his attitude low as they drove through the streets of Dallas, Texas. Between the pressures of hiding the pain from Jace and his inability to move, he constantly bit his tongue. His only recourse was to voluntarily take the drugs he'd been denying himself, which just made Jace unreasonably happy.

The funny part was Dr. Knox had his medicines ready. There was no pulling bottles, checking doses. The pills were in his hands, waiting for Colt to give in. Clearly, Dr. Knox could see how Jace acted and actually whispered to Colt that he held out longer than Dr. Knox would have in the same situation.

Mitch rode with them the entire trip. The guy stayed in full official enforcer of the law mode. He didn't crack a smile or chat the entire way. He stayed focused and vigilant. He took this seriously and for some reason that bothered Colt the most. If Mitch was so worried, did he fear another attack? Was there something Mitch knew about the accident that he wasn't telling them?

The Dallas Broncos finagled things to where Colt was going into his rivalry team's camp to hide. The team spared no expense in providing care for Colt. They gave him the best hospitals with the best staff and most up-to-date equipment, and all while almost no one knew Colt Michaels was on the premises. The privacy wouldn't hold, but every extra minute Mitch had to continue the investigation in private was better for them.

Other than the hovering new husband, Colt's intense pain, the investigation, and the hiding, the other big white elephant in the room had to do with how extensive his injuries were. Colt would work hard, do everything they said to do, but he knew this next season was a wash for him. His right arm was shot. It was too badly broken. He'd be going under the knife again in the morning to place all the screws and rods just right. The operation would last hours, mending three solid breaks along just that arm.

In Colt's mental, never to breathe out loud again, estimation, the Compartment syndrome was the final nail in his throwing arm's coffin. At best case scenario, he was faced with many, many months just to get his arm back to functional. There could be a random miracle and Colt would work for it, but he wasn't delusional. He knew the odds were stacked against him.

Since he was a man in love, even to a protective mothering type, Colt never had time to get too far down. He had actually taken on the full attitude of being thankful he had been in that car, not Jace. His entire attitude focused on live, laugh, love Jace Montgomery, and keeping him safe was paramount in his overall plan.

Besides, that cheerleading gym was Jace's life. For him to be incapacitated, and so solidly out of the day to day operations, would have done damage to the gym's reputation and crushed everything he'd worked so hard to achieve. The idea of Jace being hurt caused Colt to want to drink again on a level he'd never experienced before. He absolutely couldn't take even the thought of Jace hurt. In Colt's estimation, things had worked out the way they were supposed to work out.

"Babe, you're locked in. We have to lift you," Jace said, pulling Colt from his thoughts. He was right in Colt's line of vision; Jace's concern visible on his face but his eyes held so much compassion and tenderness Colt could easily lose himself in them.

"I love your eyes," Colt responded. Jace's cheeks turned red, and his gaze darted up to the two Medical City staffers who stood by to help Colt into the bed.

"He's on pain meds," Jace immediately spoke up, tucking his arms under Colt's torso and almost lifting him onto the bed himself. Jace moved him with care, but the pain became too much for even the medicine to help and Colt hissed.

"Goddamn motherfucker," Colt yelled out into the room, his body recoiling as he tried to move away from the agony. Dr. Knox picked that moment to enter the room with a new doctor in tow and Mitch trailing close behind them. Mitch chuckled as Dr. Knox ran to the bed to help Colt.

"Shit, Doc, they're trying to kill me!" Colt said once he was in bed. He pulled in a slow measured breath, calming himself as the pain started to dull. Laying his head back against the pillow, he closed his eyes. Jace was right there, fussing over him again. Colt could smell his cologne, but never looked at him. He needed the minute to gather himself.

"We can give you more pain medicine, Colt. You aren't taking enough," Jace said, gently lifting Colt's legs to get the blanket up around him.

"Jace, I need some water," Colt said. He kept his eyes closed, not wanting to look at anyone in the room. He hated being so helpless.

"Okay, ice water?" Jace asked, moving around to the other side of the bed.

"Yes, ice water," Colt said, thinking he would take longer to find both ice and water. He finally opened his eyes to see Jace staring down at him, apprehension etched all over his face.

"I'll be right back," Jace finally said, turning to Dr. Knox. "You'll stay?"

"Of course. Mitch, go with him, show him around." Colt prayed that meant, show him the furthest ice machine away. Colt wanted a minute alone with the doctors.

"Sure thing, Pops."

"Remember, I'll kick your ass," Colt tossed out halfheartedly at Mitch. He was really starting to like the guy.

"Waiting... Bring it," Mitch said over his shoulder, laughing as they left the room.

"Colt, this is Dr. Hauser, he's your new orthopedist," Dr. Knox said, coming closer to the bed. Dr. Hauser could be Dr. Knox's twin. He was older, white-headed, and just had that scholarly look about him. The look always made Colt feel like his care was in good hands, but he didn't have time for that right now. He needed answers.

"Hi, Mr. Michaels, I'm sure sorry to hear about all this—"

"We don't have long, Jace'll be back soon. Do we have a plan? I know this can't be good." Colt cocked his head toward his right arm.

"With surgery and rehab, you have a chance." Dr. Hauser looked down patiently.

"What kind of chance?" Colt went straight to the bottom line.

"I'd say with lots of work you have a good chance."

"Give me the numbers," Colt said, clearly getting frustrated. These minutes without Jace were rare. No time to be pussyfooting around the truth!

"Fifty-fifty," Dr. Hauser shot back.

"Really, that good? I wouldn't have thought so," Colt said, thinking over the answer.

"Colt..." Dr. Knox began.

"No, really, I'm thinking an injury like this might be a small miracle to recover from and still continue to play," Colt said, looking from doctor to doctor.

"We're going to do everything in our power to get you where you need to be. You're young and strong, Colt. Let's take this day by day. I'll be upfront with you, and you stay upfront with me," Dr. Hauser said, effectively navigating around the issue.

"I don't want Jace to know how bad it is. We need to talk when he's not here. He's already blaming himself. I don't like it," Colt said. He wasn't certain Jace blamed himself, he hadn't come out and said it, but he knew how Jace thought. Okay, so yes, thinking from Jace's viewpoint, he'd most definitely be blaming himself.

"Jace already knows your condition," Dr. Knox began again, but stopped as the door opened and Jace came in carrying ice, a pitcher of water, and several empty disposable cups. Mitch was a couple of steps behind him, shrugging as he came through the door. It was a guy code shrug, one that said he had tried to keep Jace gone but wasn't successful. Jace moved quickly, pouring Colt water and positioning everything close to his bed.

"It's tap water, I can get bottled water when you're resting," Jace said, hovering again.

"I'm gonna sleep now," Colt said.

"I'll see you two in the morning. Right now it looks like we'll put that arm back together tomorrow afternoon. We'll discuss those plans more in the morning. Rest tonight, you got a long road ahead of you," Dr. Hauser said. He nodded and shook Dr. Knox's hand before leaving.

"Guys, I'm heading back to New York in the morning. I'm needed there when they brief the team. We're also going to have to tell your father. Coach Atkins and I talked about it, thought we might drive out to his place tomorrow after the meeting, before word gets out. Mitch will be coming with us. He wants to question your father. I'll be back by the weekend to check on you, Colt," Dr. Knox said.

"I don't want my old man here at all," Colt specified. He was as convinced as Jace of his father's involvement.

"We're going to let him know he's restricted, pending the completion of the investigation. By the morning, a restraining order will be issued. I'll put it in his hands myself," Mitch stated, a smug grin lit his face by the end of the statement. Mitch gave an exaggerated wink toward the room, making sure everyone knew he was looking forward to that exchange.

"He doesn't have to know where I am, right?" Colt asked.

"Of course not. We'll tell him about your desire to have him stay away," Dr. Knox assured him. Colt knew if the team backed him, they could flex their muscles, and that alone was bigger than anything he could do on his own.

"I also have someone on this door. None of that changes," Mitch added.

"Can I pay to have someone on Jace? Is that possible?" Colt asked.

"I've taken care of it."

Colt nodded at Mitch, reassured by his answer, before flipping his head straight to Jace.

"I want you to go home, too. Get some rest." It took a second for Jace to realize Colt spoke to him, then he immediately started shaking his head no.

"I wanna stay here with you."

"You haven't slept in days," Colt scolded. He knew if he wasn't firm, Jace would drive himself right into the ground.

"Yes, I have," Jace shot back. The exhaustion on his face gave a completely different answer.

"No, you need to go home. Mitch, can you get him home?" Colt shot out.

"Of course, I can..." Colt totally got this was one of those relationship moments where you weren't sure who to side with.

"It's for the best, Jace. I'll sleep better knowing you're sleeping tonight. Get your car and come back tomorrow."

"Colt," Jace began.

"No, I'm serious, Jace. You were supposed to be home yesterday. You have a business and life here. You have to get back to it. Come back tomorrow, but rest tonight. Check in at the gym. You have Worlds coming up. They need you. You deserve to take it all this year," Colt said.

Jace was silent as recognition dawned and Colt grinned. "I told you, I've followed your life. I know what's going on in it."

That earned Colt a kiss, right on the lips, and he loved they were past the point of caring who saw them.

"All right, but just because it'll be better to have my car. If you can't get me home, I can call Haley," Jace said to Mitch.

"No, I'm heading out. I can take you now."

"Take your medicine. I'll be back as soon as I can," Jace advised and tucked his covers, making sure Colt was settled before he took off.

"Remember, he's taken. And I'll kick your ass," Colt called out as a nurse entered the room. He knew Mitch was harmless, but he still hated the fact Mitch was such a good-looking guy, leaving with his own good-looking guy.

"Blah, blah, blah," Mitch teased, sliding his arm across Jace's shoulder and giving Colt a parting wink before the door closed behind him.

"Doc, your son needs a spanking. I know you raised him better than that," Colt joked with Dr. Knox.

Chapter 33

"You're good at reading people. Is he trying to protect me or push me away?" Jace finally asked about halfway to his house on the ride home. Until then, he and Mitch had stayed relatively quiet.

"Definitely the first one," Mitch said. "He's worried about you."

Jace let Mitch's words sink in, trying to convince himself he spoke the truth. And if that were the truth, Jace wanted to go straight back to the hospital. If it wasn't the truth, then Jace needed to give Colt space. Damn, what should he do?

"He doesn't blame you. It wasn't your fault," Mitch said, never taking his eyes from the road.

"Someone cut my brake lines, so yeah, it was meant for me. His dad hates me. I made Colt call him." There Jace said it, and his eyes stayed focused on the dash.

"It's an open investigation, Jace. I can't really talk about it. But here's my problem. You definitely have that whole angle of his fucked up dad. It's solid. He had motive, you can't discount that. What you don't know is that you weren't the only ones targeted. There're a few others. Could they be tied together? Don't know yet. Your face was all over the news when ESPN highlighted your gym. That same segment still airs," Mitch said matter-of-factly, his eyes never leaving the road.

"Should I worry about the kids or the gym?" Jace asked. He turned completely toward Mitch. That had never occurred to him.

"It's why I brought it up. I honestly don't know if it's connected. I swear I don't, but I'll find out. Until then, it might be wise. Especially when it gets out that you and Colt are a couple. For the time being, I have someone following you. He's designed not to be seen, but he's there if anyone makes contact, or you need him." Mitch still hadn't looked at Jace. They rode another several minutes in silence. Jace worked at his phone, sending immediate messages to his security company, asking if they did things like security guards and twenty-four hour surveillance. He scrubbed a hand over his face and through his hair. His long hair that had done nothing but get in the way since all this happened.

"Do you think security guards are enough?" Jace asked.

"For now, it should be fine. If things change, I'll let you know." Mitch didn't say another word as he pulled to the front of Jace's townhome.

"Sleep wouldn't kill you. You need to be rested for the long haul, and trust me, it's gonna be a long ass haul. Call if you need me," Mitch said as Jace got out of the car. Sleep wasn't likely.

"Thank you for everything. Call us once you talk to his father," Jace said. How had it never occurred to him the gym and teams could be in danger? Jace tugged his stuffed backpack from the backseat and slammed the door. He waved as his phone sounded off that he'd gotten a new message. Security could be arranged as early as tonight.

Now, he needed to get a haircut, ASAP. He dialed quickly as he entered his townhome.

"Haley, who do we know that can give me an immediate haircut?" Jace asked.

"I'll arrange it if you tell me what's going on?" Haley shot right back.

"Arrange it. I'll be at the gym in about twenty minutes." Jace ignored everything else, hung up, and headed straight to the shower. He wanted to be back at the hospital before dark.

The parking lot was packed as Jace drove to his reserved parking at the front doors of the gym. Tonight was open gym, which generally meant hit and miss on how full the classes were. But school cheerleading tryouts were beginning, and everyone who wanted to tryout was at the gym sharpening their skills, hoping to increase their chances of making the team. Jace barely got the driver's side door open before several young girls came running over to his car.

"Hi, Jace," they said in unison. That was the thing about young girls. They weren't shy, but they also didn't come with talking points, which required that he continue the conversation.

"Are y'all coming or going?" Jace asked, working his way through the five or six of them, while keeping his target on the front door.

"Going," one said.

"Are your parents here?" Jace paused, looking down at their upturned faces.

"Yep, bye, Jace!" The crew took off to one of the cars waiting in the circular car lane, and Jace took the second to scan the parking lot, looking for anything out of the ordinary. That was damn hard to spot when hundreds of cars were everywhere. Hell, he couldn't even identify his own detail. Should he send some sort of note home with the kids?

"Hey, you, welcome back. You're looking suntanned!" Haley greeted him at the front door.

"Did you find anyone?" Jace asked, bypassing her, heading straight to his office. He nodded several times as his name was called, but he didn't engage in conversation with anyone.

"Hellllooo…" she said, and pivoted around, following him. His office was locked, and he fumbled with the key before he was allowed inside. He waited for Haley to bounce in, and he shut the door behind him. Thank God the blinds were drawn.

"We're going to have a stronger security presence around here. Two or three armed security guards both day and night. I think I need to draft a letter to the parents. I'll work on that tonight and send it to legal. We probably need to send it out as soon as possible," Jace said, nothing but business in his tone. He dropped his keys and phone on the desk and pushed his sunglasses back on his head as he booted up his desktop computer.

"Whoa, mister! What's going on? You look super tired, not like a man who just got back from a two week, restful vacay," Haley said and plopped down in the chair across from Jace's desk. "Except, wait! You do look like a man that got nice and laid. Good job," Haley said and extended a hand for a high five across the desk. He reached across, slapped her hand, and looked at her inquisitively. How much did he tell her? What would she say? Deciding his right hand man, or in this case, woman, might need to be on the lookout for possible problems, Jace gave in and decided to give her small details.

"Laid and married." Jace winced at his brazen response, a little surprised how he just dropped it out there.

"What?" Haley was up out of the seat, rounding the desk, hugging his neck tight as he sat there. "Congratulations! It's a good thing, right?"

"I think so, we'll see," he said, sitting back in his seat.

"Was he why you were so messed up before you left?" Haley stood in front of him, crossing her arms over her chest, smiling from ear to ear as she leaned back against his desk.

"In a roundabout way, I guess, but I need to meet with legal. You should probably go with me. There's a lot going on, and we need to stay ahead of it," Jace said, pivoting back around to the desktop, ignoring her standing there gawking at him.

"Okay, no problem. So why the security?" she asked, staying close to him.

"There's been some hate crimes. I'm guessing they're all pretty violent, and I want to protect the gym with all the press we've gotten lately," Jace said, typing an email.

"Sounds reasonable. I'll let the coaches know to be on the lookout. So who is he?" Haley asked, half-sitting on, half-leaning back against Jace's desk. Her arms were still crossed over her chest, the big grin still right there.

"I gotta get going tonight. I'll fill you all in tomorrow. You might meet him soon. I don't know. I'm gonna need you to keep things moving around here for a while, pull some extra shifts to cover for me. Is that a problem?" Jace asked.

"No, not at all. I'm happy to do whatever you need," Haley said. She watched him closely, clearly confused, but she kept that to herself. He liked that about her.

"Did you get someone to cut my hair?" Jace asked.

"Yeah, but I like your hair long," she said.

"It's in the way right now. I can grow it back out," he said, not really paying attention to her. He finished typing a quick message to his legal advisors asking for time as a knock sounded at the door.

"That's her, but I still think you need to leave it long," Haley said, rounding the desk to let her in.

"It's just hair, let her in." Jace hit send and pulled his T-shirt over his head. It was killing him not being at the hospital. The sooner he got this done, the quicker he'd be there.

Jace worked his way through the secured hospital entrance that led directly to Colt's room. He showed his identification, used all the correct names, and by ten-fifteen, he pushed open the hospital room door. Colt was sleeping, with the television blaring on ESPN. Jace entered slowly, placing his bag, pillow, and blanket on the sofa. He quietly walked to the bed and peered down at a sleeping Colt. Thick dark lashes fluttered against bruised cheeks. He didn't wake.

Jace hooked up his laptop, made his bed, and sat at the small desk in the room. It wasn't until he started typing away at the computer, answering some of the hundreds of emails he had missed while away.

"You're supposed to be sleeping in your bed. Why are you back?" Colt's voice was gruff, and Jace glanced at him over his shoulder.

"I'd rather be here than home," Jace said and shrugged, before turning back to the screen and hitting send on the email he'd just typed. He left the computer sitting open and made his way over to Colt.

"I'm not an invalid. I can handle things until you can come back," Colt grumbled. He was still irritated and most likely in pain. Jace looked up at the clock on the wall, measured time, and wondered if Colt had called for his pain meds. Probably not, saying something about his alcoholism and addiction. No matter how Jace insisted taking these meds didn't cross that line, Colt argued. He'd worked too hard at staying sober. He didn't want anything to mess him up.

"Yeah? You can't even wipe your own ass," Jace said, winking at him, and pressed the nurse's call button. "That technically makes you an invalid. You need me here."

"Why'd you cut your hair?" Colt asked in that same gruff tone.

"You're just picking at me now." Jace looked around the room, and then back down at Colt. "Did you eat dinner? I don't see a tray." Jace reached back and fluffed Colt's pillow, and responded to the nurse when she beeped in, asking for his pain medicine.

"No, really, why?" Colt asked again.

"What's it matter anyway? You didn't like it long," Jace said nonchalantly. He stood close to the bedrail. Those ice blue eyes staring back at him melted his heart every single time he looked at them.

"I did to like it long," Colt fired back.

"It was in the way. I can grow it back out," Jace reassured and leaned over to kiss Colt's lips. "I couldn't stay away. I need to be here. Are you okay with it, or would you rather me leave?" Jace asked in a rare moment of honesty. Something flashed across Colt's face.

"I'm worried about you, Jace. This is a lot to deal with, and I think you think it's your fault, and that's why you're hovering like this," Colt replied.

"I don't know whose fault it is, I just know I need to be wherever you are. It's easier to be here in Dallas. I know I'll get pulled away for work, but I want to be here with you. When they allow you to leave, I want you to come home with me. I want us to be together. I want to be the one to take care of you." Jace leaned in across the bedrail and lightly brushed his knuckles down Colt's jaw, running the pad of his thumb gently across Colt's bottom lip. His eyes implored Colt to understand. He wanted Colt living with him permanently.

"You promise if this is too much you'll take a break." Colt's voice shook, maybe broke a little, but he leaned into Jace's touch.

"Absolutely, and stop fusing over me. Focus your energy on getting you well, so I can take you home," Jace said. Colt puckered like he had done so many times in the Hawaiian hospital, and Jace leaned in to kiss his lips.

"You look like we did when we met. I'm having the same reaction as I did when I sat in that stupid pep rally," Colt whispered. He tilted his head toward the center of the bed, where the sheet was tenting. Jace laughed until the nurse walked in, and he quickly lowered his hand, awkwardly pushing Colt's erection down, reaching for anything to place in his lap.

Jace didn't dare look Colt in the eyes, especially not when his husband's warm cock was pressed against his palm. Colt chuckled, then immediately winced in pain.

"Fucking ribs," Colt cursed. It was all it took, Colt's hard-on deflated to Jace's relief.

"So you're hurting?" the nurse asked and reached for the small hand sanitizer dispenser on the wall, wiping her hands as she turned back to Jace. She hadn't paid them any attention; nothing more than business as usual. Thank God. Jace knew his cheeks were colored from the embarrassment of the moment, and he still refused to look back at Colt.

"I think it's time for his pain medicine," Jace blurted. She nodded and went directly to the computer stationed close to the bed and pulled up Colt's information.

"You're right. I'll be right back," she left and Jace turned back to Colt.

"You are so... naughty. I don't know what I'm gonna do with you!"

"I know exactly what I'm gonna do with you the very first chance I get." Colt grinned.

# Chapter 34

Mitch sat across the living room from Colt's father. His elbows on his knees, his eyes trained on the old man. He'd watched every move Larry Michaels made from the time they entered the house. When they first arrived, Colt's father had shown concern. As they spoke, Mr. Michael's even showed deep remorse. He wanted to become immediately involved in Colt's care, even asking if he should apply for conservatorship. When Mitch explained about the marriage and resulting restraining order, Larry got pissed off angry. As they sat in the old man's living room, Larry became visibly upset. His pretty young bride sat perched on the arm rest right beside him, trying to soothe his ruffled feathers.

"So you're saying my fag son married that little cocksucking cheerleader?" Colt's father roared, standing.

"Sir, I need you to sit back down. You need to remain calm, and I need to know about your whereabouts six days ago," Mitch said, standing at the same moment Larry had. The coach stood also, Mitch caught the move out of the corner of his eye.

"Fuck you and fuck him! He's dead to me! You tell him he's dead to me. He should've died, it's better than having a cocksucker for a son!" Spittle flew out of Larry's mouth along with his words as he palmed his phone, made a call, and brought the phone to his ear.

"You make me sick! You should have died—"

Mitch leaped into action. He had Larry down on the ground, wrestling the phone away and pulling the handcuffs from his back pocket simultaneously. He'd gotten really good at quickly subduing his suspects. He loved this part of his job.

Mitch wasn't absolutely certain Larry Michaels was responsible for Colt's accident, but damn this scene pissed him off. And it sure seemed like papa Michaels could benefit from time spent behind bars. If they were lucky, he'd get the much needed attitude adjustment he so clearly needed.

Mitch went through all the motions of arresting Larry Michaels and formally turning him over to local authorities, outlining the case against him. Mitch needed to get back to headquarters and present this case with all the evidence before anyone else could be targeted, if that were even the deal here. Mitch wasn't sure how many people Larry might have on his payroll. Hell, all he knew for certain, this case was a giant fucked up mess, with no clear fingers pointing anywhere except an irate father that just wished his son's death over the reality of him being gay. Damn, that was pretty clear. Why did Mitch think there was more to this? Because his gut insisted there was more.

"How's our boy doing," Dr. Knox asked seconds after Jace answered the phone. Jace sat to Colt's left, watching him sleep for the last few hours.

"He's sleeping now," Jace whispered, moving away from the bed, not wanting to wake Colt.

"Has he woken from surgery yet?" Dr. Knox asked.

"Yes, sir. He came around pretty quick; he was funny. I got some video of him after surgery. I think he'll appreciate it later." Jace covered his mouth, trying to keep from laughing too loudly.

"I doubt that very seriously," Dr. Knox replied, chuckling too. "I spoke with Dr. Hauser, he's encouraged."

"Yeah, that's what he said. He came by a little while ago. If everything keeps going this smoothly, Colt can come home in a few days." Jace kept his eyes on Colt's sleeping form.

"It'll be a lot for you, Jace. Think real hard about that," Dr. Knox advised.

"I know, but he'll be more comfortable at home, I think. It's his call, so whatever he wants." Jace watched as Colt's eyes fluttered, and he began to stir. "He's starting to wake. Do you want to talk to him?"

"No, I'll call in the morning. Take care of him and be sure to take care of yourself too, son."

"I will, thanks for everything, Dr. Knox." Jace disconnected the call and went straight back to Colt's side. Colt's eyes weren't much more than slits, but he kept them on Jace and gave him a sleepy smile.

"I was trying to be quiet," Jace said, leaning down, giving Colt's puckered lips a kiss.

"You weren't. Was that Doc?" Colt gave a small laugh at his little joke.

"He says hello. He's gonna call back in the morning to talk to you." Jace leaned over the hospital bed and straightened the rumpled covers.

"Did he tell the team?" Colt asked.

"Babe, I didn't even think to ask. Want me to call him back?" Jace moved to pick up his phone.

"No, just come hold my hand. I feel better when you're beside me." Colt eyes closed again, only giving a small smile when Jace took his hand, already on his way to falling back to sleep.

"Thank you for being here. I love you," Colt mumbled.

"I love you, too." He lowered his head to kiss Colt's forehead.

Dropping his head in his hands, Mitch kept his eyes glued to the computer screen split into four sections. Four very different victim's files shared the monitor. All gay men victimized by someone. This same crime happened every day, but not to this extreme, and no matter how he tried, or how he twisted the information, he couldn't find a shared motive. Except they were all gay.

Why did his gut insist they were all connected? Starting over, for the hundredth time tonight, Mitch went into his own head, ticking off what he knew. They were all reasonably publicized professional men, who had made the national news for assorted reasons over the last few months. They were an actor, an attorney, a county judge, and a football player, but Jace should have been in that car.

Two died, two didn't. They didn't appear to know one another. They weren't in the same circles. They also weren't obvious hate crimes, and they shared no connection. Except the lack of connection may be the connection.

They were all deemed brutal accidents, and in each individual case, there was absolutely no suspects.

So they were connected. Damn.

Mitch fired up his email and began typing a message to his superior. He pecked away at the keyboard, laying out his findings and why he needed more funds and bodies to make this a special assignment of the department. Succinctly, he bullet-pointed the case and added the files before hitting send. Now it was up to administration to allow him the time and resources to dig deeper. Who knew how that would turn out?

## Chapter 35

*Eight months later*

Colt walked through the halls of Cheer Dynasty with both the cheerleaders and their parents waving as he passed by. In a short amount of time, he'd become an accepted member of the gym. One where people actually looked forward to seeing him. How cool was that? With open arms, they completely welcomed Colt into their little cheer family, and he was grateful for their acceptance.

Cheerleading and football went hand in hand, yet the two worlds couldn't be more different. He officially came out about thirty seconds after the New York State marriage license went public. TMZ posted the breaking news by going straight to his father for confirmation. To date, that video had over eight million views on YouTube. It wasn't good, nor was the heart attack his father suffered by the end of the hateful, ugly rant. His father hadn't died, and to this day, still continued to place blame on Colt for his massive coronary.

A handful of Colt's teammates stayed in touch, a couple had even flown to Dallas over the last few months, but the majority stayed away. Colt got it. His father turned him into a media circus, and no one wanted to be involved in something so vile. And that was okay too, because Jace had stuck by him, and he was truly happy for the first time in his adult life. Interestingly enough, he hadn't thought he could love Jace more than he did before flying to Hawaii, yet his love had only grown since they arrived in Texas, and Jace seemed to feel the same way. They were a tightly woven unit, working together on almost every aspect of their lives. Even better! Damn, it felt good to be a functioning member of society.

A few months after he'd settled in Texas, they held a small reception so their close friends and Jace's mom could celebrate their union. Colt's father had been absent for the festivities, which wasn't a big surprise since he hadn't been invited. Mitch, Doc, and his wife all came. The evening had turned out beautifully; he couldn't have asked for anything more.

Recently, they were even considering the natural next steps of a married couple. They were looking at puppies to help grow their family. Some struggles were coming from this decision. Colt wanted something big, like maybe a Lab. Jace wanted a smaller dog, like maybe a Boston Terrier. Should be interesting to see who won that particular battle.

The investigation into his accident was still open, but Mitch couldn't talk about it, except to say they had a few leads. Both he and Jace were shocked to learn his father wasn't behind the attempt on Jace's life. Which left even more questions needing to be answered, but Mitch assured them they were working hard and Colt would be called to testify when they finally made a case.

Colt tried the doorknob to Jace's office, which turned easily, and he stuck his head inside to see he was in a heated meeting. Everyone involved looked up at Colt's interruption. Damn.

"Sorry!" Colt began, ducking his head back out the door. He'd shown up unexpected after his daily therapy session.

"No, we're done, come in," Jace said, motioning Colt forward, visibly trying to change his facial features from stern to soft. He was kind of funny to watch.

"Yeah, come in. He's always happier when you're around, and we were just getting an earful. You need to stay in here!" Haley took the excuse, bounded up and on her feet, already making her escape.

"I'll make sure the girls are watched better," she said as the door closed behind her and the two other coaches who had made a run for the door when he first stuck his head inside.

"What happened?" Colt asked. Jace stayed sitting behind his desk, and Colt took the chair Haley had abandoned. The seat was warm, which meant they must have spent some time in there, clearly having Jace chew on them.

"Nothing really. Two girls got caught going out back to smoke when they should have been practicing. I got chewed on for a full hour by their parents. Apparently parents still hate that kind of thing," Jace stated. His brow relaxed and his whole demeanor changed. His lips lifted into that silly grin, the one that usually lit Jace's face when Colt was around. Colt loved that smile. "What brings you here? Aren't you supposed to be at therapy?" Jace asked.

"I came to a decision. I'm pretty solid on it, and I wanna make sure you agree before I move forward," Colt said.

"All right, shoot." Jace rose and walked around the desk to stand in front of Colt. He propped his hip on the edge and leaned back, crossing those beefy arms over his chest.

*Shit!* Jace always had one hell of a hot look, but through all Colt's therapy, he'd gotten bigger, added more mass to his already thick frame. Every time Colt worked out, so did Jace. In fact, they did just about everything together. And damn, he wanted those arms wrapped around him right now. Colt ignored the pull and fought to stay focused on the topic at hand.

"I think it's time I throw in the towel." Colt stayed seated, pretending to be relaxed, but the anxiety of the decision coursed through his mind, robbing him of even the thoughts of Jace being the hottest guy he'd ever seen.

Everything they worked for since the accident centered on getting Colt back on the field. They'd succeeded remarkably. Jace had been like a dog with a bone, never letting Colt get down or frustrated. He pushed Colt, and through all the rehab, he finally understood why Jace had flourished in cheerleading—he was one to his core. Jace was Colt's personal cheerleader, encouraging and supporting him like he'd never been uplifted in his life.

With loads of rehab over the last few months, it looked as though he could possibly get back to playing some serious football. The problem he found with achieving his goal? He didn't want to leave Jace for the extended time he'd be required to if he went back to New York. Colt just didn't want to do it. He loved the life they'd created. He loved being here in this gym, having Jace come home to him every night, traveling when the gym traveled.

"This is sudden," Jace said, his brow narrowed, his smile fading. Colt had no idea what that meant.

"Not really," Colt interjected, keeping his relaxed stance, and damn, was that hard to do with this nervous energy coursing throughout his entire body.

"I don't understand. You've worked so hard to get back. You're close, Colt. I know you can do it. We can work out more together. I can make time in the morning. It's not a problem," Jace started, but Colt lifted a hand to stop him.

"Babe, they're going to officially release me this afternoon. I didn't fight them this time. I know I can get to where I was, and I will, but that means I'm away from you. I don't wanna be away from our life for months at a time," Colt spoke softly. He rose and came to stand in front of Jace.

"We can make this work. It's different now," Jace said, bringing his left hand up to cover his chin. Colt could see Jace silently contemplating all the options, mentally willing himself to find a way to better help Colt achieve his goals. Jace wore his wedding ring. He actually never took it off, and the resolve in Colt's decision firmed. He wanted to be here, nowhere else.

"Let me say this differently. If you're all right with it, then I'm done with playing professional football. Are you all right with it?"

"You'll go stir crazy, Colt. I don't want you to resent this decision someday."

"I was thinking about maybe doing more broadcasting. ESPN sent over the market numbers this morning. They said I did a pretty good job when I did the guest spot. I can do more of that." Colt watched Jace intently but his lover had gone quiet. "Babe, I want this, what we have right now. I like you videoing my progress, working with me, making me a part of this family you have here at the gym. I get told all the time that the moms like me here, because the dads come talk football. I like being wanted! This is where I want to be. I just need you to agree to keep me." Colt stepped closer to Jace, wormed his way between his parted legs. Got right up in his personal space and wrapped his arms around him. "Say yes."

"Okay, yes," Jace said, doubt still on his face.

"Perfect." Colt leaned in and pressed his lips to Jace's. The tender, sweet kiss deepened quickly. Jace's tension faded, and he finally wrapped his strong arms around Colt, making this moment perfection. The squeal of young girls drew them apart, and they both turned their heads toward the commotion. All the girls were standing outside the office windows clapping, giggling, with big smiles showing on their faces.

"Kiss, kiss, kiss, kiss!" they chanted in unison. Colt grinned as he took Jace's face in his palms and turned his head to give a good showy chaste kiss.

"We'll finish this at home, cheer boy," he whispered against Jace's lips.

"I'll hold you to that, Michaels," Jace said, kissing Colt again.

The End?

Coming soon... *Full Disclosure* (book 2, Nice Guys series)

# About this Author

Best Selling Author Kindle Alexander is an innovative writer, and a genre-crosser who writes classic fantasy, romance, suspense, and erotica.

Send a quick email and let me know what you thought of *Double Full* to kindle@kindlealexander.com. For more information on future works and links, check out my website at www.kindlealexander.com. Come friend me on all the major social networking sites.

# Books by Kindle Alexander

**If you loved *Double Full*, then
you won't want to miss Kindle Alexander's
bestselling novels:**

*The Current Between Us*
*Texas Pride*
*Up in Arms*

**Coming Soon:**
*Always*

# Everyone's talking about
## *The Current Between Us*

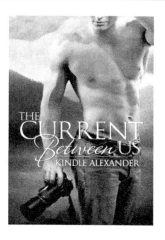

"Ms. Alexander has become one of my favorite M/M authors; check that one of my    favorite authors. Her characters are mature, well rounded and seem to find a    place in my heart."
—Denise, *Shh Mom's Reading*

"I will recommend this to those that love family stories, hot men coming together   and discovering love, a twist that will raise eyebrows and a very happy ending." —Pixie, *Mmgoodbookreviews*

"I loved this book! Everything about it was just perfection...great characters,    suprises, and the story...seriously, it was so sweet and romantic and just really good reading."   —Christi Snow, *Author*

"Kindle Alexander has given us another great book. The characters Trent and Gage grabbed my heart and haven't let go. This isn't just a love story, it has a mystery going on that keeps you hooked." —*Teri - The Bitches of Eastwick Book Reviews*

"Loved this book!!! This is the second book I've read by Kindle Alexander. The first one was *Texas Pride*. I was hooked right from the beginning. It's an amazing love story."
—Brenda Wright, *Twinsie Talk Book Review*

"This book is an excellent love story, where even the most hardened heart and disillusioned soul can find the romantic streak hidden deep within and see it   blossom into something neither thought possible. I fell in love with the   author, her writing      and the characters... just go read it!!!"
—Monique, *Sinfully Sexy Book Reviews*

"This is my first book by Kindle Alexander and I have to say that I loved it! I am a  fan of the m/m genre especially when there is a beautiful and touching story   behind it."
—*Three Chicks and their Books*

"If you enjoyed Texas Pride you will love *The Current Between Us!*" —*Swoon Worthy Book Reviews*

# Rave Reviews for
## *Texas Pride*

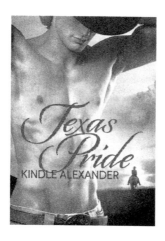

"I would DEFINITELY like this to be a series...hint hint to Kindle Alexander!!!" —Brenda, *Twinsie Talk Book Review*

"I have a severe case of book hangover. Seriously readers – you need to read this book. Ten stars for me!" — *\*Foxylutely\* Blog*

"The end of this book was so well done!" —*Shh Mom's Reading*

"Definitely a great read...I didn't want this sweet story to end." —Christi Snow, *Author*

"Recommend this to those who love cowboys and movie stars ...and a very happy ending." —*Mmgoodbookreviews*

"I highly recommend it." —Samantha, *Passionate Books*

# What readers are saying about *Up in Arms*

UP IN
**ARMS**
Kindle Alexander

"*Up in Arms* is a compelling, fascinating drama that honestly explores the conflict of love in the military without taking away from an enchanting romance." —*Joyfully Reviewed*

"This story not only follows these men's love affair, which is sweet and sexy, but we also see the aftermath of how they deal with tragedy. I love these boys, how they interact, how they over come, how one of them blushes *sigh*." —*The Bitches of Eastwick*

"This is a tender love story.... She taps all the sensory elements that binds a romance reader to the narrative, characters, conflicts and resolutions." —*Blackraven's Reviews*

CPSIA information can be obtained
at www.ICGtesting.com
Printed in the USA
BVOW06s1939261116
468971BV00013B/523/P